To Edna

The Slaughter of Leith Hall

from Lexie Conyngham

Banchory, 2022.

Lexie Conyngham

The Slaughter of Leith Hall

First published in 2020 by The Kellas Cat Press, Aberdeen.

Cover design by Helen Braid, www.ellieallatsea.com

ISBN: 978-1-910926-59-8

To Eleanor, for freely presenting me with the idea for this story – I hope she feels I've done it justice!

ACKNOWLEDGMENTS

Thanks to Anne for her usual help with sailing times and habits. Thanks, also, to the staff at Blackwell's University Bookshop, Aberdeen, for (mostly unwittingly) providing the names of many of the characters – and I absolutely promise that apart from the names the characters bear as little resemblance as possible to their namesakes!

Dramatis Personae

John Leith of Leith Hall
Harriot Stuart of Auchluncart, his wife
Mary Hay, known as Lady Glastirum, his mother
Charlie Rob, his manservant
Phoebe Clark, maidservant

His uncles:
Lawrence Leith
Andrew Hay of Rannes
Alexander Hay

John Leith of Leith Hall's friends and former fellow officers:
Gregory, Lord Watt
His sister Ciara
His manservant, Mr. Holland

James Abernethy of Mayen
Jean Duff, his wife
Michael Pringle, his majordomo

Walter Dalgarno
Matthew Keracher
Lang Tam Main, their manservant

Gordon of Cobairdy
Forbes of Brux
Patrick Byres of Tonley

Sarah Dilley, widow of Captain Robert Dilley
Margaret, her bunkwife

Alan McFarland in Stonehaven

In Amsterdam:
Josse Gheertzoon
His daughters Luzie and Anna Katerina
Jeemsie Ogilvie

Chapter One

No doubt this would be the last of these mornings before winter set in properly. Or the last when they could all be together like this, laughter steaming from their lips in the startling bright air.

James Abernethy, their host here at Mayen, laughed more than anyone, which was no bad thing, Charlie Rob thought, for James Abernethy of Mayen was easily the worst shot of all of them. He was a great affable man, good enough to make sure there was hot wine around the firing point for the servitors as well as for the gentlemen. Charlie Rob was fairly new to the game of attending his master, John Leith, in his business and his pleasure, but he had seen enough to know that servants were not always treated so generously, and he already felt well disposed to Abernethy of Mayen – not that Abernethy of Mayen was ever likely to notice him.

'Charlie, reload that, would you?'

Charlie Rob shook himself and took the pistol from his master's outstretched hand.

'Aye, sir.' He was aware of John Leith watching him, a little absently, as he carefully packed the charge into the pistol. It was a new skill, and his master had taken pains to teach him. Charlie did not mind being watched: he would rather get it right, and the pistols frightened him. There was plenty to try to remember in this new job, and though he was doing his best, he was fairly sure there were mistakes he was making. But if he did make a mistake, John Leith would be kind enough in his correction.

Leith nodded in satisfaction as Charlie handed the pistol back, and returned to take his turn with the other gentlemen, their easy gossip punctuated by the metallic pops of shots in the clear air. Charlie Rob, relieved, felt a nudge at his elbow.

'Aye, it's no so bad when your master's a good shot, eh?'

Charlie grinned, turning. It was Lang Tam beside him, the

1

black haired, skinny servant of little Matthew Keracher. Keracher was notorious, his shooting almost as bad as Abernethy's - in practice like this, at any rate. Lang Tam swore his master was a danger in battle, when his blood was roused, but it was never clear whether Tam meant a danger to his enemies or his friends. Matthew Keracher took his place now on the firing point, the pistol already wavering in his hand. There was a sudden interest from the crowd, both gentlemen and servitors. Was it time to duck?

'He'd be better of a few draughts of that strong wine, I reckon,' Lang Tam remarked judiciously. The gentlemen, too far away to hear Lang Tam, burst out laughing nevertheless as Keracher was reduced to seizing the pistol butt in both hands, squinting along the swinging barrel. He snatched at the trigger as though plucking a fiddle string, and a bottle three yards to the left of the one he was supposed to hit wobbled slightly. The gentlemen cheered, and Lang Tam sighed.

'Aye, well: at least I ken never to put money on him.' He rubbed at his scrawny upper arms. 'Think they'll be much longer? I haven't felt my feet this last hour.'

'Another round at least, I'd say,' said Charlie, glad to be asked his opinion. Gentlemen assumed that if they were friendly with each other, their servants would enjoy time spent in each other's company, too. It was not always so, but Tam always seemed happy to see Charlie. 'That's both of Mr. Leith's pistols loaded just now.'

Lang Tam nodded, and stamped his feet dejectedly.

'Aye,' he acknowledged. 'I've just reloaded Mr. Dalgarno's too.' He sighed. Charlie had heard the minister say that a man could not have two masters, but Lang Tam managed it: he served both Matthew Keracher and his friend, Walter Dalgarno. To Charlie, that gave him a dangerous, even a glamorous, air: a man going against what the kirk said with such ease! 'And his turn's at least two away. See them two!' His voice dropped abruptly, the practised hush of a servant not wanting his betters to hear his opinions. He made the slightest gesture at the next two gentlemen lined up to shoot. 'You'd near take them for twins, eh?'

Charlie looked at the two gentlemen, as he realised that Lang Tam's words were intended sarcastically. Lord Watt was the closer, and to see him you would wonder what he was doing amongst the others, for you could tell straight away that he was a superior being.

2

The very lace at his collar was whiter and stiffer than anyone else's. The velvet of his coat looked, to Charlie's eye, freshly brushed, and even his boots shone despite a morning spent outdoors. His perfectly carved profile angled for a moment, turning to see where his servant was with his pistol – Flemish, of course, silverwork glinting, wood so polished it dazzled. Long, pale lids almost concealed his eyes, but he must have been able to see clearly enough, for he turned back, raised the pistol, and in the same instant it seemed the bottle on the distant branch shattered. Unsmiling, he returned the pistol to his servant, and made a little bow to the next man, allowing him to take to the firing point.

Lord Watt's twin he was not, unless one believed in fairies and changelings. Where Lord Watt was sombre stillness, Patrick Byres of Tonley was constantly in motion – and from what Charlie Rob had heard, he needed to be, for Byres of Tonley was not short of enemies, some more powerful than others. He already had his pistol in his hand, dangling at the end of an arm that seemed too long and undulating for his short body. Still joking with the other gentlemen, he seemed to sidle up to the firing point, only half-glancing at the target bottle as if he hoped to take it by surprise. His eyes seemed to be everywhere, his grin mobile too. He fired in mid-conversation, catching the bottle on its flank – Charlie saw it spin frantically before it smashed. Byres congratulated himself heartily, and danced away from the firing point again, allowing poor Mayen, their host, to take another wasted shot.

At last the turns had been taken, and despite Mayen and Matthew Keracher there were no more bottles left to smash. Charlie hurried with the other servants to fetch the horses, tethered out of harm's way nearby to try what nourishment they could from the frosty grass. Caught here in a tilted valley in a loop of the Deveron river, they had been sheltered today, but the light was fading fast behind the hills. John Leith favoured both Charlie and horse with a smile as they returned, and thanked Charlie for his boost up into the saddle. The gentlemen settled themselves, the servants following behind on foot, several carrying their masters' pistol cases. Lord Watt rode ramrod straight, of course, a long-nosed hound following gracefully at his horse's heels. Charlie found himself tripping over Leith Hall spaniels, and Lang Tam caught his arm to stop him falling. Byres of Tonley, leaning dangerously to one side, poked Abernethy of Mayen sharply in the ribs and seemed to whisper something before touching his spurs to his horse's flanks and galloping off. With a cheer, a few of the others followed, racing towards Mayen House. Abernethy of Mayen, though, edged over to John Leith, neither of them out of a walking pace yet.

'Twenty-first of December, they tell me,' Charlie heard him say, as he tried to sort the spaniels out. Mayen's voice was low, and grave for once. 'At Campbell's inn, in Aberdeen. Can you be there?'

'Aye,' said John Leith. He smiled, but Charlie noticed a serious look in his eyes. 'I mean, Strathbogie would have been handier, but aye, I'll do my best, of course.'

'Grand!' Mayen reached a hand across and laid it briefly on Leith's shoulder. 'Not the best time of the year to travel, it's true, but it canna be helped. Secret, of course, I needn't say to you. Coming?'

Leith nodded, and the pair of them cantered off in the wake of the others. Lang Tam watched them, shrugging.

'Aye, and then we dander along behind. I hope they'll leave us a bite of dinner!'

You could tell the Abernethys had been at Mayen for a long while. A round tower, with two wings snuggled at its foot, sat with an eye to several directions and a view of the curling Deveron below. There was a walled garden outside a courtyard, where Charlie could see rows of winter kale still dark amongst other, withered stems, but the mains farm must have been a distance away and everything else here was couried safely into the courtyard – stables, store rooms, brew house and bake house, the dairy, a narrow, defendable entrance to the house itself. It was all well enough looked after, but there was none of the expansion and improvement that was fashionable just now: at Leith Hall there had been all kinds of changes. Charlie half-envied the servants here, with a smaller house to run around.

John Leith dismounted and gave his horse a farewell pat, and Charlie, blinking in the steam of all the gentlemen's mounts crowded together, waited his turn to find shelter, food and water for Leith's horse. One or two of the gentlemen stood about the doorway, discussing the horses and how they had run on the way back: the others hurried inside the house, eager for warmth and refreshment. Charlie made a face into the horse's flank: he was starving. As soon as their horses were settled, he and Lang Tam fairly ran across the courtyard to the door, Tam laughing at their open desperation.

Inside, they found Mrs. Abernethy, a neat wee body with a pretty face, lingering in the hallway to welcome even the servants and make sure they knew where to go. She must have had enough to do without hosting a whole army of her husband's friends here: she was cluttered about with children, the biggest surely not more than nine or ten, the smallest in her arms, not counting the one on its way. But she managed to find smiles for everyone and a kind word, and the warmest smile of all for her husband, touching his hand as he passed and smiled back. It gave Charlie a cosy feeling to counteract his hunger.

At last they were drummed into a dining room, plainly decorated and with nothing that Charlie could see that looked as if it had been bought in the last ten years, barring the food. There did not seem to be money here, but there was generosity – not perhaps the best of combinations – and the gentlemen were soon well served, with Mr. Abernethy at the head of the long table and his pretty wife at the foot chatting to the men on either side of her with a good mixture of friendliness and propriety. Charlie knew it was not his place to do so, but he approved very much, as he took his position with the servants in the room.

But it would be a while yet before they could eat. While the gentlemen were settled with hot food and plenty of drink, the servants stood about, each near their master's chair, ready to attend, waiting their turn, stomachs wrenching at the fine smells coming from the masters' table. After a while - and maybe faster than it should have, for Mayen was generous with his wine - the conversation amongst the gentlemen grew louder, the laughter less controlled, and when Mrs. Abernethy went to kiss her husband good night and retire from the company, the servants were able to step back a bit and gossip, too. As John Leith had been given a seat near the top of the table, close to his friend Abernethy, Charlie found himself next to Abernethy's own majordomo.

'Aye, three centuries, so I'm told,' said Mayen's man, a whiskery, wrinkled body by the name of Pringle. His hair was so thick and straight that it stuck out of the loop of ribbon on the back of his head like a paintbrush. 'King David came into the matter, you ken.'

Charlie, more interested in when he might get his own dinner, was hazy about history. The only King David he had heard of was the one in the Bible. His eyes widened, impressed. Pringle nodded.

'And like to be here three centuries or more to come, too,' he added in satisfaction. 'The master and the lady have nine bairns between them, and another on the way.'

'Aye,' said Charlie, feeling the need to stand up for Leith Hall. 'My master's got the three. And all boys.'

Pringle gave him a look, as if to say Charlie had overstepped the mark, competing with a more senior servant.

'All boys, eh?' he said. 'All boys. Aye, that's grand, I suppose. We're all gey fond of the wee lassies here, though, you ken.'

'I'm sure,' said Charlie, reprimanded.

Pringle looked away, and drew a long, considered sniff.

'I think we could clear the meats now, and leave them their drink,' he said, and signalled to some junior staff. 'And we can start to take our ease, you ken. Would you be wanting something to eat?'

'Yes, please!' Charlie said at once.

'Well, find yourself a stool over yonder, with the other men, and I'll have something brought in for everyone.'

A cluster of attendants had settled in a corner of the dining hall, Lang Tam amongst them. Charlie hurried over, not wanting to miss anything. In a moment, they were brought broth, good bread, and boiled onions, and a cup of ale each with a full jug left for them to start with. No one held back: they were all famished, and the food did not last long. Like rooks at a dead lamb, Charlie thought suddenly, and did not like the idea. He set his bowl aside, and sipped at his ale.

The gentlemen, for the most part, looked like sacks that had been untied. Most slumped back in their seats, while others leaned heavily on the table, fiddling with the remnants of meat or bread left behind, oblivious to the servants now. Charlie saw that John Leith was brighter-eyed than most, his face not quite so flushed, smiling at the others' jokes rather than laughing immoderately. Charlie felt a pride in his master. He could take his wine, as well as being a competent shot. He let his gaze tour the rest of the table, seeing how the friends Keracher and Dalgarno were bickering over a jug quite near him. Byres of Tonley let his arm trail carelessly around the back of his neighbour's chair, almost fond – yet it put Charlie in mind of some kind of ivy, curling destructively about some innocent man, insidiously seeking his downfall. Charlie shook himself. Such fancies

– he had had too much of that spiced wine while they were outside, he thought. He was not used to it.

He turned to watch James Abernethy, next to his master, always a more cheerful prospect. Abernethy of Mayen seemed to have had plenty to drink, but he had a strong grip still on sobriety for he knew his duties as host. He poured another cup for John Leith from the jug in front of him, which Pringle the majordomo took to refill. John Leith took a sip, no more, then paused and raised the cup to Lord Watt with a friendly smile. Lord Watt, pale as ice on a water barrel, lifted his own glass in response.

'A toast!' cried Walter Dalgarno, seeing the movement. 'A toast, gentlemen, to our good host, Abernethy of Mayen!'

The men rose and drank, most still steady enough on their feet. Mayen saluted them, then rose to respond.

'To my good friends here, and to your lordship for gracing us with your presence!' he said, raising his glass to Lord Watt. Lord Watt looked down his long nose, yet Charlie thought that with him that might just be a sign of approval. The gentlemen toasted Lord Watt, then each other, refilling their glasses with more generosity than accuracy. There was a general air of jollity already, and Charlie began to relax, putting aside whatever strange mood had taken him. A few more toasts were exchanged, tangled with jokes about Matthew Keracher's shooting, and James Abernethy's even worse shooting, and Walter Dalgarno's debts, and Byres of Tonley's efforts to evade the government in all its guises. Then Lord Watt managed to make his voice heard through the chatter.

'Gentlemen,' he rose to his feet like a young birch sapling sprouting, 'to the King!'

'The King,' the others obediently repeated. Then Byres of Tonley, a look of supreme mischief on his face, added clearly,

'Over the water.'

There was a moment's grim silence.

'Go on, then!' he urged them, grinning wildly. 'A room full of loyal Jacobites, and not one of you man enough to toast our true King!'

'Och, man,' said James Abernethy, slipping back down into his seat, 'why did you have to bring that up?'

'Aye, come on.' Walter Dalgarno made a face, too, and emitted a gentle belch. He scrabbled in his waistcoat pocket and drew out a battered silver watch with one round dent in it that almost pierced the metal through. 'That's all past. See I keep a lock of his bonnie hair in my watchcase – it took a shot for me in America and all, so I can well believe he's magic. But now he's away in Italy, the man's lost altogether.'

'Till next time,' said Byres, his voice soft but somehow deeply unpleasant. Charlie shivered, and tried to look away, but something about Byres made it difficult to ignore him. John Leith cleared his throat.

'We all know what way we would have liked things to happen,' he said, his tone conciliatory. 'Everyone in this room fought, or had family that fought, or has lost financially because of the uprising. But sir, times have changed, have they not? There is no hope of such an outcome now, and we must make the best of what we have: many of us had to fight in the name of King George just to set our estates back on to prosperous terms, and that is what happens. We must look to our friends and our families, to good company here,' he raised his glass just a little, quickly scanning the others to see if they were with him, 'to good health, and to quiet times for the future. These last years have not been easy for anybody, not the last hundred years. It would profit all of us to live peaceably for a while.'

'Hear, hear!' Abernethy of Mayen slapped the table in approval, and Charlie realised he had been holding his breath. He let it out in a rush, and took a gulp of ale, choking. Lang Tam reached over and whacked him between the shoulder blades and as conversation revived around the gentlemen's table, he leaned over.

'I like your master,' he murmured. 'He's a man to be proud of, eh?'

Charlie nodded, wiping his mouth on his sleeve.

'He is that, I believe,' he agreed. But he had seen the look on Byres of Tonley's face as Abernethy poured more wine for John Leith, and he had not liked it at all.

Chapter Two

Winter was drawing in: there was no more talk of expeditions up beyond the Deveron to Mayen just for a bit of target practice. Snow had fallen since the beginning of November, and by the end of the month the roads were thick with it, the hills invisible presences, grey against a grey sky. Leith Hall, snug in its own valley, drew the blankets over its head and used its dried logs prudently. Harriot Stuart, lady of the household, though she would not condemn her little boys to an uncomfortable home, was not one for wastage, particularly not at the onset of the cold. The brewing, the smoking, the drying, the pickling with which the late autumn had been frantically busy had now filled her pantries, and she counted over jars and barrels, and watched the servants' use of any precious commodity more severely than any army quartermaster.

She was well built for supervision: tall, with a nose that even in a long face was prominent, and eyebrows in the high, plucked fashion that gave her an air of one whose expectations of disappointment had been somehow surpassed. She had been mistress of Leith Hall for almost eight years – young, it was true, when she had married John Leith, but well trained, and with all the self-assurance of an heiress in her own right, bringing the estate of Auchluncart to the family at Leith Hall. John Leith had worked hard to make the place worthy of her arrival, too: somehow, despite his father's generation and their allegiance to Prince Charles Edward Stuart, John's inheritance had been a good one and he had added elegance to his home's courtyard, a decent garden up the hillside on the drive, a marriage lintel for them. He had married for love, and wanted to impress. She, too, with a realistic eye to their two estates, and no ambitions for anything grander, took delight in his suit, and assumed her place as Leith Hall's mistress and Leith's wife with the greatest of pleasure.

There was no outdoor work to be done today: the snow was halfway up the ground floor windows, and though the men had dug a path from the door the women could do little after the cows had been milked and the pigs fed. The light was not good enough for anything but the roughest needlework. Harriot set her women to spinning, and took Phoebe Clark, her particular maid, up to the attics with lamps to check for moths.

'I want each piece gone through inch by inch, and straightened as flat as you can, and every seam felt right along,' she directed Phoebe. 'You know how they burrow themselves into folds.'

Phoebe nodded, placing her lantern on the corner of a convenient chest and finding a place to kneel on the floor.

'Shall I start with this trunk, my lady?'

'Yes, that's best. That's sheets, so they won't take so long. Undo every fold, though!'

'Aye, my lady.' Phoebe pulled open the trunk, and began her work. Harriot watched for a moment. Phoebe, a slight thing, was stronger than she looked, flipping heavy linen sheets back and forth. Still, it would have been more practical to bring two of them to sort the sheets together.

'Phoebe, would you fetch Chrissie to help you with that? I should have thought. And I want to do this trunk myself.'

Phoebe stopped and curtseyed as she left, and Harriot turned to the trunk she had just opened. The contents bloomed scarlet in the lamplight, and she reached out a thin finger to stroke the soft wool.

Prudence had always been a watchword in their marriage: they were not some extravagant family in Edinburgh, she often told John, flinging away their money on balls and gambling, and the political and economic climate still did not favour any families who had had strong Jacobite connexions - and John's uncles had certainly made

10

themselves known, and unpopular, with the Government side in the uprising. Harriot frequently reflected, and was sure John agreed, that the uncles, generally, had not enough wits between them to make one sensible man. Be that as it may, once Harriot had given birth to two healthy boys, John, with her encouragement and consent, took up a commission in the army – the very army his uncles would have destroyed – and in the blink of an eye, it seemed, he was off across the ocean to the Americas, in his smart scarlet coat.

She lifted it out carefully. What a mercy, that it had come home again unscarred – that no shot or sword blade had ever penetrated it! That none of the terrible fevers, that had killed so many, had seized her husband! She touched the breast of the coat, as if thanking it for its protection – though what it might have done against a fever she had no idea, and smiled a little at herself for the thought. Then she shook out the coat, and began feeling along its lining for damage or moths, checking the threads behind the glowing buttons, the hooks for the epaulettes, the moleskin and lace of the cuffs.

John had come back safely, despite the risks. Her delight when she had received his letter, telling her he was safely arrived at the regimental headquarters in Cork – Cork! That had been an almost unimaginable distance from Leith Hall before he had gone so much further – and would be home in a couple of months, once he had discharged his duties and resigned his commission. The soldiering life was not for John, she knew now. He was content with his home, his family, his bit of land here in the shallow glen by Kennethmont, his friends about a generous table, his tenants with whom he had grown up and seen the estate flourish. She wondered at herself: she would have thought, as a girl, that she would have been the kind of wife wanting to push her husband into greater success or prominence, that she would have been a partner or a pusher, instrumental in her husband's shining career, but that was before she married John. She knew, now, that where his happiness lay, that was where she should concentrate all her efforts. And so she did – rather successfully so far, she thought, lips pressed into a little satisfied smile. Another child on the way, nestled behind her slightly loosened stays. Another boy, no doubt. Security for the estate, succession for the family – away from John's shilpit uncles and their careless destruction. Between them and their sons they could continue to build up their position, improve their land in the new fashion, look after their tenants – all that John most desired, and all with her by his side.

Though he had looked very handsome in his regimentals ...

Her thoughts were interrupted, and probably just as well, by the return of Phoebe, clattering up the attic stairs.

'My lady, there's a messenger come!'

'Well,' said Harriot, irritably, 'what is the message?'

'It's a package for the master,' said Phoebe.

'In this weather? Is the messenger awaiting a reply?'

'He's in the kitchens, my lady, thawing out. He'd come all the way from Glasgow!'

'From Glasgow!' Harriot had to see for herself. Closing the lid carefully on her husband's army chest, she chased Phoebe down the steps in front of her and then took the lead, skirts swishing against the railing of the curling main stairs, back to the kitchens below.

A man stood by the fire, a bowl of broth in his hand and a wooden spoon in the other, while the cook fussed about him.

'Look at the state of your boots, man!' she exclaimed. 'You'll need to get them dry before you ever go outside in that again! And get that cloak off till we dry it a bit. If not for your own sake, then for ours – see those puddles all over my floor! Oh, my lady,' she finished, turning to see Harriot enter the room. With a curtsey, she conceded authority.

'Indeed,' said Harriot, 'give the man a blanket while his clothes dry. He is in no state to continue like that. What is your business here?' she addressed him directly at last.

'My lady,' said the messenger, 'I am here with a package for John Leith of Leith Hall.'

'From whom?'

'I don't know, ma'am,' the messenger admitted. He was a small man, with a quick, efficient look to him. Harriot had an image of him squirrelling through obstacles to bring his messages unfailingly to their recipients. 'I was only told to give it to John Leith of Leith Hall.'

'Where is the package?'

'In the hall, my lady,' Phoebe told her. 'Near the fire.'

'Not too near, I hope. Do you know what is in it, sir? Will it be spoilt by heat?'

'I believe not, ma'am, but I don't know exactly what's in it.'

'Yet you brought it all the way from Glasgow?'

'Aye, ma'am.'

'So who gave it to you?' Harriot found she had less interest in the contents of her husband's parcel than in the strange way it had arrived. To send a parcel in the depths of winter, out here – it almost spoke of eccentricity more than urgency.

'Another messenger, ma'am. He'd brought it far enough, he said.'

'And where had he brought it from?'

The messenger, who had perhaps not expected such a level of interrogation, allowed himself a slight shrug.

'Somewhere further west, ma'am.'

Harriot looked about her.

'Where's Charlie Rob?' she asked.

'Gone to fetch the master, ma'am,' said Phoebe.

'Good. Make sure this man is dried and warmed and paid for his trouble.' She turned and made for the hall.

'My dear!'

John Leith appeared at the front door at the same moment as his wife entered the hall. Charlie came behind him, closing the door carefully against the snowy landscape outside. He had been lucky this morning, set to work at hauling sacks of vegetables in the pantries rather than following his master outside on a tour of the estate. The unaccustomed cold bit at his face and hands.

'I hear there's a parcel for me?' said John Leith. 'From points west?'

'That's the story,' said his wife. 'The messenger downstairs brought it from Glasgow – heaven knows what he'll want to be paid for that – and says he had it there from another messenger who brought it from the west. Who do we know in the west, John? I can't think of anyone.'

John Leith had already shrugged off his outdoor cloak and pulled his gloves into a heap, handing them both to Charlie. His focus was on the lumpy package on the hall table. Charlie watched him, even as he fiddled the soft leather of the gloves back into shape. The master turned the package over, looking, presumably, for any writing on it, but seemed dissatisfied with the result.

'Just my name, and the direction,' he said. 'Nothing about where it came from. And the seals are quite plain.'

'Is it heavy?' asked the mistress. John hefted it, considering.

'Not really,' he said. 'It's not books, nor lead weights, nor a set of pistols. Well,' he said, 'I suppose the best way to find out is to open it!'

He took a knife from his belt, and slit the string in several strategic places, then pulled away the cloth carefully. Whatever was inside, it was well wound-about: the cloth was in a tangle on the table by the time the master had freed the object from its wrappings.

'Look,' he said, 'it's a powder horn!'

He held up a large, curling horn, turning it slowly in his hands.

'What's that on it?' asked the mistress. 'It looks like fine decoration.'

'It's empty, anyway,' John Leith commented, 'from the weight. It's – oh! I see what it is! Look, it's all carved with what we did in America, the campaign – you know, the sites of all the battles! And someone's put my name on it – look, underneath!' He handed it to the mistress. She took it and examined it closely, particularly the place he had pointed to.

'Did you buy this?' she asked. Charlie half-expected a sharpness in her tone, the kind of voice she would have used on a servant who had made some error of judgement, but no: she was only curious, and a little – well, he might have said intrigued. Her long, pale fingers held the shape of the horn, traced the carved patterns. She seemed to be reading what it said: 'JOHN LEITH OF THE 1ST. BATTALION THE ROYAL HIGHLAND REGT. 1759'.

'I didn't buy it,' said the master. 'There must be something here to say who sent it.'

'A gift from a fellow officer, probably.' Lady Harriot's voice was light, but Charlie thought he saw her grip on the horn tense a little. John Leith worked his way systematically through the swaddling cloths that had wound about the horn, examining them on both sides either for paper stuck there, or for pen marks on the cloth.

'Probably ...' he conceded at last, with a frown. 'There's nothing to say. But I should have thought that anyone likely to make me a present of such a thing – with my name on it and all – would be one of my friends here. Glasgow?' He took the horn back from the mistress, examining it more closely. 'Unless they commissioned it when we were still in America and this is it arriving now, straight to me, instead of delivered to whoever paid for it to give me in person.'

He unlatched the delicate little fastening on the lid, and glanced inside. 'Empty, aye. I suppose they would not have sent it full of powder, anyway!' He handed the horn back to his wife.

'It's taken a while,' Lady Harriot remarked sharply.

'Aye ... maybe it went to Cork first. Maybe whoever commissioned it said to send it to the regimental headquarters, and when it arrived and I had gone, someone sent it on. No one official, by the looks of it, though!' he added, making a job of folding the cloth. Charlie wanted to take it from him and sort it out, but even if he had had the nerve, his hands were still full of gloves and coat. He should probably have taken them away by now, but the mysterious parcel had drawn him as much as it seemed to fascinate the master and the mistress. 'Well,' said John Leith eventually, 'I can see no clue on it. When I see the others next month I shall ask them, I suppose. But it's a fine piece, and a keepsake of an interesting time in my life, I suppose: I can't see myself using it to carry that weight of powder again unless there's another uprising –'

'Hush, John! Don't joke about such things!'

He patted her arm.

'We're preserved thus far, my dear: the Lord seems inclined to be merciful to us. All I'm saying is we can have the horn set here on the table where all can see it, and maybe even learn something about what happened in America – the boys will like it as they grow old enough to understand it.'

'This young one may be a girl, you know, John,' said the mistress, and her voice had gone low, the way she never spoke to the servants. The master drew closer to her, and Charlie, blushing already at the mere thought of them standing so near to each other, decided it was past time to sort out the coat and gloves. He slipped away from the hall to find a fire to dry them by.

Phoebe found him later near the same fire, fixing holes in his master's gloves. He glanced up to see her standing watching, a little smile on her pretty face. She was a clever one, Phoebe: he never quite knew where he stood with her.

'Hello, there, Charlie!' she said, drawing closer. 'You're making a fine job of that!'

'Och, I'm all fingers and thumbs,' he said, feeling himself redden.

'That's fine and fitting for fixing gloves, then, is it no?'

He looked up at her, thought through what she had said, and gave a little laugh.

'Aye, I suppose! It's an awful fiddle, though, back and forth between the fingers.'

Phoebe considered the task, as Charlie showed her the places where the old stitching had gone. He was, as always, more aware of her nearness than he was with any of the other servants. She had a neat wee figure, sure enough, but that cleverness kept him edgy. Not that he was that easy with girls anyway, he had to admit.

'I could help if you like,' she said at last. 'If you leave it with me. It won't take long, and anyway, I came to tell you the master wants to speak to you, in his bookroom.'

'Would you do that? The gloves, I mean,' he asked. There was a look in her eyes, when he managed to meet them, that would not clearly say if she was being friendly or flirting. How was he supposed to know?

'Ah, get on and go and see what he wants!' she laughed, holding out her hands for the gloves. 'I'll have these done by the time you get back!'

He stood, half-reluctant to leave her company, but found himself passing on the gloves all the same.

'The bookroom, you say?'

'That's right. On you go!'

She gave him a playful nudge with her elbow, and he trotted off obediently, still feeling the brush of her fingers on his – and the dent in his side where she had prodded him.

The bookroom was a wonder to Charlie. One wall was lined with what, when he came here, he had first taken for a kind of leather panelling, folded and flecked with gilt. It was mostly a soft brown, but there were red and green bits, too. It had been quite a shock to him one day to find the master pulling out a fold of the panelling to show him that the leather was the spines of books – books like the Bible in church, but more books even than the psalters there, and all different ones. He had no idea that so many books existed, or that so many people had been able to write them. How did you go about writing a book? The very idea made his head stuff up and stop working.

Today, however, though a few of the books lay about the room as if John Leith had tried them out and cast them aside, the master was standing at the window, staring out at the snow and the bare trees and the grey hills. Despite his decision earlier to leave the new powder horn in the hall, the thing lay on his desk in its nest of cloth. Charlie was close enough to see strange words written on it, and little drawings, cut into the horn's yellow-white surface then, it seemed, blackened with something to make them stand out. It had taken some skill.

'Ah, Charlie.' John Leith interrupted his thoughts, turning from the window. He was smiling, but there was an anxiety behind his eyes. Charlie considered. It might just have been the odd snowlight reflecting in them. 'Charlie, I have to go to Aberdeen, and I'd like you to come with me.'

Charlie swallowed.

'To Aberdeen, sir?'

This time John Leith definitely grinned.

'Aye, that's right. We'll be there for two or three days, I think. I'd like to set out tomorrow.' He paused, then asked gently, 'Have you ever been to Aberdeen, Charlie?'

'I've been to Strathbogie,' said Charlie, hoping that that would be enough.

'Then I'm sure you'll be able to manage in Aberdeen,' said John Leith kindly. 'I'll keep you nearby till you learn to find your way around, anyway. I expect I'll be travelling to Aberdeen regularly now, what with being one of the Commissioners of Supply, and I'll need you to attend me when I go, so you can think of this as a practice, if you wish.'

'Aye, sir.'

'I shan't need anything very smart this time: I want to visit my mother, and thereafter ... well, we'll see how matters unfold.' He tailed off, his thoughts clearly drifting. Then he pulled himself together. 'Anyway, yes, my mother, and some other places, and if Dalgarno and Keracher are in town, which they likely are, we might see them. You're friendly with their man Tam, are you not?'

'I am, sir.'

'No doubt he can show you a few things about the town, too,' said the master. 'I should say he's the kind to know his way about the place. We'll stay in the house in the Castlegate. No doubt it will need airing, but I'm in a hurry – in case the weather worsens – so we must just thole if the beds are stale. Now, do you think you'll be able to pack up a small kist for me by tonight? We'll need to leave just before first light.'

'Aye, sir, I think so.' Charlie was starting to make lists in his head. He wondered if Phoebe had finished mending the gloves yet. A house in the town? He had no idea the master had any such thing. Would it be the size of Leith Hall? How would he manage, as the only servant? Would there be food? Would he be expected to cook it? But the master was still issuing instructions.

'Tell the stablemen we'll need the chaise ready. Have you a warm cloak for travelling?'

'Aye, sir.' Fairly warm, anyway, he thought to himself. Would his boots be good enough – for the journey and for the town?

'Good. And the cook can prepare us something hot to take for the journey, too. If you're not sure about anything, come back and ask me. I'm not going out again today. Now, off you go.'

'Right, sir.'

'Oh! Wait – Charlie, will you take this horn back down to the hall? Leave the cloth. Set it on the hall table to good effect. It's a fine thing, isn't it?' he added, as Charlie hefted the horn reverently in both hands.

'I've never seen anything like it, sir.'

'No? Well – it's travelled a long way to get here.' And as Charlie left the room with the horn cradled in his hands, he could feel the master's eyes, following it out of sight.

Chapter Three

Charlie's fingers clenched as he watched two lads from the stables load the heavy kist on to the back of the chaise. He prayed the whole thing would not heel over. The master had not given any further direction on what he might need in Aberdeen or how long he might stay, and Charlie knew he had panicked, stuffing every corner of the kist with anything he could think of that might be required. What if he had to unpack half of it again here, before they left? The master would not be best pleased to be delayed.

But at last the kist was counterbalanced by the two of them in the front of the chaise, and John Leith was making remarks about a fine heavy load steadying the horse and vehicle on slippery roads.

'I hope you've taken a good breakfast, Charlie!' he laughed. 'We need to keep her low on the wheels!'

'But take care, John,' came the mistress' voice. She stepped warily on to the icy cobbles of the yard, a hand on her stomach. Phoebe was at her side, ready to support her. Charlie, bundled about with his own bit of luggage and the hot food they had brought for the journey, hoped he did not look a complete fool, an extra piece of makeweight with no other use. He even half-hoped she would smile at him the way she had yesterday when she gave back the perfectly-mended gloves, and half-wished she would not notice him at all. John Leith bent to kiss his wife, and Phoebe slipped a quick look past him at Charlie. She winked. Confused, he tried to wink back and smile at the same time, and somehow ended up with a kind of staggered blink and a grimace. He prayed she would think it just a joke, and she was certainly grinning before she turned away.

Then the master flicked at the reins, called to the horse, and they were off.

The road to Aberdeen, whatever Charlie might have fancifully expected, looked no different from any other road in the parish, particularly in the snow. John Leith was a careful driver and took the way at a steady pace, not pausing even as he called out to acquaintances in Kennethmont village and beyond. The sky was easing from darkness into a solid grey, but it threatened no more snowfall just yet: just the usual low pearling roof of a winter's day. Rooks, and the occasional buzzard, observed them from on high, and from his elevated perspective as the light improved Charlie was able to see quantities of deer tracks in the fields they passed, and the places where the herds had scraped away at the snow to nuzzle out sustenance underneath. He tried to concentrate on the birds and the deer and ignore the fact that his face was freezing hard, the nip in his cheeks and the way his eyes were watering. It was extremely cold, and the speed the horse was settled at did not help.

'Aye, the frost has hardened the road just enough!' said John Leith happily. 'We should make good progress if the sun does not come out and soften everything.'

The master's mood seemed as bright as usual, yet he did not appear much disposed to conversation, and occasionally, when Charlie glanced at him, there was a little frown, more of puzzlement than anything else, caught on his high forehead. But then he gave himself a shake, and asked Charlie to pull out a couple of the cook's hot pies for a snack as they drove on. Charlie's fingers soon thawed around the greasy pastry and he felt much the better for it as the meat and gravy slid welcome down his throat. There was brandy, too, and the master encouraged Charlie to take a mouthful.

'No more, just now: it can go to your head very quickly in the cold.'

Charlie was happy with just a sip. He was not used to spirits, and did not quite like the sound of them. But the brandy certainly warmed him, a different kind of warmth from the honest, sensible, and much more flavourful, pie.

What light there was in the sky was ahead of them as they made their way south east. The land grew flatter and wider, and John Leith pointed out the broad sweep of the River Don carving a path through snowy fields. He named the towns and villages they passed through, Insch and Inverurie, Dyce and Bucksburn, half-known names of places he had never been. The road rose at last as the river fell away into its valley: the way was mucky now and well-used, and the traffic much busier. At every moment Charlie thought the master would say they had arrived in Aberdeen, and at the next he realised the houses and the people had grown more dense yet.

But at last they found themselves in a kind of wide square, into which Charlie reckoned you could fit Kennethmont village and still have room for kailyards round the edges. Mind, you would have had to take the people out of it first: never had he seen such a seething mass of humanity. He almost clutched at his master's arm, terrified they might lose each other and never be found again. There was a market on, he saw: he could smell cooking and leather, apples and beer, animals, dead and alive, all wound about together. It was impossible to see any individual stall through the crowd: people with barrows, or carts, or on horseback, shoved their way through, on snow turned to grey water. He caught sight of a well head with an odd little statue on it, with women and buckets gathered at its foot – there was a great gossip going on. Not far off stood a strange little round house construction topped with a stone spike – it must be the tron, he thought, where dealers brought their goods to be weighed, to make sure they were not selling short measures. There was no sign of a church, confirming his suspicions that they had arrived in a godless place, but the buildings he could see were grand indeed, the height of Leith Hall and wrought in great blocks of hard stone. Besides the scents from the stalls and the smoke from what must be hundreds of household fires, an odd smell of fish was in the air, and when he glanced down a side street he was astonished to see water at the bottom of it, and boats. Of course: Aberdeen was by the sea. A chill ran up Charlie's spine. He had never seen the sea, and he was not quite sure, from all he had heard, that he would like it much.

But the sea was not John Leith's present concern. He guided the chaise through the crowds, around the great square to a part of the buildings in the far corner, and drew to a halt.

'Here's the town house, then, Charlie. Here, take this key and get the door open. When we have the luggage in I'll show you where the stables are.'

The house – Charlie would not have called it a house at all – was tall, indeed, but so narrow he wondered how he and the master might pass each other. It seemed to be all stairs, and chambers barely fit for a servant. He took the kist and hauled it into the ground floor room, unsure as yet of the room's purpose, then flung his own pack and the almost empty bag of food after it. The horse must be exhausted, he thought, and it would be good to get it to its stable.

The master led him, with him leading the horse and chaise, back across the square towards a smaller, broader building with an archway to one side in its stern grey wall.

'This is the Castlegate, Charlie, if you need to ask your way back. The Plainstanes, where the markets are, is that bit there. And here, before us, is Campbell's inn, which will be our cook, our washerwoman and our stableyard while we are here.'

Charlie blinked, confused. John Leith led the way through the opening in the stone wall, and Charlie brought the horse and chaise through to find a generous stableyard, with plenty of room to store the chaise until they needed it. If the rest of the inn's accommodation was as fine, Charlie had little need to worry about his duties in Aberdeen: he would have no more to do for his master than he had at Leith Hall.

'I'll go and see who is about,' said the master. 'You go back and air the house, and see if there's anything you think we need. I'll be back in an hour or so.'

Charlie hesitated at the inn's archway. Could he really cross that great square all on his own? And which (oh, heavens, he should have paid more attention!) which of the tall, thin houses on the other side was his master's? He found he was clutching the gatepost like a man about to jump off a bridge. He marked with his eye the house he believed he should be aiming for, took a deep breath, and plunged into the crowd, hands deep in his pockets, trying to watch everything at once: his goods and gear, the people around him, the cobbles beneath his feet (littered with kale leaves, scraps of meat too noisome even to be hidden in a pie, twisted rags, a discarded shoe, and almost anything one could think of that might be hazardous to stand on) and the house on the other side of the square. When he reached the right row of houses, he stopped, staring up at them, trying to remember any detail that might distinguish one from another – it must be one of these three, surely? Any further along and he would have noticed. Wouldn't he?

Then, just as he was about to try knocking at doors, he recognised the shape of the door handle at the third house – it was a shape the estate carpenter liked to make, and there were several examples back at Leith Hall. Leaping at it almost as if he thought the house might escape his clutches, he thrust the key into the lock, shoved the door open and slammed it shut behind him. He drew breath and almost laughed at himself, then shivered a little as he paused for a moment in the stillness. He had never been in a house on his own before. He could, he thought, do anything he liked. Within decency, of course.

He began to explore, starting his duties as he went. The house branched upwards into four storeys, each seeming smaller than the last. There was a basement, too, with a kitchen, and there he put his own pack: he would sleep there beside the kitchen fire, he thought, not miles up in the air in the dusty attics. What if such a thin house fell down in the night?

For his master there was what was clearly the best bed chamber, and he lifted dustsheets from a chair and table, and shook out the bed hangings. He lit a fire in the grate – there was plenty of wood, and even some coal, in a room off the kitchen – then he found what seemed just about large enough to be supper room and parlour for the master and lit a fire there, too. Finally he set the largest fire in the kitchen: the heat would rise through the rest of the house, and if he needed to boil a kettle he could do so quickly. Seeing all the fires settled and going, he went to the parlour window and stared out at the Castlegate, at the thinning mob outside, at the hurrying figures on the Plainstanes, at lamps being lit in the gathering dusk. Lamps in the windows, lanterns in people's hands, but also lamps in the street, outside the inn and outside other grand buildings, too. He stared in awe before closing the shutters firmly against the cold. Imagine lighting the street! It seemed terribly extravagant. And what would the minister say, if God's own darkness were being confronted like this? Defied?

He climbed the narrow stairs again to the next floor, checked the fire in the front bedroom, then went to the smaller chamber at the back. Here the window looked over the harbour, grey water darkening as the light faded. And beyond that was the sea itself, and that he could not quite comprehend. It seemed so close. The harbour was prickly with masts, and a tall ship was angling itself into the berth, making an end to its voyage as the day ended. He was surprised how slowly and smoothly it travelled: he had thought ships rough things, from the tales he had heard, tossing about all the time, beaten by waves the height of mountains, constantly being wrecked with the loss of all hands.

He shivered, not at all at ease with the closeness of all that water – were there not tides and things, that caused it to rise and fall? Would it come up to the house? But surely there were plenty of buildings lower down the hill even than their basement: they could not flood all the time and still be inhabited. Perhaps tides only happened in some places. He shrugged. He had to admit he knew almost nothing about it.

Back in the kitchen he found a warming pan and filled it with hot coals, and carried it up carefully to his master's bed. The covers were just as fine as those at Leith Hall, and just as new. He wondered how often his master stayed here. The rooms might be pokey, but there was nothing shabby about them, and they were barely dusty. Until he had been promoted to be the master's new manservant, he had been mostly unaware of the master's comings and goings, except when they knew he was in America. Aye, he grinned to himself, that would be a bit further than Aberdeen! He hoped his master's stravaiging days were over: Aberdeen was as much excitement as Charlie wanted. He unpacked his master's kist and shook out anything susceptible to creases after their short journey, then returned to the kitchen to tackle the remainder of the food they had brought with them. John Leith would not want any of it now, and Charlie, after all his excitement, was famished.

He had just about swallowed the last crumbs of pastry when he heard the door open upstairs, and ran to attend it.

'Ah, Charlie, finding your way about?'

'Aye, sir.'

'Good. I'll take a change of clothing and a drink, and then we'll go across to the inn. Dalgarno and Keracher are there and your friend Tam, you'll be pleased to know. And Lord Watt is to join us, I believe, which will give the evening some dignity, no doubt!' John Leith smiled. Charlie remembered the cool, upright gentleman at

Mayen House. Another man, Charlie thought, might be resentful of such a curb on his festivities as Lord Watt might seem to be, but the master seemed to be fond of everyone. It was part of the reason Charlie liked him, if he could be allowed to like his master.

Campbell's inn was every bit as well appointed inside as Charlie had expected from the quality of the stableyard. There were a number of rooms, some private, some open to all, and the public one into which John Leith familiarly led the way was as comfortable as Leith Hall or Mayen or any gentleman's home into which Charlie, in his short experience, had ventured. Wooden partitions about the walls formed cosier, or more private, spots for conversation. He at once saw Lang Tam, propped against a wall next to a table in the corner, and as expected John Leith headed for the same table. Both Keracher and Dalgarno rose to embrace him, and even Lord Watt stood and bowed his head politely. He, too, had an attendant, though Charlie had never particularly warmed to him: like his master he was quiet, polite, and a little superior. Nevertheless, he leaned past Lang Tam discreetly to shake Charlie's hand, his own cool, despite the warmth of the room.

'Good evening to you,' he said, not unfriendly.

'Good evening, Mr. Holland,' said Charlie.

'Aye, Charlie.' Lang Tam grinned, and gave him a slap on the shoulder. Charlie smiled back. 'I thought you never ventured into the town, lad?'

'I never have before,' Charlie admitted. The gentlemen were already busy with their own conversation, paying no attention to what they were saying. Mr. Holland raised his thin eyebrows carefully.

'Your first time in Aberdeen?' he asked. 'Then please take my advice: be most careful where you go and whom you trust, young man. The town will not be like your home village. Be particularly mindful,' he added, leaning in closer, across Lang Tam's stomach, 'that the women in town are not always what they appear to be.' He nodded meaningfully. Charlie nodded back, wondering what on earth the man meant. How could a woman be something she didn't appear to be? Lang Tam patted him on the arm again.

'Dinna fret, lad. Stick with me, and I'll make sure you stay safe.' He winked at Charlie, with the slightest of nods at Mr. Holland. Charlie decided that even Lang Tam spoke a different language in the

25

town, and that it was one he had no idea how to begin to understand. He smiled politely, and leaned back against the wall, looking about him at the room, the gentlemen in what he thought were probably their second-best coats and lace, the servants bringing wine to the tables with practised ease, trays full of bottles high in the air. There was so much bustle he had never seen the like, not even in Strathbogie on market day. He found he had pretty much flattened himself against the wall, determined not to get in anyone's way, anxious not to cause offence in any direction.

'We'll take another couple of bottles here!' John Leith cried out as one of the inn's servants passed. The man nodded and spun on through the crowd, presumably to fetch more wine. 'Charlie, why don't you men take that table there and get yourselves some food?'

Lang Tam and Charlie glanced at each other and as fast as thought Tam had folded himself on to a bench by the adjacent table, hand up for the inn's servant. Mr. Holland joined them more reluctantly.

'I'm afraid this may mean they are settling in,' he said, with an anxious glance at his own master. 'I do hope they remember to eat something, too.'

'Is your master likely to make a night of it?' asked Lang Tam conversationally. 'I dinna think I've ever seen the man drunk.'

'Oh, I was thinking more about your gentlemen,' said Holland. 'I shouldn't like my master to be embarrassed at all.'

'Aye, well, no doubt he'll step away from anything that might make him look bad,' said Lang Tam. 'I shouldna think dirt clings to him anyway.'

'No, no indeed! He is a most respectable gentleman!' said Mr. Holland eagerly. Charlie was sure Lang Tam had been being sarcastic, but it did not seem to have occurred to Mr. Holland.

'Cobairdy and Brux are in the town tonight, too,' said Lang Tam, naming another couple of gentlemen by their territorial titles – the way John Leith was often called 'Leith Hall', and Mr. Abernethy 'Mayen'. Charlie struggled to think who Cobairdy and Brux were – had they been guests at Leith Hall? He hoped he might recognise them if so. 'When they arrive, your master can make his excuses.'

'Aye, aye, Gordon of Cobairdy's a decent man,' said Mr. Holland. 'His lordship will be pleased enough to see him.'

Broth arrived in deep wooden bowls on the table, and for a

few minutes nothing else mattered much to them but eating their fill. Charlie as always was starving, and finished his first, trying not to stare at Mr. Holland's still half-full bowl. He looked about him instead: the large room was filling up, the tables lined with noisy, comfortable men mostly of the better sort – he thought many were prosperous tradesmen, like the miller down the road from Leith Hall, who dressed almost as well as John Leith himself, and had given a new stove to the church. But the booths about the walls seemed reserved for the gentry, and there were greetings and cheerful insults exchanged one booth to another around the room. He saw no women at all, not even amongst the serving staff, and was not surprised: he would not much like any sister of his, if he had any, working amongst the tight packed bodies in here. Or Phoebe, either. But Phoebe would be a match for any nonsense, no doubt.

Or maybe not any nonsense. Charlie felt his neck tense when he looked to the door and saw the three figures standing there. The first two were faintly familiar: one was middle-aged, blond, thickset, carrying himself as if he thought himself worth carrying. The second was darker, with messy hair and cheaper clothes and the air of an impoverished junior cousin come to town to beg for funds. The third was the endlessly mobile, slyly grinning, don't-turn-your-back-or-he'll-have your-silver-buttons, Byres of Tonley.

He jumped as his master called him to the gentlemen's table. 'Aye, sir?'

'We'll be here for a while,' said John Leith, grinning at his friends. 'Order more food for yourselves if you wish, and a jug of claret – keep the cold out. Oh, Cobairdy!'

The master stood, holding out his hands in welcome: the stocky blond man bowed to him, clearly pleased to see him, and the dark haired one followed.

'I had no idea you were in town, Leith Hall!' he said, and Charlie, watching him from nearby, thought that the dark haired man perhaps had less idea of most things than other people. He had a look on his face that Charlie had seen once on a man kicked in the head by a pony.

'Brux, I'm glad to see you are, anyway!' said John Leith. 'Come, sit with us. And Mr. Byres, too,' he added, his hospitable tone only very slightly awry. Charlie did not like to be standing so close to Byres. What was it about the man? But whatever it was, the master seemed to feel it, too.

Chapter Four

It started as a late night, and by the time it finished, it was an early morning. It would have been around three, he remembered later, for he saw a longcase clock over by the kitchen door, when the sound of his name repeated, and repeated, finally roused him from his slumbers. He lifted his head from the table where he had eaten the broth, then some very fine beef and gravy, and wondered for a moment who could be calling him. Then he saw his master, pink in the face and distinctly unsteady.

'Charlie Rob!' he was saying, and now that the general level of noise in the inn was quieter Charlie could sort of hear him.

'Aye, sir?' he said at last, mumbling his lips and teeth to clear them for speech.

'Away back to the house and get a fire lit – I'll be no more than half an hour now. Do you still have the key?'

Suddenly alarmed, Charlie patted his waistcoat pocket, and felt the metal safe and sound.

'Aye, sir,' he said. He intended to leave at a smart pace, but his feet betrayed him, whether affected by the claret or by a few hours motionless in an odd posture, he was not sure. He caught his foot on the leg of the bench and stumbled.

'Hi, dinna dae that!' cried Lang Tam, rolling off the bench with a slow, languorous sprawl. He crawled back up off the floor and lay back on the bench again, face down, embracing it like a lover, with his legs hanging off the end by more than a foot. He instantly began to snore. Mr. Holland, and Lord Watt, were nowhere to be seen. Charlie steadied himself on the table, made a face at Lang Tam, and managed to carve a fairly straight line to the door of the inn.

Outside snow had obliterated much of the detail of the daytime Castlegate, and the lights at the inn door and its stableyard gate were caught in globes of still-falling golden petals of snow. For a moment Charlie stopped in awe: then the cold bit at his bare hands and face, and he pulled his coat tight around him and made for the other side of the square. This time he found the house straight away, and proudly turned the key in the lock as though it were his very own property.

It was the work of ten minutes or so to revive the kitchen fire, revive the fire in the master bedroom, slip the warming pan out from the bed and take it back to the kitchen for refilling with fresh coals, and return it to the bed. Then he filled a kettle from the barrel of water he had drawn at the well earlier and set it to boil, and ran back upstairs again to set the master's nightshirt and nightcap to air and warm by the fire. He hoped John Leith would be too tired to ask for a bath, but at least one kettle would be a start. When he had seen his master off to bed and banked up the kitchen fire once again, he would finally have reached the end of his out-of-the-ordinary, exhausting day. It could not come soon enough.

It was not early the next morning, not by normal standards, when Charlie tiptoed up the stairs to the top of the house to take a brave look at the sea by daylight. It was no more comforting than it had been at dusk the night before, and the tangle of ships and boats, their masts and all those bits of rope looked dangerous enough in themselves without adding high winds and waves the size of mountains. He thought about the story of Jonah in the Bible, and considered that if he found himself out at sea in one of those little wooden trays wrapped about with canvas and string, he would probably prefer to be swallowed by a whale. He would not say that to the minister, though.

He paused at the master's chamber door on his way back down the stairs, and heard dense, steady snoring from within. He tiptoed into the room and saw to the fire, then observed his master for a moment. It would be as well to have his hot water ready, but he would not bring it upstairs yet. His master looked set to sleep till supper time.

He could not go far until his master was awake and had no need of him, but it occurred to him that the market stalls were not far from the front door, and the market yesterday had sold pies, pies which had smelled, at least at a cursory sniff, sweet and wholesome. He went to the front door and laid his hand on the latch, then darted out with his farthing ready, seized a pie from the nearest stall and rushed back into the silent house. The pie was piping hot and he retreated with it to the kitchen and the fire, where he helped himself to a draught from the barrel of small ale he had found in the pantry. It tasted fresh: it could not have been there long.

He was licking the last of the pastry from his fingers and wondering what duties he might have to perform today, when there was a bellow from the first floor.

'Water, please, Charlie!'

The day had officially begun.

'We are going to visit my mother,' said John Leith, wiping the juice from a plate of beef from his lips. Charlie had run to fetch it from Campbell's inn. The small ale had apparently been good enough for the master's breakfast, too: he was on his second tankard. 'She is Mary Hay and the wife of John Gordon of Glastirum, up in Banffshire, but she has a house here in the Schoolhill. Mark you the way to it and back here, so that you will know it again.'

'Aye, sir,' said Charlie, trying to stretch his tired mind into something that might be ready to receive more knowledge.

'Not a soul last night knew anything about that powder horn,' John Leith fell suddenly to musing, as if it had been on his mind all night. 'I expected as much.' A little smile tickled the corner of his mouth, and Charlie was sure he had forgotten that his servant was there. Then he roused himself. 'Come, I must dress respectable for my mother! A clean shirt, and free use of the brushes, Charlie - and I must be shaved as neat as a judge!'

Charlie had never much thought of his master as vain, but he was certainly careful with his clothes that day, and Charlie tied the ribbon in his hair four times before he was satisfied with it.

'I have not seen my mother for a twelvemonth, I believe, and

I must pay her the courtesy of looking as well as I can! That and all the news of Leith Hall and her grandsons – that is what will please her.'

Charlie, from the thought of grandsons, set out (memorising the route as best he could) with a vision of an elderly, white-haired lady in his head, frail, perhaps, and a little fussy. Lady Glastirum was as far from that as she could be.

'Johnnie!' she cried, leaping up from her sewing the moment he was announced. She was the prettiest lady Charlie had ever seen. Neatly built, a little on the tall side but not ridiculously so for a lady, she had curling brown hair with a golden hint to it, a clear complexion and one of the sweetest, most charming faces that could be imagined: she seemed born to happiness and made for fun and laughter. She embraced her son with delight and the pair of them hugged tightly before parting, holding hands and examining one another's appearance closely.

'A few grey hairs, there, Johnnie! You'll have to take to powdering it!'

'Aye, Mother, for I can have no grey hairs when you have none! How is my stepfather?'

'He is very well, very well indeed. He is out this morning with his man of business, and he will be sorry to have missed you. But when did you come to town? How long are you here?'

'Only a few days on this occasion, Mother, but I shall be back before Christmas.'

'And who is this with you? Oh, pull the bell, dear, and let us have some tea. Harriot wrote that your man had had an accident.'

'That's right,' said the master, mouth pulled down in sorrow. 'He broke his leg and it will not heal properly. This is Charlie Rob – you'll remember his mother, no doubt.'

'His father, too, yes. Charlie, will you step closer? Thank you. Yes, you have a look of both parents about you – a cottar family, were you not?'

'Aye, my lady,' said Charlie, astonished that they should have been remembered by so magical a creature.

'I remember you as a little boy. I'm glad you have found a place at Leith Hall. I hope you will always be happy there, Charlie.'

He bowed his head, trying to hide the smile that blossomed on his face when he looked at her. It would be most improper to smile at her, but he could not help it.

'You can go down to the kitchen now, Charlie,' said the master, but Lady Glastirum shook her head quickly.

'Oh, no, he won't like that at all! My housekeeper has all her gossips in, and they have been known to tear handsome young men to shreds! Charlie, there is a seat by the window in the hall outside: you will be much more comfortable there.'

'Thank you, my lady.' Charlie retreated, awkward, not sure if he should go to the kitchen anyway as all proper servants should, or take advantage of Lady Glastirum's kind offer. It might not be so cosy as the kitchen, but it would be comfortable. He surveyed the hallway, found the seat near to the parlour door, tucked himself half behind a heavy red curtain, and endeavoured to stay awake. He set himself dutifully to try to remember the route from the master's house to here, as instructed, but he felt his eyes closing even as he tried to picture it.

But Lady Glastirum's voice, light as it was, proved very audible, and he seemed unable to sleep through his master's conversation here, in a well-appointed hallway, even though he had been quite capable in the noisy inn last night. He caught, he supposed, most of their conversation, though fortunately little of it was about anyone he knew: there were degrees of eavesdropping, and he could hardly sit here with his fingers in his ears. Besides, he was a servant: he was expected to hear things and never to speak of them. He straightened his shoulders and abandoned taxing his memory.

'Have you seen any of your uncles since you arrived?' Lady Glastirum was asking.

'My uncle Hay? No, I have not seen him for a couple of months at least.'

'No, my dear, not my brother: I believe he is in the country somewhere. Goodness, it should not be hard, if need be, to find a man so huge! But no: I meant your father's brothers.'

'Oh!' There was a hesitation, and Charlie wondered what the matter was: there evidently was a matter. 'Which of them is in the country, then?'

'Oh, I think Patrick and George are still abroad – and long may that continue! But Lawrie is home, of course. I hear Anthony might also be somewhere about. Just, dear, don't let him touch you for any money. And none of them is to be relied upon for anything, unless it be to empty a cellar.'

'I know, Mother, you've always said so.'

'Well, some of them are quite charming, when they are sober: just beware! Your father was by far the best of the family,' she added, a little wistfully. Charlie thought it might be nearly forty years since old Mr. Leith had died: he had heard tell of him, but remembered only his own master. The family had been Jacobite and all had fought in the '45, and even been taken prisoner at some point, except for old Mr. Leith, the master's father, already dead. Lady Leith as she was then had quietly kept the estate in order and done her best to provoke no one. Charlie felt his eyes close, thinking back to old stories of battles and scrapes and sorrows he had heard at the kitchen fire.

John Leith cleared his throat, sounding awkward. Charlie woke.

'Have you heard or seen anything of your friend Mrs. Dilley recently?'

There was something about his voice that made Charlie sit up properly and pay attention. This, he thought, was the question that had brought the master to Aberdeen to see his mother. But who was Mrs. Dilley?

'How strange that you should ask! Poor Mrs. Dilley. Her husband fought with you in America, did he not?'

'He did: that was how I met her, too.'

'I say it is strange that you asked, for I heard only yesterday that she has returned to Aberdeen at last.'

'Has she?' If Charlie had not known that only his master and the lady were in the room, he would not have recognised his master's voice.

'Well, so I hear. I have not seen her, and she has not visited. But perhaps she has business to complete, or is recovering from her journey: I know not.'

'Will you visit her?'

'I should do, of course,' said his mother. Charlie pictured her flitting about the town, bringing light and joy wherever she went.

'I take it she is staying in a respectable part of the town?' asked the master, sounding concerned for the woman's welfare, whoever she was.

'She is, I am told, staying in a little lane off the end of Ship Row.'

There was a little silence.

'Perhaps you would do better not to visit her there,' said John Leith. 'Send her a note and ask her to come here.'

'Perhaps that would be better,' his mother agreed. 'I assume that Captain Dilley's death has left her in an impecunious condition.'

'We may be able to do something for her. I could ask the other officers and we might make up a fund for her. He was well liked, Captain Dilley.'

'I'm glad to hear it. Yes, perhaps that would be for the best – I should not like to see her living in discomfort of any kind. And perhaps that is why she has not told me herself that she is here, if she is embarrassed by her circumstances.'

'Well, I shall make some enquiries,' said the master. 'She has perhaps been in touch with the wives of other officers: they may know more about the matter, before we jump to conclusions.'

Charlie's head nodded again but he thought it was probably not long after this exchange that the parlour door opened and woke him. He slid to his feet, pushing away the curtain, and tried to look alert. John Leith bade his mother farewell, with another embrace, and as if her cheer were spreading he beamed at Charlie before making for the front door. Charlie followed, sorry to leave his comfortable seat and the musical lilt of Lady Glastirum's voice.

'We were lucky to find her in and unengaged, even in this weather,' the master remarked as they reached the street. 'My mother is a popular woman. Right, now ... we're going down here,' he finished, half to himself.

The house in Schoolhill had been smart, clean as to its doors, windows, and stonework, and the street had apparently the attention of a scaffie to keep it clean. The same could not be said of their destination, though the buildings were substantial enough. They were uncomfortably near the harbour for Charlie's liking, he noticed: he hoped he would not take a wrong turn. Here, particularly in the lanie off the main street, the snow was lumpy and brownish green in places, concealing, treacherously, irregular heaps by the walls and at the side of the road, then dissolving altogether into brown puddles of glour. No doubt it did something to mask what in high summer would have been a very particular odour. Charlie, growing used to the finer smells in life, wrinkled his nose, then felt his face contort as John Leith spotted his expression.

'Sorry, sir,' he muttered.

'Aye, well, it's not savoury,' said the master, and Charlie could see his teeth were gritted. 'I'd not like to see my mother visiting anyone here.'

'Och, no, sir!' said Charlie, shocked at the thought. The master smiled, clearly used to the effect his mother had.

'Well, we're looking for the lodgings of a Mrs. Dilley,' he said. 'She's a friend of my mother's, and the widow of an old fellow officer of mine. He was a fine man, Captain Dilley.' Charlie tried his best to look as if he had never heard of either of them before. Phoebe had told him it was the most important thing to learn as a servant, to keep your face blank as could be – then she had told him he had a long way to go to perfect his own expression. But she was being helpful.

But now the master was looking about him, no doubt trying to find someone here who might reliably tell him where this Mrs. Dilley lived. The choice was not impressive: there were two small boys, apparently oblivious to the cold, poking sticks into the worst of the puddles, and an old woman in a grey mob cap, seated on a creepie stool on her wet doorstep, smoking a clay pipe and knitting a stocking from coarse brown wool. Kennethmont, the village by Leith Hall, was full of stocking knitters, and Charlie thought she would not get much for that one, though she was quick. She watched them, her fingers not pausing on the needles. The master looked again at the boys, then made his choice.

'Madam, do you live here?'

'Aye.' Her eyes rolled about, as if looking for a wittier answer, but none came to her.

'I'm looking for someone who has taken lodgings around here recently. A woman by the name of Dilley?'

'"Dilly, dilly, come and be killed!"' the woman crooned suddenly. Charlie stared at her. Was she mad? The woman saw him stare, and cackled. 'Never heard of her,' she said firmly.

'Do you know anyone around here who takes lodgers?'

'Ha! Around here? Oh, aye, all the gentry want to come live down here!'

'I didn't say if she was gentry or not,' said John Leith. 'Who takes in lodgers?'

'A'body,' said the woman. 'A'body that can get one.'

'What about you?'

'I've been kenned,' said the woman, drawing herself up on her stool as if lodgers conveyed a certain status, 'to accommodate certain persons.'

'Mrs. Dilley among them?' asked the master.

'Maybe aye, maybe no.'

'Och,' said one of the small boys, without even looking up at the conversation, 'you ken fine she came here last week, Grannie.'

His grandmother let her knitting sink to her broad lap for a moment, the better to look daggers at him.

'Is she in just now?' asked John Leith, pressing home his advantage. A coin appeared magically in his hand and for a second it looked as if the old woman would snatch it. Then she shrugged.

'She's no. She's away out.'

'Did she say when she might be back?'

'She never tellt me,' said the woman, offended at the recollection. John Leith stood back a little, pondering, staring up at the house with its blackened walls.

'I'm reluctant to leave even my name here,' he said in an aside to Charlie. 'I daresay it matters little around here, but I should not like to bring any stain to her reputation. And a note would no doubt be common property before we reached the end of the street.' He sighed, then turned back to the woman. 'Very well,' he said, 'I shall hope to return tomorrow, perhaps. Has she any established pattern of going out or staying in?'

'She's no been here long,' said the woman. 'No long enough for any *established pattern* of a'thing. If she gets herself an *established pattern* of any kind at all I'll be sure to put an advertisement in the *Journal* for you, and a'body else that's interested.'

'How very kind of you,' said John Leith, choosing to take her at her word. The coin, the subject of much interest on the part of both boys and old woman, at last changed hands. 'I look forward to making your further acquaintance.'

'Och, and the same to you, sir!' said the woman, mocking a curtsey without getting off the stool. 'I daresay we shall meet at the ball next Wednesday!'

The cackling followed them all the way back down the street. It seemed not to bother the master, but Charlie half expected a snowball, at the very least, until they were out of range.

Candles were already appearing in windows as they made their way back up to the Castlegate, appearing and disappearing again as the inhabitants closed their shutters firmly against the cold and the dark.

'I'll perhaps go back tomorrow,' said the master thoughtfully. 'It cannot be the pleasantest place to stay. Her husband was a very fine fellow: I am sure he would not have liked to have seen her like this.'

'What happened to him, sir?' Charlie asked, sensing that the master might be trying to encourage a little conversation.

'He was killed in the war over in America, in a skirmish after we took the fort of St. Frédéric. Mrs. Dilley, as some officers' wives do, had elected to travel with him to America. They stayed with headquarters, for the most part: sometimes they can be most useful, but at least they make life more pleasant for the officers – the company of a lady or two amongst all the rough men is a civilising thing. Anyway, it was a most unlucky thing: Mrs. Dilley had had a letter concerning her sister, who was very ill in ... London, I believe, and she had decided to travel home, so she had gone ahead of her husband. By chance I was on the same ship, for I was about to resign my commission: I wanted to be at home, too. Anyway, we had landed at Cork, where the regimental headquarters was, and had been there a day or two when word reached us that Captain Dilley had been killed. She was most tremendously upset, poor lady. Have you the key?'

They had reached the house. Charlie was poking into his waistcoat pocket when he noticed that the door was very, very slightly ajar.

'Sir!' he cried. 'Look!'

'Oh, that's not good,' said the master at once. He listened at the opening for a moment, then put a shoulder to the door and entered the house at a run. Charlie was at his heels.

In the low front room, feet up in front of a fine fire, was a long-legged, shilpit creature, with unbound hair and two days' stubble on his chin. He glanced up at the noise, straightened in his chair and waved to them.

'Aye, Johnnie, in you come! Come and have a news with your old uncle!'

Chapter Five

'Uncle Lowrie!' cried John Leith. Charlie, who had been bracing himself to evict a tramp, instead prepared to run to the kitchen for whatever refreshment the master thought appropriate – not that there was much in the kitchen. He would have to run to Campbell's, no doubt, instead. He kept his coat on.

'Aye, it's grand to see you, lad,' said the man, rising awkwardly to his feet. 'I hope you don't mind that I made myself at home. It's a grand cosy wee room here, on a cold day.'

'That's – that's all right, Uncle. Of course you are welcome any time.'

The man – Lowrie Leith, presumably, for Charlie was sure this must be one of the uncles so derided by Lady Glastirum, and could be no brother of that lovely lady – the man held the back of the wing chair for support, worn fingers pressing into the upholstery. Now that Charlie could see him more clearly he realised Lowrie Leith had a great look of the master about him, the long face, the amiable mouth – weaker here, though, he thought – the kindly eyes. Lowrie was wearing a very full-skirted silk coat in a shade of deep pink matching that of his nose, and much in need of attention. His breeches and waistcoat were blue, and his shirt and neckcloth gave evidence of several past meals. Yet he had a certain dignity, even as he swayed a little. The smell of sweat and stale brandy was only enhanced by the

41

heat of the fire.

'Now,' he said, with an air of benevolence, 'I'll not expect any kind of hospitality from you, for I ken fine you've neither food nor drink in the house – barring a barrel of small beer that would not excite a bairn, and a few pastry crumbs.'

He had been through the kitchen? Charlie was not sure about the etiquette of the matter, but he thought that even an uncle should not be quite so inquisitive. Certainly if any guest tried to do that at Leith Hall, he would not like to see the mistress' face when she found out. And where had he found the crumbs? He was sure he had swept up after his pies.

'That's right,' said the master, 'I'm not here long, and I've plenty of people to see.'

'Oh, aye, your mother, no doubt! It's a long while since I've had the pleasure of meeting her. Give her my best brotherly regards – Mary Hay, eh? As pretty as she ever was. I should maybe make her a call.'

'She's leaving for Glastirum imminently,' said the master at once. Charlie found he had to practise his expressionless face again. He was sure Lady Glastirum had said no such thing.

'Aye, well, I suppose I'll catch her next time. Did I hear tell you were away down to the foot of the Ship Row the day?'

'Who told you that?' asked John Leith, more sharply than he had spoken so far. He had still not sent Charlie to fetch food or wine. Charlie stood by the parlour door trying to look useful.

'I canna mind,' said Lowrie Leith innocently. 'So you were away there? Now, I wonder who it might have been that you were visiting there? I canna see that you'd have many acquaintances in that part of the town.'

'An old soldier from my regiment, fallen on hard times,' said John Leith, and Charlie was taken aback at the ease with which he told the lie. Sometimes he wished he could be so clever so quickly. He was useless when he tried to avoid the truth – people always knew.

'And you'll have been generous with the charity, no doubt,' said Lowrie, and sighed. 'Aye, your father was aye the same: generous to a fault.'

'I fear you are too kind in your description,' said the master. 'I merely called to see how he was.'

'Och, Johnnie,' said Lowrie suddenly, and his eyes were

pleading, 'would you no let me in?'

Charlie had no idea what he meant, and by the looks of things the master was as confused as he was.

'Let you in to what? It seems you need no letting in to a house, anyway – you can manage that yourself.'

'Now, now, Johnnie, dinna be unfriendly! Listen, man, since I came back to this country there's been no fun to be had – well, once the Government settled down and realised they hadna a hope of catching me and sending me back to the plantations, anyway. Aye, I enjoyed leading them a dance or two about the place! But man, I'm near fifty: there's been nothing to keep me awake for ten years or more now. I ken I maybe drink a wee bittie too much but that's pure tedium, for there's nothing to do. If you're into anything the least wee bit dangerous or exciting, would you no let me in on it? I'd sober up, I'd no be a liability! I was always gey clever, on my day. But I'm bored, Johnnie!' He ended on a wail, punching the back of the chair with a bony fist.

'I'm not involved in anything like that!' said the master, looking alarmed. 'I'll not risk myself and Leith Hall going against the Government. And I've fought enough on their behalf, too: I was glad enough to resign my commission and lay aside my red coat: that life is not for me. I want to die peacefully in my own bed at Leith Hall, with my family around me and the estate in good order. I've seen enough action.'

'Och, man, there must be something! You're a Commissioner of Supply now, are you no? Surely there must be something exciting there.'

'That? I've barely started that. There's nothing, Uncle. Nothing at all.'

But if John Leith lied well earlier, something squirmed in his face now – and his uncle saw it.

'Well, then,' he said, and his tone had changed. He looked hurt. 'Very well, you say there's nothing, and you want to die in your bed. Whatever you say, Johnnie. I'll away out of your sight, and look for my excitement elsewhere.'

He picked up a hat with an excessive brim from the other chair, and bowed unsteadily to his nephew.

'Good day to you,' he said, and marched, cutting between man and servant, to the door.

'Oh, uncle,' said the master in despair. He stepped close to the old man, and took his hand. Lowrie Leith turned in anticipation, a glint in his eye, but all John Leith did was to slip a few coins into his hand.

'My mother said –' he began, but the look on Lowrie's face turned thunderous.

'I didna come here looking for money!' he shouted. 'What do you take me for, begging from my own nephew? I don't need it!'

And he cast the coins hard against the wall of the hallway, opened the door and slammed it behind him.

Charlie stooped and silently picked up the coins, setting them on a shelf. His master looked aghast, shame-faced, and leaned hard against the wall.

'He's never been slow to beg for money from me before,' he muttered to himself, but he did not look as if the thought gave him much comfort. But Charlie was more struck by Lowrie Leith's strange request for excitement – or at least, not so much that, for Charlie supposed that even men as old as Lowrie thought longingly of their youth and all they had done. But why should he think that his nephew John could provide excitement of any sort?

On the other hand, thought Charlie, there was that odd arrangement with Abernethy of Mayen, the secret meeting in Aberdeen – oh, yes, in Campbell's inn! – set for some time in December. That had sounded very suspicious, at least. And then why had they gone to the lanie at the foot of Ship Row? What was his interest in Mrs. Dilley, and why had he lied about looking for her?

Yet Charlie found himself hoping that none of that turned out to be the least bit exciting. He was a great enthusiast for the quiet life himself, and even the thought of another night in the rowdy room at Campbell's did not appeal so much as his own bed, as early as his master would let him. Even as he thought it, the master straightened up.

'I don't much feel like going out this evening, Charlie,' he said. 'In an hour or so, go over to Campbell's and bring back a couple of dinners, a bottle of wine and ale for yourself.'

'Aye, sir,' said Charlie, very happy with the arrangement – as long as one of the meals was for him. John Leith turned and went to the seat his uncle had left, and crouched by the fire, staring into the flames.

But next day the master seemed to have shaken off his unaccustomed gloom: he rose early, penned his usual letters, and when he was finished he sent Charlie out at once to find the carrier for Kennethmont and for some breakfast. The carrier proved tricky: Aberdeen, despite his growing familiarity with the great square of the Castlegate and the streets each side of it, was still much bigger than he had ever imagined. When he finally returned with a covered plate of bread and beef from Campbell's, John Leith had managed to shave himself and was dressed in the best suit of clothes Charlie had packed for him, a brown topcoat, a sky blue waistcoat and brown breeches. Charlie hoped he would keep the bonnie silk well away from any muddy puddles – or indeed Ship Row in its entirety. But once breakfast was done, the master sprang to his feet and announced that they were going to see whether or not Captain Dilley's widow was at home. Charlie managed, he was almost sure, the immobile servant face he aimed for: nevertheless he thought John Leith picked up far too easily Charlie's reluctance to return to that noisome lane. He grinned.

'I hope not to be there for long,' he said, as if Charlie had actually spoken. 'And if I can see the lady, I hope to persuade her to move to somewhere more appropriate. It is the least I can do for the widow of a fellow officer, don't you think?'

Charlie was so taken aback at being asked his opinion that he could do no more than nod, and felt himself blush. This serving business was very difficult, he thought: sometimes he longed for the days he had spent as a lad, running about the kitchens on tasks for the higher staff, the Leith family only distant figures with whom he had nothing directly to do. It was not that long ago, but it felt like a lifetime away. He was lucky to have an indulgent master, he knew, but he wondered just how far that indulgence could extend.

He almost had to run behind to keep up with John Leith's long stride when they set off. The master was clearly in a rush – hoping to get his visit to the Ship Row over with as soon as possible, Charlie thought – but he did not walk so fast that he could not bow and smile to every acquaintance he met along the way. His odd mood of last night was certainly over. Charlie could almost believe that the sun had come out, but alas the sky was still November grey.

Even sunshine would have been unlikely to improve the lane,

though. It was just as miserable as it had been the previous day, though a little more of the revolting brown snow had melted, revealing tantalising glimpses of unguessable detritus beneath. A couple of dogs of indeterminate colour had replaced the two boys of yesterday: Charlie could not quite rid himself of the impression that they were, in fact, the two boys, just in a different guise. Where the boys had sticks, the dogs had their noses, but the solemn interest in anything unspeakable was much the same.

The woman who claimed to be Mrs. Dilley's bunkwife was not in her place, but the door was open and somehow she must have recognised their footsteps, for she appeared, arms folded over her shawl, before they had a chance to set foot on her step.

'Good morning, madam!' said John Leith, his cheerfulness not even dimmed by this apparition. 'I trust I find you well?'

'You've wasted your journey in your fine, fancy coat,' said the woman dismissively, catching a glimpse of the blue silk under the master's warm cloak. 'She's away out already the day.'

'Already? Did she say where she was going this time?' John Leith was not to be deflated yet.

'Aye, a' course, she tellt me she was away off to see the King in London, and she would be back till her supper Tuesday week,' said the woman, sour as earwax.

'Well, when did she go out?' the master persisted. 'I'm sure an observant woman like you noticed.'

Charlie did not think there was much benefit to be had from flattering the old carline, and indeed all she offered was:

'I was out myself and when I come back she was away.'

'And what time might that have been?'

The woman looked about her, and flapped at her skirts as if looking for a pocket.

'Och, michty! If I havena lost my good gold watch and chain! Away off with you, sir, and stop bothering respectable women.'

'Then I shall wait a little here,' said John Leith, kind enough to grin at her joke.

'You can please yourself, as long as you're no under my feet,' she said, 'though I'm sure a fine gentleman like you could find better places to wait. For all I ken, she's away for the day.'

The master nodded, absolving her of any responsibility for him, and settled to stand where he was. Charlie, looking about at the state of the walls he might lean on, decided he could stand without support. They waited.

The old woman, who eventually announced that her name was Margaret – perhaps in hope that John Leith would introduce himself – came and settled on her creepie stool on the doorstep and took up her stocking-knitting, occasionally flinging a remark or a question in their direction. After what must have been a couple of hours, the master sent Charlie to find a pie shop – advising him not to try a local one. Charlie relished the chance to stretch his legs, but he was dutiful enough to hurry back with his prizes and they stood each holding the hot pastry for a long moment before tasting it. The day was growing colder.

'Aye, well, I suppose.'

Margaret took her stool and withdrew, presumably to a warm room within. The next two hours crawled by, marked by the clock on the town kirk, though Charlie was prepared to believe it had stopped altogether. He and the master stamped up and down the lane as the old snow began to freeze again, and Margaret poked her nose out now and again to see if they could furnish her with any more entertainment. But eventually, as the light dimmed, the master gave a sigh.

'I doubt she's away somewhere for the night – in better accommodation than this, I hope!' He cast one last scrutinising gaze at the building before them.

'What if Margaret wasn't telling the truth, sir?' Charlie ventured. 'Maybe the Captain's widow isn't here at all.'

'Aye, well, dilly, dilly, come and be killed,' said John Leith surprisingly. 'It's from a play that was in London a month or so ago. Where would Margaret have heard it, unless her lodger had sung it near her?'

'I didn't know, sir.'

'Come on, then, let's go to Campbell's and warm our bones. I'm sorry to have made you stand out all day, Charlie: I hope you don't take ill of it.'

The climb back to the Castlegate was unpleasantly slippery, and Charlie's numb feet were like boards beneath him, his hands not much better clutching any support that offered. Campbell's big bright room was startling when they arrived, the heat almost as painful on their faces and hands as the cold might be when they went outside again. Charlie's eyes watered and for a moment or two he had no idea where he was going: he rubbed at them until he had some notion of where the tables were in front of him, and where the master's friends might be in the crowd.

As it turned out, they were early, and once again only Lord Watt sat, silent and sombre, at the back of a booth, a king waiting for his courtiers. John Leith went over to him at once, and raised almost a smile from the older man, while Charlie spotted Mr. Holland, Lord Watt's manservant, at an adjacent table. A solid-looking glass filled with a yellowish liquid sat before him, steaming a little. Still a little nervous of him, Charlie stood politely and asked if he might be allowed to join him. Mr. Holland glanced up, surprised.

'Of course, of course, Mr. um, Roberts, isn't it?'

'Rob, sir, yes. Leith Hall's man.'

'Yes, yes. The broth is fine this evening, Mr. Rob.'

He took a sip from his goblet. Charlie, growing more confident, stopped a servant and ordered a bowl and some bread. Mr. Holland sat regarding his master dolefully. Charlie wondered if he ought to watch John Leith as attentively as this, though it looked a little strange. But when the broth arrived, Mr. Holland returned his attention to his own table, and his goblet.

'Forgive me,' he said, 'I have a rheum coming on, and the only thing that will burn it out is toddy, hot as they can make it.' He nodded, agreeing with himself, then said, 'I am right glad to see it is your master who has arrived first this evening. He seems a kind man.'

'He is, I believe,' said Charlie, all too happy to praise John Leith. 'Are the others not?'

'Och, they're a wild crowd,' said Mr. Holland dismissively. 'Well, old Mr. Gordon of Cobairdy is not as wild as many, but he goes the other way: too nervy to disagree or to make trouble, even when it might be the right thing to do.'

Charlie found this incomprehensible, and let it pass.

'My lord Watt seems, um, melancholy this evening.' He hoped this would not be taken as impudence, but Mr. Holland agreed very readily.

'He is indeed: I'm glad he found it in himself to come out, but I was anxious that rowdier company, which he disdains, would cast him even lower. But Leith Hall is the ideal man to cheer him. I hope he succeeds before anyone else arrives.'

Charlie could feel the heat of the broth warm him from nose to toes. He was glad to have a quiet conversation with Mr. Holland: it made him feel older, more established, part of the group. It was good to have Lang Tam as a friend, looking out for him, but Mr. Holland conveyed a respectability that Charlie was sure would be desirable in a senior servant. He could learn from Mr. Holland, particularly as he seemed to be in an uncharacteristically expansive mood.

'Is he often subject to melancholy, then?' he asked.

Mr. Holland's mouth turned down a little, regretful.

'He has always been a quieter kind of man, standing on his dignity. But he has suffered in the last few years.'

'Is he ill?'

'He is not, no. He lost his only child, and then his wife.'

'Och, no,' said Charlie, doing his best to sound mature. He tried to imagine what such a loss would be like. He had lost his parents, true, but that was the natural order of things: the minister had explained that, and it seemed clear to Charlie. And his sister – well, children did die. He had been lucky to be spared himself, when the typhus came. But Lord Watt's wife could not have been very old, surely?

'Was it childbirth?' he asked, his voice lowered. He was sure Mr. Holland would appreciate such discretion.

'No, the lad was seven, and a promising boy,' said Mr. Holland. He glanced around, as if to check that the other gentlemen and their servants were not nearby, and summoned a refill of his toddy glass. 'He was killed in America, when Lord Watt was with the army there.'

'The boy was killed?'

'Yes: there was an ambush at the headquarters, where the wives and families were. The boy ran out, perhaps, to fight: he was always a brave one.' He broke off, and Charlie looked up, surprised to find tears in the servant's eyes. 'His wounds were terrible. Terrible.'

'That's ... terrible,' said Charlie awkwardly, looking away, back at his broth. 'Did they find the men who did it? Was the ambush, um, defeated?'

'They fled,' said Mr. Holland, simply. 'Lord Watt's friends tried their best to discover who might have boasted of such a valiant slaughter,' his voice turned bitter, 'but none could be found. And such a minor attack: we only lost one officer, besides the poor boy.'

'And Lady Watt?'

'A broken heart,' said Mr. Holland. 'My master is a good man, but he is not a warm one – you will not be repeating this, Mr. Rob, I know. You have an honest face.'

'Thank you, sir. No, I shall not repeat it, I give you my word.'

Mr. Holland nodded solemnly, and went on nodding a little longer than was necessary. The toddy appeared to be working well on his cold.

'I wonder if matters might have turned out differently. Lady Watt had a good friend amongst the other officers' wives, but she had gone on to leave the country, having received bad news from home. There had been talk of Lady Watt and her son travelling with her, going home early, but it came to nothing. That regret, and the fact that she had not her friend when she needed her, I cannot help feeling they made everything for Lady Watt so much worse.'

'Aye, you could see it would,' Charlie agreed. The broth was gone, but he was not going to interrupt Mr. Holland by ordering another bowl yet.

'And then, of course, it didn't help that the officer that died in the same ambush, he was the husband of her friend. Aye, it was a bad day, a bad day altogether.'

Charlie frowned. Something tickled the back of his mind, something his master had said that day, he was sure.

'What was the name of the poor officer that died?' he asked.

'Oh, now, wait a moment,' said Mr. Holland, tapping his fingers on the table to aid his memory. 'That was it – he was Captain Dilley. Captain Robert Dilley.'

Chapter Six

A strange coincidence, thought Charlie, at last summoning
some more broth and bread. But then he supposed that most of these
men had been in America together, fighting with the Royal Highland
Regiment. Not Byres of Tonley, perhaps: the thought of serving in
the Government army would not appeal to him. Maybe indeed he
would not fancy the thought of being anywhere he could not please
himself, Charlie wondered suddenly, for Byres seemed a kind of
independent individual, with rules of his own. But Charlie knew that
Walter Dalgarno and Matthew Keracher had been in America, from
all Lang Tam had told him: Mayen, as well, like Dalgarno and
Keracher trying to improve his fortunes by placating the Government
and by making a bit of money for his estate. And now Lord Watt, too.
Cobairdy and Brux? He was not sure: both, he thought, were of
Jacobite families, and may have found it useful to show a little loyalty
to the King in London for a change. But Mr. Holland was right about
Cobairdy, anyway: he was a nervous sort of fellow, and older than the
rest. And Brux tended to follow where Cobairdy led – both, he knew
now, had been at Leith Hall for a stay, and Charlie had seen them at
close quarters, though he had been so nervous serving the guests that
he might not have been the best observer. He remembered Mr.
Gordon of Cobairdy being quite kind when he spilled soup on his
shoulder, but he could not remember ever having heard mention of

either of them fighting in America. But he should not be surprised to find that John Leith was interested in helping the widow of a fellow officer who had also served with Lord Watt. That made perfect sense. No doubt the master was rallying support for the impoverished widow amongst his friends and former comrades even as they gathered at the table.

Dalgarno and Keracher had arrived: Lang Tam saw them settled like a tutor with his bairns, and came over at once to where Mr. Holland and Charlie were sitting.

'A grand evening!' he said, rubbing hard at his skinny arms to bring back a bit of warmth. 'I doubt if you shot me now I'd no even bleed: the blood's all frozen in place!'

'You should warn any likely assailants to wait till you've thawed,' said Mr. Holland, not quite humorously. Charlie was pleased to see that he was munching on some of the bread Charlie had ordered: it would help with the toddy.

'Would that be true?' asked Charlie, puzzled. 'If you shot someone when they were really cold, would it not kill them?'

'Och, Charlie lad,' said Lang Tam, 'you can try it if you like! What way has your day been?'

'Cold,' Charlie admitted. 'My master was waiting for someone and they never appeared.'

'Oh, aye? That's gey uncivil,' said Lang Tam, arranging his spider legs under the table with difficulty. 'Could they not let you into the hallway, at least? Or was it one of those hallways with the draughts blowing all directions and no fire lit?'

'I'm not even sure there was a hallway,' said Charlie mournfully, wanting sympathy for himself and, by extension, for his master. 'He wanted to help her, and all. She –' He broke off, wondering if he should even mention a lady's name in this kind of conversation. 'She's an old friend of his mother's, and has fallen on hard times,' he finished, hoping that this was obscure enough. And it had the benefit of being true, as far as he knew. Lady Glastirum had mentioned her.

'Oh, right enough, that'd be Lady Glastirum's doing, sending your master to see she was all right!' said Mr. Holland, the kind of look on his face that Charlie suspected had appeared on his own face when he met Mary Hay. 'She's a fine lady, no doubt about it! Kindness itself.'

'And where's the poor old woman living, then, if she's hit bad times?' asked Lang Tam.

'The foot of the Ship Row,' said Charlie without thinking this time. The memory of Lady Glastirum had distracted him. Lang Tam made a disgusted noise.

'Aye, no lady would be there by choice, right enough!'

'And how are your gentlemen?' asked Mr. Holland. 'Oh! There's the master up and away. Excuse me, Mr. Main, Mr. Rob.' He gave a little bow, and hurried off to help Lord Watt with his coat, pulling on his own muffler and gloves even as he held open the door for Lord Watt to leave the inn.

'Aye, he's no bad,' Lang Tam remarked, watching him. 'A bit of an old mother hen, though, eh?'

Charlie laughed.

'Aye, I suppose so. Mind, he was telling me just now about poor Lord Watt and his son and his wife. That's a gey sorry tale, is it?'

'Oh, aye.' Lang Tam tutted, sinking his head on to his hands. 'That was a bad couple of days, no doubt about it. Aye, you can understand why the man has a face like a session clerk on the Sabbath.'

'I'd no fancy going for a soldier myself,' Charlie admitted.

'No? It's a fine life when it's all going your way,' said Lang Tam. 'No so good after the battle when your pals are dead and the enemy are having a party. Or when you're on sentry-go in a snowstorm and you think your fingers'll break off if you have to raise your musket.'

'Or when people are trying to kill you?'

Lang Tam grinned.

'Oh, that's no so bad! That gets the blood running – there's no feeling like it! Especially if they don't succeed, of course.'

'Aye, well, I suppose,' agreed Charlie, laughing.

'You think I'm joking?' asked Tam, then he grinned ruefully. 'Aye, well, maybe I am, indeed. Maybe I am.'

He called for more ale, and the evening progressed.

They had not stayed out so late this time, and the next day the master was keen to return to the Ship Row.

'Last day, Charlie,' he said reassuringly. 'If she does not

appear today – and surely that old quine will have told her I waited all day yesterday – if she does not appear, then I shall go home and write to her instead. Or ask my mother to,' he added, a pinkish tinge to his pale face.

Once again he dressed smartly, his hair well brushed and his boots polished. The night had been clear and bitterly cold, so at least the streets were less muddy than the day before. But it was a hard walk along the Castlegate and down the long, sweeping curve of the Ship Row: the sun behind them cast shadows of impossible length ahead of their feet, and dashed dazzling reflections from the frozen puddles, windows and slate roofs. They had to walk with eyes half-closed, the brims of their hats pulled low.

The door of Margaret's building was still shut. John Leith sent Charlie to chap at it.

'Och, she's no here!' came Margaret's voice, before even she opened the door.

'When did she go out?' the master asked, when Margaret opened the door, her knitting still in one scrawny hand. She shivered, and pulled her shawl more tightly about her shoulders.

'I dinna ken. She has a key. She maybe didna come back last night, for all I heard.' She looked as if she might try a salacious comment, then saw the master's face and thought better of it.

'Are you sure she's gone out?'

The woman sighed.

'It's me that cleans her room, makes up her bed, takes out her leavings,' she said with emphasis. Charlie thought then that she might have noticed if the lady had not spent the night in the house. 'Unless she was hiding in the close stool I doubt she wasna there.'

'I'll wait,' said John Leith.

She rolled her eyes.

'You're on your own the day. It's no the weather to be sitting out here, not at my age.'

She closed the door smartly, not quite slamming it. John Leith began to pace up and down. Every now and then they caught a glimpse of old Margaret, keeking out the window to see if they had given up yet.

And eventually John Leith did: he stopped his pacing, cast one last look at the house, and nodded to Charlie.

'Come on, then,' he said, 'early to bed tonight. We'll start tomorrow back to Leith Hall. I've a few things to get for the mistress, and you can go to Campbell's and tell them to have the chaise ready for us at first light in the morning.'

Though he had never, of course, participated in one, Charlie could not help thinking that by comparison with their journey from Leith Hall into Aberdeen, the ride home felt like an army in retreat. He was not quite sure why – surely the master had not gone into the town purely to find his old comrade's widow? – but whether his mood was a consequence of his failure to see her, or just a coincidence, John Leith made a gloomy companion.

Charlie had been up late cleaning up whatever mess they had made in their short stay in the town house and packing what he could of the master's things before the morning, trying to make sure that nothing muddy was against anything still fresh. And he was up again before first light, fetching a hot breakfast, boiling water for the master's ablutions, turning back sheets and curtains, and closing shutters to leave the house secure. Upstairs on the top floor he took one last look at the harbour and the charcoal grey sea, and shuddered, glad to be leaving it again for the safety of the countryside far inland.

He fetched pies, too, for their journey, and wrapped them well, feeling rather proud of himself for remembering without being told. But John Leith was not interested in food: he drove in silence, barely communicating, and Charlie ate the pies himself – something which, on the whole, he did not regret.

Still, the pies at Leith Hall were much better, and it was with a sense of great relief, bordering on excitement, that he found himself once again recognising landmarks in the snow, like the church spire. He waved eagerly even to people he only half-knew, taken aback at their casual friendliness, feeling as if he had been away for a year and they should have been astonished at his safe return. When they reached the point on the driveway where he could at last see the house through the trees, he found he could not speak. He was a home body: there was no sense in pretending otherwise.

'So what did you bring me from the town, then, Charlie?' Phoebe came upon him later in the passage outside the kitchens. 'Is it ribbons? Or sweetmeats?'

Charlie felt himself burn from head to foot. A present for

Phoebe was not something that had occurred to him, and there had been so little time.

'Oh ... oh, I'm sorry, Phoebe. I never thought ...'

'Did you no, Charlie?' Her face assumed a look of deep disappointment.

'Oh ... I never realised you would be, um, I mean ...'

She burst out laughing.

'Och, Charlie, dinna fret! I'm only pulling your leg! Was it fine, though, the big town? What were the ladies wearing? Is the mistress up to date?'

'The only lady I saw was Lady Glastirum, the master's mother, and she was very fine indeed.'

'Was she now? I've never seen her. Is she very grand?'

'Not grand so much. But she's just – I mean, she's very fine.'

Phoebe nodded, and removed a tiny piece of down from the shoulder of his coat.

'I'll know her from that, if she ever turns up at the front door in her carriage,' she said, smiling. She tossed the feather into the air, and they watched it as it floated sideways and off. 'Next time, Charlie, it'll have to be ribbons. Blue, I think – don't you?'

'Of course, Phoebe,' he said, contrite.

However, Lady Glastirum was not the first to turn up at the door of Leith Hall. Charlie was crossing the entrance hall the following Monday evening when he heard hooves on the hard ground outside – more than one horse, too, but without the sound of wheels. He opened the door a nervous chink, blinked at the cold draught that slipped in, and to his relief identified Abernethy of Mayen, with Walter Dalgarno, Matthew Keracher, and their servant Lang Tam Main. Not one of the horses was of the first quality - Tam's looked ready for the boneyard - and all four men were cold and tired. Charlie waved an urgent hand to the boy that waited in the hall, and the boy ran out to take the horses while Charlie bowed to the gentlemen, indicating the seats by the hall fire and holding out his hands for their cloaks. The men were noisy, relieved to have arrived, to be in to the heat and shelter, already congratulating themselves and calling out for John Leith. Almost at once Charlie was in a muddle as they piled his waiting arms with hats and gloves and mufflers, and he had to take them all aside to the kitchen passage and dump them on the top of a chest for sorting later. He turned to find that Tam had followed him.

'Good to see you, lad! Kitchens this way?' he asked, rubbing his bony hands together.

'You're welcome here! Aye, come on this way and get warm by the fire.' He hurried ahead of his friend, head in three different places at once.

'This is Lang Tam Main,' he announced in the kitchen without ceremony. 'Would we do hot wine for three gentlemen just arrived in the hall?'

The cook, already working on something spicy for the dinner, looked around and nodded to Phoebe.

'Good day to you, Mr. Main. Phoebe, get the wine from Charlie and warm it in the jug.'

Phoebe smiled at Lang Tam, then followed Charlie to the cellar door, waiting there for supplies of wine and brandy. As soon as Charlie had handed them over and locked the door again, he stumbled up the back stairs to find the master.

'Mr. Abernethy of Mayen, sir, Mr. Dalgarno and Mr. Keracher.' He hoped he had them in the right order: at least none of them had a title he might get wrong. John Leith had been looking over some papers with his farm manager in the bookroom.

'What, here? Now?' He regarded Charlie with surprise and delight.

'Aye, sir, in the hall. I've called for hot wine and ... um.' He knew an experienced servant would not feel the need to report every small move to his master. The master knew it, too.

'Well done, Charlie – horses being seen to?'

'Aye, sir.'

'I'll come at once. You'll excuse me, Jack,' he added to the farm manager, who was already folding up papers.

The bookroom door was pushed further open.

'John! Who is that in the hall? Is there something the matter?'

Charlie did his best to back out of the way as the mistress appeared. Mrs. Leith had a flushed look to her.

'Mayen has just arrived, with Dalgarno and Keracher!'

'Were you expecting them?' The mistress sounded far from pleased.

'No, not a bit of it! A surprise,' said the master, grinning. 'We have enough to go round, do we not? You said we had plenty in for the winter, didn't you?'

'Well, yes, we do ...'

'Well, then! Let us go and welcome our guests!'

Down in the hall John Leith was greeted with great enthusiasm by his friends, still buoyed up by their triumph in reaching their destination.

'Had to change horses in some gloomy settlement east of here – thought we'd never find anything with four legs!' Keracher's Fife accent stood out.

'Inverurie,' Mayen told him. 'I told you it was Inverurie. Nothing wrong with the place.'

'But what are you all doing here?' John Leith asked. 'Come on, come up to the parlour. Charlie, is the fire lit up there?'

'Aye, sir.'

'But Leith Hall, I think you're forgetting something!' said Keracher, coming to a halt in the middle of the hall.

'Oh, goodness, yes!' John Leith gestured to the doorway, where Mrs. Leith stood like a wooden doll, the stiff gatherings of her skirts and structure of her long bodice just so much bark on a tree. She had adopted a welcoming smile for their unexpected guests. 'My dear, this is Matthew Keracher, and this is Walter Dalgarno, both comrades in arms through the American campaign. Gentlemen, my wife, Harriot Stuart of Auchluncart.'

'Madam,' said Dalgarno, bowing elaborately. He was handsome, Charlie had to admit: though his hair was grey the roots were dark and strong and made him very striking. Keracher, a smaller man, almost disappeared behind the hall chair in his own bow. Mayen came forward, too.

'Mrs. Leith, you must forgive us for arriving unannounced! And if it is not convenient to entertain us then do not hesitate to show us the door!'

'Mr. Abernethy, it is a pleasure to see you again. How is Mrs. Abernethy?'

'She is very well, thank you – blooming! But wisely staying at home in this weather. May I enquire after your own family?'

The mistress flushed with pleasure.

'They are all very well, I thank you. And yours?'

'Och! I've lost count!' Mayen laughed at himself. 'I think they're all braw: they seem to run rings around me!'

She laughed: Mayen, Charlie thought, was probably amiable enough to counter any reluctance to entertain him. Yet he was not one of those deliberate charmers: he just always seemed friendly.

'Come upstairs, as my husband says, Mr. Abernethy – and Mr. Dalgarno and Mr. Keracher, too – make yourselves comfortable. Did you come straight from Aberdeen save your stop in Inverurie? It's a long ride!'

Led by their hostess, the gentry disappeared upstairs just as Phoebe appeared with a tray of hot wine from the kitchen.

'They're away up to the parlour now,' Charlie told her. 'I'll take that if you like. Can you warn the cook there'll likely be three more for dinner, and a late night? But I'll let her know if I hear different,' he added, not wanting to be responsible for the cook overdoing or underdoing the quantities. The thought of being on the receiving end of her wrath, passed on, no doubt, by the mistress beforehand, was alarming. He took the tray from Phoebe and carried it with great care up the stairs to the parlour, where he was relieved to see he had been right about the fire – it was blazing nicely in the great hearth, and the room was cosy. Charlie served the wine, leaving the jug by the fire, and retreated to an inconspicuous position by the door, casting a quick glance at his master and mistress in case they were sending him any signs of disapproval. They were not: in fact, the lady gestured him over to her side.

'Charlie, can you tell the cook to add three more to dinner?'

'I've done that, my lady.'

'Have you?' There was an edge to her voice.

'Just in case, ma'am,' he added hastily. 'I said I'd make sure, but I just thought ...'

'Well, go and tell her it's definite. And no doubt for breakfast tomorrow. You can be decanting a half dozen bottles of the burgundy and the same of the claret for later. And Phoebe needs to air three beds and set fires in the guest rooms. Tell the stable lad the horses will be here overnight. Was there a carriage?'

'No, ma'am.'

She sighed.

'Very little luggage, then. Best have Phoebe put out nightshirts, too.'

'Aye, ma'am.' Chastened, he bowed and scuttled off to do her bidding.

Not long before dinner time, he was summoned back to the parlour to show the visitors to their rooms: Phoebe had left jugs of hot water and he had the challenging task of shaving Abernethy of Mayen. He had only just built up enough confidence to shave John Leith, and had to struggle to stop his hands from shaking, particularly when he took a fine slice off his own knuckle working round Mr. Abernethy's long chin. He hid the blood in the towel, finished off his work and bowed his way out, sucking his finger as he hurried down the corridor. He had to see to the silver for the dining table.

Phoebe, finishing arranging dishes, found him in the pantry, still trying to stop the bleeding while pulling out knives one-handed from their box.

'What have you done?' she demanded, putting out a hand for his injured finger. 'Och, that'll sting! Here.' She drew a clean rag out of her apron pocket and wrapped it around the offending knuckle, tying it neatly. They stared at it for a second or two, but no blood showed through. 'If your finger starts going blue come back to me and I'll loosen it,' she said, and he was sure that she briefly squeezed his hand. 'Are you all set, or do you want a hand?'

Between them they finished the table, setting a cushion for the mistress at her seat and giving a final polish to the glasses. The wine was arranged on the huge sideboard, with the great chamber pot underneath it: from previous experience witnessing dinners in this room, Charlie wondered sometimes why the gentlemen didn't simply take the wine from the top of the sideboard and pour it straight into the chamber pot below. The door opened and Lang Tam stuck his head around it.

'Am I in the right place?' he asked.

'Aye,' said Charlie with a grin. 'I'll be fetching them down in a mintie.'

'And here's young Phoebe again,' said Lang Tam with every sign of delight. 'Would you no think of a wee change, lass, and come and work for two gentlemen in the fine town of Aberdeen? We'd treat you awful well.'

'I'm very happy where I am, thank you, Mr. Main,' said Phoebe stiffly. Charlie's heart gave a little jerk, surprised at seeing Lang Tam put down by a girl, alarmed at the thought that Phoebe might leave, and relieved that for now she said she would stay. He rubbed his forehead, glanced around the room, wondering what he had forgotten, then abandoned worry and went to tell the mistress that the dinner was ready.

The gentlemen were relatively abstemious while Mrs. Leith sat with them, though they ate three times the food she did. Charlie thought she looked pale, and wondered if she were still angry at the men arriving unannounced. But travel in the winter was never predictable, and if Dalgarno and Keracher were daft to go with him, Mr. Abernethy at least had the excuse that he wanted to go home to Mayen to see if his wife and children were well. And it was good of Dalgarno and Keracher all the same to save Mr. Abernethy travelling on his own. But she did seem tired, and Charlie was not surprised when, as he and Phoebe cleared the pudding dishes, she announced that she was going to retire for the night.

'So you may enjoy yourselves here as long as you will!' she added, smiling graciously as she rose from the table. Abernethy leaped up and the other gentlemen followed, bidding her good night as she left them. Phoebe cast a quick look at Charlie and abandoned him and Lang Tam to go to her mistress, as expected. Charlie set the dishes on the sideboard, and lifted the great round of cheese to the table. Dalgarno and Keracher took their seats again, but something had caught James Abernethy's eye.

'That's a fine thing!' he cried, with two long steps to the fireplace. 'I haven't seen that before!'

He picked something up and turned with it to the table, holding it up for all to see.

It was the American powder horn.

Chapter Seven

'Haven't you seen it before?' asked John Leith, only half a heartbeat late. 'One of my souvenirs from America. Perhaps the boys had it in the nursery when you were here previously.'

'I'd not let my boys play with a fine thing like that!' Abernethy laughed. 'Your lads must be greater respecters of things than mine!'

'Let's see?' Keracher had his hand out for it. Abernethy handed it over with care. John Leith reached out for the wine jug, and casually refilled all their glasses, but Charlie, watching, saw that his eyes barely left the powder horn.

'Weren't you asking about a powder horn when you came to Aberdeen week before last?' asked Abernethy.

'Oh! Aye, but that was a feeble thing compared with this. That was probably some soldier with fond memories of fighting, sending a sentimental gift. I just wish he'd put a note in to say who he was!'

Keracher handed the horn to Dalgarno, who peered at it with some interest.

'Where did you say you'd had this one done?' he asked.

'I can hardly remember,' said John Leith. 'Probably in New York – yes, that was it, just before we left.'

'You left early, didn't you?' said Keracher. 'Not that I'd want to cast any aspersions, you ken!'

'Aye, running for home!' Abernethy mocked genially.

'I didn't know how much longer we were going to be there,' said Leith, smiling. 'Maybe if I'd realised there wasn't much left, I'd have stuck it out to the end.'

'Aye, and maybe you'd have been killed. You were wise enough to go,' said Keracher, more solemnly.

'Aye, happy days,' said Dalgarno, handing the horn back to Abernethy with a sigh.

'Sad, too,' said Keracher, his mournful ginger brows turned up. 'I lost a good friend or two there, buried in American soil.'

'That reminds me,' said Dalgarno, 'didn't you say you'd seen Mrs. Dilley in Aberdeen, Leith Hall?'

'Mrs. Dilley?' Leith had taken the horn from Abernethy and was setting it back carefully on the mantelpiece. 'I don't think – oh, you mean Captain Dilley's widow? Is she in Aberdeen?'

Charlie was astonished at his confidence: the master was so convincing Charlie himself began to wonder if he had been mistaken about the name of the woman they had waited for in that lanie at the foot of the Ship Row. Could it have been something else? Davey, perhaps? Dandy? And how had the master learned to lie like that? Charlie was torn between deep admiration, and a strong conviction that the minister would not like it at all.

'Someone said she was about,' said Walter Dalgarno, pursuing the question of Mrs. Dilley's whereabouts. 'Was it you, Mayen?'

Abernethy frowned, and shook his head.

'I didn't know till you said just now.'

'Wasn't she some friend of your mother's, Leith Hall?' Dalgarno persisted.

'She was,' said John Leith. 'She was for a year or two my mother's companion, up at Glastirum. I think she had been left an orphan, and my mother took her under her wing: she was from a respectable family, of course.'

'Did she and Dilley have any children?' Dalgarno asked. He was showing a lot of interest in the lady, Charlie thought.

'No, they never did!' said Keracher, eyes wide. 'So if you're thinking she might be a rich widow, Walter, you'll not have to share it with any of Captain Dilley's bairns! Walter's on the lookout for a marriage to take him away from his debts, gentlemen, so if you hear of a likely prospect send the ladies in his direction!'

'You should maybe advertise in the *Journal*, Dalgarno,' Leith suggested.

'I remember she was a fine looking woman, Mrs. Dilley,' said Abernethy, nodding as Charlie refilled his glass. 'No doubt she's spoken for again by now, if she's thoughts of another husband.'

'Are you telling me she's too good for me?' demanded Dalgarno, and it was not quite clear how annoyed he might be.

Abernethy sat back to give him an assessing look, and shook his head.

'Who's to say she might not take a fancy to you, after all? Stranger things have happened. My own wife is a bonnie lassie and she still took me on,' he added, unable, it seemed, to make an unkind joke without taking the sting from it. 'I'm only saying you might be too late to woo Mrs. Dilley if someone else has got in first!'

'I never said I was going to woo her anyway,' said Walter Dalgarno, now assuming a smug look. 'I may have other fish to fry.'

'Oh, aye? Who might that be, then?' asked John Leith, and if he was relieved at the conversation turning away from the mysterious Mrs. Dilley, he did not show it. 'Anybody we know?'

'I should think so,' said Abernethy, as Leith refilled their glasses. Charlie replaced the jug, and met Lang Tam's eye: the gentlemen were settling in for another long one. Lang Tam shifted subtly so that he was leaning against the wall. 'Who would Walter know that we don't?'

'Nobody,' said Keracher. 'Decent society would never let him through the door.'

'Aye, but who is there? I mean, that must mean we do know her.'

'Gordon of Cobairdy's daughter!' John Leith suggested, keeping a straight face.

'She's spotty, she's no more than twelve, and she's promised to Forbes of Brux when she's of age,' Dalgarno protested. 'And she'll no have much of a dowry, anyway.'

'Och, she'll have more than you do, anyway,' said Abernethy. 'What about Lord Watt's sister? Ken, what's her name – something peculiar.'

'Their mother was from Donegall,' said John Leith. 'She's cried something like Cara, Cora ...'

'Tara?' Keracher suggested.

'That's a place, is it not? Ciara, that's the name.'

'Who was she married to last, then? Is he dead?'

'Aye,' said John Leith, who seemed to know these things. 'She married a man from down your way, Fife parts, Sir .... Oh, aye, Sir David Murray. He fell off his horse, and she came home and was married next to a Gordon – I can't mind which one.'

'There's herds of them,' Dalgarno agreed.

'Cluny, maybe? Anyway, he took a fever and died, and she's

home again.'

'Bairns?' asked Keracher, checking again for competition.

'Not a bit of it, not from either of them. It's beginning to look like more than bad luck, poor lady.'

'Aye, well, it might just take a real man to deal with that problem,' said Dalgarno. 'I heard Davie Murray was a cripple.'

'So is Miss Watt a candidate, then, Walter? Or is it someone else we know?' asked John Leith.

'You might know her, you might not. Or there might be more than one of them,' said Dalgarno, winking broadly. 'I might be hedging my bets.'

'Spreading your favours,' said Abernethy, nodding as if acknowledging the wisdom of the strategy. 'That's fine until they find out about each other. Even kindly lassies don't take well to finding out they're not the only yow in the flock.'

'It'd be a gey funny flock with only the one yow,' Keracher remarked thoughtfully.

'Have you land, then, Matthew?' John Leith asked, surprised. 'Or hopes of it?'

Matthew Keracher snorted.

'No, my brother got all of that. That's why I took a commission – to make my fortune,' he added sardonically. 'Tried that, now I'll have to try something else. Or hey, Walter, if you have two or more well to do ladies on the go, can you give me one of your spares? That would suit me nicely – and if she maybe has yellow hair and a neat wee figure then all the better.'

'And not too tall, eh, Mattie?' said Walter Dalgarno, nudging him with his elbow. 'You'd want a wife who can look up to you without you standing on a chair.'

'Aye, and you'd want one that's hard of hearing, for the way you snore she'll never get a night's sleep from her marriage night till her death – or yours!' said Keracher ominously.

Dalgarno, already muddled with wine, opened his mouth as if trying to decide whether to insult Keracher in return or make some remark about sleeping on marriage nights – Charlie held his breath, prepared to be shocked – but Abernethy had been distracted by talk of flocks and ewes and begun to discuss farm improvements with John Leith, and he had lost his audience. Charlie tried to emulate Lang Tam's neat posture against the panelled wall, bumped his head and decided he needed to be taller – though he was not as short as Mr. Keracher, he thought. He established himself a little more firmly on his feet, one hip propped against the substantial sideboard, and tried not to fall asleep as Dalgarno and Keracher sniped at each other with dwindling coherence, and the master and Mayen drew up plans for a farm that would cover the whole of the north east of Scotland.

The mercy of winter was that however late you drank into the next morning, the chances were you could still go to bed in the dark. Charlie blearily tidied the dining room after the gentlemen had staggered to their beds, almost too tired to give instructions to Lang Tam when he offered to help. Between them they locked away silver and covered the cheese against rats, brushed off the table, and extinguished all but one candle, finally sagging into dining chairs by its soothing light to share the remains of the last jug of wine before they, too, headed to Charlie's chamber for a few hours' rest. Phoebe had made up a bed on the floor for Lang Tam, and Charlie wondered if it was only his imagination or if she had deliberately made it a little thin and unwelcoming. He was quietly pleased – and ashamed of himself for being so – that Phoebe had not taken a shine to Lang Tam.

It seemed only five minutes later when the stable lad whose job it was knocked smartly on the chamber door to wake them. Charlie was on his feet long before his eyes were open, and managed to trip over Lang Tam. Tam grunted in alarm.

'Is that how you waken guests in this house?' he demanded. 'Kicking them where it hurts? I'd best go up quick and warn my masters!'

'Sorry,' said Charlie, grinning. He rubbed his eyes open, and lit the candle on the table. 'Were you up in the night?'

'Was I?' Tam looked confused. 'Oh, aye: well, I didna want to use your pot, so I slipped outside to the midden.'

'Oh! You'd no need to do that,' said Charlie, but he was grateful all the same. 'No doubt you can lie for a bit: I doubt the gentlemen will be up for a whiley yet.'

'Och, no,' said Tam, crawling out of the tangle of his blankets like some elongated spider caught in its own web. 'They were talking last night about setting off early, for we've to get to Mayen by dark. And the roads'll be worse from here, no doubt,' he sighed. 'Why my masters couldn't just stay in the town, this time of the year in particular, is a mystery to me.'

'I thought they just came to keep Mr. Abernethy company on the road,' said Charlie, who was already into his clean shirt and brushing his hair back to tie it with black ribbon. His chamber seemed less than half the size with Lang Tam in it, and it was not large to start with. Tam, sitting on the nest of his blankets still with his arms and legs everywhere, seemed unaware of the space he was taking up. He scratched his head thoughtfully, and stared into the middle distance.

'Aye, I suppose,' he replied eventually, and Charlie was not even sure he had remembered what Charlie had said. 'Mayen had to get home, anyway: his lady's expecting again – it's easy seen there's gey little to do of an evening up by Mayen, for that'll be their tenth – and he has no like of a farm manager. You ken he runs the place himself? The man has no money at all. But he's careful, I'd give him that, from all I've seen: he's not a spendthrift like my two. He's doing his best.' He stopped, as if he had lost track of what he was saying. Charlie fastened his waistcoat and tucked his neckcloth into the top of it, then pulled on his heavy brown coat and his boots, ready, he hoped, for whatever the day might bring and the master might require. He loved that coat, he reflected, making sure he had all he needed in the pockets. When he wore it, he almost felt as if he was a proper servant, smart and intelligent and experienced: the weight of it on his shoulders made him straighten up, head back, proud of his position. Then he glanced down at Lang Tam, shabby and dilapidated, with his years of experience behind him and his cleverness and charm, and with no need of a well-brushed brown coat to prove anything.

The gentlemen did indeed rise just before dawn, demanding breakfast in low tones. Keracher's normally pasty face was greenish in the candlelight, and Dalgarno had a shaky look to him. Abernethy was the healthiest of the guests, munching his way happily through a plate of mutton in company with the master, while Keracher and Walter Dalgarno, slumped in their chairs, toyed with a lump of bread each. Lang Tam caught Charlie's look and rolled his eyes, despairing of his two masters: he himself had managed two bowls of porage and a cup of ale at the kitchen table before he had roused both his gentlemen and shaved them each with a steady hand. It was solely to Lang Tam's credit that they were even at the breakfast table, let alone in clean linen with their buttons done.

Not long after first light, after Abernethy had chivvied them for half an hour and checked the horses three times, Lang Tam handed first Dalgarno, then Keracher – precariously small on a tall horse – up into their saddles, and swung himself on to his own horse. Abernethy kissed Harriot Stuart's hand with genuine fondness, and turned to John Leith.

'Thank you again – it was more than good of both of you to take us in.'

'Not at all, not at all!' The master was generous. 'I'll wish you a safe onward journey, though: it looks very much like snow again.'

They walked together over to where Charlie was holding Mayen's horse steady, leaving Mrs. Leith in the shelter of the doorway. Above them the sky, pinkish and swollen, did indeed threaten, and it was a little milder than it had been: there would be snow by dinner time. Abernethy checked the girth, and put a hand to his stirrup.

'I'll see you on the twenty-first, then, in Campbell's – you'll remember?'

'Of course,' said the master, his voice as low as Abernethy's. Mayen laid a finger on his lips, and winked solemnly, and John Leith nodded, equally sober. Charlie looked away, pretending not to have heard, and only when the master tapped his arm did he turn and bend to help Mayen up into his saddle. Dalgarno and Keracher edged up to them, murmuring their thanks and farewells, eyeing the sky through sideways squints. The fresh air may or may not have been doing them good. John Leith waved, and the party set off down the drive, quickly becoming shadows amongst the trees. At the last Lang Tam turned and raised his hand in farewell, and Charlie waved back, sorry to see his friend go.

Still, it sounded as if he might see him again in a week or so, if the master took him once more to Aberdeen. Though what the nature of their meeting might be, or why it should be so secret, he could not imagine: it seemed that Abernethy of Mayen and John Leith were perfectly capable of meeting in Campbell's inn without any secrecy attached, but this seemed to be long-planned. He considered for a minute, then shrugged. What business was it of his? Except for taking him back to Aberdeen, he could not see that any meeting, however secret, would have any effect on him.

Somehow, John Leith's next expedition to Aberdeen was talked of in the household as a journey in search of some particular sweetmeats and delicacies to be purchased for the celebrations at Hogmanay: a tradition had developed over the last few years of the tenants coming to feast at the Hall to toast the master and the New Year, and other guests came too. Harriot Stuart was in her element, cleaning and organising with an energy that the cook, with a sniff, said was typical of a woman in her condition. John Leith and Charlie, once more seated in the chaise, took a list of some twenty items from the mistress for their marketing, and Charlie folded it carefully and slipped it into his pocket. The bundle of hot pies on his lap was damp, but wonderfully warming: the snow had cleared again but the frost was hard.

Charlie spent the journey this time squinting into the light, struggling to recognise features he had noticed on his first trip, trying to learn the route particularly now it was less obscured by snow. The sky was high and hard and bright, the bite in the air bitter, and the shadows cast by the blade of the sun were sharp and black. John Leith was not in quite as excited a mood as he had been the last time, but he did at least seem quietly cheerful, less cast down than on their journey home before.

'You go to the kirk on the Sabbath, don't you, Charlie?' he asked unexpectedly at one point. They were passing through Inverurie at the time and the kirk there stood prominent on the main street, so it was not so surprising that his thoughts had turned that way.

'I do, sir, of course.'

'And what do you think of our minister?'

'I like him fine, sir,' said Charlie, not altogether sure that it was up to him to express an opinion on a member of the clergy. 'I believe he's a good man.'

'I'm sure he is, Charlie.' The master looked thoughtful. 'That's a very old kirk there,' he added, nodding at the church. 'Long before ministers and presbyteries were thought of, in the time of priests and bishops.'

'And popes, sir?' Charlie was anxious. The minister at Kennethmont had made mention of a pope, and it had not been flattering.

'Yes, and popes, too. A pope is a kind of bishop, really.'

70

Charlie was not very clear what a bishop was, so that was hardly helpful. He only knew that bishops and those associated with them were not too popular and there were things called penal laws to do with them – what these were was even more perplexing than bishops. He made no reply, and the master's thoughts evidently wandered on on their own.

The drive seemed shorter than the last time, perhaps because it was not so new. Once they reached the point where before Charlie had thought they were already in the middle of the town, it was only a matter of minutes before they were drawing up outside the narrow townhouse in the Castlegate. Charlie took the baggage inside and then headed back out to lead the horse and chaise over to Campbell's stableyard.

'No doubt I can manage the lighting of a fire myself,' said the master reassuringly, removing the pistols he had worn for the journey and knocking back his cloak to kneel unimpeded at the hearth. Charlie left him to it.

When he returned a little later, the fires were lit but the master was still in his cloak, hovering near the door like a worried buzzard eyeing its prey.

'I'll go out for a little, Charlie,' he said. 'I'll probably be no more than an hour. But if I am, don't worry.'

'It's growing dark, sir,' said Charlie. 'Do you not want me to come with you?'

'No, no, Charlie, it's fine. You do whatever you need to do about the house, and when I come back we'll go over to Campbell's for our dinner.' He was edgy, that was clear. When they had been in Aberdeen before, he had taken Charlie everywhere, and Charlie thought he had made himself useful. But perhaps the master had just been helping him to learn his way about the town, and now his education was over.

'If anyone calls, sir, am I to tell them –'

'You are to tell them that I am out, and will be in Campbell's this evening if they wish to speak with me.' Charlie flushed: the master's voice was rarely so sharp. As if he had taken confidence from the exchange, John Leith pulled his cloak about him and seized his gloves, making for the door. Charlie watched as he disappeared down the darkened Castlegate, then closed it softly after him.

He lit the kitchen fire, aired the beds, opened shutters and closed them again, all without thought. Then he went and stood at the little window on the top floor and stared out at the black emptiness that was the night time sea. Where had his master gone? When would he return? Should he have insisted on going with him? No: he could not see himself insisting on anything the master disagreed with. He would never be able to, not in a lifetime. But what if his master never came back? What would he do then? When would it be right to go home, and tell Mrs. Leith what had happened? Not that he would know what had happened.

But wait, he told himself, when he was dizzy with anxiety. He could find out at Campbell's where Mr Dalgarno and Mr Keracher lived: he could go there, easily, and ask Lang Tam's advice. But he would not do it just yet. He would wait a little longer: after all, the master had said he would likely be an hour, and it was scarcely an hour yet.

He found the muscles in his neck ease at this plan, and he turned to go back downstairs. But even as he did so, he heard the front door open, and the distinctive sound of his master's step in the hallway. John Leith was home again, safe and sound.

Chapter Eight

Supper was a gloomy meal. None of John Leith's usual circle seemed to be at Campbell's – he muttered something about Mayen coming the next day with Byres of Tonley – and besides whatever he had done while he was out seemed to have left him in a state of distress. Charlie prayed that Lady Glastirum was not ailing in some way, but he could not think what else might have brought the master so low. A quarrel with a friend, even, would surely not have caused this. The presence of Charlie standing behind him, attentive as a servant should be, seemed to drive him to distraction and he made Charlie sit at the table beside him, gesturing to him to eat as his appetite required. Charlie was very happy to oblige.

He thought that the master might prolong his dinner, or at least order more wine, to see if anyone else turned up late, but as soon as Mr. Leith had finished his meal and drained the last drop from his jug, he instructed Charlie to bring another jug of wine with them and follow him home.

Outside the air was steel sharp, the cold moonlight harsh, the cassies slippery underfoot. The inn servant had slipped a white cloth over the top of the jug, and as Charlie slid about he could see the dark stain of the wine spread a little where the jug had slopped. For a moment in the ice-white light he fancied it looked like blood.

The jug was empty next morning, and the master's bed had not been slept in. Instead, Charlie found him lolling in one of the armchairs in the parlour, head propped loosely in its wings, coat and waistcoat unbuttoned. It was not like him, in Charlie's experience. John Leith was a neat man, not given to careless living, however much he might enjoy a glass or two with his friends. Charlie was almost embarrassed to waken him, feeling he should not have seen him like this, mouth agape and snoring. But whatever had brought him to Aberdeen, Charlie remembered – though perhaps he was not supposed to know – that it was to happen today. He had no idea at what time the secret assignation was to take place, and so it seemed best to kneel noisily by the fire in the parlour, near the master's sprawling legs, and clatter at the fire irons a little while coaxing the flames back to life. In a moment or two, gratifyingly, there was a grunt behind him and the abandoned legs jerked back towards the chair. John Leith groaned.

'Oh! Oh, Charlie, I beg your pardon – I nearly kicked you. What time of the day is it, do you know?'

'Almost noon, sir. I have bread and beef ready when you wish for it, sir.'

'Ugh – is there water hot?'

'In just a moment.'

'Then I shall address it in my chamber as soon as may be. When I am cleaned and shaved, then it will be time for bread and beef, I think. My grey suit today, Charlie: and the cleanest and finest of my shirts and neckcloths. I have an important meeting to attend.'

'Aye, sir.'

John Leith gathered himself and went upstairs, and Charlie hurried to the kitchen to fetch hot water. There, he had officially been told there was a meeting – a sober affair, by the sound of it. The grey suit was a new one and so far Charlie had only put it out for him for going to church. He had been a little surprised to have been asked to pack it, but it was ready and aired, too. He poured water into a weighty jug, and trotted upstairs in his master's wake.

The master seemed to be in no great hurry, nevertheless. Carefully placing a large napkin about him he tucked into the beef and bread, washed down with ale, and considered a copy of the *Journal* for which he had sent Charlie out into the Castlegate again. Charlie could read, even the elaborate lettering of the newspaper's title if he took it slowly, but the close print further down the page muddled his head and he took no interest in it. After his breakfast, the master hovered by the door, in much the way he had done yesterday, but today his chin took on a look of determination, and he went to the chair by the parlour fire with a book he must have brought from Leith Hall. There he remained, sitting carefully so as not to crease his coat, until Charlie heard the town kirk's clock strike a quarter to four. Then he rose.

'I shall go to my meeting now, Charlie. At half past five you may meet me at Campbell's for dinner. Until then you may amuse yourself.'

'Aye, sir,' said Charlie. Whatever the master's destination, Charlie felt fewer misgivings about him today: John Leith was going to Campbell's, for that was where Mayen had told him the meeting was, whatever it was. He was dressed decently and had not that bright-eyed, edgy look he had had yesterday evening. If there was still a look of anxiety about him, he seemed to have it under control. And he had told Charlie to amuse himself: and Charlie had brought some pennies with him from Leith Hall for that very purpose.

He watched John Leith cross the Castlegate to Campbell's, a tall, slight figure in grey, almost ghostlike amongst the crowds, then fetched his own hat and locked the front door. Somewhere here, in this brisk mass of stalls, had to be the perfect ribbon for Phoebe, and he was going to find it.

In the end, indecisive as ever, he found he had bought four, and spent all his money. He would have to give them to her one at a time or she would not receive another present from him for months. But he had nothing else to save for but himself: many a cottar's child, sent to serve in the big house, had to take his savings if he had any back to his mother. For him, all that was gone.

For the rest of his free time, then, he wandered the streets of Aberdeen, making sure to be able to trace his way back. He even descended one street that led to the harbour, but did not approach too closely: from where he clung to the wall, gazing in wonder, he took in the vast size of the wooden ships – vast, yes, but could they be strong enough to withstand all the sea could throw at them? From all he had heard, no: they could not. The sunlight glared across the constantly busy surface, as though trying to polish knives on a moving table. The glitter and the gulls' cries and the constant thump, thump, thump of hull on hull on harbour gave him no peace, and though he made himself watch and consider it, in the end it made his head sore and his stomach as restless as the waves. He retreated to the Castlegate, and went about the house to make sure all was well – he realised that John Leith's fine pistols still sat on the parlour table, and for practice as much as anything he carefully examined them, saw they were unloaded – the master must have hoped the threat would be enough if they were attacked on the road – and laid them in their case, taking them upstairs to the master's chamber for safety. Then he sat down to wait for the clock to strike half past five.

Campbell's seemed even busier than usual, which surprised Charlie on a Wednesday night. It had been so cold as he crossed the Plainstanes that his eyes watered in the warmth of the entranceway, and for a moment he could not see more than colours and lights. But as things cleared, he found that his master, and almost all his master's acquaintance, seemed jammed into their wooden booth, elbowing each other in their efforts to tackle a fine looking dinner. Lord Watt was at the back as usual, in the manner of a presiding host: Gordon of Cobairdy and the shabby Forbes of Brux, apparently his son-in-law elect, were on his left, and at the outside of the booth on that side, ready to vanish if the moment required it, was the mobile Byres of Tonley, eyes everywhere. Opposite sat Abernethy of Mayen and the master, with Dalgarno beside John Leith and Keracher perched on the end of the bench like a pet monkey. The only face Charlie did not know was the man sitting on Lord Watt's right, a slightly-built man with a cheerful expression and a neat grey wig. Charlie wondered if he were yet another officer from the American campaign: no doubt he would find out sometime. Around the table hovered Mr. Holland and Lang Tam, making sure the inn's servants were furnishing food at the right speed and refilling jugs of wine promptly. Charlie took his place with them, and Lang Tam grinned.

'All well, there, Charlie?'

'Aye, not bad. Am I late?'

'Not a bit of it. They've not long sat down.'

'Then where have they been all afternoon?' Charlie asked. He had assumed that this was where they had sat for their mysterious meeting.

'Oh, upstairs, I think,' said Lang Tam vaguely, then turned to wave a servant closer with an ashet of roast beef. 'There's broth for us already if you're hungry. The gentlemen are well seen to for now: no doubt they'll dismiss us in a mintie anyway.'

'Charlie! All well?' The master had just noticed him.

'Aye, sir, all well.'

'Then find yourself some dinner, Charlie.'

'Aye, sir, thank you, sir.' Lang Tam winked at him, and Charlie went to their usual table where a bowl of broth stood steaming enticingly. Soon Mr. Holland and Lang Tam joined him.

'They're all in good form tonight!' said Mr. Holland. 'I doubt we'll be in for a long session! Or you will be, gentlemen: his Lordship will want away a bittie earlier, if I'm lucky.'

Lang Tam made some remark about not minding a late night, while Charlie looked again at the table of gentlemen. It was true, he thought, that his master and Lord Watt seemed content, and the stranger, too. But he thought he sensed a tension about the table. What was it, and where? If he could sense it, it must be quite strong.

'The mannie in the wig is a Mr. McFarland,' Lang Tam told them generally. 'Aught else about him I do not know, but he's a visitor in these parts. Is he staying with his Lordship?'

'No, not at all,' said Mr. Holland, peering over at the man in the wig.

Charlie only half-listened. What about Mr. Gordon of Cobairdy? He looked no more anxious than usual, but that was quite anxious. And Forbes of Brux seemed as dim as ever. Mr. Dalgarno and Mr. Keracher were joking with Tonley – not a very nice joke, Charlie thought, to judge by Tonley's laughter. But Abernethy ... Abernethy was paying no attention to the laughter, nor to the stranger Mr. McFarland, nor to the chatter of his friends. He ate, steadily and neatly, as if he feared the food might be taken away. And any attempt of John Leith's to draw him into conversation seemed unsuccessful, and eventually John Leith turned away and talked across the table to Brux, who had to squint at him to make out his words. At this rate, Charlie thought, he and the master might well be going home early.

But both his hopes and those of Mr. Holland were worn away that night, for however cramped they were in their booth, the gentlemen cleared their plates, ordered cheese to be brought, and at last seriously confronted the wine. Past midnight they continued: Charlie, struggling to stay awake, tried to see the clock with first one eye, then the other. Past two: past three. John Leith was pink in the face. Tonley seemed to have drunk nothing at all, his movements as constant and random as ever. Cobairdy had his head back and was snoring, till Brux nudged him hard in the stomach with his elbow. Dalgarno and Keracher were singing, quite tunefully, an old ballad into which Keracher seemed eager to insert new words, but Dalgarno was trying to stop him. Lord Watt was talking seriously, though a little unsteadily, to Mr. McFarland. And James Abernethy of Mayen, white as a sheet, toyed with his glass, and spoke to no one.

Something about his face pulled Charlie into wakefulness. For one thing, the gentlemen had all changed places, and Mr. Abernethy was now at the outside of the table, Leith Hall still beside him.

'What's wrong with Mr. Abernethy?' he asked Lang Tam. But Tam had his arms around some lassie he had found, and had no interest in considering Mayen. Briefly Charlie pictured Tam with his arms around Phoebe, scowled, and tried to replace the image with one where he had his own arms around Phoebe. But he was unconvinced: when would he ever have the nerve to do something like that? He turned to Mr. Holland.

'Do you think Mr. Abernethy looks himself at all?' he asked. Mr. Holland, three-quarters asleep himself, dragged his eyes open and considered.

'Drunk,' he said.

'Well, aye, but then maybe no. The poor man's looked miserable all evening long, and I dinna think he's touched much wine at all.'

'Dyspepsia, then. I'm more concerned about his Lordship. He's not used to late nights like this any more. What time is it, anyway?'

'Four o'clock,' said Charlie. 'Four o'clock in the morning.' When he had been the most junior servant at Leith Hall this was the time he had risen, stunned by the new day, staggering on his bare feet, completely sober. Any stunning and staggering this evening had come out of those wine jugs that seemed to keep appearing, regardless of the hour or the state of the gentlemen, on the table – and just as remarkably, kept being emptied.

'Did I not hear that Mayen's had a financial hit?' said Mr. Holland, coming back to wakefulness. 'Or am I mistaken?'

'I don't think he's very rich,' said Charlie cautiously. He did not understand much about money: he just knew who had it and who had not.

'Something about something that happened at Strathbogie mart,' Mr. Holland persisted. 'What was it now? Had someone accused him of adding cheap beremeal to oats, or something? Goodness, how these stories float past and only sometimes do they leave their details behind!'

'I don't think I heard that one at all,' said Charlie, 'but then we're quiet enough out at Leith Hall. But Mr. Abernethy was there a couple of weeks ago, and nothing was said about it then.'

'Well, I don't suppose anybody would say anything to his face,' said Mr. Holland sensibly.

'And I don't suppose,' said Charlie, suddenly feeling a little brave on behalf of the gentleman he thought well of, 'that Mr. Abernethy would do such a thing. Not knowingly, anyway. He doesn't seem like a cheat to me.'

'Ah, no, indeed,' Mr. Holland shook his head sadly. 'But sometimes, when a man is drawn into desperate circumstances – and his ever increasing family must place great demands on his purse. I sometimes think that it is better for a poor man not to be a gentleman. He has so many fewer obligations in life.' He paused, chin drawn in and his nose a little in the air, allowing Charlie the full benefit of his opinion. Charlie considered the idea carefully, and thought that there might be something in it, after all. Mr. Holland might not be as clever as Lang Tam, but he always seemed a sensible man, and he had many more years' experience than either Tam or Charlie. And where was Tam?

He stood up with care, and looked about him. After four in the morning, and the room was still busy, or at least still full of people – not all of them were talking, or drinking, or even conscious. None of them, however, looked like Tam. He sank back down, and took another look at the gentlemen's booth. Byres of Tonley was not there, he noted – and just the thought of not quite knowing where he was and what he was up to made Charlie glance quickly around the room again. But there was no reason to think, barring instinct, that Tonley was up to no good: he was probably off outside at the midden, where the fresh air made the process sweeter than using one of the reeking chamber pots inside – and come to think of it, that was likely where Lang Tam was, too.

Even as he watched, Tonley sidled back into the room from somewhere near the side door, the one that would lead to the stableyard and indeed the midden. Charlie watched him for a moment as he made his way round the room, looking like a nasty rumour. The man could probably not help himself, he thought. It would be terrible to be a decent man and look as untrustworthy as

Tonley – how could you ever make friends?

Abandoning his study, he turned back to the booth again. Lord Watt now seemed to be asleep, and the man next to him, Mr. McFarland with the grey wig, looked as if he would rather like to leave if he could have thought of a way of getting past the men between him and the exit, short of crawling under or over the table. There was some kind of covert game of cards going on between Cobairdy, Brux, Dalgarno and Keracher, which Brux appeared to be losing: there were only pennies on the table, though, so the stakes could not be high. John Leith was watching and commenting, which seemed to add to the entertainment of the game. Abernethy, though, was ignoring them, slumped on his fist with his elbows on the table, staring down at his glass. When Tonley came back and inserted himself into his seat, Abernethy jumped – Charlie had the impression Tonley had kicked him under the table by accident. Abernethy glared at Tonley, then gave an immense sigh.

'Listen,' he said, tugging at John Leith's shoulder. 'Listen, I ken what you've been saying about me.'

John Leith turned, mid-laugh.

'What?'

Abernethy drew a longer breath.

'I ken what you've been saying about me. That I sold my grain short at Strathbogie mart.'

'What?' John Leith repeated, looking baffled.

'Man, you've been telling a'body I'm a dish – a dishonest man. That's no right – that's no friendly.'

'Mayen, I have never even thought you might be dishonest, let alone told anyone else – and what's that about Strathbogie mart?'

'There's word goin' roun',' said Abernethy, downing his glass of wine almost as he spoke. ''Sword going roun' I cheated wi' the meal at the mart. And see, Leith Hall,' he said, pushing himself awkwardly to his feet in the restricted space and glaring down at his friend, 'Ahm calln yout.'

Mayen's words were barely words at all. John Leith blinked. Byres, eyes glittering, leaned in.

'He says he's calling you out. To fight him.'

'Aye.' Mayen nodded quickly, and swayed on his feet. 'Na jool.'

'In a duel,' added Tonley, helpfully. 'Let's take a walk on the

Plainstanes, eh?'

'But - I have no pistols here!' John Leith clutched at the excuse. Charlie could see he was beyond bewildered.

'Then you'd best have them fetched, eh?' said Byres. There was a horrible pause. Charlie felt as if they were in a wee hole of black silence, all by themselves in the still rowdy inn. Lord Watt, Cobairdy, Brux, Mr. McFarland - none of them seemed to have heard. Then John Leith, barely turning towards him, said, flat-voiced,

'Aye, Charlie, will you away and fetch my pistols, please?'

'Aye, sir.'

With a deep breath, Charlie burst from the bubble of silence, half dancing with relief, half longing to drag his master after him, away to safety. A duel? Where had that come from? Why had his master said nothing in return? Was that what gentlemen did?

Surely John Leith would be safe, anyway, he told himself as the ice-cold air of the Castlegate hit him. Somewhere over there in the darkened square a lamp showed Leith's front door. He squinted to identify it, tried a few cautious steps in that direction, then bitten by urgency he broke into a slithering run across the frozen cobbles. Everyone knew Abernethy of Mayen couldn't shoot. And John Leith could. He'd be all right, wouldn't he? But somehow, he could not rid his memory of Byres' grinning, knowing face.

It took an age to unlock the door, then where were the pistols? Upstairs, in the pistol case - his hands felt like winter mushrooms, flabby and useless. And then - oh! Were they loaded? Surely not - no, he had checked. The mushroom fingers shook as he sorted out shot, powder, ramrod - what order? How could he not remember? But somehow he did, as if suddenly some stronger force had taken over. Was this Providence? Was John Leith meant to fight this duel? If he failed to bring the pistols, would the matter just fade away?

For a moment he sagged, propped against the hard, high side of the bed. What if he never went back with the pistols?

Mayen would forget all about it, he was sure. Mayen had probably forgotten already. And John Leith was his friend.

But Byres ... there had been a fire in Byres' eyes. Charlie had not liked that look at all. Whatever Mayen might do, Byres was not going to forget the challenge. And that meant that he could not leave his master unarmed.

He gave himself a resolute nod. Yes, a decision. He pushed

himself to his feet, lifted the pistols with almost reverent care, and headed back to the inn.

It was easier going back, even with his anxiety over the pistols. The inn was still well lit, glowing in the frosty air, and he could see figures moving outside it. One was tall, swaying and sliding in the ice – Mayen. Beside him, imp-like, menacing, constantly on the move – that had to be Byres. Over by the mercat cross, that funny little building, there were more figures – or was it only one? It was hard to tell. It looked a bit like a servant he had seen with Mr. Abernethy.

And then - oh, Lord! - the neat, unobtrusive figure of his master, John Leith. Regardless of the pistols and the treacherous cobbles, Charlie broke into a run.

But even as he reached the other side of the square, an echoing shot rang out - or was it two? – and his master, a hand out as if to prevent it, crumpled slowly to the ground.

Chapter Nine

Charlie felt as if the frost had taken him, while he watched the rest of the world move on. Tonley, his whitish clothes clear in the uncertain lamplight, stepped over to John Leith where he lay, stooped, and picked something up. Light glanced off the silver furnishings of a pistol – but not one of the master's, surely? Charlie almost looked down at his own hands to check he was holding his master's guns himself. Then Tonley glanced in his direction, turned deliberately, and took Mayen by the arm, starting to walk him away. Charlie, no longer sure where to put his feet or what to do, focussed on them and followed. He would not look down at the master. He would not, even as he passed. It was too soon to know the worst, and the longer he put it off, the better it might be. He stared at Byres and Mayen, the bulky figure in the blue coat and the slight, edgy man in grubby white. They were heading for the side entrance to Campbell's, but there was some hiatus as Tonley seemed to grab at Mayen's thigh – Mayen stumbled, but made no exclamation, and they moved on. Charlie took the chance to catch up, but Byres turned his head a little and remarked loudly to Mayen,

'Knock the rascal on the head.'

Charlie stopped in his tracks, heart beating fit to be heard at Leith Hall. Mayen glanced around, and Charlie's jaw dropped: the man looked as if he had caught a glimpse of hell.

Then, as if the sky cleared above him Charlie came back to the reality of the matter, turned, and ran back to his master.

John Leith lay white as the frost on the ground by the Plainstanes, almost in a ditch. Blood, slowed by the cold – Charlie's mind turned briefly to Lang Tam and his frozen blood – had run from his head and pooled on either side, soaking his hair, his ears, his collar. And the front of his head was knocked in, the hole made by the ball clear but the damage around it almost as if some heavy heel had pressed down on the man's skull. Charlie let out a yell that shocked him as much as anything. Then he ran to the main door of the inn.

'Help me!' he cried to anyone who would listen. 'Help me! Leith Hall has fallen!'

Back outside, he laid the pistols gently on the ground, pulled off his coat and laid it over the master, then crouched and began to rub his hands – in his haste to meet the challenge, perhaps, Leith was wearing no gloves. Footsteps echoed behind him, and in a moment a confusion of hands, feet, faces gathered, offering advice, giving orders, lifting, supporting, gathering the master up and bearing him back into the inn. Charlie grabbed the pistols again, solemnly, as if taking care of those might make any difference.

'Upstairs.' Archibald Campbell himself, the innkeeper, gave directions now. The narrow staircase pruned his bearers from either side but still John Leith swept upwards, leaving bloody hands and cuffs in his wake. In a moment Charlie found himself in a small bedchamber, crowded with men eager to help, eager to see, to be a part of whatever exciting tragedy might be happening. He longed to throw them all out, but he needed them: he had no idea what to do.

'Benjie,' snapped Campbell at the inn's servant, arranging blankets over John Leith's still form, 'away and run for Dr. Skene. You can put those pistols down there, on the night table, man: no one will take them from you.'

'Oh. Yes,' said Charlie, and did as he was told. A doctor, of course. That was what was needed. He tried to look about the crowded room. Where were the master's friends? Who would tell him what to do? Where was Lang Tam? He could see no familiar face at all, but then they all seemed to be a blur.

'Right,' said Campbell – Charlie had hardly been aware of the man before, but now he seemed like the officer of a regiment, in charge and competent. 'Everyone out unless you have a good reason to be here. Not you, son,' he added to Charlie, just in case. The crowd began to seep out by the door, casting looks back at the bloody figure on the bed. 'Ann,' he called to a serving girl amongst them, 'clean that blood off the stairs: we canna have folks walking that around the place.' Gradually the room emptied, and Charlie was left alone with Campbell, staring down at John Leith. The master was breathing – he really was, snoring almost, snuffling at the back of his throat. Charlie was about to allow himself to hope, when Campbell, with a sigh, said,

'Aye, that's no looking good, is it?' He looked at Charlie, and nodded to himself. 'You're no looking so good yourself, lad. I'll send up some hot water and a clout for cleaning him up before the doctor comes, and a glass of brandy for the shock.'

'I can't afford –'

'Och, it'll go on your master's bill, no doubt,' said Campbell with an attempt at a grin, then shook his head. 'He was a fine gentleman, I always thought. How this could happen - and here and all - beats me.'

He left the room, and Charlie sagged against the side of the bed, as if his bones had melted. He would clean his master's face, when the water came, he thought, trying to make his head work. That would help him, refresh him. And the doctor was on his way. Charlie had never met a doctor before, and he was not sure what to expect: something awfully grand, who might tell Charlie it was all his fault. And some of it was, anyway. He should have been quicker, fetching and loading the pistols. He should have run faster, been cleverer with the fiddly rod and charge and ball, not taken that moment to contemplate before running back. In Charlie's mind, that moment stretched out to five, ten, fifteen minutes. Had the master been pacing the Plainstanes, wondering where he had got to? The idea made Charlie's heart shrink inside him. Had he let him down?

But even as he found ways to blame himself, Charlie began to wonder. Why had no one else stopped the duel? And who had been out there with them – the figure, or figures, by the mercat cross?

The maid Ann appeared with a large bowl of steaming water and a couple of cloths under her arm. Her hands were shaking – Charlie could feel the tremor as he took the bowl from her and set it carefully on the bed beside his master.

'I'll be back with the brandy,' she said, with a look of horror at the bed. With the back of her hand pressed to her lips, she hurried out. Charlie swallowed hard, and told himself he was just going to shave the master, that was all: wash his face and shave it, just as usual.

The water was red in seconds. The blood had begun to dry, but the warm water eased off the black stains, diluted the oozing crimson. Charlie bit his lip as he worked, concentrating on not causing any pain, on not thinking too hard about the strange shapelessness of John Leith's high forehead. He rubbed the cloth gently down the master's hair, clumped and sticky, as John Leith's breathing rumbled and rasped under his elbow. Something splashed on to the master's grey cheek and Charlie wiped it with the tail of the cloth before realising it was his own teardrop.

The brandy and the doctor arrived at the same time: Charlie wondered if the maid Ann had waited until Benjie the servant was back with Dr. Skene so that she would not have to return to the grim little chamber. Dr. Skene was plump and assured, and had even found time to shave – Charlie was surprised until he thought that it was now early in the morning, a reasonable time for a professional man to be up and awake, not the middle of the night.

'Now, what have we here?' said Dr. Skene, approaching the bed. 'A gunshot, the servant said, I think?'

'That's right, sir,' said Charlie, hoping he was using the right form of address. Should it be 'my lord'? But the doctor did not look offended. Indeed, all his attention was on the master, except when he threw a glance at Charlie's bowl of filthy water.

'Take that away and fetch clean water, would you?' he told Benjie, the servant. 'And you – you're Leith Hall's servant, are you?'

'Aye, my lord,' said Charlie.

'What's your name?'

'Charlie Rob, my lord.'

Dr. Skene's lips twitched very slightly.

'"Sir" will do nicely, Charlie. Was your master the only one injured? You're gey pale yourself.'

'Aye, sir, he was. I was – I was too far behind ...' He felt more tears fall, and was ashamed. But the doctor made no comment on them.

'I'm sure you did your best,' he said. 'Is that brandy? I'd drink that down, if I were you.' He must have seen Charlie's nose wrinkle. 'Think of it as physic, man. It's for the shock.'

Charlie turned from the bed, and sipped at the burning spirit. It tasted only a little better than the first time he had sampled it, on that first run into Aberdeen with the master. He should have known then, should have listened to himself. No good came of leaving home, of going to the big town. What were they going to do now, all of them? The master was going to be sick for a long time.

Benjie had returned with a bowl of clean water and a very white towel. Dr. Skene must have been probing at the master's wound, for he washed his bloody fingertips in the bowl and dried them on the towel, his gaze still on his patient, thoughtful.

'Are his family in town?' he asked.

'No, sir. They're at Leith Hall.'

The doctor pursed his lips.

'Can anyone be sent for them? Or as a member of the household perhaps you should go yourself, Rob. I'd go at once, if I were you.'

'Will he be all right, sir?' Charlie asked, though his lips and tongue numbed over the question. The doctor turned to him.

'His family should be told,' he said with clarity, 'that if they want to see him alive in this world again, they need to make haste.'

Charlie swallowed, eyes wide and wet.

'I will. I'll go at once, sir.'

'That's best, lad. Now,' he turned to Benjie, still holding the bowl of water, 'let's get a fire lit in here, and someone to sit with him. There's a chance he'll say a few words, and someone should be here to hear them.'

But his own words were already fading in Charlie's ears, as he stumbled down the narrow wooden staircase and made for the stables.

It seemed better to take the chaise.

It was a decision he regretted several times over the next few hours.

He thought it was clever, because if he was to fetch the mistress she would need something to travel in. And if he had just taken the horse – well, he had only ridden a little around the estate with the master, and he did not consider himself very safe high on a horse's back, particularly if the road were slippery. But he had never, ever, driven a horse before, and while the master had made it look easy, that had evidently been because the horse knew to co-operate with him. Whatever signals John Leith had been sending to the horse were not now getting through.

When they had come to an accommodation, and made some progress along the road, another problem became clear: when Charlie took a wrong turning, it was much harder to turn the chaise than it would have been just to turn the horse. He could not calculate the time he was wasting trying to bend the horse in two, or curl the solid shafts, in some narrow mistake of a lane. All the time he tried his hardest to stay calm, for the master had told him several times that a calm man gets more out of a horse than an angry one, or a frightened one.

A couple more problems struck him, when the sun finally emerged and began to melt the ice into mud: the wheels began to stick, even though the road was generally a fair one. And even though the day seemed to promise a warmth they had not felt for a week or so, it was still bitterly cold, and he had not brought that cunning provision of hot pies that had sustained him on previous journeys. If he had been riding, he would at least have benefitted from the horse's warmth. As it was, he felt he had frozen to the wooden seat, and dreaded the pain he knew would come when he finally warmed his feet and hands. But most of all he dreaded breaking the news to the mistress.

As the route grew more familiar in the daylight, his mind dwelt more and more on what he was to say, and whether or not he could persuade Phoebe to take the message for him. After all, the mistress could not blame Phoebe for anything that had happened, and by the time she had to see Charlie the shock, at least, would have diminished. Would Phoebe do such a thing for the gift of the ribbons he had bought her? But that had been intended as a gift of - well, of affection, not as a bribe. It didn't seem quite right to use it to avoid an unpleasant situation for himself. But on the other hand, if the mistress blamed him for the master's injuries ... He would be put out of the household, no doubt about it, and he might never see Phoebe again - or if he did, he would not be able to afford any more ribbons for her. What was he to do?

In the end he was so cold by the time he reached the driveway he could no longer think, beyond that he had never thought he would be so reluctant to arrive home. The dark windows watched his approach expectantly and he fixed his bleary eyes on them as he advanced towards the house, then, numb, he abandoned the reins to the stable boy, and headed indoors. He marched straight upstairs to the parlour, knocked once, and went inside.

Afterwards he had no recollection of what he said, only that whatever he managed seemed to cause a great whirlwind about him. In the parlour had sat not only Mrs. Leith but also two immensely tall men, and as they birled about him, asking questions and shouting orders, what drew his attention most of all was their massive feet. He felt he had happened in a dream into a land of giants, and as it was a dream, he had no need to do or say anything until he woke up.

But after a while, after a buzz of confusion and blurry activity, the taller of them leaned down next to him and handed him a cup of hot wine. As he had expected, the very feel of the cup seared through his fingers, but it did begin to waken him.

'There, is that better?' said the man. 'You're Charlie Rob, are you? John has mentioned you.'

'Aye, s- ... my ... your majesty,' said Charlie, unsure as to how he should address a giant. The giant laughed, but gently.

'I'm Hay of Rannes,' he explained, 'Leith Hall's uncle.'

Leith Hall's uncle ... this, then, was Lady Glastirum's brother. That made no sense whatsoever, Charlie thought, but then he saw a gentleness in the man's huge face, and thought perhaps it did. But what way were her brothers giants?

'Aye, sir,' he muttered, and sipped at the wine. He felt its warmth tumble all the way down to his stomach.

'You didn't even stop on the way, did you?' Rannes asked. 'Good man, Charlie. But from what you say, things are bad.'

'Gey bad, sir.' Charlie could feel thawing tears welling again in his eyes, and blinked them back hard.

'And who did this?'

'Well ... the thing is, sir –' He hesitated, but that kindness was still there in Rannes' face. 'The thing is, it was Mr. Abernethy of Mayen, but I dinna see how it could be. I mean, sir, they were friends.'

Rannes frowned, but not, Charlie was sure, in anger. Maybe his impression was not so foolish.

'And Mr. Byres of Tonley was there, and all.'

'Byres of Tonley?' said Rannes at once. 'Back in the country?

Of all men!' He turned away, and paced a mile or two across the room. Charlie could not take his eyes off the man's feet. His shoes were the size of the cradle in the nursery. He wondered the floor could take the weight. Then Rannes turned, and seemed about to say something, but Harriot Stuart burst back into the room.

'We are ready, Uncle Andrew,' she said, breathless but in control. 'Will you come with us?'

It seemed to be assumed that because Charlie had managed to bring the chaise back, he could drive it again to Aberdeen, and since it was likely the only way he would be allowed to return to his master's side, he made no complaints, even if he did offer up a prayer for their safe return to the town. He should not pray so much, he thought: he had been nagging the Almighty for John Leith's life and recovery all the way home. Even the Lord must run out of patience with his petitioners. Then he wondered if that was wrong, to think that God might have a fault, and returned to his silent prayers.

It was a different horse, of course, and he had to get used to that for the first part of the journey: then there was the impending darkness to contend with, and the proximity of Lady Leith Hall beside him, separated only by the slight figure of her eldest son. Young John was only six, and prone, as the whole household knew, to coughs: he was wrapped as tight as could be and still breathe, and all three of them had hot stones on their laps. Mrs. Leith was motionless, staring straight ahead almost constantly, as if she were trying to see her husband even from this distance, as if making that link with him would keep him alive. Hay of Rannes and his brother rode on either side, and sometimes a little ahead if the road seemed uncertain. They seemed to know the way well, and Charlie could allow himself to worry less about the journey, and more, much more, about his master. Who was seeing to him in Charlie's absence? Should he have taken him over to his own house? Had he let him down again?

Rannes and his brother tried to persuade Lady Leith Hall to stop along the way for refreshment, but she was determined and the horse seemed content. Little John's white face peered out dark-eyed from his wrappings, staring about him but patient, not pestering as some children might. It crossed Charlie's mind to wonder if the child had been to Aberdeen before, or was this a journey tinged with excitement as much as dread.

The sky had weighed in heavy and grey by the time they were as far as Inverurie, and it was fully dark when they entered Aberdeen, grateful for its occasional door lights and candlelit windows. Charlie felt as if he had been driving all his life when they turned in at Campbell's gate: the Hay brothers dismounted smoothly and helped Harriot and the boy down from the chaise. Charlie led the horse over to the stable men, and as quickly as possible followed the family into the inn.

Archibald Campbell, by some wizardry of innkeeping, knew at once who they were even before Charlie caught up with them, and led them straight upstairs to the chamber where John Leith lay. Charlie saw clearly that there had been no change since he had left: he did not know whether to be pleased or dismayed, but at least there was still life there. The room was small enough but with the two Hay brothers in it it had shrunk to the size of a snuffbox: Charlie slipped back out on to the landing, and waited for his orders.

Waiting was all they could do that day, and the next. Lady Glastirum was summoned, but she had returned north and would take some time to arrive. Under the supervision of Dr. Skene and a couple of his colleagues they moved John Leith from Campbell's, no doubt to the innkeeper's relief, to the Leith townhouse across the Castlegate, moving with immense care and a slow pace that caused one or two passersby to look twice, as if they were accidentally present at a funeral. A bandage lay over the master's forehead, and the boy John walked beside him, clutching his father's hand: not strong enough to help he had been given that as a solemn duty. Rannes and his brother hardly seemed to fit in the stairway of the narrow townhouse, but somehow they took the master up to his chamber, where Charlie had gone ahead and lit the fire.

The change of scene may have jogged something in Leith Hall's damaged mind, for that evening he stirred a little, and reached out a hand. The mistress took it, pressing her other fist to her lips, then managed to hold his hand in both of hers.

'John, dearest, can you hear me?'

John Leith's eyelids flickered a little, as if he were trying to open his eyes wide, but they closed again.

'John? John, my dear,' she persisted. She stroked his hand

with her thumbs. Charlie wondered, watching her, how he had ever been afraid of her.

Then John Leith tried to raise his head, and his lips parted.

'Charlie, the wine,' said Mrs. Leith at once, breathless. Charlie stepped forward and held out the cup he had ready. She dipped a finger in it, and touched it to John Leith's lips. He almost licked them, and drew breath. Everyone else froze.

'D-' he began, and stopped. After a moment Mrs. Leith prompted,

'What, my dear?'

'D ... D ...'

'What begins with D?' asked little John, wonderingly. 'Dog?'

His father's eyelids flickered again, and his lips worked.

'Dilly, dilly, come and be killed!' he said, with unexpected clarity, and sank back on to the pillow.

Chapter Ten

John Leith of Leith Hall died on the morning of the old feast of Christmas, having never said another word.

Harriot Stuart of Auchluncart, stiff as buckram, did not weep, though as they realised that the last staggering, struggling breath was gone, she gripped her son tightly around his thin shoulders, so that Charlie thought for a moment she might break his bones. Then she released the boy, and her whitened knuckles grew pink again. She rose, and kissed her dead husband, and drew up the sheet to cover his broken face, then turned to his uncles. The giants had not left the house since John Leith had been moved there, and Charlie was almost grown used to them. They stood now, as best they could, heads bowed out of respect as well as necessity.

'Right,' said Mrs. Leith, briskly, and everyone jerked in shock at her tone. 'I want my husband's murderer brought to justice. Forthwith.'

Rannes was the first to collect himself.

'My dear Mrs. Leith, of course we'll seek reparation. But you know that John and Mayen were good friends ...'

'What's that to the purpose? Mayen killed him. Even in a duel, that is murder.'

'But ...'

'And Abernethy of Mayen is not a rich man,' Rannes' brother

Alexander Hay added, his voice soft. 'There is little reparation he can make. You know his large family, and his small estate.'

'He should have thought of that before he drew a pistol on my husband,' said Harriot, tight-lipped.

'Have you considered the funeral, my dear?' asked Rannes, trying to change the subject. 'Will it be held here at the town kirk, or at Kennethmont?'

'At Kennethmont,' she said at once. 'In the family tomb. I shall write the minister today.' She had clearly spent her sorrowful sickroom watch in planning. Charlie felt he should say something, but in the face of the mistress' grim preparations he was speechless.

Downstairs, though, when the giant uncles followed him like a couple of byre walls to the kitchen to give him his instructions for transporting the master's body home, he found the nerve to impart his information.

'Sir, word is that Abernethy of Mayen has fled,' he said.

The Hay brothers exchanged looks.

'Wise man if he has,' said the younger, Alexander. Rannes nodded.

'Any idea where he has gone?' he asked Charlie. 'Has anyone said?'

Charlie shrugged.

'I only know that Lord Watt sent his man Holland to seek him where he was staying on, er, the Gallowgate,' he said, hoping that he had the place name right: he was not sure he had ever been there. 'The fellow that has the stables where he was staying, he said that they all went off in the direction of Old Aberdeen. Is there an old Aberdeen, sir? This one scarcely looks very new to me.'

'Aye, the Aulton. It's north of here,' explained Alexander Hay, always kind. Charlie did not have to remind himself now that he was Lady Glastirum's brother. 'You'll have come through it on the way here: there's a college?'

'Oh, aye!' said Charlie, nodding in recognition.

'He might go there to cross the Don at Balgownie, then head for maybe Peterhead or Fraserburgh. What do you think, Dandy?' he asked his brother.

'Who is "they"?' asked Rannes, astutely.

'Mr. Abernethy of Mayen, his man, and Mr. Byres of Tonley,' said Charlie. 'Mr. Byres was there when the master was shot. I think

_'

'Tonley, eh?' said Rannes, clearly not pleased. 'Where that man is, there is always trouble. And he has kin at Stoneywood – they could have gone there if they crossed the river further inland. Tonley is trouble,' he repeated.

'Yet no one disputes that Mayen fired the shot,' said Alexander.

'No, indeed.' Rannes sighed heavily, the weight of the world on his huge shoulders. 'But I cannot see why. From all accounts they were good friends.'

'If he is out of the country – and a wise man would be – then he will never stand trial,' said Alexander. Charlie felt his mouth twitch in dismay. He had no wish for Mr. Abernethy to hang – even if he had killed the master, for surely that had been some kind of mistake – but the thought of having to go out of the country was dreadful. To America, like the master and his friends! And so many of the Jacobite fighters had gone to the Continent, which was nearly as far, from all he had heard. He had only a hazy idea of what either might entail but danger was certain. How desperate must Mr. Abernethy have been, to abandon his home and leave for abroad?

Charlie shook his head and tried to listen to the Hay brothers in case he could be of any further help: they seemed wise men, and good, and in any case even with the master dead Charlie needed a position in which to serve. He would do his best to be useful.

'He will not stand trial, no,' Rannes agreed. 'Not unless he returns for some reason. They will put him to the horn. No, it will have to be financial compensation from his wife, poor innocent soul.'

'Could we not persuade Mrs. Leith to leave it be? With her estate and Leith Hall put together she could buy and sell Mrs. Abernethy: she must have nearly ten times Mayen at her disposal. She need have no fear of even the younger boys being in want, or of lacking a dowry if the bairn she's carrying is a girl.'

'Do you think you could persuade her?' asked Rannes grimly, eyeing his brother. After a moment, Alexander shook his head, ruefully.

'No,' he agreed, 'I'm not sure I could.'

'Aye, well,' said Rannes. 'We'll just have to see what can be done, I suppose, with the least ruination to all. Charlie, what other news have you heard?'

'I dinna think I've heard anything much,' Charlie admitted, though it was nice to be asked. 'They've washed the blood off the road - they had that done quick enough. There's gossip all about - ken the master was a popular man, altogether, and nobody can believe someone shot him. They're blaming the drink, mostly.'

'Aye, well,' said Alexander, nodding sadly. 'That's no far from the truth, I daresay.'

'I'm no sure that Mr. Abernethy was drinking that much,' said Charlie boldly - or boldly for him, anyway.

'Is that a fact? Still, I'm sure it had something to do with it. I'm surprised Lord Watt didna try to stop him, though. Did he?'

'I think it all happened too fast,' said Charlie. 'And they had all been drinking, even Lord Watt.' He tried to remember the details of that horrible morning: he had felt uncomfortable long before the three men had headed out for the Plainstanes. And there was a thing, he thought: they had talked of meeting on the Plainstanes, and walking on the Plainstanes, but when John Leith had fallen he was down in the street. Had he stepped down over the edge? Why would they have a duel when one person was high up on the raised ground, and the other lower down? It could not have been to balance a height advantage, for Mayen was only a little taller than Leith Hall and in any case it was Leith Hall who had gone lower. Was the master walking away from the duel when he was shot? Was he walking away to see where Charlie had got to with his pistols? Why had he been mad enough to agree to fight his friend at all? Charlie had barely slept for the last four days and nights, and with four gentry to attend to not to mention the young lad - the new John Leith of Leith Hall, he thought with a shock - he barely knew what house he was in, and any reflection he had made upon the events of that awful morning had been at best confused. He wanted a good night's sleep, and then peace to consider the whole thing from start to finish, what he could piece together of it. But peace in particular seemed likely to be in short supply for a good while yet.

The Hay brothers, having ascertained that he could read enough to manage, made out a list of things for him to do, besides fetching more food from Campbell's. He was to go to the printers in the Broadgate and have a card made up - Alexander Hay was writing out its contents with great care, so that Charlie could simply pass the instructions over to the printer - which would be delivered to various addresses about the town announcing Leith Hall's death. He was to visit a carpenter recommended by a neighbour, who would come to measure the master for a coffin. He was to call, with the greatest of respect, on the minister at the South Kirk, to come and pray with the mistress while the master was being kisted. He was to arrange with Campbell's for a decent cart that would carry the coffin to Leith Hall, with reliable and steady horses unlikely to make any kind of fuss along the way, whatever the weather: the ice had thawed, but reports were coming into the town of roads lost in mudslides, and rivers overflowing their banks.

'The nine men's morris is filled up with mud,' said Rannes, incomprehensibly, 'and the quaint mazes in the wanton green for lack of tread are undistinguishable.' His brother Alexander nodded sombrely, so that Charlie thought it must be something from the Bible. He bowed his head, too, and took the list to see if he could find everywhere he needed to be.

The next couple of days were busy ones, though only Charlie and Rannes left the house at all, Charlie on his various errands, and Rannes, reportedly, to talk to a lawyer, some kinsman of Mrs. Leith. Though he had no manservant of his own with him, he did not take Charlie on the visit: there was plenty for Charlie to be doing.

Callers began to arrive, coming to pay their respects to Leith Hall and to his widow, and to poor little John who sat in grim black on a chair slightly too tall for his short legs, looking as washed out as an old rag. It was hard on him to stay in a cold room with his father's corpse, so he and his mother had removed to the parlour so that he would not cough so much. Alexander Hay watched over the body, and Charlie was constantly directing visitors up to the bedchamber, hoping they would not stick on the narrow stairway. When he was not doing that, he was taking in food which arrived in a constant stream, it felt, from Campbell's, only to disappear into the maws of the visitors and have to be replaced again. He was so busy he barely recognised Lang Tam when he chapped at the door on behalf of his masters, Mr. Dalgarno and Mr. Keracher, and ushered them inside. Charlie announced the gentlemen at the parlour door, then backed into the hallway.

'Have you a chopin of ale for a dry throat and an old friend?' asked Lang Tam. 'I've no seen you since this miserable business.

How are things?'

'Come quick to the kitchen, then,' said Charlie, and poured him a tankard from the barrel there. 'It's a bad business, Tam: I've never known the like.'

Tam scowled.

'Your master was a fine man, and you were lucky to have him. Will you stay on with the family?'

'Oh, aye, if they'll have me! It's the only situation I've known!' said Charlie at once, distressed at the very thought of leaving Leith Hall. 'It's my home, and all.'

'Aye, aye,' said Lang Tam soothingly, 'if it's that way, with your family on the estate and all, no doubt they'll keep you. You'll be grand – though changed times, eh? Changed times.'

'They are that,' said Charlie fervently. 'Can you believe Mr. Abernethy would do such a thing? I canna comprehend it.'

'Nor can anybody, Charlie,' Tam agreed, taking his ease at the kitchen table. 'But for Gordon of Cobairdy, who is going round telling anybody who'll listen that that Mayen was a danger to his friends and it was only a matter of time before someone was hurt – and apparently he warned us all. Which is not something I can call to mind, I have to say,' he added, smiling gently, 'but perhaps it was only the gentry he warned.'

'Poor Mr. Abernethy. I mean, my poor master, but he was the innocent party. But I cannot think that Mr. Abernethy meant to do it. And now they say he has fled, and his wife and children abandoned.'

'He'll send for them, no doubt, wherever he settles.' Lang Tam was reassuring, but it did not work on Charlie.

'Can you imagine that? Having to up and leave your home and live abroad, and for poor Mrs. Abernethy it's not even for something she has done? My, but that would break my heart!' He called to mind the pretty lady, swamped by bairns and sweet with her guests.

'To leave home?' Lang Tam was interested. 'Why's that, then?'

'To leave home, aye,' Charlie confirmed. 'What more is there to be said?'

Before Lang Tam could reply, there was a terrific rattle at the risp, and Charlie hurried off to open the front door once again.

This time the man outside almost poured himself into the hallway.

'Mr. Lawrence Leith, to pay his respects to his nephew's widow,' he announced, with loose grandeur. As far as Charlie could see, Uncle Lowrie was wearing the same clothes he had been on his previous visit, without apparent benefit of any cleansing – of either clothes or self – in between. The scent of old wine was several layers deep. Charlie hesitated. 'Come on, man! My kinsman's dead, most horribly – you canna keep me hanging about on the threshold in all this –' he shook sleet from his cloak 'and no let me in to the warmth!'

Charlie stood back, and hoped that Mr. Dalgarno and Mr. Keracher would save the mistress from any embarrassment.

'Mr. Lawrence Leith,' he announced at the parlour door. Uncle Lowrie stumbled past him, just as sodden as he had been last time, when he had tried to persuade the master to – to what? To involve him in some secret matter? Whatever it had been, John Leith had refused. Would the master have wanted him here now? It was too late now, anyway.

And Uncle Lowrie did not last long in the parlour. There was a thump as of something falling, a cry of irritation from the mistress, and the shilpit figure staggered back out into the hallway and made with determination for the stairs. Up there, Alexander Hay would be more than capable of dealing with him. Charlie decided to make sure all was well in the parlour.

'It's only a stool, Charlie,' said Mrs. Leith, as Dalgarno attentively picked up the offending piece of furniture and returned it to its place. 'Uncle Lowrie – finds details difficult to focus on. Perhaps you should see to it that he discovers the dead room successfully – and the front door again afterwards.'

Charlie hurried off to the stairs, conscious that the mistress was telling him to make sure Uncle Lowrie left fast.

But upstairs Lowrie had had no problem in finding out where his nephew was lying, and was paying his respects surprisingly appropriately. Charlie stopped at the door, unnoticed by the visitor, though Alexander Hay caught his eye.

'My poor nephew,' said Lowrie, holding the master's pale hand. 'Ken,' he added over his shoulder to Hay, 'ken I always knew it would come to this, though, eh?'

'What's that?' asked Alexander Hay, surprised.

'To an end like this. A tragedy for the poor lad, and for his pretty wee wife, and his bairns.'

Charlie would not have called the mistress either pretty or wee, but he supposed that Lowrie was being gallant.

'Why should you have foreseen tragedy?' asked Alexander, still confused.

'Oh aye! Oh aye!' said Lowrie. He had kept his voice respectfully low before, but now it sank to a breathy hiss. 'That's right! That's the way of it - say not another word! You never know who might be listening!' He spun uncertainly, bent at the waist, as if looking for spies in the corners of the room - and jumped when he saw Charlie at the door. 'What's your name, lad?' he demanded, still in a whisper.

'Charlie Rob, sir,' said Charlie, nervously.

'Charlie, aye, a fine name, that. We'll have the bonnie lad back on the throne afore long, will we no?' He managed somehow to nudge Alexander Hay with a bony elbow, leaning over precariously.

'Hush, now, Mr. Leith,' said Alexander, striving to make his tone light, 'some of us are not long back in the country - like yourself, no doubt. There's no call for talk like that, or we'll all be back in France again for Hogmanay.'

'There's truth in that,' said Lowrie, nodding enthusiastically. 'Much truth. Let me shake your hand, my friend.' He seized Hay's hand, seemed astonished at the size of it, and shook it several times. 'Now, then, Charlie, no doubt there's a glass of wine to be had in the house?'

'Kitchen, Charlie,' said Hay quickly, under his breath. Charlie blinked, and nodded.

'What's that?' Lowrie swayed, trying to catch the words.

'I'm suggesting the kitchen,' said Hay, a little more loudly. 'You ken yourself what it was like, times past. Sometimes the kitchen's the safest place, eh?' He caught Lowrie's eye and made a very firm wink. Lowrie, astonished, allowed a look of cunning to spread over his long face.

'Aye, that and all. Oh, aye, I mind the days. The kitchen it is, then, and no doubt fine company there!'

Well, Lang Tam and a tankard of ale, thought Charlie, but better there than the parlour, anyway. He guided Lowrie down the stairs, and with elaborate care along to the kitchen, depositing him at the table opposite Lang Tam. Tam stared at him in surprise, and then at Charlie, winking at him over Lowrie's shoulder.

'We can have a nice wee chat about old times, eh?' Charlie suggested. 'This here's Tam, a friend of mine. Tam, this is Mr. Leith – Mr. Lawrence Leith – not long back from points abroad in the service of, um, the King over the seas.' He dropped his voice conspiratorially, and hoped he had used the right words. He tried to remember them from Tonley's toast at Abernethy's dinner, long ago.

'Oh, aye?' said Lang Tam, then hunched over the table and leaned in. 'And where did you fight, sir?'

'Och, all parts,' said Lowrie in a low voice, but proudly. 'My brother Anthony and I were well-kent thorns in the side of Cumberland. He couldna stop us, so he shipped us off to America to the plantations.'

'My,' said Tam, looking impressed. 'When did you come back?'

'Now that, my friend, would be telling!' said Lowrie, pleased with himself. No doubt he had returned before he was supposed to, unlike Hay of Rannes. 'Aye, the whole family is in it, ken. We four brothers – and then the eldest kept himself clear so the estate was safe – but that doesna mean, just because he didna fight alongside us, that he wasna ... of assistance to the cause, if you take my meaning.'

'Was he indeed?' asked Tam. 'Good man, good man.'

'Though he was dead long before it happened. And now, see, his son ... my nephew ...' Lowrie threatened to turn teary. Tam reached out a long arm and upended the bottle into Lowrie's glass. Charlie opened his mouth to protest, but the effect was definitely cheering. 'Aye, young John, there, well, he was up to mischief just as much as any of us! Aye, he was grand ... but then look where it got him.'

'Charlie, I think maybe Mr. Leith needs to be helped somewhere to sleep it off now,' Tam suggested. Charlie looked at Uncle Lowrie. He did not seem far gone to him, but Tam undoubtedly had a better estimation of a man's capacity.

'There's a room upstairs, with a bed made up, but it's in the attic,' Charlie suggested.

'Or I could take him to his home, wherever that is,' Tam suggested. 'No doubt my two will be here for a while – in fact, thinking about it, there's a rich widow there in yon parlour that Mr. Dalgarno probably has notions about already.'

'You're joking!' cried Charlie, shocked. Tam shrugged apologetically.

'Aye, I suppose I am. Sorry – it's a bit early, even for that.'

'But I think we should let Mr. Leith lie down here – it's the family house, after all,' said Charlie.

'Are you sure your mistress would want that?' Tam asked. It was a fair point, but Charlie had no wish to bother her. She was like a hedgepig these days.

'No, come on, let's get him up there between us, before anybody else appears at the door,' said Charlie, making his mind up – or at least, taking action before his mind could change back again. He took Mr. Leith under one arm, and Lang Tam took the other: between them, with Lang Tam coming behind on the narrow stair, they levered the visitor up to the attic and the last empty bed that Charlie had aired. Charlie closed the shutters firmly against the cold and rain, and they pulled Lowrie Leith's boots off and wrapped the covers about him. Soon he was snoring comfortably.

'As long as Mrs. Leith doesna hear him snoring before you get the chance to explain, or send him home,' said Lang Tam cheerfully, as they slipped back down to the kitchen again. 'I wonder where he lives? I mean, I ken he's a gentleman, but he doesna have a very refined look to him, you have to admit.'

'I have no idea,' said Charlie honestly, 'but I doubt there's a bath there, anyway. Och, no: there's the door again. Away and have your ale in peace!'

And Tam happily retreated to the kitchen, while Charlie opened the front door to yet another set of mournful visitors.

Chapter Eleven

The journey back to Leith Hall, to home, was not what
Charlie had expected, somehow. Travelling with care, moving the cart
– hastily painted black – at a decorous pace along roads glutinous with
mud and standing water, took two days rather than a brisk one, with
a night at the inn in Inverurie's straight street. How old had the master
said the church was? Charlie wished he could remember, if only to
preserve a small fragment of what the master had been. They made
quite a procession, the chaise, the two Hay brothers as outriders, and
the cart, and then behind them those from Aberdeen who felt it right
to attend the funeral: Lord Watt had brought his carriage, and in it
were also Gordon of Cobairdy and Forbes of Brux, though Charlie
had noted Dalgarno and Keracher hanging about as if they would
have liked the offer, too. Instead they had once more hired horses
which they changed at the inn in Inverurie, muttering complaints just
as before. Lang Tam, attending them, had only been able to secure a
mule, and his thighs must have ached from the single task of keeping
his feet off the ground. There were others, too, all sombrely attired,
and though sometimes the road took all Charlie's attention he was
constantly called back to their purpose by men on the side of the road
baring their heads, or children stopping to stare.

The Inverurie inn was small, with only a few free rooms into
which the gentry squeezed themselves in various combinations: Mrs.

Leith and the boy went to one and the Hays to the other, and both Lang Tam and Charlie, not the only servants there, retreated in weary silence to the kitchen downstairs. There Lang Tam stretched his cramped limbs out on the floor, while Charlie curled himself into a corner, watching the fire dim.

He remembered other years where as soon as the solstice was passed, the days lightened with almost excited haste, but it seemed this year was not one of them. The heavy sky loomed lead grey above them, never really growing light. In the chaise the boy huddled under his mother's cloak and coughed miserably, and the carter was damp and morose. Charlie dreamed of hot pies, then felt it was disrespectful and tried to stop.

When at last they turned in at the gates, he could see that candles had been lit in the windows to guide them. The letter Mrs. Leith had sent to the minister had also contained instructions for the household, and in the hallway a trestle had already been set up with a black cloth on it for the coffin. The master would lie here overnight, at home for the last time, before the interment tomorrow. The household staff were already dressed in black, and Charlie, his new town black almost bright by comparison, did not feel he stood out too much. The minister, always in black, of course, was in the hall to meet them, along with a few of the master's friends or family who had met there from parts around, to attend the funeral.

The gentry and the minister retired to the parlour, leaving a serving boy to watch the coffin, pale faced in the corner of the hall. A good quantity of hot wine had been prepared in advance, and Charlie retreated to the kitchen to find out what was happening with regard to dinner.

'Aye, it's near ready for them,' said the cook. 'I'm glad to see yez are all safe back, this weather. But you'll need to be getting on and laying the table and all. Phoebe says there's sixteen of them altogether, including the minister.'

So Charlie wearily set to to decant more wine and bring out the silver, and Phoebe joined him. There seemed to be no words easy enough to say, and it was not a moment for the giving of ribbons, though they were burning a hole in Charlie's coat pocket: they worked in silence, laying plates and cutlery around the great long polished table, and Phoebe adjusted the silver candlesticks and the white china ornaments for the centre. The nymphs and shepherds, to Charlie's eyes, looked dead.

'Oh, the cheese!' said Phoebe, breaking the silence suddenly and leaving the room. Charlie turned his back on the white figures, and went to the fireplace to give the fire an encouraging poke. On the mantelpiece, level with his eyes, lay the elaborately engraved horn from the North America campaign. He reached out a cautious finger and touched his master's name, the letters browned into the creamy horn perhaps with soot, perhaps ink.

JOHN LEITH OF THE 1ˢᵗ. BATTALION ROYAL HIGHLAND REGT. 1759

What had it been like, he wondered, to fight so far from home? The towns and battles were marked there, not one of them a familiar name. Had the master thought he might die there? Yet he came safe home, to die almost in an Aberdeen street – killed by a man who had fought alongside him.

His mind slipped back to the night that Abernethy, Dalgarno and Keracher had dined here with the master, and their interest in this very horn. And the master's – what? Wariness? Was he afraid they would drop it? Break it? Could you break a horn like this? You could break off the silver lid, with its hinge and figuring. Charlie dared not touch it. It must have been expensive, all this fine engraving, and then to send it all the way from America? John Leith's eyes had never left it until it was safely back on the mantelpiece again, away from their unsteady, drunken fingers.

Dalgarno and Keracher – they were not close friends of the master's, and Charlie had not thought much about them beyond they were Lang Tam's masters. But Abernethy: he and John Leith were good friends. Abernethy was kind, generous within his capacities, a sensible man. John Leith, and Charlie's eyes pricked at the thought, was the best of masters, wise, thinking of the comfort even of his servants, and good to his friends from all Charlie had seen. Why, why had they fought? Why had they even risked such a terrible outcome: one friend dead, the other exiled?

In due course Phoebe reappeared, struggling to carry the great cheese through the door. He ran to help her, then went to summon the guests – the mourners. More would appear in the morning, no doubt, the locals, or the late arrivals. These ones here now were a blur: some he had never seen before, some he knew, like the minister, like the giant Hay brothers, like the mistress. They ate and they drank, they reminisced and, occasionally, they laughed a little, reflectively, and he served them without thinking, half-looking out for the master, for his directions, then remembering it was his mistress he should watch. It was not to be a night for drinking late: most of them would sit up in the hall downstairs, in quiet conversation, keeping John Leith company on his final night. Chairs had already been arranged, and the fire banked up to last. Charlie wanted to sit up, too, but the mistress had told him to be sure he had a good night's sleep, for the next day would be a long one. She had meant it kindly, no doubt, but who could ever really be sure they were going to have a good night's sleep?

Next day, New Year's Day, dawned in steady rain. The Aberdeen cart was pressed into service again to bear the coffin to the kirkyard, for the ground underfoot was clagged and slithery and the mistress, talking it over with the Hay brothers, feared that the bearers would slip and drop the coffin. Besides, both brothers wanted to help bearing, and there were no other men to match them for height. Instead the intended bearers could walk on either side of the cart, and be ready to help if it stuck in the mud.

Mrs. Leith watched them from the front door as they walked, slow and steady, down the drive. Charlie could feel her gaze on them, fierce, almost hungry, and on the coffin they escorted, all the way to the gate, and he wondered how much longer she would stand there after they disappeared from sight. It was almost unbearable. He did not want to imagine how he would feel if, when they returned with the empty cart, she was still there, staring fixedly out into the rain.

At the kirkyard there had been no need for gravediggers, who would have had a miserable task in this weather. Instead, the Leith family tomb - the mausoleum, he had heard it called - lay open, as one of the gardeners had been sent ahead with the key to give it to the session clerk. Both men stood, heads bared in the soaking downpour, waiting, and now the Hay brothers could do their work. They and two others slid the coffin from the cart at hip height - the brothers hunched over to reach - and eased the long black box under its mortcloth into the tomb. Charlie closed his eyes. He had no wish to see what lay within that little stone hut. In a few minutes, the living emerged, leaving the dead behind: the session clerk locked the door and handed the key back to the gardener, who looked alarmed and gave it to Charlie. Then each Hay brother produced a bottle from a vast pocket, and passed it around. Brandy again: Charlie, who was surprised to be handed the bottle early in its circuit, hoped he was not growing accustomed to it and to bad habits. He took only a sip, and passed it to Mr. Dalgarno, close behind him. The gardener and the session clerk each took their share, and fled, probably to a warm fire if they had any sense. Then it was time to turn the cart, and make for the hall and a hot meal.

In Charlie's experience – he would be the first to admit it was not broad – at this point in a funeral everyone would go home. But the gentry were staying at the Hall and could not be expected to set off home at this time of the day. Besides, from what he had been able to gather from the Hay brothers' talk even when he had tried not to listen, John Leith had died very organised: perhaps his fear of being killed in North America had swayed him, but he had made sure that his will was in order and that guardians had been appointed for his sons in the event of his death. Both Hay brothers were guardians, which Charlie thought was certainly a good choice on the master's part, but there were others, too, and Mrs. Leith wanted as many as could be brought together to meet after the funeral and discuss all that had to be done. Even for the cottar class like Charlie's family, it was a lot more straightforward when parents died after their children had reached the age of reason: how much worse was it, he told himself, when there was an estate to be managed, employees to be paid, staff to be fed and watered, and schooling still to come. He hoped the other guardians were as kindly and sensible as the Hays.

He was called to bring wine to the master's bookroom late that afternoon, after dinner had been cleared but before there were any thoughts of supper. Mrs. Leith sat behind the master's broad desk, and candlelight warmed the brown leather spines of all those bewildering books. The Hay brothers were there, like pillars holding up the ceiling of the small room: another man sat neatly nearby, and Charlie realised he was John Gordon of Glastirum, the master's stepfather and husband of the wonderful Lady Glastirum, who had come from near Banff for the funeral.

'My dear Lady Leith Hall,' he was saying, his expression concerned but his face, plump and comfortable looking, nothing like the image of a heroic archangel Charlie had pictured for Lady Glastirum's husband. 'I have to say again how much my wife regrets being unable to be here. She was already suffering from a chill, and then to add to that the terrible news – terrible news – of John's death, completely overthrew her. An it please you, as soon as the weather is better and she can travel, she begs leave to visit Leith Hall once more and the site of her son's interment, and to talk with you, if she may.'

'Aye, of course,' said Harriot Stuart, with a gracious nod. 'She must come, when she is well. No doubt she will agree with me on the course of action I intend to take.'

'Have we enough guardians to act?' asked Alexander Hay, ever the cautious one.

'We need four of the total,' said Harriot. 'My husband's uncle, Leith of Blackhall, will be here shortly, which will make us five.'

'Well, now, I daresay, as perhaps the eldest here,' said Glastirum, preparing to take charge of the meeting at least for now, 'I'd advise that the first things we need to do are to find poor John's will, and arrange for an inventory to be taken –'

'Forgive me, Mr. Gordon,' said Harriot, in a tone that made Charlie wish he was allowed to leave, 'but the first thing that has to be done is to find James Abernethy of Mayen and bring him to trial for murder.'

'Oh!' said Glastirum, so completely set off balance in his run of thought that he actually wobbled in his seat. The Hays, of course, had heard it before.

'A trial which will, of course, find him guilty,' Mrs. Leith added.

'But will it, though?' asked Glastirum, recovering. 'Are we sure he did it? I mean to say, the man has no reputation for hotheadedness. Quite the opposite, in fact. He's always seemed a decent sort of fellow.'

'He was drunk, like the rest of them,' said Hay of Rannes. 'He may not have known what he was doing.'

He was not so drunk as the others, thought Charlie. He remembered Mayen that night, fingering his glass, staring into it – but he had no recollection of that glass being refilled more than maybe twice. Abernethy had certainly not seemed drunk until the very last minute, as if he had made a sudden decision to be drunk. In fact, there were a few of them that were nowhere near as far gone as he had seen them before – Tonley, for instance, and the master himself. Had they just sobered up over the course of the night? Or was there some reason for it? In his head, Charlie half-connected it with the strange, mysterious meeting, whatever it had been, that had been the cause of their gathering at the inn in the first place. What had that all been about?

Coming to with a start he realised that the mistress had addressed him: a tiny squeak of fear escaped his lips, and he prayed that no one else had heard.

'Aye, ma'am?' he said.

'Your master left you this: it's his third best waistcoat. You may as well take it now. It's a good thick winter one – make sure you take good care of it.'

'I will, ma'am. Thank you.' He took the bundle from her, the dark woollen cloth with its winter padding as familiar to him as his own clothes. But the mistress had not finished with him.

'You were there. Tell us what happened. These gentlemen and I have heard your account, but Mr. Gordon has not.'

'Oh ... well, aye, there were words in the inn,' said Charlie, trying to remember in how much detail he had told the story before, 'and Mr. Abernethy called the master out. He was slurring his words, sir, so Mr. Byres had to explain what he had said.'

'Byres of Tonley was there?' asked Glastirum.

'He was, and I gather he has vanished, too,' said Rannes. Glastirum shook his head heavily.

'My, oh, my, that's a bad business. Byres of Tonley, eh?'

'He was Mayen's second, apparently.'

'And who was John's second?'

'Well, Charlie? Who stood with the master?' Rannes prompted him.

'No one, sir.' Glastirum gave a little gasp. 'It was the three of them out there by the Plainstanes. The master sent me back to make up the fire and fetch his pistols, but when I came back they were already facing each other.' He swallowed. 'And then, just as I was crossing back over the Castlegate, I heard a shot and the master fell.'

'You heard a shot? Did you see it, too?'

'Aye, sir, Mr. Abernethy's pistol flared, I think. There were the lights outside the inn behind them so it was hard to see what light was coming from where.'

'Just the one shot?'

Charlie hesitated.

'Well, man?' Glastirum prompted him. Charlie closed his eyes, trying to hear the sound again.

'I don't know, sir. I didn't know then. There was a shot, but it sort of echoed. If it was two, they were gey close.'

'Which can happen, of course, in a duel,' said Rannes sensibly. 'Did you see the master fire?'

'What would he have fired with, sir? I had his pistols.'

'He could have been offered one of Mayen's,' Rannes explained. 'If they were in a hurry.'

'Why would he have been in a hurry, sir?' The words came out before Charlie could stop them, but it made no sense to him. 'They hadna been in much of a rush up to then: they were just walking up and down. And he'd sent me for his own pistols, so why would he no wait?'

There was silence for a moment, and he feared he had spoken out too much. He hung his head, wishing he had been dismissed from the room before they could ask him any questions. Then he remembered something that had not come back to him before, and it needed to be said.

'Only ...' he began, 'only there was a second pistol.'

'Well, of course! Abernethy would have had a pair,' Glastirum said.

'Sir, I mean, the second one was near the master. When I was going over to him, Mr. Byres stooped down and picked something up from near the master's feet – and I'm almost sure it was a pistol.'

'So John may have fired back?' Rannes was serious, but Harriot looked delighted.

'Was Abernethy injured, then?' she demanded, but Charlie could only shake his head.

'I saw nothing like that, ma'am. I followed them a little way as they went back towards the inn, but then Mr. Byres – Mr. Byres said they would hit me, so I ran back to the master.'

'He's a very unpleasant character,' said Glastirum solemnly. Charlie thought he could have put it more strongly than that and not been far wrong. 'Were they all staying at the inn?'

'No, sir. I believe that Mr. Abernethy was staying in a place on the, um, the Gallowgate.'

'Cruickshank's stables,' Alexander Hay put in. 'Cheaper, I suppose.'

'Oh, aye,' agreed Glastirum.

'Still, it makes no difference whether or not John fired back,' said Mrs. Leith, recovering from her dreams of some serious injury for Mr. Abernethy. 'It is still murder on Mayen's part.'

'It looks very like it,' Glastirum agreed. 'It's a real tragedy. His poor wee wife!'

Harriot opened her mouth to reply, and it did not look as if she intended sympathy, but Alexander Hay spoke before she could.

'It's an odd world, right enough, where John and Mayen fire at each other and John misses, while Mayen is right on the target. Don't you think?' His mild expression cast about the room. Charlie remembered at last Mayen's reputation as a truly awful shot.

'Do you think that's why John was prepared to face him? He maybe felt safe?' asked Glastirum.

'He'd have needed to be drunk if he was prepared to take that risk,' said Rannes simply. 'Apart from anything else, I don't imagine Mayen had the best of pistols.'

'How drunk was the master, Charlie?' Harriot asked. She had asked before, so this was also for Glastirum's sake.

'Not very, ma'am,' he replied. 'He seemed to know what he was doing.'

'Yet he accepted the challenge, and went outside to the Plainstanes with Tonley and Mayen,' said Rannes. He, too, had been over this ground before. 'What did he think he was doing?'

'They were just talking, sir,' said Charlie. 'And the master wasna even on the Plainstanes. He was down on the street. Only Mr. Byres and Mr. Abernethy were up on the Plainstanes. And Mr. Abernethy's servant was over by the well ...'

'Was he, indeed? You didn't mention that before,' said Rannes at once.

'I'm sorry, sir. I've only just remembered.'

'So there was someone else about. Do you know this servant?'

'No, sir. I'd only seen him that evening. He wasn't – I mean, he was just a servant that rode with Mr. Abernethy when he went about, not a household servant.' It was difficult not to sound a little superior, but to be honest Charlie had not thought much of the man.

'Was he alone? When he was by the well – or are there others you haven't remembered till now?' asked Mrs. Leith, a little sharply. Charlie's forehead creased.

'I canna mind, ma'am. There might have been someone else. But not many, no. I mean, there couldna have been more than maybe three altogether. No more than that, I swear, ma'am.' He could feel himself sweating. What a fool he looked, remembering all this now! Did they even believe him, or did they think he was making it all up? He could not look at them, and hung his head again.

'Do stand up straight, Charlie,' said the mistress with a sigh. He tried to, but kept his gaze low.

'So we have other witnesses,' said Rannes, at last, 'witnesses who might be able to tell us more. They might even have heard what Johnnie and Mayen spoke about as they walked, or whether Johnnie really took Mayen's pistol. We need to find Abernethy's man - what was his name, Charlie?'

Charlie thought hard.

'Murray, sir. Hugh Murray. He was from Sutherland, I think he said.'

'And do you know who any of the others were?'

'I canna even swear they were there, sir. They were only shadows.'

'Very well.'

'I shall write this evening to John's man of law in Aberdeen,' said Mrs. Leith, 'and tell him of these witnesses, and inform him that we are proceeding with the court case. Even if Mayen has truly fled the country, we shall insist on reparation. And if Tonley was involved, then he will be punished, too.'

No one else spoke. She nodded to Charlie in dismissal, and with his heart pounding half in relief, half in fear, he left the room, clutching his new waistcoat.

Chapter Twelve

'I just canna believe it, even yet,' said Charlie.

'I canna believe the master's dead,' agreed Phoebe.

They had hardly had the chance to speak with the house full of guests and the funeral, and there was plenty to do today with most of the visitors leaving, rooms to be cleaned, luggage packed, keeping the mistress informed when people set off. But the pair of them had met in a corridor, suddenly quiet: he was returning from a summons to Glastirum's chamber to clean grease off a waistcoat, and she was taking hot water to Lord Watt. They paused, staring out at the rain.

'I canna think how it happened.' Charlie had been turning the whole night over now in his head, now that the gentry had set him off. Before that he had not had time. 'Why would he quarrel with Mr. Abernethy, of all people? Now if you had told me that that Mr. Byres had shot him, I might have believed you.'

Phoebe glanced about her hurriedly.

'Be careful what you come out with, Charlie! They say that man's everywhere!'

'Aye? Then he'll ken what they're all saying about him. I doubt he'd bother himself with a wee serving man like me.' He sighed. 'Anyway, Mr. Byres didna shoot him. He didna even have his hands out his pockets, when the shot went off. He was easy to see, in his odd white coat.'

'White?'

'It was white once, anyway,' said Charlie. 'They were all dressed up, see, in their finery. All the ones who'd been to that meeting ...'

Phoebe frowned at him, and he knew he was making no sense to her – probably no sense at all. He rearranged the waistcoat over his arm, then thought of something.

'I've – I've something here for you,' he said, before he could lose his nerve. He fished in his own waistcoat pocket, and brought out a piece of the ribbon he had bought for her. 'I'm sorry, you'll no be able to wear it for a while. Not till the household's out of mourning, anyway.'

She smiled, and took it, curling it sleek around her fingers before folding it carefully into her own pocket.

'Not in my hair, no,' she said, with that funny look women sometimes wore. She winked at him, then glanced about again, leaned towards him and kissed him lightly on the cheek. 'Thank you, Charlie! That one is worth a kiss!' Then she hefted the jug of hot water, and disappeared into Lord Watt's chamber without a backward glance, all at once demure again. He half-smiled, and hoped he had not done anything stupid. It was good to be home, though: if he thought Phoebe was confusing, how would he ever cope with a town girl?

But he was not to be allowed to stay at home for long, he soon discovered. Even as the various guests were finding their horses and packing their kists and bags, he was summoned once again to the master's business room. Outside it, the Hay brothers were deep in low conversation.

'Well, Glastirum will probably do as she tells him, even though he won't like it. And the others ...'

'Charlie,' said Rannes, catching sight of him, 'my lady is waiting for you. Go on in.'

Nevertheless, Charlie opened the bookroom door with caution. Mrs. Leith was once again seated behind her husband's desk. It was an odd place for a woman, he thought, but it suited her. If anyone had feared that the household would be masterless after John Leith's death, they were wrong.

'Charlie, I have a letter for you to deliver,' she said at once.

Indeed, the letter lay ready on the desk. 'You are to take it to Aberdeen, to my man of law, and you will stay there to make your precognition.' Charlie knew he looked blank, and she managed to contain her impatience. 'Your statement of what happened the night the master was attacked.'

'Am I to stay overnight, ma'am?' he asked.

'Of course you are: there is no need for you to be travelling back and forth in the dark at this time of the year. There is no sense in opening the house just for one, though: it will be cheaper if you stay somewhere.' Charlie felt his heart beat hard at the thought of returning to Campbell's, but Mrs. Leith had other ideas. 'Cruickshank's, on the Gallowgate, is a reasonably priced establishment, and should have space for you at this time of the year. You may take the grey mare, and see to it that she is properly tended to. These places can distract you with a warm fire and broth, so that you never think to check that your horse is adequately fed and watered.'

'Aye, ma'am.' He had never had such warnings from the master: perhaps the master had thought he should know without being told. He told himself to listen and learn. And rather proudly he thought he remembered the name Cruickshank and the Gallowgate: perhaps he was growing to know the town, after all. At least a little.

Only one night in the town: he packed very little, and went to ask the stablefolk to prepare the grey mare for him, while he made sure all his duties would be carried out by someone else in his absence. Then he returned to the stable, viewing the horse with trepidation, and made sure for the last time that the mistress' letter was safely in his pack. On the front of it was the name and address of the man of law: Alexander Stuart, in the Upper Kirkgate. He had no idea where that was, but no doubt Mr. Cruickshank could tell him, or could tell him where to find out.

'Are you going to be all right, Charlie?'

His heart bumped as he turned to find that Phoebe had followed him out into the stableyard, treading carefully in the outdoor muck, her skirts held just clear of the glour. She dropped them on one side and laid a hand on his arm.

'Och, yes, I think so,' he said, trying hard to sound more relaxed than he felt. If he had been relaxed, he would have been on the horse by now, and plodding down the drive with the departing guests.

'You've never gone in on your own before, not to the town. Not to stay in an inn, and all.'

'This'll be my fourth visit, though, in a way.' He laughed, not sure if he was trying to reassure her, or himself. 'Och, it's not too bad. I'm getting to know the place, bit by bit. It's just like a big Kennethmont, when it comes down to it: churches and inns and rich and poor, gentry and clergy and tradesmen and all.' He was quite pleased with this fancy: he knew he would use it later to reassure himself. Phoebe had let go of her skirts with the other hand now, and held her fingers to the mare's warm muzzle.

'She's bonnie,' she said. 'She'll look after you, Charlie.'

'As long as I look after her,' said Charlie. 'If I don't, I'll have the mistress to answer to.'

'She's watching from the window – don't look round! – She told me to come and make sure all was fine with you.'

'Oh.' He had imagined, fondly, that Phoebe had just come out of her own concern for him. But he caught a little smile at the corner of her mouth, and wondered if - hoped that - indeed he had at least been partly right.

'She says to tell you that Mr. Dalgarno and Mr. Keracher are heading off just now, and if you wait you'll be able to travel with them. That way at least you'll no miss your way!' This time she was definitely smiling, but it wasn't unkind. He smiled back, and wondered if he would ever have the nerve to kiss her. Then he wished the thought had not even occurred to him, as he felt his face burn at the very idea.

But Phoebe, like all the servants, had plenty to do this busy morning and was already looking about her to go back across the mud into the house.

'Come back soon, Charlie!' she murmured, then raised her skirts and skipped back to the door. She lighted there, like a teasing bird on a twig, then waved, and vanished into the hall.

He checked his pack once more, told himself where he was going, and made sure he had the money the mistress had given him for the inn, the stabling, and food while he was in town. Then he glanced around. The mistress had been right: she was at the door now, seeing off Mr. Dalgarno and Mr. Keracher, with the kind of stiff courtesy that Charlie realised meant she was pleased enough to see the back of them. No doubt she would be pleased to see most of the guests go: she had plenty to be getting on with, by the sound of it, and there were only a few she trusted to help her. Charlie hoped he was one of them, though of course he would not be as handy in the matter as the gentry. They were the ones who would know all about testaments and inventories and the like: the ones who would read those books with the brown leather coats to them.

'Come on, Charlie lad, are you ready to go, too? Mount up and travel with us!'

Lang Tam was already draped over his mule, grinning. Charlie sighed and finally led his horse over to the lepping-on stane, climbed the steps carefully for they too were wet and muddy, and did his best to mount his horse as if he knew what he was doing. The mare was kind, and did not, in front of everyone, immediately bolt or throw him, so he gathered the reins and moved off to let the next man use the stane.

The journey back to town was surprisingly pleasant: they did not rush themselves, and while no doubt there was a lingering air of grief about them the funeral, for Charlie's companions, had signalled an end to the matter and they were almost jovial. Charlie himself could not quite reach that level of content – nor anything like it – but he was happy to allow the others to converse casually, even frivolously, as he let the mare drift along behind them. His thoughts still lingered on more mournful subjects.

It was hard to know what to do, if anything. The Hay brothers, he was sure, were just as shocked as he was that Mr. Abernethy would have picked a quarrel with the master, but they were somehow prepared to accept it as an odd thing – tragic, but no more than odd – that had happened when the men were drunk. The mistress could see nothing but that Mr. Abernethy was guilty: she seemed to care nothing for the circumstances. And as far as Charlie had seen, as he ran back across the Castlegate with the master's pistols, it had been Mr. Abernethy that had fired the shot that had killed him. But ...

But what kind of terrible luck would it be if the second worst shot in the north-east of Scotland took aim and actually hit you?

And how drunk had Mr. Abernethy really been?

This time they had left Leith Hall early enough to arrive in Aberdeen in the one day, with no need to stop at Inverurie. It was dark, though, by the time they reached the low houses and silent college in Old Aberdeen, the students away for the New Year holiday.

'Where are you staying?' asked Lang Tam. 'Campbell's?'

'No,' said Charlie, 'I'm for Cruickshank's on the Gallowgate.'

Lang Tam turned in the dusk and looked at him.

'What for would you stay there? Come and stay with us, and take the horse to Campbell's. I'll no say the masters live in luxury, but you'd be warm enough and there's a decent pie shop next door.'

It sounded very tempting, and for a moment Charlie thought of saying yes. But he was not his own man, and when he thought what might happen if the mistress discovered he had not done as directed ...

'Aye, it's good of you, Tam, thank you,' he heard himself saying sadly. 'But it's Cruickshank's for me.'

'Truly you'd be more comfortable with us! And the horse would be better off at Campbell's, ken. You have to take that into consideration. If Lady Leith Hall has given you coin to pay for yourself and the mare at Cruickshank's, then spend that money on the mare at Campbell's and come to us where you don't have to do more than maybe buy me a pie!'

This time Charlie knew he should not allow himself to hesitate.

'She's made arrangements,' he said. 'I have to go to Cruickshank's place. She maybe has her own reasons for it.'

'Oh, well, if you're really sure,' said Lang Tam, reluctant to let him go that easily.

'I am, really, Tam. Not that I'm not grateful for the offer.'

Aye, it was good to have friends like Tam, Charlie thought, as Tam pointed out the gateway of Cruickshank's stable on the Gallowgate. They waved good night and Tam followed his masters slowly down into the Broadgate and the town. It would have been fine and cosy, probably sleeping on a chair in Tam's masters' flat, gossiping into the night. But at the same time, this way he would get a quiet night's sleep for a change, and no serving at a table or drinking or watching everyone else drink. A bit of peace to himself to think.

It turned colder overnight – Charlie was well aware of it as Mr. Cruickshank did not believe in petty details like having his window frames fit the holes in the wall for them, or in weighing down his curtain poles with heavy bed curtains. When Charlie pulled back the creaking shutters, he saw without surprise that it was snowing silently, great weighty fluffy flakes that, for now, vanished as they settled on the wet cobbles of the Gallowgate. There was a persistence to their constant descent, though, that made him feel they might soon cover the ground again in a coat of soft white. He decided not to linger too long over his morning ablutions, and to pay an early call on Alexander Stuart.

Busy people on the street were well bundled into shawls and cloaks when he ventured outside. He had directions to the Upper Kirkgate from the surly Cruickshank, and knew that first he had to head down towards the Broadgate as Lang Tam and his masters had done last night. And that was another college there, so someone told him when he asked – the Marischal College, called for an ancestor of the Earl Marischal that had been attainted in the '45 just like so many of the master's friends – a dark archway lined with snow and set amongst lowly dwellings, and not at all what he expected of such places. But when he reached the head of the Broadgate, he did not turn right towards the great kirk, but could not resist going left, along a road he knew, that opened almost straightaway into the wide expanse of the Castlegate. It was busy as usual with traders and travellers, with stalls up on the Plainstanes and gossips lingering around the well, even as the snowflakes caught on their hats and shawls. He paused, surveying the scene, remembering the first time he had seen it as his master steered the chaise skilfully through the throng – then remembering it again as he had seen it that awful night, the lamplight and the tickly smell of gunpowder, the looming figure of Mayen and the nasty little pale goblin that was Byres of Tonley, and his master lying on the gritty cassies, almost in the ditch, no more respected than a dead dog. The sudden anger that surged in his throat knocked back his tears, and he walked on to the front door of Campbell's, open and welcoming as always.

Here the two lampposts stood, the ones that had lit the scene that night. He glanced up at them, fancying that they could tell him more than he already knew, if only they could speak. Then a man, sweeping the front step, darted snow over his boots and he jumped back. He recognised one of the inn's servants, but the man did not seem to know him.

'Och, sorry, lad. I didna mean to spray you like that!'

'That's fine,' said Charlie, though he could feel cold spots on his breeches and tried not to look as if he was brushing the snow off.

'Are you looking for the shot hole, then?'

'The what?' Charlie was alarmed.

'Och, I thought you were one of these sightseers. Ken, a week or so ago there was a duel out here!'

'Was there?' Charlie let his eyes open wide.

'Aye, a couple of the gentry, no more sober than they should be, either of them. And one shot the other, and the shot went into yon lamp pole!'

'Is that a fact?' Charlie tried his best to look as if it was all news to him - though, to be fair, this last bit was. 'And what happened the gentlemen?'

'The one who was shot died - not there on the street, but away in his own house,' said the man, sounding just a little disappointed that he could not point out the exact site of the death. 'The other saw what he had done, and he fled. They say he's away in America now, or he will be - it takes a gey lang time to cross yon Atlantic, ken.'

'I should think so,' Charlie agreed. He peered up at the lamp post. It was true that the wood, smoothed and grey with weathering for a number of years, was at one point gouged as if by something sharp, or fast. The wound looked fresh. 'Is that really a shot hole from that duel?' he asked.

'It certainly is,' said the man, 'for I cleaned up the bitties of wood myself the next day, while the maid scrubbed away the blood from the cassies,' he added, with relish.

'My,' said Charlie. 'Well, thank you for showing me that. I'd never have seen it otherwise.'

'Well, a fine-dressed serving man like yourself,' said the man, showing his powers of observation, 'will no doubt be able to show his gratitude.' He stood innocently, hand not quite out for a reward but certainly ready to move if one were proffered. Charlie drew out, hiding it as much as possible, the bag of coin that the mistress had given him, and gave the man one of them. He hoped it was enough, and hoped even more fervently that it was not too much.

It was only when he turned to walk away, back to the head of the Broadgate and off to find Alexander Stuart, that it struck him what he had discovered. The ball that had killed John Leith had lodged in his head - all the doctors agreed, and he himself had seen the master's head bathed and bandaged. There had been no exit wound, Dr.

Skene had called it: no hole at the back for the ball to come out.

So if there was really also a ball in the lamp post, and it could not be the same one, then there really had been two shots fired that night.

He made his way to the house behind the great town kirk where he had been directed by Mr. Cruickshank, still pondering the problem. Two shots. Had the master fired back? But surely ... surely he had been in front of that lamp post, or at least between it and Mr. Abernethy. So what had happened? Could Mr. Abernethy have fired both his pistols, and one shot went into the lamp post and one into the master's head? That seemed the most likely, but then ... then why did Mr. Abernethy only have one pistol in his hand when Charlie followed him and Tonley back towards the inn? And what did Tonley pick up, the thing that had looked so much like a pistol, from beside where the master lay? He shook his head: none of it made any sense, and just now he needed to concentrate on finding his way or he might lose himself as well as the house he was seeking. This was a strange part of town to him, not surprisingly, and he had to watch his path.

But the house, it turned out, was easy enough to discover, and he waited in a cold hallway while a maid took the letter written by Mrs. Leith upstairs somewhere, her boots clacking on the stone stairs. Just when he was beginning to wonder if Mr. Stuart was asleep, or in the house at all, the maid clattered back down to his level and jerked her head at him.

'Up to his study, if you please, Mr. Rob. He says he'll see you now.'

She was a little frightening, and he very quickly did as he was told. The man of law was short and whiskery, but younger than Charlie had expected and with a reddened face that perhaps showed he spent more time out of doors than the usual lawyer. He had several blank sheets of paper in front of him, as well as the mistress' letter, and fiddled with a pen as Charlie explained briefly what he had seen on the night of the master's duel. Then he asked one or two questions, probing for anything that Charlie might have missed or, as Charlie thought, that he might be for some reason concealing. Then he began again, in as much detail as he could, and committed Charlie's whole story to the sheets of paper, with names and descriptions and even, in places, Charlie's opinions and impressions.

121

Charlie complied dutifully with everything, wondering why the man should want his opinion on anything, and when he was dismissed the maid took him back down and saw him firmly out at the street door. He found he was exhausted.

For a moment he simply stood, propped against the front wall of the house, staring sightlessly at the passing crowds of strangers. Then, just as he was about to move, he saw a face he knew.

What had been her name again? Margaret, that was it. The landlady of that lady for whom John Leith had waited for so long, but whom he had never seen.

Just then, the woman looked round, somehow aware that she was being watched. She saw at once who it was, and crossed the street to stand face to face with him.

'Well?' she said. 'You're that gentleman's servant, are you no?'

'Aye, that's – probably right,' Charlie agreed, though the description had been vague enough.

'Right, then, tell me this,' she said, standing on tiptoe so as to come nearer to meeting his eye. 'What has he done with her? For she's never come home yet!'

Chapter Thirteen

'I don't understand,' said Charlie, looking about him to make sure it was really him she was talking to.

'She never came back! I've to get a new tenant and everything. I'd have sold her wee bits and pieces to make up the rent due but –' Here she hesitated, and Charlie realised she was kinder, or fonder of Mrs. Dilley, than she wanted to be seen to be. Margaret cleared her throat, and finished sternly. 'I'd have got nothing for them, anyway. But where did they go?'

'What makes you think they went anywhere? I mean, together,' Charlie asked, playing for time in the hope that he would suddenly realise what all this was about.

'He was the only one came to see her all the time she lived at my house,' Margaret said. 'I mean, not that she wasna a handsome woman and all, but she was respectable. I won't have that kind of business in my house, ken. But anyone could see that he was an admirer.'

'The master?' cried Charlie, nearly choking on the suggestion. 'But he's a married man!'

Margaret stared at him, then laughed hard.

'What difference does that make?'

Charlie tried to shake off that idea.

'He never saw her, though, did he? Not when she was at your

house.'

That brought Margaret back to gravity.

'No, he did not, you're right. Neither when he came with you
– you poor wee soul, standing there in the snow all the day – nor later
when he came on his own.'

'When was that?' Charlie asked in surprise, but then he
already knew.

'A week or so ago. But she was long gone by then.'

'Then why,' said Charlie, thinking of something clever, 'would
you think he would go to your house to see her, if he'd already taken
her off somewhere else?'

'Och, to pretend he had nothing to do with it, nae doubt,' said
Margaret dismissively. That was a stage further than Charlie's clever
thought. 'No, he'll have her in some wee comfy house somewhere,
ready to receive him when he can get away from his wifie and all the
responsibilities of home.'

Charlie was aghast.

'But that's – that's sinful!'

'Well, it's no right,' said Margaret, 'and forbye, he should
have sent for her things and let me clear the room for another tenant,
that or paid the rent there too.'

'But the master would never do a thing like that! The mistress
would kill him!' he added, hardly knowing what he was saying, but it
made Margaret laugh again.

'Oh, she's that kind, is she? Aye, nae doubt, if she ever found
out!' she admitted. 'All the more reason for some discretion, do you
no think?'

'I canna believe it,' said Charlie firmly. 'I'll no believe it. The
master's a good man.' He realised he was still talking of John Leith as
if he were alive, as if Margaret's ignorance of the master's death
allowed him a few weeks more of existence. And the master had been
a good man, he was sure of it.

'Aye, even good men have their wee wants and desires,' said
Margaret philosophically. 'Are you his trusted doer, or are you just a
rider with him?'

Charlie hesitated.

'A trusted doer, I think,' he said slowly. He was, wasn't he?
John Leith had taken him to that lanie off the Ship Row in the first
place, and if he hadn't taken him that last time, maybe that was

because he didn't want to make Charlie stand pointlessly in the snow again. He was always considerate. Wasn't he?

'Well, then,' Margaret was going on, 'nae doubt you'll soon find out where she is, where he's put her. It's a wonder he didna get you to set the place up, but he maybe had somewhere ready for her. You've no been with him long, have you?' she asked, with an astute look.

'Not as a trusted doer, no,' Charlie agreed. 'I've been in his household since I was a bairn.'

She nodded.

'Aye, well, you'll get to know, sooner or later. He'll have you running messages to her, nae doubt, and mebbe sending her on her way when he's found a younger replacement.' She sighed, and Charlie could take it no longer.

'Margaret, he'll no be doing that -' he held up a bold hand as she made to interrupt '- for he's dead.'

'Dead?' That stopped her in her tracks.

'He was killed in a duel. He died on Christmas Day.'

She stared at him, mouth open, then found her voice.

'Yon John Leith of Leith Hall? The duel on the Plainstanes?'

'Aye, that's the one. My master's dead.' He felt tears well up again, and swallowed hard. It was a strange conversation altogether to be having on the street, with the world and all going by. He need not make it worse by greeting.

'My,' said Margaret. Then, after another pause, 'Ken they're already writing ballads on that one.'

'They are?' He should find a copy – probably on the Plainstanes at the market. Should he show it to the mistress? He'd better read it first, and perhaps ask Mr. Hay of Rannes to take a look at it, too. If the ballad made out that John Leith had provoked Mayen, she would not be pleased. It occurred to him that Lang Tam might know about it, and that might save him buying a sheet if it was not going to be well received. A ballad, eh? He wondered how the master would have felt about that.

'Well, it'll make it harder to find her,' Margaret was saying, 'unless there's a'body in the household that kens of a house he might have used. Thing is, she might not even ken he's dead.'

'Of course,' said Charlie, wondering how he might ask around, still not remotely convinced himself that John Leith would ever have kept a woman in a house apart from his own wife. Margaret turned to go, then spun back, scowling.

'What was the duel about?'

'What?'

'What was the duel about?'

'Well ...' Charlie tried to think. What had set it off? He was not even sure that he knew.

'They're saying it was something to do with one of them saying the other was selling oats with rubbish in it, is that so?' Now that she knew the names, it seemed Margaret had much more information about the whole business than he had.

'I dinna ken ...'

'Aye, or you're no to say.' She sighed sharply. 'It's aye the same. The high heidyins tell you to hold your mouth shut, and that's you, you can say nothing even to an old friend like me.'

'A what?' That took Charlie by surprise, and Margaret laughed again.

'Och, away with you. I doubt you'd tell me what colour my own eyes were if your master tellt you not to: you're that sort. You always do what you're told, do you not?'

'Well – if it's sensible ...'

'You'll always think it's sensible, if your master tells you,' she said. Charlie tried to think of a time he had been told to do something he had not thought sensible, but his mind went blank. But then John Leith had been a sensible kind of a master.

'Aye, well,' she said, 'no doubt you have your business – or your master's business – to be getting on with.'

'I told you my master's dead,' he interrupted, suddenly anxious that she had not understood.

'Oh, you'll have a master again, I'm sure. There'll always be someone telling you what to do, laddie. Now, off you go about his business – and if you find yon Mrs. Dilley, tell her if she's lucky I'll maybe still have her things when she comes back.'

She nodded sharply at him by way of farewell, and marched off. Charlie tried to take in all she had said, as he wandered along the street back towards the Broadgate. Could the master really have had Mrs. Dilley accommodated in a cottage somewhere? Or perhaps in a flat in the town, for when he came into Aberdeen? Could she even be in the Leiths' town house?

The thought alarmed him, somehow, the idea that he was stuck at Cruickshank's inn while someone was staying in a house he had looked after, possibly unattended, perhaps making free of the place – but that would have been all right if the master had installed Mrs. Dilley there.

Which he would not have done.

Yet ... if Mrs. Dilley was there, no doubt she would be expecting the master to return to her. What if Mrs. Leith came into town and found her there? Charlie winced at the very thought: if Mrs. Dilley was there, then she was there for all the wrong reasons, but to have Mrs. Leith angry with you was not something many deserved. Should he go and make sure she was warned to leave? If she went quickly now, she could go back to Margaret's and carry on as she had done, whatever way that might be.

Or was his duty to his mistress now, to report Mrs. Dilley's occupation of the town house to her?

His duty to his master might well be to conceal Mrs. Dilley's occupation from Mrs. Leith, though. His thoughts were so contorted he almost tripped over his own feet as he walked.

His duty to Leith Hall was to go and make sure the town house was secure, as he was staying so near by and it was unused. As his master had not been the kind of man to go against his wife and take in another lady, there would be no one there, so that was all right. He had the key with him on his set of keys since the master had handed it to him in the autumn: it would be the work of a few minutes to take a look through the building, make sure everything was sound and dry, and lock it up again. He had nothing else to do, anyway: he was to be here in the town for another night, and to travel back first thing in the morning.

Resolved, and confident that he would find nothing to concern his mistress or defame his master, he trotted back through the muddy slush towards the Castlegate again.

But when he let himself in to the narrow house, the first thing he saw was a pair of muddy boots in the hall which had certainly not been there when he had closed up the house and followed the master's coffin back to Leith Hall.

To be fair, they did not look like women's boots, not at all. But sometimes, in the winter, if they had to go out and about in bad weather, women did wear heavy boots that could be mistaken for those of a smallish man. Charlie peered into these ones, noted a fairly ripe odour, and felt even more uneasy. He had never met Mrs. Dilley - was she the kind of woman who did not know tricks to take the smell out of well-worn boots?

He glanced into the parlour, and saw it was empty, with the shutters closed. The fireplace smelled cold and sooty, and was not cleaned out. On the table next to the chair by the fire was the flattened remains of a candle, as burned out as it could be, and a bottle which had, by the smell, contained wine. There was no sign of a drinking vessel of any kind. He progressed, soft-footed as could be, to the kitchen, in case empty glasses might have been left there. Instead he found the remains of a pie - beef, he thought - which he would hesitate to offer to a dog. Mrs. Dilley was certainly not tidy in her habits.

But where was she, if she had left her boots in the hall? The flagged floor of the hall was dry, as was every other floor he had seen: she could not have been out of the house and returned in the last couple of hours, anyway. And she would not have gone out without her boots, surely - not in the snow.

An alarming thought, quite unworthy of him, sprang up in Charlie's innocent head. Could the boots belong to someone else? Someone who had perhaps stayed the night in the house with Mrs. Dilley? She might have allowed a friend to stay, perhaps. His thought modified even as it occurred to him. There were several bedchambers upstairs: one of them might easily accommodate a friend, and Mrs. Dilley another. After all, perhaps the master had encouraged her to move quarters to more comfortable surroundings in all innocence, and she had invited a friend to stay. But if the friend owned the boots, then even if Mrs. Dilley had gone out, the friend was still somewhere upstairs.

Or perhaps Mrs. Leith knew all about this, about whoever was staying here and why, and that was why she had sent Charlie to stay at Cruickshank's inn?

He turned the problem over in his head. He was Leith Hall's steward, and it was his business - well, he thought it was probably his business - to know who was staying at Leith Hall, or indeed here at the family's town house. Therefore he should look upstairs.

If Mrs. Leith knew who was here, and had not wished Charlie

to disturb them, then he should not look upstairs.

But then, he could just look without disturbing them, couldn't he? And if something did happen, and he disturbed whoever it was, well, she would indeed be annoyed. He might have to be a little roundabout, say he had seen lights on in the house as he was passing and was concerned. Something like that, anyway - he would have to find some way of explaining his anxieties without, necessarily, mentioning Mrs. Dilley to her. He was fairly sure the master would not have wanted that.

But if Mrs. Leith did not know who was here, then she might well be pleased to find that Charlie was looking after the family property. Unless it was Mrs. Dilley, in which case it was unlikely that Mrs. Dilley would tell her.

Charlie pressed his cold fingers to his temples, considered his options at some length, and with considerable trepidation – but some curiosity – began to climb the stairs.

They were stone, and the only sound he made was a soft scuffing which he did his best to minimise. On the first floor, the door to the master bedroom, where John Leith had died and which Charlie clearly remembered closing before they left for Leith Hall, stood half-open. Thick, glutinous snoring issued from within.

Charlie hesitated at the door: the room was in darkness. He decided to check the rest of the house first and make sure he had as much information as he could about the situation. There was no point in waking whoever was in there if he found a servant sleeping in the attic who might tell him what was going on with less awkwardness all round.

But he could find no one else in the house at all. He paused for a moment, as had become his habit, right at the top of the house, to look over the snowy harbour and the flaky grey water beyond, as if he wanted to tease himself over his dread of the sea. Then he took a deep breath, lit a candle, and trotted back downstairs to the doorway of the master bedroom. Shielding the flame a little, he edged inside.

The room was stuffy and unpleasant, as if a number of heavy drinkers with an aversion to both washing and laundry had spent a fortnight there, eating food which had not agreed with them. He thought again of the relic of a pie down in the kitchen, and hoped quite hard that the occupant of the room was not Mrs. Dilley. It was not the picture he had in his mind of a lady who was not only an acquaintance of the master, but also a friend of Lady Glastirum. He stepped carefully forwards towards the bed, saw a leg, long and bare, protruding from beneath the bedclothes, and stopped again, embarrassed. Then the snoring gave way to an alarmed snort, the leg kicked and disappeared, and with a cry a figure plunged from behind the bed curtains, wild as a savage. In its hand was a sword.

Charlie yelped, managed to retain the candle, and backed rapidly towards the door. The figure – a man, definitely a man, for its nightshirt was on the short side – swayed, the sword uncertain.

'Who in the name of the wee man are you?' he demanded.

'Ch – Charlie Rob, sir,' said Charlie, now on the landing outside the door, ready to dive sideways if the sword approached. 'I'm Charlie Rob, and I was servant to Leith Hall – I mean, the late Leith Hall.' He had recognised the figure.

The man pushed a hand through his unkempt hair, with some difficulty.

'You were Johnnie's man?' he asked. 'Have I seen you afore?'

'Aye, sir, but only for a short moment.' Now was no time to be offended. 'You're Lawrence Leith, are you no, sir?'

'I am,' said the man, drawing himself upright, a movement which made his nightshirt rise up even further. It must have been draughty, Charlie thought. 'Lowrie Leith, at your service ... and Johnnie was my nephew, may he rest in peace.' His shoulders sagged again at the thought. 'What time of the day is it?'

'It's gone midday, anyway, sir,' said Charlie, not quite sure. 'I'm sorry I disturbed you. I had no idea there was anybody staying in the house.'

'Aye, well.' Lowrie Leith laid down the sword and pulled a robe over his half-covered body, tying it tight. Charlie recognised it as the master's. 'There was a minor difference of opinion with my landlady, you see, and since I knew nobody would be using this place for now ...'

'A minor disagreement?' asked Charlie, wondering if he would need to tell the mistress.

'Aye, she felt strongly that I should be paying my rent on time, whereas I had a more, well, open-ended approach to the matter. She was going to get the money eventually, the silly woman, and now she won't. Very short-sighted, some of these people,' he added, suddenly meeting Charlie's eye as if he were conveying business information of considerable importance.

'Aye, sir, I should think so.'

'Well,' said Lowrie, 'open the shutters and let's see what the day brings, eh?' He flung his arms wide as if they themselves were the shutters, and Charlie blew out the candle and did as he was bid – after all, Mr. Leith was family. The open shutters displayed to full effect the heavily falling snow, and let a block of cold air into the bedchamber. Lowrie Leith shuddered.

'Have you a fire going down in the parlour?' he demanded. 'And is there any drink in the house?'

'I can light one straight away,' said Charlie, 'but apart from the ale in the kitchen I don't think there's much. Oh, there might be a bottle or two in the pantry, for we had guests here before – before we left.'

'Och, they're long gone,' said Lowrie Leith sadly. 'Light the fire, and I'll keep an eye to it while you get away out and find some more – the same kind would be grand. No doubt the family has an account somewhere nearby?'

'Shall I fetch you some breakfast, sir, while I'm out?'

Lowrie put a grubbily pale hand to his brow.

'I don't think there's a kind of food I could face just now,' he said faintly. 'Just bring me the wine.'

Nevertheless, when Charlie returned with the wine and with some bread and butter for himself, Lowrie ate three large slices. He then set to with the wine.

'How did the funeral go?' he asked, after a long swallow. 'I meant to go, but ... there was business in the town I couldna very well leave unattended.'

'It went off well, I think, sir,' said Charlie. It had only been two days ago, but it felt much longer.

'A sad business. A very sad business,' said Lowrie, nodding solemnly. 'And the wee wifie? I mean, Harriot Stuart, Mrs. Leith. How's she managing? Is she keeping well?'

'I believe so, sir.'

Lowrie took another swallow.

'They're saying it was Mayen that did it. Jamie Abernethy, ken.'

'Aye, sir. It was: I was there myself,' he said, though the words sounded more certain than he felt.

'Whyfore would he do that, do you think? Was there a quarrel betwixt them?'

Charlie considered what Margaret had told him, not long ago.

'They're saying there was, sir, but I was in the inn that night, and I saw no sign of a quarrel till Mr. Abernethy called the master out.'

'Is that a fact, now?' Lowrie's lips tightened. 'Was there many others there, in the inn? Campbell's, was it?'

'Aye, sir, Campbell's. There was Lord Watt, and Mr. Keracher and Mr. Dalgarno, and Mr. Byres of Tonley, and Mr. Abernethy, and a man called McFarland I've never seen before.'

'Oh, aye,' said Lowrie Leith, as if he knew the man. Charlie waited for further information, but nothing came.

'And that was all the party, except for Lang Tam who's servant to Mr. Dalgarno and Mr. Keracher, and Mr. Holland who's servant to Lord Watt, sir.'

'Hm,' said Lowrie, and his wracked face seemed, for once, to show some keen intelligence. 'I wonder now if it was any of them.'

'If what was any of them, sir?'

'See,' said Lowrie, 'when you're a fellow like me, ken, Charlie, everybody thinks you're drunk the whole time. Ken what I mean? So I was there in Campbell's one night, on my own, and I was in one of the wee booths. It was quiet, like, so I had it to myself. And I'd maybe just shut my eyes for a mintie or two. And I daresay anybody looking in at me would have thought I was away with it. But see, Charlie, I wasn't!'

'Right, sir,' said Charlie, after a moment. 'And what were you, sir?'

'I was listening!' hissed Leith, and suddenly Charlie remembered Uncle Lowrie's plea to the master, to let him in on anything that might give him some excitement in his life. It seemed he was still looking for something.

'And what did you hear?' Charlie whispered, too.

'I heard a man say that he needed John Leith of Leith Hall dead, Charlie – and that a made-up duel would be the best way to go about it.'

Chapter Fourteen

Charlie turned ice cold.

'What do you mean?' he quavered.

'Just that,' said Lowrie Leith, sitting back in his chair. Charlie tried not to clutch the chair for support. 'There was a mannie wanted Johnnie dead, and that was the way to do it.'

'Could the man he was talking to – could that have been Mr. Abernethy?'

Lowrie thought about it for a moment, emptying and filling his wine glass as he considered.

'I dinna think so,' he said eventually.

'Why not, sir?'

'I had the impression, when I passed the booth later, that neither of the men was the size of Abernethy. He's no small, you know.'

'Aye, I know that, sir.' Charlie thought hard. Was there any chance that some other party had planned a fake duel, even as a real duel was about to happen? 'When was this, sir?'

'Och, I canna mind,' said Lowrie carelessly – then seemed to change his mind. 'Wait, now, let me think. It would have been – well, it was after the time I last saw your master, and then it was before he died.'

'Aye, sir,' said Charlie, not particularly impressed by this.

'No, wait, I can bring it down further than that. I was just starting wide. It would have been after I quarrelled with yon fellow in the Castlegate, because that was the reason I was drinking on my own in Campbell's – I'd no like you to think I've no friends to drink with me, Charlie. And that was – when was that?' There was a long pause, while he emptied and refilled the glass once again, and frowned horribly. For a moment Charlie thought he had forgotten altogether what he had been saying. But at last he shook his unwashed grey locks, and placed a long fingertip on the table as though pinning down his prey.

'It would have been the seventeenth of December,' he said firmly. 'Aye, that's right. That's when I heard them.'

'Did you hear anything more?'

Lowrie scowled again.

'There was talk of money – a reward. I canna mind the details. Something as a deposit?' He seemed to question his own memory. 'Aye, something like that. They were no shouting, ken: I had to concentrate to hear them.'

Which is a lot harder, Charlie thought, when you've had a bottle or two of Campbell's best red wine. It seemed that there was no more to the account for the moment, anyway, unless something came back to Lowrie Leith later. Charlie hoped that if it did, Lowrie would remember to tell him.

'The thing I don't understand, though, sir, is why anybody would have wanted to kill the master. That makes no sense to me,' he admitted.

'Well,' said Lowrie, 'Johnnie's dead, so someone must have.'

Charlie was not quite sure that followed: the whole thing could still have been an awful misunderstanding, but he was not going to argue. If there was a chance that the master had been deliberately lured into a place where he could be shot, and by his close friend, then the people who had conspired against him were much more to blame than ever Mr. Abernethy was – and much more worthy of Mrs. Leith's anger and vengeance.

'See,' Lowrie was saying, and there went the last of the wine into his glass, 'see, I had a notion that Johnnie was involved in something interesting. Or exciting. You might remember the time I was here before and I asked him if he would ever let me in on it. But I wonder, now ...'

'You wonder if that's why someone wanted to kill him?' Charlie prompted. But Lowrie shook his head, sleepily.

'I wonder if there was ever anything in it, at all,' he finished with a puzzled frown, and sank into a heavy doze.

Charlie found a cushion and propped it under his head, and surveyed him for a long moment. Was there any chance that anything Lowrie had said was true? After the master's death, when he had staggered into the house to pay his respects, he had gone on at some length about the master and his exciting, secret activities, but none of it had made much sense, and the next day Lowrie had let himself out of the house early and disappeared without saying goodbye. Charlie wondered what he should do now. He could hardly prevent Lowrie from staying in the house – he seemed to have his own key, in any case, and he was a member of the family. But he had no directions to remain here and act as his servant, either. He had to return to Leith Hall, first thing in the morning, now that the lawyer he had come to town to see appeared to have finished with him. But that was first thing in the morning – should he stay here and look after Lowrie this evening? And if he did, would Lowrie remember anything else to tell him? Looking at the man asleep on the chair, mouth gaping, grey flesh sagging, he did not hold out much hope. And was anything he remembered reliable anyway?

Charlie let himself quietly out at the front door, into the still snowy Castlegate, and looked up at the sky. It was already late dusk, on this wintry day, and he wondered if there would be anyone he knew in Campbell's, for a bit of company before he returned to Cruickshank's inn. Cruickshank's felt less of an inn and more of a stable with a few rooms: there was little cheer there, and while that was likely to make for another undisturbed night's sleep, just for the moment he longed for warmth and friendliness more than a quiet bed. He began to trudge across to Campbell's, while his mind wandered back to what Lowrie Leith had said. Could there be any truth in it?

What if someone, for whatever reason – whether connected with activities so secret Charlie himself knew nothing of them – really did want the master dead, then a duel might be a reasonable way to go about it. Charlie could not imagine wanting to kill someone, but it made sense – well, as long as you were a good shot, and you managed to shoot your enemy before he shot you. The trouble with that was that Mr. Abernethy was well known to be a terrible shot.

Then he stopped short in the middle of the street. A handcart swerved to avoid him, the boy shoving it swearing imaginatively as he passed.

The master had been involved in something secret, hadn't he? What about that meeting, apparently upstairs in Campbell's inn, for the purpose of which he had come to Aberdeen? He had told Charlie nothing about it, and as far as Charlie could remember, as John Leith had left Leith Hall for the last time, he had not mentioned anything to the mistress except some vague commissions he was to purchase. Charlie remembered the master's sober demeanour as he left the house that evening, his clothing sombre and smart. And some of the others had been at whatever it was, too – it had been Mr. Abernethy himself who had given the master the information about the meeting, hadn't it? Quietly, confidentially, as they had ridden back to Mayen House that evening in October. Who else had been there? Had they all gone to the meeting before joining to drink downstairs? That would mean Mr. Byres of Tonley, Mr. Dalgarno and Mr. Keracher, and Lord Watt – oh, and that little Mr. McFarland. Who was he, and why had Charlie never seen him before?

He entered the main room of Campbell's inn, and looked about him, as if Mr. McFarland might still be there in the corner. Instead, he saw no one at all that he knew. It was very strange, for a moment: he felt almost as if he had wandered into the wrong inn, in the wrong town: he glanced across at the booth where Lord Watt had previously hosted the table of friends that had included John Leith, but it was full of strangers. He shivered.

The servant who had earlier pointed out the ball in the lamp post came past, and stopped to find out what Charlie was looking for.

'You're back, then?'

'Aye, I'm looking for ... well, Mr. Dalgarno and Mr. Keracher? They usually sit over there, I think,' he added.

'Och, they're no in tonight, or not yet. Sit yourself down and have a drink, and no doubt they'll be here before long.'

'Um ...' said Charlie, looking about him.

'Mind you, they only live down in the Green,' the servant went on. 'You could find them down there, if it's urgent. Have you a letter for them, or something?'

'No, no,' said Charlie, 'it's nothing like that. Whereabouts in the Green, though?'

Charlie left the inn a minute or two later, setting out confidently for where he was sure the Green lay. Like the Castlegate it was a centre of commerce in the town, but it was older, narrower and darker. But Campbell's servant's directions had been very clear, and it did not take long before Charlie was chapping at the door on a tiny landing, and Lang Tam was opening it with a look of delighted surprise on his bony face.

'Charlie, lad! It's good to see you – did you change your mind about coming to stay here?'

Charlie grinned at Lang Tam's enthusiastic friendliness, and followed him as directed into a kind of boxroom crossed with a kitchen, which was evidently Tam's own territory in the flat.

'No, I think I'm best to stay up at Cruickshank's, thanks. But I went into Campbell's to see if there was anybody there and there was not a single face I recognised.'

'Oh aye – well, Mr. Keracher is eager to get up there and start drinking, but he's waiting for Mr. Dalgarno to get home.'

'Oh? I sort of thought they went everywhere together,' said Charlie, half-joking.

'Aye, well, when a man's heart is in it sometimes he likes to head off on his own, and not have to find an occupation for his friend.'

'Oh aye?' Charlie thought about this. 'Is Mr. Dalgarno courting, then?'

'He is.' Lang Tam's eyes widened in solemnity. 'He's courting very seriously and all. I think he asked permission at your master's funeral – well, I hope he maybe waited until the journey home.'

'He's not courting Mrs. Leith!' cried Charlie. Lang Tam put out a hand to hush him.

'No, no, man, he's not that quick off the mark. It's Lord Watt's sister he's after – yon one with the funny name. Kee-ra? She's a widow twice over. Mind they were on about her when they dined at Leith Hall?'

'Oh, the one with no children,' Charlie remembered.

'Aye, no children, but plenty money. Mr. Dalgarno's desperate for that. Aye, and the lady's bonnie enough, so I hear.'

'Will Mr. Keracher go and stay with them, or will you just

have the one master, then?'

'It's a good question,' said Lang Tam, sucking his lip. 'I'll maybe go for a servant in Mr. Dalgarno's household, a grand one like yourself - I'd be a majordomo, ken, and no more of this cooking and cleaning. I'll have a whole staff to tell what to do, and I can just polish the silver and check the wine for quality!'

'Hi, there's a deal more to it than that!' said Charlie, laughing. 'As you'll soon find out, if you take it on.'

'Well, we'll see,' said Tam. 'I doubt there's a good chance the lady would prefer a more refined manservant about the place, and I'll be left with Mr. Keracher and maybe only half my money. Aye, well,' he sighed. 'What about a cup of ale, then? While we're waiting to see if Mr. Dalgarno will leave the lady tonight, and Mr. Keracher cools his heels in the parlour.'

Several ales had been consumed when at last there was a clatter at the door and Lang Tam jumped up, raising his eyebrows at Charlie. He disappeared into the hallway, and Charlie heard voices, not only Tam's and Mr. Dalgarno's, but also Mr. Keracher's, presumably emerging from the parlour.

'Mr. Leith's servant - that's to say, the late Mr. Leith's servant, sir, is in the kitchen,' Charlie heard Tam say, 'wondering why there was no one up at Campbell's the night.'

There was a pause when none of them spoke. Their voices seemed loud, coming all the way through the thick door.

'I'm not going to Campbell's till this matter is settled,' came Dalgarno's reply. 'Let Lord Watt see me as a sensible gentleman, not one to fling his money about on drink.'

'But that's exactly what you are!' Mr. Keracher called from the parlour, and by the sound of things he had been flinging his own money about in much the same way. Charlie wondered how much wine he had had in there, sitting on his own and waiting. 'You're a spendthrift and a drunkard, and that's the very reason you need to wed his sister!'

'Aye,' said Dalgarno, 'but I don't want him to think that. Or her. Just at the moment she's charmed by my handsome looks and attentive courtesies. If her brother goes home and says 'Oh, by the way, yon Dalgarno emptied his purse into Campbell's coffers again, and then he fairly boked up his drink this evening - the gutters were flowing with it', then it's going to cloud her judgement the least bit, wouldn't you say?'

'So we're not going out?' Keracher's voice was plaintive.

'You can go if you like, but I'm staying here. Give us a glass of that stuff, if there's any left,' he snapped, and the parlour door shut hard. In a moment, Tam returned to the kitchen.

'They're no going to Campbell's. I'm thinking Campbell will maybe send a fellow down to see if they're all right, or if the world has ended or something. I can barely mind the last time they were here and not there of an evening.'

'Well, I'd better be heading off, anyway,' said Charlie. 'I've to go early tomorrow and get back to Leith Hall, or the mistress will be having words.'

'Aye,' said Tam, 'I'd say she's not one to cross. I wonder what this Lady Key Hole will be like, when it comes to the bit?'

Thoughtfully, and generally sober, Charlie walked up the hill to the Gallowgate, glad on the whole that they had not all resorted to Campbell's. When he reached his own inn, Mr. Cruickshank opened the door in his nightshirt and robe, though it was barely nine o'clock, and looked him up and down, grimfaced.

'I'm sorry I'm late, sir,' said Charlie at once. 'I had to go and see someone, but I'm back for the night, now.'

'Aye, that's grand,' said Cruickshank as he reluctantly let Charlie past, 'for I'm locking all the doors the now.' He suited action to word, turning an intimidatingly large key in the back of the door. The hallway was ill-lit, and not over-tidy. Charlie had to watch his step, particularly as the well-rounded Mr. Cruickshank stepped past with his candlestick. Charlie caught his foot on something soft, and bent to pick it up. It was a glove.

'Mr. Cruickshank, there's something here that maybe a man has dropped? One of your guests, I mean?' He held the glove out.

In the candlelight they could see it was black, leather and well made, but repaired a little between thumb and finger. Charlie recalled his own master's gloves sent for mending, and warmth ran through him when he remembered Phoebe taking them from him to do the work for him. But for Cruickshank, obviously, the glove brought back a different memory.

'Yon's Mr. Abernethy's glove,' he said, his face suddenly softened.

'Mr. Abernethy of Mayen?' Charlie asked at once in surprise.

'You ken the gentleman?' asked Cruickshank, glancing dubiously at Charlie.

'I've met him, and I've been to Mayen,' said Charlie. He went no further, for to talk of his master and the duel did not look as if it would go down well with Mr. Cruickshank.

'A very nice, couthy gentleman,' said Cruickshank precisely, his eyes on the glove.

'He stays here, does he no, when he's in the town?'

'Aye,' said Cruickshank, and Charlie could see real sadness in his face. 'But I doubt he'll be here for a whilie now: he has business of another kind to deal with. Aye, sad times, sad times.'

Charlie nodded solemnly, and as always looked for a way to be of service.

'I could take the glove back to Mayen, if you like,' he said. 'I bide up that way, as you know.'

Cruickshank turned his yellow eyes on Charlie again.

'You'll no be expecting me to pay you for such a thing, will you?'

'No! No, not at all.' In fact he had no idea how he might finance a journey from Leith Hall to Mayen, but there was always the chance that he could pass the glove on to someone else going that way. He was sure that a missing glove was among the least urgent of Mr. Abernethy's concerns just at the moment.

'Aye, well, then,' Cruickshank was saying, 'take it, then. And if he comes back for it,' he added in a moment's bravado, as sure as Charlie was that Mr. Abernethy would not be popping back in for the glove any time soon, 'I'll be sure to tell him who took it.'

'Aye, sir,' said Charlie, and arranging the glove carefully in his hand, he retired to his chamber.

The next day he made his way back, starting early, for Leith Hall. It was a quiet journey, giving him plenty of time to think along the way. The glove rested in his pack.

It seemed to him that more people than he liked Mr. Abernethy, and found it hard to believe that he would have quarrelled with one of his best friends, a man who was also, incidentally, kind and decent. The notion that Margaret had voiced, that one of them had accused the other of adulterating grain at the market, was incredible.

And if you took that objection to the duel, or what the duel had looked like, seriously, then you had to start thinking about what Lowrie Leith had said – what he had overheard in Campbell's, that a man wanted to kill John Leith and thought a duel would be a good way to do it. And that man, if you could believe Lowrie, was not Mr. Abernethy. And that meant, as far as Charlie could see, that unless there had been a huge mischance and while one false duel was planned another real one actually happened, Mr. Abernethy had somehow been put up to challenging the master to the fight.

That seemed to make sense, and perhaps Mr. Abernethy had needed money.

No: there he had taken a wrong step. Charlie would not believe that Mr. Abernethy would have shot John Leith for money.

But the two shots: the two shots. Mr. Abernethy might have accepted money to fight a duel with John Leith, knowing that John Leith would almost certainly aim wide, and that he himself would never be able to hit him. So Mr. Abernethy's shot went into the lamp post, and the man who had arranged it all, the man who wanted John Leith dead, he had hidden in the shadows of the Castlegate and shot past Mr. Abernethy, catching John Leith right in the head.

He saw again in his mind's eye the look on Mr. Abernethy's face as Tonley led him away, a little demon dragging him off to his own particular hell. Mr. Abernethy had not expected John Leith to fall, had not wanted, Charlie knew, John Leith to fall.

Charlie felt himself shake, and the horse picked up on his twitchiness. He stopped the chaise and tied up the reins for a minute, slipping down to stride along the side of the road and back several times. It made sense: that was the frightening thing. No: he was wrong. The frightening thing was the thought of trying to explain all this to Mrs. Leith.

'Well, Charlie, you met with Mr. Stuart?' the mistress asked, having summoned him once again to the book room. Alexander Hay was there, but his brother Rannes was not.

'I did, ma'am, and gave him a full account as he asked for it.'

'Did he send any message?'

'A letter, ma'am.' Charlie drew it out from his coat. Mr. Stuart had written it in front of him and he knew it contained only sympathetic words and assurances of business being done. Mrs. Leith opened it, read it swiftly in silence then repeated it aloud to Alexander Hay.

'He'll see to all the legal side,' said Alexander Hay, comfortably.

'Is there anything else, Charlie?'

He ran quickly in his mind through all that had happened in the last couple of days. He could not tell her about looking for Mrs. Dilley in the town house, and somehow he was reluctant to mention Lowrie Leith anyway: it would only make her cross. He would have to make sure that if she intended a stay in Aberdeen, he would get there first to evict Lowrie and tidy up. He could not tell her about the master's secret meeting at Campbell's - there was no point, anyway, until he knew more about it himself. He could not tell her about Mr. Abernethy's glove.

'Here is the money left after I paid Mr. Cruickshank, ma'am,' he said, taking out the purse she had given him. She took it, and began to count the contents, and as she did so something seemed to click in his head.

'Ma'am, I believe Mr. Abernethy was not entirely to blame for the master's death. I believe someone put him up to it. And I don't even believe that it was Mr. Abernethy's shot that killed the master.'

Mrs. Leith's fingers froze. There was a terrible silence. His eye was caught by the candlelight reflecting on a cross she wore at her breast, how it flashed as she breathed, deeply and steadily.

'Let me make it clear,' she said at last, and her voice was low and hard. 'I shall see justice done for my husband's death. I shall see Mr. Abernethy hanged, and his family ruined. If you have no interest in assisting me - in serving your late master who only ever showed you indulgence - then you had better leave our service forthwith.'

Chapter Fifteen

'You're really leaving?'

Phoebe's eyes were wide as pewter plates, standing in the doorway of Charlie's room. Charlie was remaking the pack he had just brought back from Aberdeen, systematically selecting the bits and pieces – and there were few enough of them – around the little room that were properly his, and not just Leith Hall things that he used in the course of his work. Even his aprons remained hanging on the back of the door.

'Aye, I'm off,' he said absently. The words did not even make sense to him as he said them. He half-laughed as he remembered the look on Alexander Hay's face: the big man's jaw had dropped like a nutcracker.

'But where will you go? What are you going to do?'

He laid down a pewter cup, reluctantly: it was the one he always used, but he was sure it belonged to the household. He wondered if it would be all right if he took a battered old one from the kitchen, one that no one ever touched, but decided that that was not right, either.

'I'm not sure,' he admitted, half-turning towards her but not letting himself look at her face. If he met her eye, he was sure he would be back upstairs pleading forgiveness from Mrs. Leith in an instant.

And what would be wrong with that? something in his head wanted to know.

Mrs. Leith had made her intentions clear, and in all conscience Charlie could not agree, that was what was wrong with that, he told it firmly.

'She really told you to go?' There was a hint of nervousness, too, in Phoebe's voice now. If Charlie could be told to go, might she

143

also be sent away? For a moment, Charlie thought of asking Phoebe to come with him, but that would not be right: he could not support her, and he had no idea where he was going. No: if he found a good place for himself, then – maybe, if he had the nerve – he would write to Phoebe and ask him to join her, as his wife.

Even the thought of that could not, for the moment, penetrate fully into his head. It required him to accept that he was really leaving, that he might one day be settled somewhere else.

'Does your friend Lang Tam know about this?' Phoebe asked, and Charlie looked up at her in confusion.

'How would he know?'

'I thought maybe you'd seen him in Aberdeen, and talked it over with him before you came back.'

'No, he doesn't,' said Charlie. 'I only decided just now. What difference would it make if he knew? He didn't talk me into it, if that's what you mean.'

'No! No, I just mean – I dinna like the man, but he has a lot of experience as a servant. I thought he might have tried to talk you out of it, in fact.'

'Well, he's had no chance to,' said Charlie, but he wondered what Lang Tam would say when he found out. Assuming he ever did find out: with the master dead there was no reason why Mr. Dalgarno and Mr. Keracher should have any further connexion with Leith Hall.

He began to fasten his pack, and a glove fell out. Mr. Abernethy's black leather glove, somewhat mended.

And all at once he had a plan – or at least the beginnings of a plan. He tucked the glove firmly into his pack, took another swift look about the room, and gave Phoebe a brisk nod.

'Right, that's me,' he said. 'I hope the next fellow in this place is good.'

She looked as if she would move out of his way, then stood her ground in the doorway.

'Charlie,' she said softly, then stood on tiptoe and before he could do anything she kissed him. He had barely felt the delicious warmth of her lips on his when she was away, out of his path and gone.

Nothing seemed real. He shouldered his pack, and slipped out by the kitchen door, saying farewell to no one. At the foot of the driveway he hesitated only briefly, then turned to take the road for

Strathbogie, the one that would lead him to Mayen.

He arrived at Mayen the following day around noon.

Darkness had soon overcome his determination the previous evening, and in desperation he had knocked at the door of a cottar's house and begged a space on the floor. He had shared the cottar's gruel in the morning and marched on, not entirely sure of his route but meeting enough people to direct him. He was pleased to see the solid white tower of Mayen House ahead of him at last, and much relieved when old Mr. Pringle opened the door to him, and, though a little puzzled, welcomed him in.

'Are you no Leith Hall's man?'

Charlie opened his mouth to agree, then stopped himself.

'I was,' he said. 'I've left Leith Hall.'

'Oh aye?'

'Aye.'

Mr. Pringle waited, and Charlie drew a deep breath.

'Look, you'll know, sir, no doubt, that Mrs. Leith is intending to pursue Mr. Abernethy for - for what he did. She told me to leave if I didn't want to help her, and, well, I didn't. So I left.'

'I hope you're no looking for a position here,' said Pringle at once. 'We've enough to do looking after our own. Here since King David, and this befalls us!'

'Listen,' said Charlie, 'do you really believe your master could have done such a thing? He and Leith Hall were good friends, were they no?'

Pringle's look was deeply suspicious.

'What are you trying to get me to say, laddie? Do you think I would tell you where he is?'

'No! No, I wouldn't expect that - why would I? No, I really want to know if you think he did it. Because I don't. Or I don't think it's as straightforward as - well, as Mrs. Leith thinks it is.'

'I have no time for young lads who think themselves better than the people they serve,' said Pringle, his nostrils wrinkling as if Charlie had imported some bad smell to his house.

'Oh, but sir!' Charlie could not believe that Abernethy's own man was arguing against him. 'Look, I served my master faithfully, and as I see it I'm still serving him. He would not have wanted his good friend punished for killing him in a duel, I'm sure. And he certainly would not have wanted Mr. Abernethy punished for something he didn't do.'

Pringle drew in a breath, looking suddenly weary.

'Look, laddie, all the gentlemen who were there say that the master – I mean my master – killed Leith Hall. I canna say I'm not appreciative of your attitude, but you werena there.'

'I was, sir. I was in the Castlegate.'

'You were?'

Charlie raised a hand to stop him.

'I canna deny it looked like Mr. Abernethy shot Leith Hall, but the thing is there were two shots. And you know, sir, that your master could not shoot straight. He was well kent for it.'

Mr. Pringle looked briefly as if he might object to this slight, but he was not that stupid.

'So what are you saying?'

'I'm saying Mr. Abernethy's shot went into a lamp post – it's still there – and someone else's shot went into my master's head.'

Mr. Pringle stared at him hard.

'Someone else shot Leith Hall? Not my master?'

'That's what I believe,' said Charlie firmly. He was pleased: all that he had told himself yesterday, when he had reasoned it out to himself, still seemed sound.

'You'd better come in and see Lady Mayen,' said Pringle. 'Leave your pack here in the hall.'

Charlie bent to retrieve something from the pack, ran a hand through his hair, and followed Mr. Pringle upstairs.

The parlour into which he was shown was full of children. It took a moment to work out what else might be there. But Mr. Pringle was announcing him to a small figure half-reclining in a long chair, a bairn in her arms and another sitting astride her skirts. Mrs. Abernethy was still very pretty, as Charlie had remembered, but her eyes were red and moist, and she flapped a hand helplessly at the children as if to say there was nothing she could do about them.

'Mr. ... what's your name again, lad?'

'Charlie Rob, sir, ma'am.'

'Mr. Rob has some theories he would like to share with us,' said Mr. Pringle, his voice much grander than it had been when he was only speaking with Charlie. 'He believes, ma'am, that the master was perhaps not responsible for the incident with Leith Hall.'

'I was there, ma'am,' said Charlie quickly, for Mrs. Abernethy looked as if she might burst into tears again – as if this might be her reaction to anything that happened at present. 'The thing is, if you look at what happened, Mr. Abernethy fired his pistol and my – and Mr. Leith fell to the ground.' There was a distressed squeak from Mrs. Abernethy. 'But there were two shots, and I think Mr. Abernethy's shot went into a lamp post and someone else fired the shot that killed Leith Hall. Oh, and ma'am, I happened to find this glove at Cruickshank's inn yesterday, and I said I should return it.'

Mr. Pringle shot the glove a suspicious look, but Mrs. Abernethy stretched out a hand for it and grasped it as if it might have been her husband's own hand in it. Charlie noticed that her fingers were calloused and reddish: she was not a lady who could not turn her hand to the domestic work around the place, then. It was another sign of Mayen's poor financial state.

'What were you doing poking about at Cruickshank's inn?' asked Mr. Pringle.

'I was staying there, as I had been instructed by Mrs. Leith –' He broke off as Mrs. Abernethy gave a cry, clutching at the child in her arms and making it squeal, too.

'She wants to ruin us! She wants to ruin my poor babies!'

The babies, the oldest around nine, were crawling up the curtains and over the furniture and looked quite capable of ruining things themselves. But Mrs. Abernethy was clearly beyond upset: Charlie wondered when she had last slept.

'I no longer work for Leith Hall,' he said firmly. 'But I had to go to Aberdeen to make my statement to a lawyer, and I stayed at Cruickshank's inn. I found the glove by accident.'

Mrs. Abernethy sobbed into it. Charlie, remembering how grubby Cruickshank's hall floor had been, winced, and waited while she made some attempt at recovery.

'Wait,' she said at last, in a more composed voice, as though she had been reviewing in her tears all that had been said so far. 'You said there were two shots?'

'I wasn't sure at the time,' said Charlie, 'but afterwards I found out there definitely had been. There was a ball in a lamp post by the door of Campbell's inn, as well as the one that killed my master.'

Mrs. Abernethy and Mr. Pringle exchanged looks.

'You know, ma'am, the master's aim has never been ...'

'Yes, yes, I know.' For a moment she stared over her baby's head, gazing at the wintry trees outside the parlour window. 'But two shots – are you sure Leith Hall never fired back? For there was some talk that my husband was wounded in the thigh.'

Charlie made himself concentrate on the lamp post and his memory of that horrible night.

'If Mr. Abernethy had a wound in his leg,' he said, 'there would have to have been three shots. The lamp post was behind my master, so he could not have hit it. I didn't see him raise his hand to aim while I was walking towards him. When I went to him, I believe there was a pistol by his side but Mr. Byres of Tonley lifted it, so I don't know if it had been fired or not.'

'And Mr. Leith's own pistols?'

'I was just bringing them,' said Charlie, suddenly desolate. 'I had them in my hands – he never touched them.'

Mrs. Abernethy sniffed back more tears.

'Did you tell all this to the man of law?' asked Mr. Pringle sternly.

'No,' said Charlie, 'I did not, for though I had just found out about the ball in the lamp post, I had not worked out the rest of it.' I had not spoken with Lowrie Leith, he added to himself. He kept leaving Lowrie out of his accounts, and he was not sure why. Was he afraid that association with Lowrie might make people doubt him?

'We'll have to tell our man,' Mrs. Abernethy said, her voice wobbly. 'This could make the difference – James could come home.'

'Well ... why would someone want to shoot Leith Hall?' asked Mr. Pringle, giving her an anxious look. At least someone was looking after her, Charlie thought. He took a deep breath.

'Did Mr. Abernethy mention, um, that he had been asked to do someone a favour?'

'What do you mean?' asked Mrs. Abernethy.

'I mean,' said Charlie, knowing he would have to choose his words carefully, 'that I thought maybe someone had asked Mr. Abernethy to challenge Mr. Leith to a duel – with neither of them likely to injure the other, of course – and took advantage of it.'

'Someone made my husband take the blame?'

'Well, yes.'

'That's dreadful!' Mrs. Abernethy gasped. 'How could anyone do such a thing?'

'Well, that's what I've been wondering,' said Charlie. 'He didn't say anything about anything like that?'

'That he would arrange for Leith Hall to be shot?'

'No, no!' Charlie said hurriedly. 'I don't believe Mr. Abernethy had any idea what was going to happen. But I think someone asked him to do it, giving him an innocent reason, see?'

Mrs. Abernethy and Mr. Pringle again looked at each other, but this time it seemed that they were trying to see if the other knew anything. Both their faces were blank.

'It makes some kind of sense,' admitted Mr. Pringle, a little grudging, 'but I cannot think of anything the master said that would have meant ...'

'Why was he in Aberdeen, ma'am?' Charlie asked. Mr. Pringle deferred to his mistress, who said, vaguely,

'I think he wanted to go to the meeting of the Commissioners of Supply, is that not so, Pringle?'

'He never said, ma'am. And I thought they were to meet in January – this month – not in December.'

'Silly time of the year to travel, anyway,' said Mrs. Abernethy. She shrugged, as if the ways of men were a mystery to her. 'But he went.'

'Mrs. Abernethy, ma'am,' Charlie crossed his fingers behind his back. 'Where is Mr. Abernethy?' He felt Mr. Pringle's sharp look. But Mrs. Abernethy grew tearful again.

'I wish I knew – don't we, Pringle? I thought maybe he would have sent word by now, to join him – somewhere. I look every day for a letter from him.'

'Do you think he's gone abroad?' Charlie prayed not.

'I suppose so, Mr. Rob. I believe he must have. It's the only place he would be safe, isn't it? But if we could get word to him – about what you believe really happened – then perhaps he could really come home.'

'I've told the mistress I'll go and look for him,' said Mr. Pringle.

'I need you here, Pringle,' said Mrs. Abernethy, favouring him with a watery smile. 'You keep the whole place running and allow me time – time to ...'

'Shall I go, ma'am?' said Charlie, before he could stop himself.

'To look for my husband?' Mrs. Abernethy was taken aback. 'Would you do that?'

'I would, ma'am,' said Charlie firmly.

'I have no money to give you,' Mrs. Abernethy said quickly, embarrassed.

'I know, ma'am - I mean, I should not expect any. I have a little put by and - well, we'll see, I suppose.'

He had a very little put by: the purse tucked into his shirt was hardly a burden. But ... but ... what was the point of leaving Leith Hall if he did not do something about all this? And what else was he going to be able to do, anyway, when his head was full of shots and lamp posts and secret meetings and dark streets - he would be no use to any new employer. He waited for Mrs. Abernethy's response, and was not surprised when she agreed to let him go.

'He took the road to Edinburgh, that's what I heard,' said Mr. Pringle, scooping broth into Charlie's dish. The kitchen was spacious, but there seemed to be few servants about. Whether he was trying to be helpful or not, Mr. Pringle seemed to be pleased to have someone to talk to over his simple meal. 'There was a fellow with him, a shilpit lad he took now and again to try and drum some sense into his thick head, but he left him behind. The fellow came here to tell us what had happened.'

'Is that Hugh Murray? Can I talk to him?' asked Charlie. Edinburgh seemed a daunting idea, vast and distant. If he could find Mr. Abernethy before he might have to go there, it would be as well. But Mr. Pringle shook his heavy head.

'He's away on - had some notion of looking for work up north. He was from Sutherland himself. I told him they were as clever there as anywhere else, he'd no find things any easier, but off he went.'

'Was he the one who said that Mr. Abernethy had been wounded in the thigh?'

'Aye, that's right, though he was no very explicit about it. It sounded more like a bruise than anything else, and he said that the master never mentioned it till later on in the day. There was no talk of it straight after the duel, and the master walked and rode as if there was nothing wrong with him. Well, that's what the fellow said, though whether he was trying to cast doubt on the story or to reassure us that the master was not badly hurt, I couldna say.' He paused, breaking a piece of bread with great care, ensuring the crumbs fell into his broth. 'Are you really going to go looking for the master?'

Charlie nodded, and tried a bit of a smile.

'I'll have to now: I've told Lady Mayen I'm going to.'

'Aye, it'll give poor Mrs. Abernethy some comfort, true enough.'

Charlie tried to think of anything else he needed to ask while he was still at Mayen.

'Why do you think he might have gone to Edinburgh? Did he say?'

Mr. Pringle shook his head.

'I doubt he was in too much of a rush to write messages, and yon lad couldna carry two words in his head from here to the door. I've given it a bit of thought, though, ken, and I think it's this: he came north to start with, when he fled Aberdeen, as if he thought of coming straight home. Then I reckon he bethought himself of earlier times and decided not to put his house and family to any risk, so he turned south again. He wanted then to fly abroad, but by that stage no doubt they'd have a guard on the ports at Aberdeen and Peterhead, so he decided to head further south to try to get round them.'

'It's not, maybe, that he has friends in Edinburgh who might help him?'

'There's no one I can think of, nor the mistress, neither,' said Pringle. There was just a touch of pride in his voice: he was in a position to talk such things over with the mistress. He was certainly a few steps ahead of Charlie on that one.

'He wouldn't –' an idea struck Charlie, 'he wouldn't be trying to take his case to some high court of law, would he? Isn't Edinburgh where all the big judges and lawyers are?'

'Now there's a thought,' said Mr. Pringle, brightening very slightly before he slumped again. 'Aye, but those fellows would be gey expensive, would they no? He could never afford that.'

'But what if Mr. Byres of Tonley went with him?' Charlie persisted. 'Didn't he start off with him? He's a friend of his, I think?'

'Well, as to that ... But he did start off with him, aye, but then they took him up and put in him in the Tolbooth in Aberdeen for assisting at a duel.'

'But he was released – they said he'd tried his best to stop Mr. Abernethy. Mr. Gordon of Cowbairdy and Mr. Forbes of Brux stood up for him.'

'Oh, aye?' Mr. Pringle nodded. 'Aye, fine respectable gentlemen, the pair of them.'

'Aye. So he could easily have followed Mr. Abernethy down to Edinburgh and helped him. He has money, does he not?'

'Aye, I believe so,' said Mr. Pringle thoughtfully. 'I suppose it's possible, right enough. Well, if you get down to Edinburgh and find that the master is up before the court with an expensive advocate, I'll be delighted. Can you read and write, by the way?'

'I can, yes,' said Charlie. 'I'll write and say when I find anything.'

'And what will you do if he's not there? If he's gone abroad?'

'Then, I suppose,' said Charlie, 'I shall have to follow him.'

Mr. Pringle whistled.

'Aye, it's grand to be young and free! You'll see the world, no doubt! He's maybe away to America like he was before – which would explain why no letter has come calling the mistress to follow him yet.'

'What would you do if it did? Would you go to America, too?'

'Och, no, laddie, no. I'm beyond that stage in my life,' said Mr. Pringle, between resignation and content. 'I'll bide here the rest of my days, or hereabouts. No, it's young lads like yourself that do the travelling about. What sights you'll see, eh?'

'Oh, aye, I'm sure,' said Charlie, scraping out the last of his broth. But he knew if he ever reached Edinburgh, that would be more than far enough for him.

Chapter Sixteen

Charlie had no idea how long it might take him to walk to Edinburgh. By the reckoning of the Mayen household, it was between a hundred and fifty and two hundred miles, maybe four to six days if the weather stayed mild and not too wet. The very thought made his feet ache, and worse, he knew that Mr. Abernethy would have been travelling a good deal faster on horseback, and if he had plans to go on from Edinburgh, whether by land or by sea, he might already have left by the time Charlie reached there. If that were so, Charlie could only hope that it was by land. And how far would his little purse of money go in the big capital? He had always heard tell that the Edinburgh markets were grand, with things you'd see nowhere else, and much more expensive than the country towns.

But first he had to make for Aberdeen once more. Mr. Pringle was all for him taking a boat from there, one of the cheap little boats that touched in at every port. Mr. Pringle seemed very keen on enjoying other people's adventures, but he was not going to get Charlie out on the sea as easily as all that. And there were no boats from Mayen to Aberdeen anyway. He adjusted his pack for comfort, settled himself into a steady pace, and set off, aware that while Mr. Pringle was watching him from the front door, Mrs. Abernethy and an assortment of children were observing from an upper window. He did not look back: it was hard enough to know what he had foolishly taken on, without feeling even more bound to it by their farewell kindnesses. But he had not resisted when Mr. Pringle slid a loaf of fresh bread into his pack, and a round of yellow cheese. He was not that foolish.

There was no friendly cottar's house this time, and the first night he slept in the corner of a sheep fank, cosily sheltered by a couple of old ewes. The second night, just outside Aberdeen, he was reduced to finding a dryish ditch, but the night was mild and dry, and the thought of the money he was saving went a long way to insulate him. He woke in the morning to realise that somehow he had missed the Sabbath the previous day, and not attended the kirk. He felt bad about that for several hours: it seemed to be all one with the commencement of his dissolute life, no work, no home, a strange, possibly pointless quest, and no church to go to. He would try, he thought, to go to both a morning and an afternoon service next Sabbath. He wondered where he would be next Sabbath.

He supposed he could have gone to that ancient church in Inverurie that the master had pointed out on the way through that time. His mind wandered a little, recalling the master's conversation on that occasion. It had seemed a little odd. Hadn't he been talking about Papists and Episcopalians, people whose services were banned just now? Maybe the master had known a few amongst his Jacobite friends – plenty of Episcopalians had come out for the Prince, he had heard tell, and that was why they were constrained now.

Turning his thoughts to more important matters – or at least more urgent ones - he tried as he went along to plan what he should do when he reached Aberdeen, in preparation for going on to Edinburgh: there was more to sorting this business out than simply finding Abernethy of Mayen. Or at least, there was more that he wanted to know. After all, Mr. Abernethy might or might not be prepared to tell him who it was that suggested Abernethy should call Leith Hall out for a duel, and he might or might not know why. Charlie wanted the blame taken from Mr. Abernethy for something he was sure the gentleman had not done, but he also wanted to know who had wanted his master dead, and why. And in order to find that out, he felt that it would at least be to his advantage to find out what the secret meeting had been upstairs in Campbell's that night, and where Mrs. Dilley had gone. The second might just mean, as Margaret had suggested, that Mrs. Dilley was accommodated somewhere that Mrs. Leith would never know about her, but it was up to Charlie at least to make sure that she was safe and well, as he believed his master would have wished.

So here he was, once again entering Aberdeen though for the first time on foot, and the town that had seemed so intimidating to him only a couple of months ago was now at least partly a little too familiar. He tramped through the college town with its own tolbooth and church, and unhesitatingly took the road south up over the hill to pass along the Gallowgate, nodding at Cruickshank's inn, and descend once again gently to the Broadgate and the centre of the town. He made once again for the Castlegate, for he had decided where he was going to start.

The shutters were closed in the Leith town house, but he knew well enough that that probably meant that Lowrie Leith was still abed – in fact, it could only have been around nine in the morning, so the chances of Lowrie being up and alert were really quite low. He could have hesitated to disturb him, but it was only the one piece of knowledge he wanted, and anyway, he was not of the household anymore, so it did not matter at all if Lowrie Leith complained to Mrs. Leith about his behaviour. And Charlie would have been surprised if Lowrie had tried.

He had of course handed back his household keys before he left Leith Hall. He rapped on the door of the town house, quite prepared to have to wait a while before Lowrie might rise to the surface and hear him. Instead, the door swung very slightly open.

Hairs rose on the back of Charlie's neck. That was not supposed to happen.

But then he reconsidered. Lowrie Leith was quite capable of having returned home last night – or this morning – drunk, and failing to secure his own front door. While Charlie the servant, still feeling his responsibilities, was not very pleased, Charlie the seeker after knowledge was delighted. He pushed the door a little harder, and walked into the darkened hallway.

There was a terrible screech, and something flew at him from the parlour door.

Charlie was smacked against the side wall of the hallway, so hard he saw dust break from the plaster – or was it stars? His jaw jerked sideways a second after his head, and his teeth grated across each other. He slid hard to the floor, tangled in the strap of his pack, and felt almost at once a bony knee in his back, pinning him down. There was a moment of gasping breaths, then he was released, flipped over with surprising efficiency, and pinned once again by the knee – but this time with a knife blade against his throat. The bread and cheese with which he had broken his fast threatened to rise back up, despite the knife, and he had to swallow hard, blinking his watering eyes. Then even against the light from the doorway, he knew his attacker.

'Mr. Leith!' The words came out hacked about and rasping. 'Mr. Leith! It's me! Charlie Rob!'

'Who?' Lowrie's grip was firm, though the smell of wine off him made Charlie gag again.

'Charlie Rob. I came in the other day ... what day was it? I got you wine. You told me, um, things about your nephew's death.'

The knife pressed closer. The voice was menacing.

'Why would I do that?'

'You were worried, sir – I think – and so was I – I was his manservant, remember?'

'You were Johnnie's man?'

'Aye, aye, I was.'

'Why do I no remember you?' Lowrie demanded, focussing on him a look of savage intensity. The knife had not moved.

'I dinna ken that, sir. But we've met three times. But not everyone remembers the servants, sir.'

For a moment, there was no sound. Then, slowly, the knife was drawn back, and with an uncomfortable jerk the knee slid back from his ribs. He tried to breathe normally, and after a minute succeeded. Lowrie put out a long hand and pulled Charlie to his feet, then gestured him into the parlour, kicking the front door shut as he followed him.

In the parlour he lit a candle and flung himself into his usual chair by the fire. Charlie, still a bit shaky, stood with his back against the doorpost with his fingernails digging into the wood. Then he looked properly at Lowrie's face in the candlelight, and drew in a quick, shocked breath.

'Aye,' said Lowrie, fingering his black eye then the long cut on his cheek. 'That's no done much for my natural beauty, has it?' He gave an ironic snort, and studied Charlie's face. 'Aye, I mind you now, now you're the right way up. You were here the other day, but you went off again.'

'I had to get back to Leith Hall, sir. What happened, sir?'

'I fell down the stairs,' said Lowrie shortly.

And that makes you nervous about intruders? Charlie thought, but did not feel he could say anything.

'Are you back to fetch me more wine?' asked Lowrie, a smile just edging on to his lips.

'I was here to ask you a question, sir, if you don't mind.'

'That very much depends on the question, Charlie. What kind of a question might it be?'

'The kind of a question that maybe would tell me a bit more about the night the master died.'

Lowrie for a moment did not move a muscle. Then he said, quietly,

'Oh, aye?'

'When you asked me who was there, sir, I mentioned a Mr. McFarland. And you nodded, as if you knew him.'

Lowrie's shoulders relaxed. It was not the question, Charlie suddenly thought, that Lowrie had been expecting. Should he have asked something different?

'Oh, aye, I ken yon fellow. Alan McFarland, that's what he's cried.'

'What is he?'

'What? A man and a scholar, no doubt.'

'Where might I find him?'

'You might find him in Aberdeen, I suppose, if he's up here again,' said Lowrie, teasing, 'but you'd be more likely to discover him in Stonehaven, where he bides.'

'And where's that?'

'Where's Stonehaven?'

'I've heard of it,' said Charlie, embarrassed at Lowrie's surprise, 'but I've no idea where it is.'

'South of here.'

'As far as Edinburgh?' Charlie asked, resigned.

'No! Never so far as that,' said Lowrie. 'It's maybe fifteen miles down the coast, a wee fishing town. Mr. McFarland bides there, and that's likely where you'll find him. Now, are you going to go and fetch me a flask of wine?'

Charlie allowed himself a little inward sigh, but he left his pack in the hallway where it had fallen, and went to the shop to fetch another bottle of wine on the Leith Hall account. He wondered what Mrs. Leith would say when the accounts came in. Then he picked up his pack, and left Lowrie Leith to it – and to defending himself against who knows what that might cause him to fall down the stairs again. If he were desperate, Charlie might return to beg a bed for the night.

So now he knew where to find Mr. McFarland, he thought he might stand a chance of finding out what the meeting was about. A scholar, though: likely he would use words Charlie might not understand. But the thought of talking to him was less alarming, somehow, than asking Lord Watt, or Cobairdy, or Brux, or (definitely) Byres of Tonley. Mr. McFarland had had a fatherly look about him which Charlie had warmed to.

But there were still things to do before he left Aberdeen – and then at least if he had to go to Stonehaven he was heading in the right direction for Edinburgh. He wanted to find out as much as he could about Mr. Abernethy's conversations that evening, and anything he said to John Leith, before calling him out, and Charlie thought the best place to start would be with Lang Tam and his masters Mr. Dalgarno and Mr. Keracher – the gentlemen would not wish to speak to him, no doubt, but Lang Tam might know what they had said afterwards.

He remembered quite well the directions down to the Green and found the flat easily. When Lang Tam answered the door, he looked gratifyingly surprised.

'Back so soon?' he asked, holding the door wide.

'I've left Leith Hall,' said Charlie at once.

'Well, aye, you're in Aberdeen – do you mean you've left his service? I mean, her service?'

'I have.'

'Oh my.' Lang Tam stopped where he was, a hand still on the door handle, staring at Charlie. Then he shook himself. 'You'd best come in and tell me why.'

So Charlie sat again at the kitchen table, drinking ale and explaining all that had happened in the last few days. Lang Tam's jaw dropped.

'Lowrie reckons Mayen was put up to the duel?'

'Well, Lowrie drinks. I mean, more than other gentlemen.'

'True – you think he might have imagined it?'

'He might. But the trouble is it sort of fits, if you see what I mean? We all know Mr. Abernethy canna shoot –'

'The second worst shot in the county, after my Mr. Keracher,' Lang Tam agreed automatically.

'There must have been two shots, because of the ball in the lamp post. So someone else fired the second one that killed my master.'

'Byres of Tonley?' Lang Tam suggested.

'No,' said Charlie. 'I could see him – he had a palish coat on, and pale breeches, too, remember? Grubby looking. And there was no flash from where he was standing. His hands were in his pockets'

'Well,' said Lang Tam, sinking his elbows on to the table. 'And you've agreed to go after Mayen and see what he says?'

'That's the idea,' said Charlie, trying to sound brave.

'All the way to Edinburgh?' Tam questioned. 'You?'

'If I have to.'

'My.'

'But I wondered if your masters had said anything about it, about that evening. Did they say anything later? When Mr. Abernethy fled, or when my master died?'

Lang Tam thought about it.

'I know they were surprised when Tonley was arrested,' he said, 'for they agreed that he'd come back into the inn carrying Mayen's pistol, and took the ball out of it, only that Mayen took it back and reloaded it. So they said you could hardly accuse Tonley of assisting in a duel when he tried to stop it.'

'But Mayen had a pair of pistols, didn't he? So what difference would it make to take the ball out of one of them?'

'Aye, well, as to that I have no idea.'

'No ...' Charlie folded the thought away in his head for later. 'What about the others? Have they said anything?'

'Tonley left town as soon as he was released,' said Lang Tam. 'He's no been around since. I suppose he's away back to his house.'

'What about the others who were there? Mr. Gordon of Cobairdy? Mr. Forbes of Brux?'

'I doubt either of them had a wee notion what was happening. I think I said to you Cobairdy's going round telling people he always knew Mayen was a dangerous man, so I suppose Brux is saying the same. Mr. Keracher said that when Mayen came back into the inn and told Cobairdy that Leith Hall had fallen, he told him in French, and then told Brux the same thing in English. Brux hasna much inside his head, I think.'

'Why French?' asked Charlie, confused.

'Aye, well, you ken these gentlemen,' said Tam with a shrug. 'Too much tutoring when they're young.'

'What else did Mr. Keracher say?'

'What did he say? It's hard to remember, sometimes, for Mr. Dalgarno talks over him. Oh, aye, he said that Mayen was complaining of a wound in his leg.'

'Was he?' That was interesting: he had heard at Mayen that the wound had not been mentioned until later.

'Aye, in his thigh. But he's a big man: it would take a good shot to bring him down, I should think.'

'So my master must have got a shot in, too. First, in fact,' said Charlie slowly. He was puzzled. He had seen no flash, and smelled no smoke near his master, and he was almost ready to swear that his master's arm had not been raised high enough even to hit Mr. Abernethy's thigh. Could the pistol have gone off as he fell? And perhaps caused a very slight injury, which affected Mr. Abernethy only a little, and was then forgotten about? He wished he had had the presence of mind to look at whatever it was Mr. Byres of Tonley had picked up from the master's side – and if it had been a pistol, whether or not it was still loaded. He was sure it had been a pistol. He remembered the gleam on the metalwork.

'Where does Mr. Gordon of Cobairdy live?' asked Charlie. He wished he could shorten their names to their designations, the casual way that Tam did, but he could not quite bring himself to that level of informality, not with gentlemen.

'Him? Oh, he's up by Schoolhill, I believe.'

Near Lady Glastirum, Charlie thought with a shiver.

'And Mr. Forbes of Brux?'

'He bides with Cobairdy, not having a town house of his own. They're next to the grammar school: I think Cobairdy's hoping a bit of the learning will rub off before Brux marries his daughter. Are you really going to go and see them?'

'Well, it's them or it's Lord Watt – I mean, I'd be talking to Mr. Holland there, of course.'

'That's a wee bit further out of the town, though. You'd be quicker talking to Cobairdy, right enough.'

'Well, I'd best get going,' said Charlie, reluctantly getting back on to his tired feet.

'Will we see you in Campbell's this evening?'

'Och, no,' said Charlie, 'I have to save my money, and my time. When I've seen Mr. Cobairdy I'll be off south.'

'Come and have a cup before you go,' said Tam earnestly. 'I'll buy it for you, as good luck for your journey.'

'Well ...' It was a comforting thought, but he needed to be outside the town before night time if he was to find cheap lodging. 'How early are you to be there?'

'How early do you want?'

They tossed times about for a minute before settling on something mutually suitable, and Charlie shouldered his pack once more and took directions from Tam along the course of the Denburn to Schoolhill.

Mr. Gordon of Cobairdy had nothing useful to say, and no wish to share it with someone as low as Charlie, anyway, though he came up with one or two sympathetic words on the loss of a fine master. Mr. Forbes of Brux grunted and nodded, and did nothing to dispel the impression that he had – with the greatest respect, Charlie added internally - very little between his ears. Charlie left the house again and after its cossetted warmth winced at the slap of cold air outside. What now?

Naturally Mr. Gordon had not invited him to sit. His legs were weary, and at last he decided that the best place to rest them might be the Castlegate, where he could sit unobserved amongst the throng of sellers and buyers and wait until it was time to go into Campbell's inn. Campbell's would already be open, of course, but he needed to guard his few coins carefully: he would wait until Lang Tam arrived later before he ventured inside. If he were really lucky, Mr. Holland, Lord Watt's servant, might come too, and then he could ask him his few questions. And perhaps then a penny bowl of broth would see him warmed for his walk to the southern borders of the town – whatever they might look like, for he had never been – and for finding a hole somewhere to spend the night.

He found a perch at the edge of the Plainstanes, only yards away from where the master's body had fallen, and stared at the lamp post with the shot hole in it. That, he thought, was where his trouble had started: until then he had only felt that there was something a bit funny about the duel, about Mr. Abernethy of all people challenging his master, about Byres of Tonley's odd looks. But that second ball – that had made all the difference. If it had not been for that, and perhaps for Lowrie Leith's mutterings about what he had overheard in Campbell's - and who would believe Lowrie Leith when he was in his cups? – then he would never have thought for a moment to defy Mrs. Leith and leave his home, the only home he had ever really known.

He felt the sting of a tear in his eye. The Castlegate was full of people, all going about their business, and he knew none of them. And this was in a town he had visited four times, now. What would he manage to do in Edinburgh, where he knew no one? Where the streets were even less familiar? His legs and feet ached, the bread Mr. Pringle had given him at Mayen was almost gone, and his purse was impossibly light, and the more he slept in ditches and could not wash himself or his linen, the less, he knew, people would be inclined to help him or talk to him. Why had he set out like this? He had been stupid, stupid beyond belief to leave Leith Hall: he could never go back now. Mayen would welcome him but could not afford to keep him, and there was nowhere else except an occasional welcome in Lang Tam's kitchen. What was to become of him?

His lip trembled, and he was just about to bury his head in his palms when a great, heavy hand the size of a dinner plate landed on his shoulder.

'Charlie? It is you, isn't it – Charlie Rob?'

Chapter Seventeen

'I'm sorry, Charlie, did I alarm you?'

He looked up, shaken, into the odd triangular face of Andrew Hay of Rannes, the master's enormous uncle. He tried to stagger to his feet, but Rannes' hand on his shoulder was firm.

'Sir, I beg your pardon!'

Hay laughed, and settled himself like a great spider on the ledge beside him.

'I'm glad to find you, Charlie: I've been seeking you for a few hours. Have you been in Aberdeen since you left Leith Hall? My brother sent me a note to say what had happened.'

'Oh, did he, sir?' Charlie shrank down even further, wondering what Alexander Hay might have said about him.

'Aye, he said you stood up to our niece, and resigned your position because you thought Abernethy of Mayen was not entirely to blame for Johnnie's death – your master's death. Is that right?'

'Aye, sir,' said Charlie, almost in a whisper. Could Mrs. Leith have sent Mr. Hay to stop him, in some way? But that would mean that she thought Charlie might actually be able to get in her way, and that seemed unlikely. But Rannes laughed.

'You're a braver man than any of us, lad!' he said. 'Look at the size of my brother and me, and neither of us can stand up to the lady. Well done!'

'Um, thank you, sir,' said Charlie, taken aback. He dared not look at Rannes' face, not this close to him.

'What made you do it? My brother said something about shot holes in lamp posts?'

So Charlie explained his theory once again about the two shots. It was easier to make plain here, where he could point exactly to where Mr. Abernethy had been, where the lamp post was, and where, though Hay knew that bit already, his master had fallen with, probably, a pistol by his side.

'And where was that wretched Tonley while all this was happening?'

'Well,' said Charlie, gaining a little confidence, 'you ken, sir, that he's never in one place for long. He was about there,' he pointed to the area just behind where Mr. Abernethy had been.

'Could he have fired the second shot?'

Charlie was interested to note that Mr. Hay looked about him, as if to see who might overhear, before he asked that. Charlie had never seen Mr. Byres with a manservant, that he could remember: anyone in this crowd might be his doer and Charlie would never know.

'I don't believe so, sir,' he said. 'I saw no flash, from either him or from my master, nor did I see either of them with their hand up to take aim. I still say Mr. Byres' hands were in his pockets. I did wonder, sir, as pistols are unchancy things, if my master's might have fired as he fell.'

'That would never have hit the lamp post though, would it?'

'No, sir, but it might have hit Mr. Abernethy.' And he explained about the elusive wound Mr. Abernethy was supposed to have had in his leg.

'Mr. Keracher saw it, apparently, sir,' he added.

'Who's Mr. Keracher?'

'He and Mr. Dalgarno live down in the Green. They were with Mr. Abernethy and the master and Lord Watt in America, so the master said.' Rannes nodded, and Charlie added, 'They have a servant, Lang Tam, who was with them there too and he's a friend of mine.'

'Ah, I see,' said Rannes. 'Do I gather, then, that you've been looking for more information?'

'Well ... aye, sir. I mean, what I told you about the ball, that just happened, I didn't go looking for it. But then I did ask Lang Tam if Mr. Dalgarno and Mr. Keracher had said anything more about the night the master was shot, and I've just been to Mr. Gordon of Cobairdy to ask him if he knew anything more ... He just says that Mr. Abernethy was always a dangerous man and should have been locked up long ago.'

'Och, Cobairdy's an old woman!' said Rannes. 'I'm not

surprised you got nothing from him. He makes up facts after the event, tries to look clever. And there's never been any harm in Mayen: he's a good man, and certainly not a violent one.'

'That's what I thought, sir. And he always seemed friendly to the master. I mean ... I miss the master, sir, I really do, and if I thought Mr. Abernethy was to blame for his death I'd serve the mistress with my last breath to bring him to justice. But I don't think he was, sir, I really don't.'

'No ... No, Charlie, I think you've convinced me. I was never very happy with the whole account of the duel anyway. And if you had told me there was a chance that Byres of Tonley had shot Johnnie, I'd be off after him in a moment.'

'I ken what you mean, sir, but I honestly couldn't say that he did.'

'And as you say, poor Mayen couldn't have shot the side of a house standing in front of him: it would have been the worst luck in the world if he had really shot Johnnie. But if he aimed just past Johnnie and hit the lamp post,' he went on, giving the lamp post another hard look, 'that sounds much more like Abernethy to me. And this second shot, the one that did kill Johnnie ... yes, we need to find out where that came from, don't we?'

'I'd like to, sir.'

'So what's your plan now?'

'Well, sir, I've been to Mayen and talked to Mrs. Abernethy _'

'Have you, indeed? You're a busy man, Charlie!'

Charlie's mouth twisted in a kind of a smile.

'They said they'd heard he'd gone to Edinburgh to try to take ship there, or maybe even to plead his case to some high up lawyers. So I'm going to follow him there,' he said, breathing in hard to stop his voice wobbling.

'To tell him you think he didn't kill Johnnie?'

'Well, sir ...' Again, Charlie had not mentioned Lowrie Leith. 'The thing is, seeing what Mr. Abernethy was like that night, and seeing he did challenge the master, I believe someone put him up to it. Not to shooting the master, of course.'

'No, indeed,' Rannes agreed.

'But to challenging him. For whatever reason - a wager, maybe, or a joke. And then whoever it was took advantage of it. I'll never forget, sir, the look on Mr. Abernethy's face as Mr. Byres led him away. I think he might tell me who put him up to it.'

'He'll have gone on horseback, no doubt,' said Rannes thoughtfully.

'I believe so, sir. They were fairly sure he wouldna take a boat at Aberdeen, for he would have thought there would be people waiting to stop him, and he did have a horse with him. The man that was with him left him and went back north with news of his plans – that was Hugh Murray, sir, that I mentioned.'

'Did he, indeed?'

'Mr. Pringle – that's Mr. Abernethy's majordomo at Mayen, sir – he didna think much of the man, and thought Mr. Abernethy had just sent him away as useless.'

'Oh, I see. If we can track him down he might be a useful witness, anyway. I've sent word to Mr. Stuart, the lawyer.' He drummed his long fingers on his knees. Each of his feet was nearly the length of Charlie's two feet. It was like sitting beside someone from a different world.

'I'm hoping maybe to get a word or two with Mr. Holland, Lord Watt's man, before I go,' Charlie said into the silence. Rannes was a comfortable man to talk to, for a gentleman and for all his size, perhaps because he didn't seem quite real. 'He might be in Campbell's this evening: he often is.'

'He is indeed,' agreed Rannes, eyeing the inn door opposite them. 'And then you plan to leave for Edinburgh, or have you further business in Aberdeen?'

'Nothing further in Aberdeen, sir, but I want to call at Stonehaven on my way.'

'Would you go by boat yourself?'

'By boat, sir!' Whatever Charlie's attempts to look brave about visiting Edinburgh, he could not hide his alarm at the thought of going by sea. Rannes laughed again, and patted him on the shoulder.

'Nevertheless I think you need to get there faster than on foot. There's a new coach that takes the mails down to London each day –'

'London, sir!' Charlie was nearly as frightened by the word as he was at the thought of sailing.

'Aye, even bigger than Edinburgh,' Rannes agreed with a grin.

'But the coach goes by Edinburgh. I'd like to buy you a place on it – maybe the day after tomorrow, if you have business in Stonehaven? It goes past not far from the village.'

'A place on a coach?'

'The outside, of course,' said Rannes. 'It'll get you down to Edinburgh with more chance of catching Mayen, if he plans to move on from there.'

'That's more than good of you, sir –'

'And I don't suppose you have a great deal of money of your own anyway, even though my nephew was a generous employer, no doubt. So here's a separate purse – and here's the money for the coach.'

'Sir!' Charlie felt the weight of the two bags, shakily. 'Why should you be so kind?'

'Tuck them safely away now, and remember not to be too trusting. It's barely kindness, Charlie. I want to find out, too, why my nephew was cut down like this, leaving his young sons, leaving his estate – leaving his poor wife with another child on the way. I've always liked Mayen, too: if someone has caused him to abandon all he loves and run away, then he has my sympathies, for I have done the same myself. Call it a commission from me, if you like, and from my brother. We're both still, ah, of interest to the Government. You are much more at liberty to move around than we are, to go to the Capital and ask questions, whatever is required. You can read and write, can't you?'

'Aye, sir, but not fast.'

'That's all right: I doubt you'll be needed to write fast! But if you need anything more, write to me at Rannes – and if you could write to keep me informed of your progress, then I should be grateful.'

'Of course, sir.' He contemplated the idea of himself, Charlie, casually posting a letter to Andrew Hay of Rannes, while Rannes swung himself to his feet. Charlie scrambled up but of course still had to stretch backwards to see Rannes' face. Rannes stepped back to allow himself to reach out an enormous hand to Charlie.

'Good luck, Mr. Rob. If your fortune is in accordance with your virtues, then all will be well.'

He bowed, his head almost reaching down to the height of Charlie's, and even as Charlie bowed in return Rannes had stepped away, already yards away towards the Broadgate. Charlie rubbed his eyes in disbelief: in a moment only the weight of the purses inside his shirt could convince him anything out of the common had happened. Brave to stand up to Mrs. Leith? Foolhardy, maybe. But at least he could now afford maybe two or three bowls of broth to see him on his way, and if he could go somewhere and have a wash in Stonehaven before he caught the coach – the coach! Him! – then he would feel a good deal more prepared to meet whatever might be in front of him. And goodness knew what that might be.

He waited another hour, contemplating his plans, watching the business on the Castlegate, calculating his fortune in Mr. Hay of Rannes finding him here, gazing again at that lamp post, before he caught sight of Lang Tam hunch-backed, attending Mr. Keracher to the door of Campbell's inn. As he stood, Tam, perhaps with some sense he was being watched, turned and spotted him, grinned and beckoned him to hurry over. Charlie grabbed his pack and followed into the warmth of the inn.

'Come on and sit down. I've news for you,' said Tam, his eyes glinting. 'Just let me get Mr. Keracher settled and I'll be back. Here's for the ale I promised you,' he added, tossing a coin on to their usual table. Charlie waited until the inn's servant passed and asked for two cups and a large bowl of broth, and the bowl was already steaming in front of him before Tam at last came to join him.

'Did you just ask for the one bowl?' Tam asked, swinging his long legs round the end of the bench.

'Sorry,' said Charlie, 'I thought you'd have eaten at home. I'll get you one now if you want one.'

'Aye, you'll have to treat me better than that, Charlie lad, if I'm going to come with you to Edinburgh.'

'I'll get you a bowl ...' said Charlie, looking about for the servant. 'Wait – what do you mean?'

Tam was grinning from ear to ear.

'There's not a hope of you managing on your ownsome all the way to Edinburgh and back, Charlie lad. You need someone with you who can keep an eye on you, tell you the safe places to stay, the safe food to eat, the safe women to bed –'

'Tam!' Charlie was shocked, even though he knew that was Tam's purpose – at least, he hoped that was all it was. 'How can you be coming with me? What about your place?'

Tam shrugged, still beaming.

'I tellt the masters what you were away to do. Mind, they were friends with your master and with Mayen, too. They thought you were doing a grand thing, and when I explained you'd never been further from home than the end of your ain neb, they said I could go with you to look after you, if I don't take longer than two months.'

'Two months!' Charlie had had no notion that it might take that long. So far he had not thought much further than the goal of getting to Edinburgh.

'Aye, I ken, it's no long. But I reckon we can do it: a week to get to Edinburgh and a week to get home, and then we have six weeks in the middle. Man, we could get to London in that time!'

'Och, not London again!' Charlie sighed, not even sure what to think of his expedition any more. 'Let's go no further than Edinburgh, eh? I mean, if I canna find him there, then where else would I look?' He was tired, he knew: faced with that possibility he was sure he would start trying to find out where Mr. Abernethy had gone from there. But what if he did have to go to London? It was a place he could not even imagine. It was where the King lived – the one that was not over the water.

'Aye,' Tam was agreeing, 'let's start with Edinburgh, anyway. Yon's a place we could see some sights, no doubt: I've been afore, so I can show you around.'

'It'll no take us six days to get there, though,' said Charlie, 'even though I've a stop to make on the way. Mr. Hay of Rannes has given me the fare to get the coach to Edinburgh, in case I miss Mr. Abernethy.'

Tam did not look as delighted as Charlie might have expected.

'Rannes did? Why for?'

'To help me on my way,' Charlie explained.

'Aye, but what's his interest?'

Charlie frowned.

'He believes my story – the idea I had about the two shots. He wants me to find Mr. Abernethy, too. My master was his nephew, remember.'

'Oh, aye ... He's that gey big fellow, is he no?'

'Gey big barely describes him,' Charlie agreed, smiling. Tam thought for a moment, then seemed to pull himself together.

'Just a mintie – Keracher's waving at me.' He looked over Charlie's shoulder at his master, and rose to attend him. In a few minutes he was back, his cheeriness recovered.

'My, the man's in a grand mood. I canna fathom if he's happy because Dalgarno's courting is going so well and Mr. Dalgarno's happy, or whether he's looking forward to having the flat to himself when Dalgarno goes. Anyway, he says if you're in such a hurry, I can go by the coach and all!' He rattled a small purse. 'That'll be you and me in the morn, Charlie lad!'

'That's wonderful!' cried Charlie. 'But it's the next day, though.' He thought for a minute. 'I know what: if you catch the coach on Wednesday morning, I'll join you further down the road.'

'Why, what are you up to?' asked Tam. 'You saying a sweet farewell to some young lassie along the way? One last night in her arms before she sends you off on your adventures?'

Whatever secret meeting the master and Mr. Abernethy had been at was still their secret, Charlie thought, and Mr. McFarland in Stonehaven was his only available source of information. He would keep it even from Lang Tam, for now.

'Aye,' he agreed, 'something like that, right enough.' He let himself imagine what kind of a lass he might be saying farewell to – a lass strangely similar to Phoebe – and flushed a little. No matter: Tam would be able to laugh at his expense.

The road to Stonehaven the following morning, after a night in a barn of winter straw, was a cheerful place for Charlie. He crossed the bridge over the River Dee and felt the unexpected warmth of winter sunshine on his face, the light glancing off icy puddles. The day was full of promise: fifteen miles to Stonehaven, a puzzle perhaps solved, a night in an inn much cheaper than Campbell's, and then the coach to Edinburgh in good company. He could not yet believe his good fortune at the generosity of Mr. Dalgarno and Mr. Keracher, to let Lang Tam come and help him with his journey and his search. Whatever courage he had tried to summon for his venture, it was much augmented by the thought of having the knowledgeable, humorous Tam with him – he had even been to Edinburgh before.

It may have been the benefit of his good mood, but he liked the look of Stonehaven as he arrived, a village cupped in a little bay with cliffs either side, and ruins of some kind guarding it a distance along the coast beyond it. The ruins were a little ominous, but the harbour round which the town was built was a cheery affair after Aberdeen's serried ships, and the bright sunlight glittered on the water – best admired, though, Charlie reminded himself, from a safe distance.

Once he had descended the steep brae and arrived in the village itself, he wondered who best to ask about Mr. McFarland. The man had looked gentlemanly enough – maybe not quite as grand as Lord Watt, but certainly better found than, say, Mr. Forbes of Brux. No one had said he was McFarland of anywhere in particular, so that did not help. He had a notion, though, that Lowrie Leith had mentioned a Christian name – what had it been, now? Alex? Andrew? Alan, that was it.

He stopped a woman who had the air about her of a maid in a respectable house, and asked her if she could direct him.

'Mr. Alan McFarland?' she repeated, and subjected Charlie to a particularly intense stare. He waited, wondering if there was anything he could say to make her more likely to help. 'You're no fae Stanehive, are you?'

'No,' he said, never one to avoid honesty if he could help it, 'I'm fae Kennethmont. Up by Strathbogie,' he added. The further he came from Kennethmont, he suddenly realised, the smaller it seemed: he might just have to say 'near Strathbogie', soon.

'Oh, aye?' She gave him another up-and-down look which took in everything from the mud on his coat to the state of his chin, which he had tried to shave in a burn along the way with, he was sure, only qualified success. 'Well, dinna make me regret directing you!'

'Um, I'll try not to!' said Charlie, surprised. Squirming her face into a look of distrust, she pointed out the High Street, and a cottage along it closer to the other end than to this.

'Mind,' she added, 'he has plenty friends here. If you lay one finger on him you'll have the lot of them to answer to!'

'I understand,' said Charlie, though he was very far from understanding anything except that she thought he posed a threat to the man. Why should he do that? The man had not looked particularly weak or vulnerable, and Charlie, he was sure, did not appear very frightening. He felt her gaze stay on him as he walked awkwardly along to the cottage. He did not even dare to turn in her direction as he rattled at the risp, and waited for a response.

'I'm seeking Mr. Alan McFarland,' he told the little maid who answered the door.

'Please to come in, sir,' said the maid, and gratefully he escaped the gaze of the woman in the street, and entered the cottage.

If he had thought the master's bookroom was well furnished with leathery volumes, it was only because he had not seen this place. True, the books here looked a good deal more used and tattered, but for every ten John Leith had had, there must have been a hundred here. Charlie wondered if the cottage had walls at all, or if they had simply plastered over the outer side of a rank of bookshelves to keep the weather out.

The maid had drawn him further into the cave.

'What name shall I say, sir?'

'Charlie Rob, please. And you could say that I was servant to the late Leith Hall,' he added, hoping that that might help.

As it turned out, it did.

The maid led him into one of the tiny front rooms, and curtseyed as she announced him. At a desk at the window, surrounded by open volumes and papers, sat the man Charlie had last seen on that awful night in Campbell's inn, his neat grey wig tied back with the same black silk ribbon, his glasses squeezing the bridge of his nose. He gazed over them at Charlie as the maid retreated, smiled, and said,

'So, are you Episcopalian, too?'

Chapter Eighteen

Charlie blinked.

'Episcopalian, sir? I go to the village kirk and do what the minister tells me to do!'

'Ah.' The man's smile faded a little. 'I had hoped, as you were John Leith's servant, you might ...'

Charlie felt as if someone had thrown a bucket of cold seawater over him.

'My master went to the kirk as well!'

'Aye, indeed, and very wise to do so – and no doubt it did him no harm. I gather your minister at Kennethmont is a good man. But there is a little more to the true church than that, you know.' He sighed. 'But I suspect this is not the time for a discussion on ecclesiology, is it? My very sincere condolences on the death of your master, Mr. Rob. I believe I saw you at Campbell's inn that night?'

'Aye, sir, you would have.'

'A terrible, terrible tragedy.' He laid one hand across his chest, and seemed genuinely to be on the verge of tears. Charlie warmed to him – but what had the master said about penal laws? Should he even be here talking to the gentleman? 'But at least he would have had the consolation of knowing that he had received Communion that very evening.'

He looked at Charlie very directly. Charlie met his eye,

confused, then suddenly realised what the man was saying.

'You had a meeting that evening? That was it, wasn't it? Upstairs in Campbell's?'

'That would not be permitted under the Penal Laws, Mr. Rob, would it? Or at least, not for more than four of us at once.'

'Not more than four ...' Charlie knew from the look on Mr. McFarland's face that what he meant was completely the opposite. He counted: Mr. McFarland, the master ... who else had he thought might be there? Lord Watt, Mr. Gordon of Cobairdy, Mr. Forbes of Brux ... it was Mr. Abernethy himself who had told the master about the meeting, long ago in the autumn at Mayen. He must have been there, too. Mr. Byres of Tonley? Seven, that made. More? Mr. Dalgarno? Mr. Keracher? He had to think about this carefully.

'If I said ... If I said, sir, that I thought that Mr. Abernethy was one of these four, with you and with my master ... well, that is only three of you, and you would be breaking no laws, would you, sir?'

'True, true,' agreed Mr. McFarland. He was watching Charlie carefully.

'So, um,' Charlie felt his way around the words, 'did they maybe have words when they were at – at this very small meeting?'

'It was not really the occasion for conversation,' said Mr. McFarland. 'But there was nothing I saw that made me think ... do I gather that, like me, you found Mr. Abernethy's actions in this matter, ah, difficult to believe?'

'I do, sir,' said Charlie, relieved to be open about it. 'I don't believe it was Mr. Abernethy's shot that killed Leith Hall, and I don't think he intended any such thing to happen. I think someone put him up to it.'

'Really? That seems unlikely.' Mr. McFarland frowned, as if he were reviewing his memories of that night against this new idea.

'Did you know either of them well, sir? Had they been to – to very small meetings before?'

'To one or two that I had attended. But I did not know them very well. You'll understand that, while things have become a little easier over the last few years we have for some time had to be very careful about where we went and who we met, so the meetings in Aberdeen have been, um, attended, by a variety of gentlemen in a position to administer Communion to one or two close friends.'

'Well, if you were breaking the law ...' said Charlie irresistibly.

He could not imagine breaking any law himself if he could possibly help it.

'I don't believe any law in this country allows the penalty of burning down your house,' said Mr. McFarland mildly, and allowed Charlie to see his left arm, hitherto concealed at his side. 'Without, moreover, checking to see whether or not you were still at home.'

Charlie looked: the hand was withered and mangled, almost like wax that had melted in the sun. He swallowed hard, twice.

'That's very bad, sir,' he muttered, when he was able to speak again. 'I had no idea ...'

'Aye, well,' said Mr. McFarland, 'I doubt a good deal of this happened before you were born, or were a mere bairn.' He tucked his scarred arm away again, looking a little contrite at Charlie's expression.

'Sir, why do you think it's unlikely that someone put Mr. Abernethy up to the duel?'

'It just sounds extremely unlikely, don't you think? Who on earth would do such a thing? And why? I cannot imagine anyone wanting to kill Mr. Leith.'

'But he is dead, sir,' said Charlie, 'and someone shot him.'

'But that was Mayen, surely? You cannot say that two men were out there in the Castlegate firing at Leith Hall. Such a notion is ridiculous! Mayen started the whole thing as some kind of joke, did he not? Such is Lord Watt's opinion anyway, and mine too. It was a horrible, tragic accident.'

'Mrs. Leith believes Mr. Abernethy should be held guilty of murder, sir.'

'She does?' He looked jarred. 'Does she? Goodness, no. No, that's no good at all.'

'And Mr. Abernethy has fled – towards Edinburgh, anyway.'

'Has he indeed? And what about his poor wife?'

'Mrs. Leith wants to sue for compensation.'

'Oh, dear me, dear me, no! No, that is not the thing to do. Oh, good gracious.'

An idea struck Charlie.

'Is there any way you could stop her, sir? Maybe help her to see ... to see, um –'

'The error of her ways? I don't know the lady, not at all, never met her. But, well ... I know Lord Watt has always had a high opinion of Mrs. Abernethy. Have you met her? Do you believe she is able ...?'

'She is a little short of friends, I believe, just now, sir,' said Charlie, very happy to think that Lord Watt might be able to help her. 'Until Mr. Abernethy is able to return home, anyway.'

'I shall send him a note this very day,' said Mr. McFarland. 'That would be the proper thing to do. But even if it was an accident, Mr. Rob, don't count on Mr. Abernethy being able to return home – the best we can hope for is that he is able to call his wife and children to join him somewhere overseas. He still killed Leith Hall in the course of a duel, and that is murder.'

There was nothing to be done to persuade the clergyman – Charlie found it hard to think of him as a minister but he was not quite sure what else to call him. Charlie saw no point in explaining once again about the two shots, and did not mention Lowrie Leith: he was increasingly dubious himself about Lowrie's account of hearing someone planning Leith Hall's death. Why on earth would anyone have wanted to kill the master? The more questions he asked, the more good opinions he heard of John Leith, and no one could benefit from his death when all his estate was left to his wife and his boys. But as he had said to Mr. McFarland, John Leith was indeed dead, and someone out there in the Castlegate had shot him. And if Charlie was determined that it could not have been Mr. Abernethy, then it must have been someone else, for some reason.

Nevertheless his visit produced more of benefit than the discovery of what the secret meeting had been about in Campbell's that night: Mr. McFarland directed his maid to make sure that Charlie did not depart before consuming bread, fish and broth – a very fine meal, which made up for the maid sitting and watching him throughout as though convinced he was going to steal the silver if her back was once turned. He made his thanks, and asked to be directed to a respectable but inexpensive inn, and she gave him the name and directions at once, very glad to be rid of him.

The rest of the day allowed him to find out exactly where and when the stagecoach would stop next day, and to take a stroll through small but pretty streets, well kept despite a strong smell of fish. He suspected the smell lingered even next morning when the coach drew into the yard of an inn a little uphill of the village. Lang Tam was waving from the roof, and when Charlie had paid his fare Tam put down a long arm to haul him up beside him.

'She's no here to wave you off, then?' he asked, laughing and looking around the yard for Charlie's imagined sweetheart.

'She's shy,' said Charlie with a grin. 'It's a gey long way up here, though, is it no? What happens when it goes over bumps in the road?'

Lang Tam showed him how to hold on tight and to press his back into the luggage stacked behind them.

'It's grand up here! You could be a giant, or king of the world!'

'There's certainly a fine view,' said Charlie, trying not to squeak as the coach lurched into motion once again.

'We'll fly to Edinburgh like this!' cried Tam excitedly, watching the horses press into their harness, pulling them up out of the hollow bay of Stonehaven.

'As long as we dinna fly into the ditch,' murmured Charlie, clinging to the handles. 'Or up to Heaven,' he added, even more quietly, as the coach reached the top of the hill and the coachman whipped the four horses up to speed. The wind caught his hair and his muffler, turned his fingers white, and snatched at his breath: he had never gone so fast before, and never so far from his home. Every hoofbeat took him further and further from all he knew. It was too easily done, far, far too easily. Downhill all the way, it felt like – how would he ever get back?

Yet there was nothing too fearful in the first few hours of the journey, anyway. Tam curled up his long legs and slept, but Charlie watched every passing cart or carriage, every house and cottage, every village and each bridge they crossed. At last, some time after dark, the coach's lamps showed denser houses than before and then suddenly, as far as he could make out, water, a broad expanse of water before the coach, and boats. He jabbed Tam's side in alarm.

'Tam! The sea! It's the sea?'

Tam woke with merciful swiftness, a hand on his knife, but looked around him at once.

'Och, it's the Tay,' he said. 'It's no the sea, it's only a river.'

'But we've to get on a boat! They're saying – the whole coach on to a boat! It must be the sea!'

'It's a wee river,' said Tam, his voice reassuring as he climbed down off the roof. 'If it wasna the night time you'd be able to see the other side, clear as can be. Only,' he added, 'we take a wee wiggly route across, ken, so we dinna get swept along. Ken what rivers are like,' he said reasonably.

So Charlie, trusting him, followed the coach on to a flattish boat with the rest of the passengers and allowed himself to be sailed across what seemed to him to be an uncommonly large bit of water to be called a river: he had crossed the Don and the Dee himself, the Dee only that morning, but this was a different case altogether.

It was true, however, that no enormous waves smashed them to pieces, and that it was not long before he could begin to see pinpricks of light on what was presumably the opposite bank: in fact, he could nearly have seen them from the dry land. Very shortly they were helping to haul the horses up on to the shore, and with renewed confidence Charlie followed Tam back on to the roof.

'So if that was the Tay,' he said, 'where are we now? Is it far?'

'We're about halfway,' said Tam comfortably. 'This place is Fife – that's where Mr. Keracher comes from, ken? – and at the end of this there's another wee river called the Forth, and then we're nearly there.'

'Does it have a bridge, or are we sailing across it, too?'

'Sailing like the Queen,' yawned Tam. 'The north Queensferry to the south Queensferry. So you'll be in good hands, just like on the Tay.' He curled up again, tucked into the baggage, and was at once snoring. Charlie could see almost nothing in the dark except the dusty winter sides of the road. A faint, unconvincing rain started, and he hugged his hands under his oxters and tried to doze, too.

The night was very black when they came to the north Queensferry, but all was arranged as Tam had said, and when they came to the south side of the river the coach stopped at an inn, where breakfast was hot and ready. They took it standing, bowls of porage burning their fingers, and clambered back on board again as soon as the fresh horses were ready.

'Not far now!' said Tam, looking momentarily excited, before slumping back again into sleep. Charlie could not be so relaxed: it was still dark, but as they neared the city he began to see lights in the distance. And more lights, and more lights – lights down low, at their own level, and lights high in the sky, fighting with the last of the morning stars, and everything in between. How tall were these buildings, then? Could they be taller even than the houses in the Castlegate? Surely not: how could anything so tall stand?

The wheels soon grated on cobbles and the horses slowed to a brisk walk. Tam woke again, and began to pay more attention to his surroundings.

'Aye, we're close now,' he said.

'Close? But surely this is Edinburgh!'

'Oh, aye, it's Edinburgh sure enough. But we don't stop till we get to the Grassmarket. And here, I believe, we are.'

The buildings around them were enormous but the square did not seem so open as the Castlegate: Charlie had the feeling of being driven into a box. The horses drew the coach smoothly in to the left of the square, and at last drew to a halt. Tam grinned from ear to ear and pulled his pack out from the heap of baggage behind them.

'Right, Charlie lad, here's the big city! You've arrived!'

Even though it wanted an hour or so till first light, this Grassmarket bustled. Passengers descended from the coach and joined the throng, greeting friends, arranging porters for their baggage, calling for refreshments. It was a moment before Charlie had the nerve to climb down himself, and even then he kept his arms around his pack and his pockets, and his eyes firmly on Lang Tam, convinced he was going to lose something either by accident or by someone's malevolent design. Not that it was entirely dark even now, for every building seemed to fling its light out into the square and there were more street lights than he had ever seen in one place before, down here at the level of the coach and again stepping higher and higher into the air. What on earth was so far above them and yet still lit up? He longed for daylight and dreaded it – what would it reveal?

'Time for breakfast,' said Tam calmly, looking about him but only as if to make sure all was as he had left it. 'I seem to remember they do a good plate of food just over there.'

'As long as it's not too expensive,' said Charlie anxiously, following behind him as close as he could. Tam laughed.

'It's no your money, Charlie! And even Mr. Hay of Rannes would not want to see you starve!'

That at least was probably true, Charlie thought, though he was sure Mr. Hay would like him to be careful with his expenditure. But the plate of eggs and ham that a plump maid laid before him a few minutes later made him forget, for the moment, about care with money.

'The porage at the Queensferry was only a stopgap,' Lang Tam said, when he had dealt with most of his own plateful. 'This is a proper breakfast, designed precisely for weary travellers with a day of business ahead of them. Do you no feel the better for that, Charlie lad?'

Charlie nodded enthusiastically.

'That was awful fine,' he agreed. 'I could eat that every morning and not be sorry.'

Tam laughed, pleased.

'Oh, there's many a fine thing about Edinburgh,' he said. 'This is just the start. Now, where do you want to go first?'

'Oh,' said Charlie, 'I'm not sure. I - well, I suppose I knew the place was big, but heavens! Where does anybody find anybody?'

'There's the harbour,' said Tam, 'down at Leith - it's like a separate wee town, but it's no far. We could try there, in case he's waiting on a ship.'

Charlie held in a shiver.

'There's lawcourts, isn't there?' he asked instead. 'I wonder if we should try there? There was some talk at Mayen that he might be trying to - I dinna ken the word, but try to get some help from the big lawyers, the advocates and all. To start a court case of his own, or to get round Mrs. Leith's.'

'Oh, aye?' Tam regarded him with interest, and licked the remains of the egg yolk from his lips. 'Well, I ken where the lawcourts are. The lawyers near run this town, and they all stick together in the one place so they can work out how much to charge ordinary folks. I can take you there, easy.'

'Then I think that's where we should start,' said Charlie firmly. 'After all, if he's trying to defend himself then the ball in the lamp post can only help him, do you think?'

'I do indeed, Charlie lad,' said Tam. 'So finish that ale, and let's get up the hill.'

The hill explained a lot. It was sharp, steep, and wedged tightly with buildings, and as the sky cleared and the city was slowly revealed Charlie realised that on the summit of the hill was a massive building, or collection of buildings, that could only be the Castle. He had seen plenty of castles in his time - Aberdeenshire was rife with them, of all shapes and sizes and ages – but this was huge.

'Close your mouth, there, Charlie lad, you're letting the draught in,' said Tam with friendly humour. They had taken a side street to arrive on a long, straightish cobbled hill, longer than any bit of a road in Aberdeen, lined with shops and houses, with steps up outside to doors halfway up the walls, and overhanging upper floors, and signs dangling to show what trades could be found within. On the front of just one building, top to bottom, Charlie saw signs showing a violin, a wig, something apparently to indicate a mantua but in effect a bit like a sleeping bat, a basket, two sheep (wool? mutton?) and a large serrated knife, painted black and as menacing as one might ever see. He noticed, while just managing not to step into it, a channel of all kinds of rubbish, solid and liquid, running down each side of the road producing, at least, probably less of a smell than it might on a hot summer's day. The place was mobbed with even more people than the Grassmarket had been.

'Is there some kind of a fair on?' he asked, for the people were of every quality, in everything from silks to sacking.

'A fair? Not a bit of it. It's just a normal day on the High Street. This is part of what they call the Royal Mile, that goes from the Castle all the way down to Holyroodhouse where the King would live – where the Prince would have lived,' he murmured in a softer voice, winking at Charlie. Charlie ignored the reference, though, and having stared up the hill, trying to see the Castle from this angle, he turned and gazed down the road. Not far off was a great tower with arches on its roof, with the look of a church about it, but the biggest church he had ever seen. Honestly, he thought, if you looked about you here you'd think the place had been built for a race as gigantic as the Hay brothers, the master's uncles. Everything was just about on their scale, and not meant for ordinary humans at all.

'So where are the lawcourts, then?' he asked, half expecting to be pointed towards some mighty chamber he had not yet noticed. But Tam took his arm, and led him down the hill towards the great church. Just before they reached its doors, in what must have been an elegant square if you could see it for all the people, Tam pulled him in to the right, to a building on the edge of the square.

'Here's where all that noblesse de la robe bide,' he said. 'We go in here – but then, I'm afraid, we'll just have to wait our turn.'

They found themselves in a kind of entrance hall, and despite the early hour there were already more than twenty people, standing and sitting, evidently waiting their turn.

'But we only want to ask a question,' Charlie objected. There was something about the others that seemed to say they were ready to wait for days if necessary – and perhaps had already done so.

'Aye, no doubt some of this lot are the same. But if you want to find out if Mr. Abernethy has been in this way, we'll just have to be patient.' Tam wedged his pack against the wall and slid down to sit on it, instantly looking settled and comfortable like a cat on a cushion. 'We're lucky: there are two of us, so one can go for food when we're hungry and all that. Sit yourself down, Charlie lad: you may as well make yourself at home.'

Chapter Nineteen

'I'm looking for Mr. James Abernethy of Mayen,' said Charlie when they finally reached the front of the long queue. They had eaten three pies each, and Lang Tam had even managed to bring cups of ale into the anteroom to the envy of some of the others queuing. After that, Charlie saw less of Lang Tam as he ran to fetch food and drink for the rest of the petitioners, making, as Charlie was shocked to discover later, a very reasonable profit.

The clerk at the doorway that led further into the building maintained a face as expressionless as a clock's, and as round and white. He had a long ledger in front of him and some kind of day book, written in a looped, regular hand that Charlie could almost read even upside down. The clerk caught him looking, and draped a wide sleeve over the pages.

'He has no meeting with any of our gentlemen,' he declared. Charlie's mouth turned down, but then the clerk added, 'But his name is somehow familiar to me. Now, why might that be?'

His gaze rolled round and up to the ceiling, and he pursed his pale lips. Lang Tam tapped his foot impatiently, but Charlie said nothing, waiting while the clerk reviewed some extensive business in his mind.

'Mr. James Abernethy of Mayen,' announced the clerk at last, as though he were reading it from a schedule, 'is to be put to the horn the day after tomorrow. Friday, that would be, the tenth day of the month.'

Pleased with himself, he nodded. But Charlie squeaked in alarm.

'Put to the horn?' In his panic he began to gabble. Hadn't Mr. Alexander Hay mentioned a horn as a joke? 'Sir, what terrible punishment is that? I thought – I mean, I was sure that there was nothing like that in this country any more! To be hanged for murder, yes, of course, though if he did not intend murder then it seems not right – but what is this horn?'

'Laddie,' said the clerk, with a calculating glance at the queue behind Charlie and Tam, 'have you never heard of a horning? When they blow the horn four times?'

'He's rarely been outside his ain village,' Tam put in, excusing him. 'He'd no seen the sea till a month ago, nor Edinburgh till this morning.'

'Truly?' The clerk gazed wide-faced at Tam for a moment, and again appeared to be reading something inside his head. He turned back to Charlie. 'A horning is when, most usually for debt but sometimes for more extreme crimes, a man is barred the country. This is signified by the blowing of a horn four times at the Cross of Edinburgh, as instigated by the issuing of letters of horning, where his name is made public. I note,' he added, running his finger down a passage in the daybook, 'that Mr. Abernethy of Mayen is to have his name called out and the horn blown not only at the Cross, but also at the port of Leith and the port of – dear me – Aberdeen, from which it is believed he may have fled. Dear me,' he repeated.

'A matter of a death in a duel,' Lang Tam explained briefly, 'and failure to pay compensation to the man's family.'

'I see,' said the clerk. 'Well, if you require further information, my lad, then go to the Cross or to the port of Leith the day after tomorrow, and you'll see everything happen just as I said. Now, unless there is anything further?'

'No, that's gey kind of you,' said Lang Tam, taking Charlie firmly by the arm. 'Good day to you, sir.'

No sooner had they shifted than the next petitioner was at the clerk's desk. Charlie wondered at the man's courtesy in the face of such a crowd, some of them far from calm or gentle with him. He allowed Tam to guide him back out into the square outside, where the dusk was already creeping back over the city, and a dazzling array of little booths was now lit up around the great church across the way. He gasped at the prettiness of the sight, and even Tam stopped and let a look of pleasure cross his cynical face.

'Aye, the luckenbooths,' he said. 'You should come and have a wander, but hang on to your pack and your pockets! A sight to be seen.'

The little luckenbooths, many of them selling delicate silver ornaments and jewellery ornamented with pearls and topaz, were charming. Charlie's thoughts flew at once to Phoebe – how she would love this! – and he wondered if there were some small thing he might be able to buy her. He paused, fingering a little double heart brooch, simple but sweet.

'What's the name of the lovely lady?' asked the stallholder cannily.

'Phoebe,' he replied, without thinking.

'The lassie at Leith Hall?' asked Lang Tam, just as Charlie was wishing he had thought to keep his voice down. 'Her as well? Charlie, there's more to you than I thought!'

'As well as what?' asked Charlie.

'Your other sweetheart in Stonehaven! Dinna tell me you've forgotten her already!' Lang Tam laughed heartily. 'You'll have to buy them one each!'

'I'll not buy any now,' said Charlie, resolute. 'I have no idea how much money I might need while we're here. And not all of it's my own, remember.'

'Aye, I remember,' said Tam, a little sour. 'Still, walk on and we'll see what we can see.'

'Hi, excuse me,' said someone, and it took a moment before Charlie realised the man was addressing him. He wore a lawyer-like wig, and had a youthful look that Charlie thought might not indicate his real age. 'Sorry, I've been trying to find you in this mob! Weren't you the fellow looking for Abernethy of Mayen?'

'I was,' said Charlie, as he felt Tam draw protectively to his side. 'Do you know anything of him?'

'Well, I'm not sure, but if you've nothing else to go on it might be worth investigating,' said the man. He had a very pleasant voice, a trustworthy kind of tone to it. 'It's just when the horning was first announced I was there, and I heard someone in the crowd say "Well, that'll be no use – the man was away to Amsterdam yesterday morning." But it could be a mistake.'

He shrugged apologetically.

'Amsterdam?' Charlie repeated in alarm. 'But that's abroad, is it no?'

'Aye,' said Tam, a hand on Charlie's shoulder.

'Take it or leave it,' said the man, glancing warily at Tam. 'You just sounded as if you needed help.' He edged away through the crowd, unwilling, Charlie thought, to turn his back on them.

'What do you think?' he asked Tam as soon as the man had gone.

'It's a bit of a coincidence,' said Tam, scowling.

'Aye, I suppose,' Charlie admitted, though he had thought the man was speaking the truth.

'There's always ears listening round these parts,' said Tam, clearly made grumpy by the encounter. 'I'd pay no heed if I was you.'

'All right, then. What shall we do now?'

'Och, just walk on and I'll have a think.'

Charlie did walk on, eyes wide at all there was on display. Tam lingered over a small purchase but Charlie kept his word and his money, and they emerged from the other end of the stalls not much poorer than when they went in.

'What did you buy?' Charlie asked. Lang Tam briefly showed a curl of dark red ribbon, smooth and shiny.

'That'll be a grand Hogmanay gift for my sister,' he murmured, folding it away, 'and no a bad price, either. You just need to know where to look. Right, where now? I doubt Mayen will be lingering in the town to hear his own horning.'

'Would it be all right – I'd like to see inside the great kirk,' said Charlie shyly. 'I missed the service on the Sabbath, and I feel bad. But to go into a place like that, even if there's no service – well, that must mean something!'

'Into the High Kirk?' Tam grinned. 'Well, why not?'

He led Charlie back round to the main door again. Charlie removed his hat and smoothed down his black hair, but his mind jumped off to his meeting with Mr. McFarland in Stonehaven. Charlie had attended his master to the church in Kennethmont more times than he could count. Was it really true that he was an Episcopalian? Brave enough for his faith to risk arrest if they were caught? Charlie went to church every Sabbath - well, apart from the last one - but he was not sure how brave he might be about it if the Government said he had to stop. But here, at the High Kirk of Edinburgh, he could be sure he was safe in the House of God.

But the interior of the great, grey building was not quite as Charlie had expected. True, the high arched ceiling took his breath away, and the broad, blackened pillars were monuments in themselves. But the church seemed to serve as a general meeting place: men milled about, chatting and discussing business, and Charlie thought about what the minister at Kennethmont had had to say on the subject of the moneylenders in the temple, and just what Jesus had done to them. Propped against a wall nearby were two particularly unpleasant-looking characters, one in a dirty yellowish buff coat and the other missing an eye. They were probably entirely innocent, Charlie told himself, but he could not help just checking that no one was at his pockets or the purse of money in his shirt.

Yet he could not help wandering further into the building, squinting into side chapels and up at high windows, until he noticed the pair again. He was about to turn to Lang Tam to ask what he thought of them when Tam muttered,

'Well, there's a thing! I wonder what that fellow is doing here?'

He drew Charlie in behind a pillar, and pointed discreetly towards a long bench with two men seated on it, their backs to Charlie and Tam. Charlie wondered how Tam could have recognised either of them, then saw that one, at first with his arms flung out across the back of the bench, was already gathering them in again and shifting to a hunched position, hardly in that when he was up and walking, poking at odd stones in the wall. No one Charlie knew fidgeted about as much as that, but for one man - Mr. Byres of Tonley.

As if Charlie had spoken his name aloud, Tonley swivelled on his heel and stared straight at them. And as he saw who they were - though Charlie had no notion that Mr. Byres would actually recognise him - a sly grin spread across his mobile face.

'Come on,' said Tam after a second, 'I think we've had enough of church life for the day. Let's go down to Leith and see if we can find anybody there who has any idea where your Mr. Abernethy went, eh?'

'He's no a very nice man, is he?' Charlie asked quietly when they were safely outside again.

'No a very nice man?' Tam laughed, a soft, secret kind of a laugh. 'Charlie lad, I think that's the worst thing I've ever heard you say about anybody! But if you were going to choose someone to say it about, then aye, Tonley's your man. Your no very nice man.'

Tam and Charlie pushed their way through crowds that not even evening seemed to diminish, down the ramp of the Royal Mile towards Holyroodhouse, though at one point Tam paused.

'Yon's the Tron where they weigh the goods for market,' he said, jerking his head to the right. But he was looking to the left, where at the foot of an even steeper slope the valley was full of wood and stone. 'Aye, I heard tell they were to build a great bridge down there. It would have made our path quicker, no doubt, but you can see they've hardly started. We'll go on this way.'

The streets were complicated and dark, now, and Charlie concentrated on following in Tam's footsteps, down and down. Leith, he thought to himself, Tam had said Leith. Funny to think of going from Leith Hall to Leith, to look for the man who had killed Leith of Leith Hall. Except that he had not, Charlie was convinced.

'Right,' said Tam at last, waking Charlie who had almost been asleep on his feet. 'This is Leith.'

Charlie could smell fish and the sea, indeed, and in the dusk could see – oh, the same kind of prickle of masts and glint of threatening water he could see from the top floor of the town house in the Castlegate.

'Do you really think Mr. Abernethy would have gone abroad?' he asked, clearing his throat to try to make himself sound less nervous.

'I think you have to face it, Charlie lad, that he might well have. He's been abroad before, after all. And you might have to go abroad yourself, if you really want to find him.'

'No!' The word burst out before he could help it. But Tam did not laugh: he patted Charlie on the shoulder sympathetically, and turned towards the buildings along the quayside.

'Well, no sense in doing that until we have a bit more information, eh? And we might as well look for a bed for ourselves at the same time,' he added, wriggling his shoulders under his pack, and

Charlie followed him gratefully towards the first of the lodging houses and inns that seemed to constitute this part of the town. 'We'll start with the best ones and work our way down.'

They had no luck in the grandest-looking inn, nor in two adjacent lodging houses run by a couple of very respectable ladies with firm ideas about standards. Tam clearly did not meet them, though they were willing to talk to Charlie briefly. They had never heard of a Mr. Abernethy of Mayen, and when (at Tam's hint) Charlie gave them a description of the big man in case he had stayed under another name, they still shook their heads. The middling grade of lodging house failed to yield information, too, and it was growing darker. Charlie swung his pack off his shoulder and clung to it, peering into the shadowy corners of the narrow streets and lanes.

'Should we stop now and find somewhere to stay?' he whispered. Tam looked about him, and Charlie expected him to encourage Charlie to go on, but he said,

'Aye, maybe so. Do you think – I mean, I just wondered if you had maybe heard someone behind us a minute ago?'

Oh, that was bad. Charlie had heard something, but as Tam had not hesitated he had told himself not to be silly. He looked about wildly.

'I'm sure there's nothing –' he said, and that was when they were attacked.

Two heavy figures, both the height of Lang Tam. One each.

'Run!' cried Tam. Charlie dropped his pack and fled.

For a moment he was sure Tam was following him. Then he thought it was only one of the men. Then again there were more than two sets of running feet. Who was where? Had the other man dealt with Tam and now Charlie had both of them after him? No: that was ridiculous. It was much more likely that Tam, canny man that he was, had dealt with the other man and was now running to catch up with Charlie.

He whirled into a more brightly lit street and risked a look backwards. Lamplight fell on a dirty yellowish buff coat. Charlie stumbled, fell, hit something soft and rolled away in a flurry of angry barking. Somehow he was on his feet again and running while his pursuer tried to get past the dog.

Yellowish buff coat. The men in the High Kirk?

He ran hard, then realised he should stop: someone looked out of a doorway to see what was going on. He slowed to a walk, no idea where he was. But downhill would lead him back to the quay, then he could find his bearings – and maybe his pack.

Yellowish buff coat, his thoughts continued. Why would they have followed them down here? He wondered how many men in Edinburgh – and Leith – wore yellowish buff coats. It might be the fashion.

Walking on, feeling his legs begin to shake with relief, he listened hard for footsteps. He wondered if it would be better to walk in the middle of the street where no one could pounce on him so easily, or whether he should sneak along the sides and be less visible. Tam would know. Where was he? He could hardly be far away.

And then as if he had tripped from one world into another, they were after him again.

Both of them this time, the buff coat and the other, and no sign of Tam. Charlie was running before he even knew it, pounding down the unknown street, still determined to head downhill. Even if he could not find Tam, the respectable women lodging keepers were there. They would look after him.

But even as the quay opened out before him, buff coat seemed to know his plans. He took on a turn of speed and somehow got between Charlie and the decent houses, cutting him off. Where should he go? To the left was unknown territory - and for all he knew these fellows might come from there and know it well. They might even be trying to push him that way. Ahead was the quay. The sea, yes, and ships, and all that he preferred not to think about, but from what he had seen earlier there was a maze of boxes and crates and piles of sacks between here and the water. Surely, if he were quick and clever, he could lose them in amongst all that?

Quick and clever – aye, that might be the problem.

He darted towards his right, as if he might be trying to get round Buff Coat. He felt something catch his own coat from the side, something sharp, but he tore free and made as if he were now going to try the left. The other fellow – was he the one with only one eye? – he slipped and stepped back, maybe allowing him to get loose. But Charlie turned again, and plunged towards those heaps of goods on the quay.

It was a nightmare.

190

How had he thought he might be quick and clever enough to get round one man, let alone two?

He dipped and dived between stacks of crates, mounds of barrels, and always one of them would be at the other end of his path, waiting for him. He was tiring, he knew: he could hardly keep his breathing quiet and his legs were as much use as the inside of a peeled cucumber. He was starting to lose track of where they were – where he was. He could not think any more.

Then he saw his path clear. From his hiding place, he could cross a very short open space, and climb on to a ship.

Even then he hesitated. The ship was on the water – that was not good. But he could see how tightly it was tied to the shore. It was not going to be overthrown by some passing wave, not there. Surely it would be safe, at least for a few minutes?

At any rate, it had to be safer than staying here.

He slipped towards it, getting as close as he could while still in shadow. Where were the men? He had no idea. He turned for a final check.

And there was Buff Coat, coming round a stack of barrels. He gave a shout, and Charlie ran.

He sprang up the dicey-looking board that led to the gate in the ship's wooden side. The board sagged beneath his feet and he could feel blood pounding in his ears as he focussed on not slipping over the side, into the black water. All at once he was on the wooden floor of the boat, head snapping from side to side as he looked for some place of refuge. Where could he go? Men were milling about, most with some busy purpose, and he was not sure he could blend in with them. Had his pursuers seen him cross to the ship? He heard shouting coming from the gate, and seeing a dark corner by a kind of wooden building he fled to it, curling himself down into the darkness, pulling his coat about him to hide his shirt and his face, neither of which, he knew, was now very clean or white anyway. He sucked in his breath, trying to control it. The shouting went on, just audible over the beat of his heart.

'Aye, a lad about so high, with black hair and –'

It was his pursuers. But they were not going to find him easily. Whoever was guarding the gate – he wondered how he himself had slipped past him – was not co-operating, though it took Charlie a minute or two to work out what he was saying.

'I have seen no one come aboard in the last five minutes,' he said firmly, with a great emphasis, it seemed, on all the noisiest bits of the words. Charlie wondered if he needed a good spit.

'There's nowhere else he could have gone,' came the voice from the shore again. 'He must be here. We'll take a look,' he said, with assurance. Charlie heard a heavy step on wood, and braced himself for discovery.

'You will not take a look,' came the voice of the guard again. 'We have no time for you to take looks.'

'A quick one – it won't take long.'

'It will take no time at all. It will not happen,' replied the guard, as if he had nothing better to do than to stand there all evening and state the obvious to the man on the shore. There was another thump, this time of wood on wood. Men cried out, odd, incomprehensible noises above and around him, but nothing sounded as if anything untoward had happened. There was an oath from the shore, but it was the oath of the thwarted, not of one in pain. Could they really have given up so easily?

There were still voices around him, voices he felt he should have been able to understand if he concentrated hard enough. They sounded almost like Scots, but somehow not quite. And there was no more sound from the shore. But still, he did not move, pressed into his corner with his coat over his face and his knees tucked up hard against his chest, breathing as silently as he could manage, wondering when he might be able again to sneak back on to the shore and see if the men had gone. Or when Lang Tam might come and fetch him away to safety – he couldn't have been far behind, surely?

Now there was splashing, and creaking, and he wondered if they were loading more provisions. Would he have the nerve, he wondered, to ask for a passage? How much would one cost? If he wrote to Andrew Hay of Rannes, would he be kind enough to send more money? He was indeed very kind, but he had probably been kind enough already without doing more for Charlie. He might have to find work in Edinburgh and save up. If he ever managed to leave this boat.

'Verdomme!'

The exclamation came from just above him, and he jumped, just as a broad fist pulled his coat from his face. Large, dark eyes stared into his from a reddened complexion under hair that looked as if it had never been brushed since it had grown there. Charlie could not move, and in any case, pinned into his little corner and with this monster before him, he had nowhere to move to.

'Hm,' said the man, as he raised his lantern, and his voice seemed to pound in Charlie's ears. 'What do we have here?'

'I'm sorry,' said Charlie. 'I'll go. I never meant to get on to your boat, never – well, not before I'd saved up – but I sort of accidentally ran on up that bittie wood, and I'll go as soon as ever –'

'Where are you going to go?' asked the enormous man, apparently politely. Charlie squirmed round until he could face him properly.

'I dinna ken,' he said, with sudden honesty. 'I was running away.'

'What are you, a dishonest servant?' asked the man with interest.

'No, sir! No – well, I am a servant. Or I was one, until – until my master died.'

'I see,' said the man, though Charlie was not sure how he could. 'Well, you're not going back just now.'

'Are they still on the shore?' Charlie dropped his voice to a whisper, not sure whether he could trust this apparent ally. But the man shrugged his bulky shoulders.

'As to that, I have no idea,' he said. 'But you see, we're away out of the harbour now. See?' He reached down a hand and helped Charlie up: his legs were stiff from sitting so long without moving. Yet what he saw across the ship's wooden floor made him stagger.

'Where's the shore gone? All the buildings and all?'

The man laughed.

'How long do you think you've been poked into your little corner, my lad? We're away down the Forth to the sea: the shore and the buildings and all is far behind!'

Chapter Twenty

He was on the water! Really, on the water, in an actual boat. His legs shook uncontrollably and he stared about him - he could only see the water to his left and his right, and he peered frantically into the dusk, waiting for the curling, disastrous wave that would destroy them. But he could see nothing. Even the wooden floor beneath his feet, wet though it was, seemed no more unsteady than it had been when they were at the dock, considerably better than sitting in the back of a farm wagon on a rough road. He was suspicious. Ahead of him was a low wooden building, and behind him a tall one: perhaps the waves were coming from one of those directions. In any case, he drew a deep breath and tried to calm his heart. He was going to die, and he would never see land, or Leith Hall, or - or Phoebe, ever again.

'The thing is, son,' said the huge man, not without kindness, 'I'll need the cost of the passage from you.'

'What?' He blinked at the man, not initially making sense of the words even though it was a problem he had been considering not long before.

'You need to pay for the passage?'

'How - how much?'

Swallowing hard, he heard the man mention a sum he knew was far beyond what was currently in his heavily protected purse.

'I'm guessing, from the colour of your face,' said the man with interest, 'that either the sea's getting to you - and us not out of the Forth - or you havena the money.'

'I havena the money,' said Charlie, already shaking at what this might imply. The very best thing would be to be taken back straightaway to Leith: he had the strong impression that this was not going to happen. 'I - I could work?'

The man laughed.

'I've no need of a servant, lad, and I doubt from the look of you you've much experience on a ship.'

'I've never been on one till this minute,' Charlie admitted miserably.

'Then we'd better come up with a better idea than that, hadn't we?' said the man. Charlie looked blankly at him, and just as he tried to imagine what on earth the man was suggesting, another voice joined the conversation.

'I'll pay for the lad, Dirkzoon. My boy's staying behind in Leith - met a girl, going to keep an eye on the business for me while he courts her - so I could do with someone helpful. You're helpful, aren't you?'

Charlie gaped round at this new person. In his voice he sounded a bit like the huge man - Dirkzoon, maybe? - but he looked different: yellow curls emerged from beneath his firmly-planted hat, and bright blue eyes gleamed. His jaw was heavy but he was friendly looking. Tall, too: where were these people from?

'I - I'm helpful, yes, sir,' he said, trying to look it. 'I've been in my master's house since I was a boy until just lately, and I was not sent away - I left.'

'Most interesting,' said the new man, handing over coins to Dirkzoon. It seemed that Dirkzoon was in charge. 'There you are - his passage. My name is Josse Gheertzoon, lad - you're Scots, I take it?'

'Aye, sir. Charlie Rob's my name, late servant to - to a gentleman from Aberdeenshire.'

'Yes, fine, and you left his service. I shall ask you about that, no doubt, when we are settled. I am an Amsterdammer, returning home - a merchant, of course.'

'Of course ... does that mean that's where this boat is going?' asked Charlie.

'To Amsterdam? Yes!' Josse Gheertzoon and Master Dirkzoon looked at one another and laughed, the laugh of satisfied men embarked on something pleasing. 'We are going home!'

'Though it's a ship,' added Master Dirkzoon, more solemnly. 'The Janetta.'

'A ship, of course,' said Charlie, wondering what the difference was, but mostly glad he had not had to pay his passage.

Why pay to die in a shipwreck? And until then, he liked the look of Josse Gheertzoon with his yellow hair and bright eyes. And he was heading where he had wanted – well, knew he would have – to go: he had left his native soil, and was bound for Amsterdam.

'So you left your master?' asked Josse Gheertzoon, sharing his supper with Charlie an hour or so later. The great waves had not yet hit them, and Charlie reckoned there was no sense in dying hungry if he did not have to.

'My master died, sir,' he explained.

'No family? A household to work in?'

Charlie wriggled a little.

'The master introduced me to a bit of the world, sir – well, Aberdeen – and so I thought I might venture further. Edinburgh was what I had in mind, but maybe not so far as Amsterdam.'

Josse smiled, an awkward, bony affair.

'Those men were chasing you, were they not?'

A pause.

'They might have been, sir.'

Josse sat back on the bench he had secured, leaving a well-wiped plate and barely a crumb of bread from what they had shared. Charlie wondered if he had eaten too much from the gentleman's supplies.

'I don't really need a servant,' he confided. 'I have a few at home – a couple of pretty girls, you know?' he nudged Charlie's arm comfortably, 'and a man for the heavy work, and a cook. That is all any household needs.' Charlie was surprised, thinking back to Leith Hall. How many people worked there, inside and out? 'But I saw what happened, what those men were yelling, and I thought, well, here is a man who may need some help, and I have been lucky in my trading this month, and maybe the good Lord does not mean me to save all of it at once for my Jakob and my girls, for they say sometimes that if you are generous to some, others may be generous to you.'

'I'm very grateful, sir. I don't know what Master Dirkzoon would have done if you hadn't come to my aid.'

'Oh!' Josse slapped the table and laughed. 'He would have waited at Amsterdam for your friends to have paid it for you! But have you any friends in Amsterdam? No, I thought not.' He had sobered suddenly. 'Did you mean to travel to Amsterdam, Master Rob? Maybe not today, but some day soon, for a purpose of your own?'

'Why do you ask, sir?' Charlie was starting to learn not to answer questions too readily. Josse Gheertzoon nodded, acknowledging his caution.

'When we told you where the ship was sailing, you looked – well, as if you were content. As if you recognised a kind of destiny in the matter.'

Charlie felt his eyebrows rise.

'Well ... I believe I may have an acquaintance there. Not one I could call friend,' he said quickly, distancing himself from any close association – and it was true, for Abernethy of Mayen was a gentleman. 'But one I might benefit from conversation with, if I had the opportunity. Ach,' he breathed out suddenly, frustrated, 'I dinna even ken if the man is in Amsterdam. I just heard a rumour he might be, and here I am – well, I'm here by accident, but here I might have been all the same even without – without the work of others.'

'What's the name of this man?' asked Master Gheertzoon.

'Mayen. James Abernethy of Mayen.' If he was to drown at sea, he had nothing to lose by telling. And if he were lucky enough to survive the shipwreck, then who knew? Master Gheertzoon might just be able to help him.

'A Scot, then?' Josse Gheertzoon asked.

'Aye.'

Gheertzoon assumed a more cautious look.

'A man of ... sympathies with the Prince in Rome?' he asked, more quietly. Charlie shrugged.

'That was a long time ago,' he said. 'Before my time. He's no been exiled on that account, if that's what you mean, sir. He's ... abroad on business, but his wife and his weans have lost track of him and they want to know if he's well.'

'Oh,' said Gheertzoon, clearly a little disappointed at the tameness of the story. 'He's a merchant, then?'

'He has dealings with merchants,' said Charlie vaguely, for it was true that all gentlemen seemed to have dealings with merchants. Where else would they buy things?

'Then when we reach Amsterdam I shall ask amongst my friends,' said Master Gheertzoon, resolved to help him anyway. 'And we merchants, we are the kings in Amsterdam! If he is there, we shall find him for you – or if he has ever been there, or ever thought of being there!'

Four days it took to reach land, though most of the last day was taken up in sight of it. Charlie stood on the floor – the deck, he had to learn to call it, though it looked like a floor to him – and gazed out at a land as flat as could be, little houses and cows clinging, it seemed, to clumps of snowy rushes in the middle of a vast puddle. But as the ships around them grew more numerous, so that he was certain they would ram each other and sink to the bottom, he saw that there were greater numbers of buildings on the land, too. He caught a glimpse of fine houses in the distance, and nearer there were waterways between great, strange edifices, some on poles that stuck out of the water, some adorned with pillars across the front as though the poles had continued up to the roof.

'Churches, factories, windmills, synagogues, theatres, brothels,' sighed Josse with a smile. 'All laid before you in the service of trade!'

'What's that one?' Charlie asked, almost at random. Josse laughed.

'That's the Stock Exchange,' he said, 'where air is bought cheap, and heated and sold on for a great profit.'

Charlie stared at the building in awe.

'This is our inner sea, which is closed off at night. I see the snow has not left us yet. These winters are terrible. Last January the canals froze so hard that even in the middle of the day a team of more than eighty horses could not drag the ice-breaker through it. And fresh water, then, costs so much! Of course, the advantage is that a frozen canal is not a stinking canal, not so much.'

The ship edged its way through the throng, gently making its way to some predetermined landing point. Charlie had no baggage, of course, and Josse's was ready to be lifted when they docked.

'Come with me,' said Josse Gheertzoon, as they stepped through the gate of the ship again and on to the board that led to the shore. Charlie tried not to think about the water beneath, and crossed with a jump and a slither. 'You can help carry my packs. Here,' and he loaded a number of small packages and bags around Charlie's shoulders, taking slightly more upon himself. 'The rest can wait for a porter. Now, we are not too far!'

I'm in a different country, thought Charlie, feeling his feet on the ground, on what seemed to be a tight pattern of narrow bricks set into the earth, infilled with mortar. A wall: they have a wall on the ground. He shrugged, as well as he could under the packs, and looked about at the people that crowded the dock. They did not look too different: there were pretty girls and ugly girls, large men and small men, women who looked as if they never sneaked out of the house and women who looked as if the men in their lives would know exactly who was in charge ... Josse had set off, and he hurried to follow.

The houses, however, were nothing like those in Aberdeen, or even in Edinburgh. Tall and thin: that was what he had thought the master's town house in the Castlegate, but oh, no: these houses were the width of a taper, and about as long – if you drew a taper out and up and as far as any taper ever went. Yet there were two or three windows on each floor, sometimes squeezed together with barely a bit of wall in between, but painting around the window frames and up to a curly edge to the roof like one of the porcelain ornaments set on the Leith Hall dining table for a grand dinner. And the windows had their shutters on the outside, like beetles' wings. And the water just never stopped – there were rivers in the streets, with boats in them and the boats were full of chickens and ducks and barrels of milk and water – that would be the fresh water, presumably – and nearly every man was smoking a pipe, giving an odd blue haze to the cold air ... and where were the hills?

He followed Josse as best he could while staring around him, listening to the odd language he was already growing used to, trying to pick out a word or two in case he might understand something. They crossed a number of bridges where the air was heavy with the stink of the water, walked along the brick bank of a river for a few hundred yards, then stopped at a panelled wooden door, painted green. Josse grinned, and pushed the door open, jerking his bony head for Charlie to follow. They stepped over a high sill, on to a tiled floor in a high, cold room with white walls and chairs around the edges. On shelves about the room stood a number of pieces of blue and white pottery, of a kind Charlie had even seen at Leith Hall: there were vases and pots and jugs, and odd-shaped vessels with lots of little spouts. He had never seen the like of those.

'Pappa!' came a cry, and two small girls hurtled out of an inner room, throwing themselves at Josse and babbling in the same odd language he spoke. Charlie laughed to himself: the very bairns could speak it and understand it, but he hadn't a clue.

In a moment they noticed him and turned more quiet, putting on their public faces. Josse must have been explaining who he was, for he heard his name mentioned, then Josse turned to him with a beaming smile.

'These are my girls, my daughters, Luzie and Anna Katerina,' he explained, though their faces had told him the same story. Both were fair and heavy-boned, with bright blue eyes and hair the colour of young cheese. Luzie, the elder, seemed shy and solemn, while Anna Katerina looked at him more boldly. 'They are the ladies of the house, since my poor wife died. And sometimes they have been known to behave like ladies!'

Charlie did not know if the girls knew Scots as well as their father spoke it, but perhaps they caught his tone. He made a low bow, as if they were indeed the ladies of the house.

'Good day to you, mevrouw, mevrouw,' he said to each in turn. He hoped he had his new words right. Anna Katerina giggled, but he guessed she would have giggled whether he were right or wrong. Charlie put her age at maybe nine or so, Luzie maybe eleven or twelve. He was not particularly good at guessing the ages of children, but there were always a few around Leith Hall.

'Come, now, girls: Master Rob is not a customer, but a friend. Let us take him into the parlour and be comfortable. He has come all the way from Scotland!' He translated quickly for Charlie, and the girls ran ahead as Josse gestured Charlie through the inner door. To the right of the entrance hall he glimpsed a rather grand room with a huge fireplace, currently unlit, and more pieces of the blue and white pottery about the room. It was quite right that he, by contrast, should be led away somewhere to the back of the house, and not into a place of such grandeur, though Josse's comments about his being a friend had taken him by surprise again. True, Josse had said he had no need of a servant, but surely Charlie could do something to help him if he were going to help Charlie find Abernethy of Mayen? Charlie was sure he would have to pay for assistance somehow.

'Here, come and sit by the fire, and warm yourself against the damp,' said Josse, nodding to Luzie. She fetched, on a tray, a very small glass of something, and offered it to Charlie. For a moment he was confused, thinking she intended him to take the tray and serve Josse, but no: for once, someone was serving him. It felt very awkward. Josse took his own glass and knocked back whatever was in it: Charlie, sensing something like brandy, sipped with care, trying not to stare around him too much. The fire at which they sat was a kind of boxed-in stove in black metal, sitting out on legs in front of another elaborate fireplace, and all around stove and fireplace were little blue and white tiles with pictures on them. He longed to get down on his hands and knees and look properly at the tantalising little figures and scenes: they were like something from a book, and he had never seen anything like them on a wall before. The floor was wooden - wood! On the ground floor! - and well swept, he noted. But to take away some of the feeling of formality, to his right was a panelled box bed, very much like the one he remembered from his parents' cottar house. It was a most peculiar mixture, he decided, then tried to pay attention to what Josse was saying.

'We are here in good time, still in business hours, so if you are feeling fit we can begin our enquiries straightaway - or once you have warmed through, anyway!' Josse laughed. The stools on which they sat had triangular seats, on which Josse managed to look comfortable. Charlie could feel the edges digging into his thighs. He would be pleased enough to be warmed through and up on his feet again, he thought, even if the floor still lurched a little as his feet grew used to the land again.

'Do you really think we'll be able to find him?' asked Charlie. Now that he had seen the size of the town, he had begun to wonder - let alone the harbour with its prickling masts, its wooden walls of shipping. Surely it would be the best place in the world for Mr. Abernethy to hide: no one could possibly have traced him here, even if they had seen him land here with their own eyes. And Charlie was not quite so confident that he was even in the right town.

'If he has set foot in Amsterdam, we will find out,' said Josse, bright eyes confident. 'There are often plenty of Scotsmen here, anyway, and they all know each other. Some are your Jacobites, who have not yet gone back - I think there are a few your Government is still hunting for, and others who have made Amsterdam their home now. And of course there are always merchants and traders, working back and forth as my son and I do, staying a while to build up the business or oversee something particular, then moving on. It's a great life!' he added, slapping his knee, then he caught sight of his daughters lingering, fascinated, in the doorway of perhaps the kitchen. His habitual grin softened. 'But it's always good to come home.'

While he fell into conversation with his daughters again, Charlie allowed his thoughts to wander, wondering what Josse's wife had been like, what it would feel like to have a house and a family, a business of one's own. He would have to find somewhere to work again when all this was over, somewhere that was not home, a different family to serve. And what of Phoebe? Would he ever see her again? Leith Hall seemed so far away, a different world: even Lang Tam, who would doubtless have enjoyed this adventure immensely, seemed a ghost from his past, here in the cosy Amsterdam parlour with those intriguing tiles. If he could share a house like this with Phoebe – share that comfortable box bed in the corner ... But that was a dream he would never be able to fulfil. Where would any man who started as a cottar's child find the money for that?

'Come,' Josse said, leaping up. 'Before we grow lazy and lose the best of the day! We'll come back here for our dinner later – for now let us go and ask a few people a few questions, and see where that gets us. You never know, you could be shaking Mr. Abernethy's hand before sunset!'

Charlie could not help smiling at that, for Josse's good humour was almost irresistible. He wriggled off his triangular stool, bowed again to the little girls, and followed Josse back through the formal front rooms and out into the street.

The day had been fair and the sky to the west was a soft blend of buttery yellow, fading to blue and pink – a bit of silver embroidery, Charlie thought, and it would have made the master a very fine waistcoat. He smiled a little, allowing the sadness to touch his heart, watching the same colours slither across the dark waters of the nearest bit of river. Then he braced himself to go about his first foreign city in the path of his friend Josse.

The next few hours were a muddle for Charlie, as Josse Gheertzoon swept him from dock to barge, from grand front entrance hall to small back parlour, and he began to realise that Josse had paid him a kind of compliment in taking him into that warm panelled room with the lit stove, the intimate family room, rather than leaving him out in what was, in many houses, really a warehouse, designed so that customers could sit and be shown stock and occasionally, if they had travelled a distance, be accommodated. In some houses that was as far as they went, with polite bows all round. In others, it was hand-shaking and back-slapping and Josse's heavy, bony grin. But everywhere it was 'Master Rob' and 'Master Abernethy – Scots – Mayen' as Josse explained their quest. Charlie himself stood helplessly by, nothing more useful to the search than a bill stuck to a wall. Sometimes, though, Josse's friends and acquaintances spoke Scots, welcomed him solemnly to their town, apologised for the weather, said they had never heard of a James Abernethy.

But at last – a little after sunset, as it happened – they hit on the scent. A Scotswoman, married to a cheesemaker and surrounded by a flock of small children like hens at her skirt tails, told them that her brother, likewise married and settled locally, had a broad acquaintance amongst the Scots in Amsterdam – the emphasis she placed on the word 'broad' made Charlie wonder if she meant their political sympathies covered a wide range. She gave them directions, and Josse, clasping her hands, thanked her with such enthusiasm Charlie was sure he was tiring of having offered to help.

'That's near the Nieuwe Kerk again,' he said. 'Sorry, we're doubling back on ourselves. But come on! That's the best word yet!'

He bounded off, leaving Charlie, footsore, to follow.

The brother, who like his sister hailed from Ayrshire, was a little more circumspect than his sister had been.

'Who is it you're looking for?' he asked, head on one side, half his attention on an apprentice working on a side of cured beef.

'James Abernethy of Mayen. A place up near Strathbogie. No so far from Aberdeen.'

The man nodded, taking in the direction but clearly adding other considerations to his thoughts before replying.

'Aha, yes. Aberdeen, eh?' He turned and spoke sharply to the apprentice, who hesitated, then turned the beef and tried again. Even Charlie could hear that the Ayrshire man left nothing of his accent behind when speaking Dutch. The Scot watched for a moment, then, almost absent-mindedly, said,

'You could try Jeemsie Ogilvie, over near Pijlsteeg. You could try. But you might not want to venture near him this time of the night.'

'Why?' asked Charlie boldly. 'Does he go out drinking?'

The man looked at him again, considering.

'Aye, him and all his neighbours,' he said shortly. 'It's no the place you want to be after dark. You'd ken that, and all,' he added to

Josse, who nodded.

'We'll be careful,' he said.

Chapter Twenty-One

Back outside in the street, Josse looked at the sky. There was still some light from the set sun, though not much. In the streets, however – and particularly, Charlie noted with gratitude, near the canals – there were lamps lit, and it was relatively easy to see where they were going and to keep an eye open for any pickpockets or other ruffians. Charlie was growing used to towns, and kept his hands by his sides where some of his valuables were in his deep pockets. His purse of coins from Andrew Hay of Rannes was tucked inside his shirt, where he was sure no one would ever find it.

'If we go quickly,' said Josse, not quite so cheerful as usual, 'it should not take us long. But it is not a good place to be after dark, around Pijlsteeg: stay close to me.'

Charlie thought back to his first encounter with the Castlegate, his ventures with the master down to the foot of the Ship Row. He nodded, but he was not too concerned. He knew how to behave, and he was sure with two of them they would be quite safe. He made sure he knew where his knife was, and once again followed Josse.

The streets were as narrow and overhung as any he had seen, many lined with wooden houses like some of those near the Castle in Edinburgh. But they were neither too crowded nor too deserted, and they moved neatly and swiftly along them until Josse paused and pointed up an alley.

'This is where we'll find Master Ogilvie,' he said, having asked a local or two. 'The third house on the right, where he lives on the fourth floor.' He took Charlie's arm to guide him, and soon they were picking their way up an ill-lit, scruffy wooden staircase, smelling of mice and stale wine, twisting in on itself and at last spitting them out, as if they had been kicked out of a cupboard. They fetched up on a landing floored with tiles – green ones, but the glaze had worn off in the middle and the plain brick underneath showed through – and against the wall they were black from a lack of sweeping, Charlie noted. Josse approached the door opposite the stairs, and knocked hard. A voice within answered in Dutch, and after only a moment the door was opened by a rotund gentleman with smooth white hair, perhaps powdered, tied into a very neat black silk ribbon. His linen was perfect, and his hands and face were almost as pale as the frills at his neck and cuffs. He looked better suited to Lady Glastirum's parlour than a little place like this.

If he had been expecting anyone, he managed to smooth over his expression and asked a question, with every appearance of friendliness. Josse replied in Scots.

'We're looking for a Master Jeemsie Ogilvie?'

'Aye, that's myself,' said the man, still affable. 'Whom do I have the pleasure of meeting?'

'My name is Josse Gheertzoon, a merchant in Amsterdam and Leith. This is Charlie Rob, who is on an errand in these parts, and we hear tell you might be able to help us.'

Jeemsie Ogilvie looked them up and down, more amused than disapproving, Charlie thought.

'Well, you'd better come in, then,' he offered, 'and not be standing out here for all to see. Will you take a glass of wine by the fire?'

'That would be very kind of you,' Josse agreed, his grin returning. Charlie saw that Mr. Ogilvie too had conceded to local taste and had furnished his hearth with blue and white tiles – good – and triangular stools, which Charlie viewed with less favour. He had sat on several since leaving the Gheertzoon house that afternoon, and none of them was what he would have called easy on the legs.

Nevertheless they perched there, and Mr. Ogilvie who, it seemed, had no servants, poured them wine from a jug that had been set near the stove. It was just the right warmth, and went well with the little biscuits he offered around.

'Now, what can I do for you?' Mr. Ogilvie asked, settling down next to them.

Charlie hesitated, but Josse gestured him to go ahead.

'Well, sir,' he began, 'the thing is, I'm from near Aberdeen, and I'm looking for a man from those parts who, I believe, came here or hereabouts.'

'Here to this flat?' asked Jeemsie Ogilvie, politely surprised.

'No, no, sir, here to Amsterdam.'

'Oh! I see. And what is this man's name?'

'He's a gentleman, sir, by the name of James Abernethy of Mayen. Mayen is –'

'Aye,' said Ogilvie, 'I ken where Mayen is.' He pursed his pale lips, and regarded Charlie in a manner that seemed to see everything about him – the suit of clothes he had lived in for five days now, the linen a loan from Josse on board ship, the results of a borrowed razor, the alarm at being so far from home, the servant – perhaps even the cottar boy, playing on the muddy floor. It was disconcerting, but not, strangely, frightening. 'Why might you be looking for the gentleman?'

Charlie swallowed, with difficulty.

'My master was John Leith of Leith Hall –'

'Oh, aye,' said Ogilvie, and Charlie was sure he knew the rest of the story at once.

'But I have left that service,' he went on, though the words still caused him a qualm. 'I do not seek Mr. Abernethy to bring him to justice – what could I do against him, on my own in a strange country?' The last words came out unbidden, though Jeemsie Ogilvie nodded. 'I am here because – because I thought he was a good man, and a good friend to my master, and I cannot see how it could all have happened. It makes no sense to me. And so I wanted to ask him, if he would be kind enough to answer – and I think he would be, for he always seemed to me to be a kind man – what really happened. Oh, and also I've been to see Lady Mayen, and she misses him sorely, and wants to know that he is safe and well.' He stopped, and made himself take a deep breath. More had come out there than he had intended, and while it was all honest, he was beginning to wonder if he talked too much to people he barely knew. Still, Jeemsie Ogilvie looked a sensible and knowing man, and would not mock him, at least.

Jeemsie took a long sip of his warm wine, staring into the middle distance.

'Aye, it's true she maybe hadna had my letter when you saw her – it can take a wee while, or it can miscarry easily enough. I wonder if I should write again, just in case? Or maybe that would make it worse, to have the news twice?' He spoke absently, then turned back to Charlie. 'I have bad news for you, I'm afraid, and for Lady Mayen if you're talking to her and she hasna had the letter. For

James Abernethy of Mayen is dead.'

Charlie had no idea how long he sat in silence. He almost felt he should have expected the news, but he still felt as if he had been punched in the stomach. Poor Lady Mayen, with all her bairns! What would she do now? And how was he going to find out what had been behind Mr. Abernethy's attack on the master? A sense of terrible failure descended on him: he had wasted Hay of Rannes' money, and he had nothing to take back to Mrs. Leith to console her, or to prove his instincts had been right – not that that mattered. He had wanted to bring something that would make things better, somehow, something that would be a final service to his master, and he had failed.

Gradually he realised that there was still a conversation going on in the room: Josse, who had been uncharacteristically quiet while Charlie explained himself to Mr. Ogilvie, was now asking questions.

'When did Mr. Abernethy die? What was the cause?' he asked.

'A week ago, or thereabouts,' said Mr. Ogilvie, and his face was sagging with sorrow. Charlie was pleased to see that Mr. Abernethy had at least died somewhere he had a friend. 'And I blame myself, at least in part. He was staying here, for we had mutual friends in Scotland. I had not met him before but he was – very likeable.' He nodded to himself, and Charlie warmed to him even more. But in what way might Mr. Ogilvie have been to blame?

'Aye, Charlie says he was a fine fellow,' Josse said, encouragingly.

'We went out for dinner one evening to a place I know near here. I should have chosen somewhere a little more ... well, well-lit, anyway.' Josse exchanged an odd look with Ogilvie, then glanced at Charlie. Ogilvie pulled himself a little more upright, ready to explain. 'I like to live here for it is lively – and well-priced. But it is not altogether a respectable area, you understand?'

'So I gather,' said Charlie, as politely as he could manage. It was not for him to judge other people's towns, or choice of places to live in them.

'We were attacked,' said Jeemsie Ogilvie, on a long sigh. 'It happens often enough around here, if you linger at night. I felt a knife, a hand on my purse, and then I heard a splash and a cry from Mayen.

And then I was in the canal myself, too. Well, there's nothing for bringing a man to his senses faster than a knife at his side and a dip in a cold canal on a January night, I can tell you. I heard footsteps running, so I knew we'd been left to sink or swim for ourselves, as you might say. I'm no too bad a swimmer, even in my clothes, it turns out, so despite the lumps of ice and who kens what in there, I pushed and pulled myself around in the water, my teeth chattering fit to smash them all, and I find Mayen and seize him about the chest, and pull him to the edge. It's almost more than I can manage to push him up on to the bank – I dinna ken how I did it, in the end, but sometimes the strength just comes to you, doesn't it? I shoved him up, and found some steps and hauled myself up and out after him, and for a moment I just lay there, peching. Then it struck me if I didna move I might freeze to death, and there was not a sound from Mayen. So I crawled over, and tried to feel for a pulse or a breath or anything. There was nothing. I thought of crying out for help, but – well, it's not always help that comes when you cry out round here, ken?'

'True enough,' agreed Josse, shrugging.

'So I pulled him along the path, until I could get him under one of the odd street lights. And I near had apoplexy when I saw him.'

He paused dramatically. Charlie held his breath.

'Well?' said Josse, not prepared for a performance.

'His throat was slit from ear to ear,' whispered Jeemsie Ogilvie.

'Oh, my,' said Charlie, and he felt sick.

'Did you tell the magistrates?' asked Josse, practical again.

Jeemsie nodded quickly.

'Of course I did! What else was I to do? But I couldna even tell them what the fellows looked like: they came on us from behind, in the dark. The only wonder was they had missed Mayen's purse when they attacked him: they certainly had mine, though of course I only carry what I need when I go out like that,' he added, congratulating himself for such good sense. 'The only thing would be if the sheriffs found my purse somewhere, though I daresay it's at the bottom of the canal by now. So, my friend, it's a sad story I've had to tell you: I'm sorry I hadna a better one for you.'

'Do you – do you know where he's buried?' asked Charlie, hesitantly. Mr. Ogilvie reached over and clapped him on the back, then poured more warm wine for all of them.

'Of course I do, my lad! Wasn't I the one to bury him? And pay for all, and act as chief mourner? I shall be - well, happy is not the word, not the word at all. I shall be honoured to be your guide tomorrow, if you wish to visit his grave. There is no marker there yet, of course - far too early for that - but at least you can take some account of it back to Lady Mayen. You can tell her,' he added, and his face was desolate, 'that I did my best for him. In the circumstances.'

So it was that the following day, in another set of clean linen borrowed from Josse and with Josse to accompany him, Charlie ventured into the district around the Oude Kerk. The day was foggy, as if the air itself had aspirations to be as wet as the rest of the town, and Charlie found himself coughing and sneezing as they walked. Josse was quiet, for him, merely pointing out places of interest they had not been able to see the previous day as the light had dimmed - though really, the fog was almost as concealing.

'I'm glad,' Charlie ventured, 'that Mr. Abernethy had a friend nearby at the end. Someone to shelter him when he came here, and someone to see to a decent burial for him. Mr. Ogilvie seems a nice man, did you think?'

Josse snorted.

'He was pleased enough with his exciting story, I'll give him that!' he remarked. 'As to paying for the burial and all the fees, where has Mr. Abernethy's money gone? I'll be very surprised if he's sent it back to - how is it you call her? Lady Mayen?'

'Aye, though Mrs. Abernethy's as good a name, too, if it's easier,' said Charlie. The layers of names and territorial designations had been new to Josse, and Charlie had spent some time on the ship explaining the system. The memory caused him to miss, for a moment, Josse's unexpected criticism of Mr. Ogilvie. He considered it: it was true that Mr. Ogilvie had told the story well, and that no mention had been made of Mr. Abernethy's money except that the robbers had not touched his purse. But then, Charlie doubted that there had been much in that purse. The robbers might, if they had been local, have thought that Mr. Ogilvie was a better option.

'Well ... he won't have sent anything back to Mrs. Abernethy unless he finds a trusted carrier, I suppose,' he tried. 'And he can't help telling a good story. He wanted to show us how sad it all was, didn't he? I mean, that was what I thought he was doing.'

Josse, who had been looking a little fierce with his heavy brow and long chin, grinned suddenly and laid a hand on his shoulder.

'Always you will see the best in people, Charlie! Always.'

'Is that not a good thing?' asked Charlie, puzzled, but Josse just laughed, and turned away to wave up at a house they were passing, where a woman was cleaning the windows. The woman smiled, and flapped her cloth back at them – yet Charlie had the least feeling that Josse had hoped to wave at her unseen.

They met Mr. Ogilvie at the foot of the alley where he lived: his linen was as spotless as it had been the previous night, and he had attired himself in a suit of black clothes so perfect they seemed like a hole in the world, not real stuff at all. He greeted them sombrely, as befitted the occasion, and remarked on the fitness of the weather for the morning.

'Mind, it was snowing the morning of the burial. I thought myself that the very snowflakes were like the blessing of heaven on his coffin, the poor man.' He glanced sideways at Charlie. 'Did you ken Mr. Abernethy well, lad?'

'Me? No, no, of course not, sir. He was friends with my master, and I had seen him on many occasions and had cause to consider him a very good man, if it had been my place to pass an opinion on him at all. Which of course it wasn't.'

'Of course not,' said Mr. Ogilvie, with a slight puff of breath that seemed only to add to the fog. 'A good servant like you would not have opinions on a gentleman.'

'That's right, sir,' said Charlie, relieved he would not be expected to have any complicated thoughts on anyone else. It would be difficult to explain to anyone how he had such a high regard for the man who had seemingly murdered his much-respected master.

They had not walked far when he became aware, even amidst the tall, skewed buildings, of a spire mightier even than them which rose above them like one of the porcelain ornaments at Leith Hall, spindly, graceful, airy, and fading into the mist. Even the High Kirk in Edinburgh was not like this: it was earthbound, firm fingers pressing down on the stony tower. Though of course the High Kirk was already on a hill: the people of Amsterdam had to make their own heights, it seemed.

'The Oude Kerk,' said Mr. Ogilvie, gesturing a little sadly up at it. 'Or the Old Kirk, in our parlance.'

'Do you mean they use the Scots words?' asked Charlie, both pleased and confused. Josse and Mr. Ogilvie exchanged a smile.

'Well, it's the same word, kerk,' said Josse, kindly. Charlie felt himself blush. He had no idea that he had known Dutch words since he could talk. He wondered what the minister at home in Kennethmont would think if he could see him now, on the point of visiting a great church like this, in a country so far from home? He shook slightly at the thought. Just how far from home was he? And how would he ever return?

They rounded a corner and entered by a gateway into a kirkyard very much like the ones at home, so that for a moment he even found the place comforting. There were plenty of headstones, and he found himself scanning them, looking for a familiar name, but of course Mr. Ogilvie was quite right to say the grave had not yet been marked. If there was little money, he wondered if it ever would be – or, if he himself made some money, somehow, somewhere, could he come back here and raise a stone for Mr. Abernethy, just as far from home as he was and never, ever to return?

'Here we are,' said Jeemsie Ogilvie, reaching a space between two much older graves – if the Dutch did their figures the way the Scots did, too, these graves were a hundred years old. A long line of black earth, the grass not even begun to disguise it, lay, marked at the end by a rough wooden cross. There was writing on it in what looked like charcoal, and Charlie squinted to make it out.

'James Abernethy of Mayen,' it read. 'Died in this town, 6th January 1764. A loyal Scot and friend.'

'Oh,' said Charlie, and could say no more. Jeemsie Ogilvie stood with his head bowed, clearly upset, too. But Josse seemed to find the little cross more curious than moving: he stepped round one of the old graves and squatted in the yellow grass to study it more closely, fingering the edges of the rough wood. Perhaps, thought Charlie, he thinks Mr. Ogilvie could have done better, even for a temporary arrangement, but then Josse did not quite seem to like Mr. Ogilvie. And as for his remarks about Charlie always seeing the best in people ... well, why on earth not? He would like to think people saw the best in him, too, though he was not sure there would be much to see.

'Well,' said Mr. Ogilvie, 'there you have it. You can tell his widow he's in good company at the Oude Kerk: lots of respectable burghers buried here, and of course it's the Reformed church ... well, he's no in with any papists, I suppose.' He tailed away, clearly not sure what James Abernethy's religious affiliations had been. It had probably not come up in conversation during Mayen's stay.

'Thank you for showing us, Mr. Ogilvie,' said Josse politely. 'Most kind of you.'

They walked with Mr. Ogilvie back again to the end of his alley, and when he invited them to step in for a drink Josse quickly declined, even when Charlie's mouth had been open to say thank you. Josse shifted Charlie onwards, back towards his own house, and when they were clear Charlie asked,

'What's the matter, sir?'

'I don't trust your Jeemsie Ogilvie, Charlie, that's what,' said Josse firmly.

'I don't understand why not.'

'I told you last night the way he told his story sounded odd. Then he takes us to see that grave this morning – and perhaps indeed your Mr. Abernethy is buried there – but that touching little cross, that was bone dry. And it rained last night.'

'Well, maybe he thought ... maybe he hadn't got around to it before ... it's only been a few days, and with offering to show us the grave maybe he realised he hadn't done it yet and this would be a good time to do it,' said Charlie, struggling.

'Aye, maybe, maybe,' said Josse Gheertzoon, but it was clear he had other ideas, whatever they might be. The pair did not speak to one another all the way back to the house, and when they reached it Charlie used the excuse of his coughs and sneezes to retreat to his chamber early. He was confused about Mr. Ogilvie, and about Josse; he missed the reliable humour of Lang Tam, and his own country, and Kennethmont, and Leith Hall, and Phoebe. He felt as lonely as he had ever felt in his life. He had failed in his task of finding and questioning Mr. Abernethy, and Mr. Abernethy was dead. Snuffling and coughing, he tucked himself into bed and cried himself to sleep like a baby.

Chapter Twenty-Two

His sleep was not altogether peaceful, and he was wracked with uneasy dreams of ships sinking and graves opening, and duels in the dark. Then a peculiar notion followed that there were people in the walls, watching him and whispering about him. The sound of their shoulders brushing the woodwork seemed to bring him back to consciousness: he sat straight up in bed, alarmed, then found he had a very prosaic need to find and use the cludgie.

It was as he was rubbing his hands on the linen cloth left out for him that he realised that he could indeed hear whispers, but that they were outside on the little landing. He listened carefully, trying not to move, for every floorboard creaked. He reckoned that it was the two little girls, Josse's daughters Luzie and Anna Katerina. Were they whispering because they were trying not to disturb him? Or did they perhaps need to get into the room for something stored there, or to clean ... what time was it, anyway? Was it night, or early morning? He knew too well how awkward it could be, when someone was lying late in a room you wanted to red out. He decided he had better see if he was in their way.

The girls both jumped when he opened the door in his stockinged feet, shirt and breeches.

'Do you need any help?' he asked, trying to look reassuring. The girls looked at each other, then back at him, then Anna Katerina, the younger, said something to him about 'Pappa'. It was then that he remembered this was the first time they had been in each other's company without benefit of Josse's translation – how easy he always made it seem!

'Pappa is here?' he tried, speaking quite slowly. It seemed to work. Both girls shook their heads. Then again Anna Katerina spoke, at first unintelligibly.

'Pijlsteeg,' she finished, trying the same principal and speaking with great exaggeration of lips and teeth.

'Pijlsteeg?' Charlie picked on the familiar words with relieved delight. Then he considered. 'But ... Pijlsteeg? I thought that wasn't a good place to go at night. It is night, is it no?'

That was too much: they looked blank. Charlie stepped back into his bedchamber and tugged open first a window, then more warily, the shutter. It was indeed quite dark, with those sounds on the air that point to late night rather than early morning, though he was not quite sure he could have described how. What on earth was Josse doing going back there at night? Unless he thought to find out more about Jeemsie Ogilvie. That might make sense: he would not like to see Charlie taken advantage of. He was so lucky in the people who had befriended him, Lang Tam, Josse, and indeed – he was sure – Jeemsie Ogilvie. But still, from all Josse had hinted, it was not the place to go at night, and it seemed that the little girls were worried. He thought hard. Could he find his own way back into that maze, and in the dark? It had been dusk when he and Josse had gone there first yesterday, and almost dark when they returned. He was growing used to noting his path in strange places, and he thought he might just manage on his own. The thought gave him the shivers, but he could not allow Josse, who had been so good to him, to head off into danger on his own on Charlie's account. Still ...

'Have you a lantern I could take out with me?' he asked, then pointed up at the sconce on the panelled wall, and pretended to carry it in his hand, using it to look about him. With a laugh, Anna Katerina beckoned him to follow her downstairs, with Luzie following, to the kitchen, where she handed him a small but useful looking light, and with a questioning look lit it for him from the fire. Luzie tapped him on the arm, as if he were deaf as well as dumb. She said something slowly and clearly, and pointed first to Charlie, then to the door.

'Aye, I'm away out to look for your papa. I'll need my coat and my boots, and then I'll away. Dinna you twa fret now: I daresay the pair of us will be back before you know it.'

The girls smiled and nodded, and bolstered by their faith in him, he went to find his outdoor things.

It was one thing being confident for the girls: it was quite another when he was only a few paces from the front door, holding his lantern high and convinced he was going to step into the canal at any moment. He had forgotten to check exactly what time it was: there were very few people about here, in a decent, respectable neighbourhood, and it felt very late. But he concentrated hard, slowed at every corner, thought about his options, and picked his route with care, noting the features he had seen both yesterday and earlier today. As he neared the vicinity of Pijlsteeg, he noticed that there were rather more people about the streets, more lights in windows, more voices raised in shouts or laughter, most, he thought, the worse for drink. His memory spun back to the night of the duel, the noise and smell of Campbell's inn, Tonley's sly, sleekit face, Abernethy's hands around his glass, the master dropping so sharply when the shot rang out ... no, it was no good: he had to focus on what he was doing here and now, or he would be lost and wandering, or worse.

One more corner, and he found himself at the foot of the alley where Jeemsie Ogilvie lived. Rather pleased with himself, he paused, his back securely against the wall, and scanned the alley and then the street around its mouth. He was sure he could find his way even to the Oude Kerk itself from here, but should he? He was looking for Josse, who was, he thought, looking for Mr. Ogilvie: if they were not here, then he was not sure where he might find them. He edged up the alley and with some effort strained to look upwards at what he believed were Mr. Ogilvie's windows, to see if there was the least light, but the shutters put paid to that attempt. It was impossible to tell.

He returned to the mouth of the alley and took a moment to decide what to do next. If Mr. Ogilvie were in, then Josse might have been here, waiting in the alley for him, and he was not. Then it was likely that Mr. Ogilvie had gone out, and Josse had followed him. That was, unless Josse had simply come over this way to try to find people who knew Mr. Ogilvie and talk to them, rather than try to follow the man himself. Charlie shivered in the damp air, and not entirely from the cold. How could he possibly find Josse here? Had he been mad to come and even try?

Well, he was here, and he might as well try. Whether Josse was following Mr. Ogilvie or not, Charlie could have no idea where he was. So the best thing might be to wander the surrounding streets, with due care both for the residents, and for his directions, and see if he could find him. It was not the most reassuring course of action (which was, of course, to run home to his bed as fast as possible, pull up the covers and pray that Josse would have turned up safely by the morning) but it was indeed probably the best. And if it took a little more courage than the other option, well, did not his friend Josse deserve a little help from him, just as he had received so much help from Josse? Nodding sharply to himself, but with one hand to the wall, nevertheless, he stepped out into the unknown. And if his sudden venture was perhaps stimulated by an odd noise in the alley behind him, then that was even better, surely?

He began by making little forays in each direction, seeing where people seemed to be congregating, observing their movements and their dress and trying to decide who might be people he could ask, and who might be people best avoided. It was a worrisome business, and several times he almost approached someone only to be plagued by doubts the next moment and back off into the shadows again. A couple of times men glanced round to see who was bearing that little lantern, and once a woman, in a broad silk gown of improbable hue, stopped, peered, and gave vent to a rich chuckle. Even in the dark, Charlie felt himself blush.

Gradually he drew a greater circuit with his lantern and his tentative steps, a growing web of darkened streets and alleys, inns and what seemed to be private houses where there was much drinking and dancing, and a good deal more women than in the inns Charlie had seen in Scotland – though, to be fair, he had not seen that many. He wondered what the minister in Kennethmont would say about women dancing like that: it looked as if everyone was enjoying themselves tremendously, so there must be something wrong about it.

It was only as he edged down a different alley to skirt a particularly noisy inn (he had already peered through the open door and was as sure as he could be that Josse was not inside) that he began to think he might be being followed.

At first he turned, pleased. Josse must have seen him, somehow, and be trying to catch him up. But as the little lantern swung he saw only a shadow, stepping back fast to blend with darker shadows: he knew it was not his friend, and despite his best efforts his teeth began to chatter. He needed to find his way round and back into that busy street, however unpleasant the inn had looked: surely no one would try to knife him and steal - well, he had forgotten his purse, in his haste - steal anything, in front of a crowd like that? He would be quite safe, surely.

He took a turn to the left, but the lane he had entered did not follow a straight line. This must be carrying him even further from the well lit street. But if there were someone following him, and by now he was fairly convinced it was not just his imagination, then they would already be between him and the corner and if he turned back to change his direction, he would just walk straight into them, wouldn't he? Och, he wished his teeth would stop clattering! Walk straight into them ... it was almost tempting. It was like something Lang Tam would do, no doubt about it. He would draw his knife, or his sword, and spin on his heel and challenge the fellow, and the man would run and all would be well, and Lang Tam would have a hearty laugh about the whole thing, and take another glass of wine, or pot of ale, or whatever was on offer. A great gulp, somewhere between a sigh and a sob, caught Charlie in the throat, and his uneasy walk turned to a trot.

He knew he was lost. At that pace, even the lantern light was not of much use to him. The people he passed, and there were one or two, did not even turn to stare at a man passing at a jogtrot, at this time of the night. Charlie did not blame them. There was not one of them he cared to stop anyway. When he tripped and whacked the lantern on the side of a building, and the light went out, he did not even pause but trotted on, still clutching the black light as if it alone might lead him back, charmed, to Josse's house and the girls who had lent it to him. But how could that happen? He was doomed, doomed from the moment he had thought himself brave enough, or competent enough, to set out alone to help Josse, to do anything useful at all. Panting, he staggered along, constantly aware of the relentless footsteps behind him, sometimes persuading himself it was an echo of his own, sometimes convinced it was the devil himself at his heels. He turned left and right, right and left, at random, no longer caring, no longer noticing that there were fewer and fewer people in the streets, that the voices were quieter ... He would run, he decided, until he could run no more, and then he would turn and face whatever fate had been sent to pursue him.

But the end came faster than that. Charlie felt the walls of the street drop away from him somehow in the dark. He carried on forwards into the open, thudded hard into something cloth-covered, and gave a cry of alarm. There was an enormous splash, a bubble of fetid air, and he toppled, winded, to the ground, thudding chin then cheekbone on cold, wet brick.

He lay there dazed, funny little lights coming and going behind his eyes, though he knew the lantern was still broken. He had it firmly grasped in one hand, even now. Then he heard footsteps, soft, near his head – the footsteps, it occurred to him, of someone not wanting to be heard. He lay very still. There was silence, then whoever it was turned with the least scuffing of boot on brick, and walked quietly away.

He looked about him. Lined up on the edge of the canal were several cloth-covered – what? Light enough for him to have moved, and heavy enough to sound like a man falling into the water. He poked the nearest one: cheeses, he discovered, great rounds of wax covered cheese, piled on a wooden tray and covered in cloth. Good enough to deceive his potential attacker – who was now making his own escape.

Somehow he was on his feet, and following, still clinging to the lantern. This was the person who had followed him, he was sure, and now he would turn the tables on him, whoever he was. Could it be, even, that this was one of the men who had attacked Mr. Abernethy? If so, Charlie wanted to catch him – well, maybe not to catch him, personally, at least to try to find out who he was so that someone important could catch him, and see him punished for the awful thing he had done. With that hope, as softly as he could he pattered along behind, helped by the fact that the person was now walking quite normally, and seemed to have no idea that anyone else was still around. In any case, Charlie had no idea at all where they might be, and there was a chance that the person might just lead him back to somewhere familiar. His chin and cheek hummed with pain in the cold, but he thought he was probably not bleeding too much – maybe his blood was frozen, he thought suddenly, remembering Lang Tam's joke. Oh, Tam would be enjoying himself here now!

He concentrated hard on not losing his pursuer, and not breathing too heavily, as the pair of them padded through alleys and along streets. He could see, on a better-lit stretch, that it was a man he was following, but that was hardly a surprise – cloaked and hatted like half the rest of the population. Then the man turned into one more lane, and as Charlie paused at the corner to watch, he pushed open a door and went into one of the houses. Charlie ran, light-footed as he could, to catch the door before it closed, already hearing the man's footsteps ascending the stair inside. Charlie knew the place straightaway. It was Jeemsie Ogilvie's flat.

He darted for the stairs, but slowed again, trying not to make the steps creak. At Mr. Ogilvie's floor he stepped on to the landing and to his surprise saw that Mr. Ogilvie had left his door open just a crack. He went to it, paused, and with his heart dancing, pushed it open.

'Come on in, Charlie Rob: I thought I had not made sure enough of you at the canal,' said Mr. Ogilvie with a sigh. 'Close the door behind you, eh? Keep the wind out.'

Charlie moved slowly into the room. One candle was lit on the table. Mr. Ogilvie stood, his face carved black and white in its light, with his back to the shuttered window. In his hand was a pistol, the barrel pointed steadily at Charlie.

Charlie felt his jaw wobble. That wasn't right. Mr. Ogilvie would not just shoot him. Would he?

'You just followed me through the streets, did you no?' he said, and he heard his voice tremble, too. He cleared his throat and tried again. 'What would you do that for?'

'You came to my house in the middle of the night. I thought you ... well, I wondered what you were up to.'

'Up to? What do you mean?'

Ogilvie smiled, as if pleased that Charlie could not work it out, which had the effect of making Charlie think quite hard. Following people through the dark – falling into the canal – Josse didn't believe his story ...

'It was you who killed Mr. Abernethy, wasn't it?' said Charlie, suddenly sure.

'It was,' said Ogilvie with a sigh.

'Why would you do that?' cried Charlie 'He was a good man!'

'You barely knew him!' Ogilvie snapped back. 'And he killed your master!'

'He was still a good man! There must have been something ... if you hadn't killed him, I'd hoped to get the chance to ask him why ... They were friends, ken.' He eyed the pistol as discreetly as he could. There was no way of knowing whether or not it was loaded. Was this what the master had felt like, that night on the Castlegate? How long would it take Charlie to die? He licked his suddenly dry lips, and made himself meet Mr. Ogilvie's eye. 'Why did you kill him, then?'

'Because I was told to!' Ogilvie's voice gave a little squeak, and Charlie suddenly realised that Jeemsie Ogilvie was almost as frightened as he was. The pistol quivered.

'Why would someone tell you to do a terrible thing like that?' Charlie asked, but this time he tried to keep his voice soft, gentle, the way you would with a horse that was out of sorts. He wondered if it would be possible to edge sideways, out of the way of the gun.

'There was a letter ... He brought the letter himself, ken? That was a laugh. He had no idea. A letter of introduction, that was what he thought it was, and he handed it over to me and inside, where the foolish man had never thought to look, it just said, 'Get rid of this fellow, James Abernethy of Mayen, as soon as can be – he is no longer useful to me.'

'What?' breathed Charlie, proud of himself for not shouting it in Ogilvie's face, though somehow he had managed to slip closer to him. 'No longer useful? What kind of a way is that to talk of anybody?'

'Aye, I ken,' muttered Ogilvie, a little wretched now.

'But you felt you had to do it?' Charlie pressed on. Ogilvie nodded.

'I did. I – had to.'

Charlie hesitated. Would Ogilvie tell him what he needed to know? He had to ask.

'Who gave Abernethy the letter?'

If Charlie had hesitated, Ogilvie nearly spat out his answer, as if the taste of it disgusted him. Charlie could almost feel the spittle on his face.

'Patrick Byres of Tonley,' he said. 'It was him.'

'Tonley?'

'Aye. I ... I owe him a very great deal.' But Ogilvie sounded less grateful, and more afraid. At the very mention of Tonley his gun hand had sagged just a little. Charlie took a deep breath, and pounced.

Ogilvie was less distracted than he had hoped. His grip on the pistol was a strong one. The two struggled, and for a moment Ogilvie had the clear upper hand. Then Charlie discovered in himself a tremendously strong desire not to die, nor to end up in a foreign kirkyard like Mr. Abernethy. He might have had the disadvantage but he was younger and fitter than Ogilvie, and he was determined. He seized the pistol in a better grip, and hauled hard.

It felt like the struggle of a week, but in only seconds he felt the gun slip from Mr. Ogilvie's moist hands, and both men staggered backwards. Charlie's elbow caught the candle on its stand, and he tried to steady it and sort out the pistol at the same time. Ogilvie lunged for the gun again, clumsy and confused as the shadows lurched around them. Charlie tried to stop him but had no third arm to do it with: the candle was perilously balanced, the pistol trembled, and there was an awful, ear-ringing bang.

When Ogilvie toppled slowly to the floor, Charlie's head whirled – back to the Castlegate, back to Mr. Abernethy's grave, back to Leith Hall, back to the kirk in Kennethmont and the great lists of the commandments on the wall: Thou Shalt Not Kill. Thou Shalt Not Kill – and now Charlie himself had killed. He dropped the pistol on the floor with a clunk, and sank to his knees. The candlelight had steadied: he drew the stand over to the edge of the table, not trusting himself to lift it, and looked down at Mr. Ogilvie, and at the hole in Mr. Ogilvie's breast, and at the blood on Mr. Ogilvie's lips. Charlie had killed.

He knelt there on the floor for a very long time. If he tried to pray, what stopped him was that thought: Thou Shalt Not Kill. How could God listen to him now?

The silence roused him in the end. No one seemed interested in finding out what had caused a loud bang in a flat at night, not around here. The streets had grown quiet. His head was still spinning, and when he pulled himself to his feet he could not stop shaking. The candle was low – how tall had it been, though? – and he licked a finger to extinguish it, barely conscious of the prick of heat as he did so, nearly knocking it from its stand. His legs seemed unsure about bearing his weight: they felt light and insubstantial, like bolsters stuffed with down. Taking extraordinary care not to trip over anything – particularly Mr. Ogilvie – in the dark, he stepped to the door, opened it, and left the flat.

He had very little notion of where he went after that. Nothing made any sense to him: walls, earth, water, all seemed strange, inexplicable. He thought perhaps he had walked for some time, or flown, or swum – it was not clear. At last he found a place to sit: the stone was cold but it did not matter, and behind him was wood but that was of no significance. He was more tired than he ever remembered being in his life before. He would sit here – lie here – float here, whatever it was he was doing, and forget everything, though he was not sure what it was he hoped to forget. Nothing mattered any more.

He woke when the wood moved – when the door behind him opened. There was a squeak of surprise, and then, distantly, he heard voices calling and debating in some language he thought he might have heard before. He felt himself lifted, not by much, and hauled off the step and then pulled across a smooth floor. He was somewhere warm. He was set down for a moment, and there was some discussion above his head – light voices, pleasant, he thought. Angels? No: no angels for him. Then something soft was flung over him, and he was rolled a little to allow it to be tucked beneath him, too. He was propped on more softnesses, fluffy and light, and then warm things were added under the blanket with him. It was all very pleasant. Someone passed a cloth over his face, a damp cloth, and he blinked, and opened his eyes, and tried to sit up.

'Master Rob?' came one of the voices.

He was on the floor of Josse's cosy parlour, wrapped in blankets, propped on pillows taken from the box bed, he realised. Before him knelt Luzie, the older girl, staring anxiously at him, holding out a bowl of some kind of fragrant broth. An angel indeed. How had he come here? How was he so cold, and so tired? He glanced down, and saw blood on his hands.

Then the memory of all that had happened came to him, and he pushed the bowl of broth away, and burst into tears.

The sobs wracked him and wracked him until he had no strength left. He had killed a man. He was no better than James Abernethy or Jeemsie Ogilvie or – or even Mr. Byres of Tonley. Not that he had ever thought himself better than any of them, really. But he had at least thought himself law abiding, an honest man, obedient to all the minister at Kennethmont had taught them. What was he now? A murderer, a killer, not fit to be in the company of innocents like these. He turned from them, staring at his bloody hands, then began to drag himself back toward the front door. He could not stay here, not in this house where they had been so kind to him. He must leave.

But he was so tired. The girls followed him, got in front of him, tried to stop him, and he was so weak they almost succeeded. But he pushed himself on, on hands and knees, through the grand hallway with its beautiful blue and white pots, its spotless furniture. He did not deserve to stay in such a place. He had to go.

Chapter Twenty-Three

The front door burst open, and Josse cried out a greeting to his daughters – a greeting at once lost when he nearly fell over Charlie on the floor.

'What's this? What's this? Charlie, what is the matter? Are you sick?'

Luzie and Anna Katerina gabbled at him in Dutch, urgent and sensible. He listened, then bent and swung Charlie up and over his shoulder. Luzie ran ahead and flung the pillows back into the box bed, and Josse held Charlie while Anna Katerina pulled off his boots. Then between them they levered Charlie into the box bed, straightened the pillows and pulled the blankets up round him. Anna Katerina washed his filthy hands with a hot cloth. Josse took the broth from Luzie, sat firmly by Charlie's side, and began to lift a spoon of it towards Charlie's mouth. Only to prevent it falling on the beautiful linen did Charlie open his lips and receive it. It was delicious.

When the rest of it had been spooned into him, he began to feel, physically anyway, more normal. He had stopped shaking, his legs felt like legs, and though his mind was filled with all he had seen at least his head had mostly stopped spinning. An immense sorrow settled on his chest, but he could at least think fairly straight, and answer when Josse asked him how he was feeling.

'Josse, I killed a man,' he said at once, knowing he could say nothing else first.

'You did?' Josse looked surprised, but not exactly as shocked as Charlie might have expected. 'Was it Jeemsie Ogilvie?'

Charlie nodded.

'I shot him with his own pistol,' he said, and felt a tear run again down his cheek.

'Well,' said Josse, 'I can see it's been a shock to you, but I daresay he deserved it. If it hadn't been you, no doubt it would soon have been someone else.'

Charlie opened his mouth, and shut it again. He was not quite sure what Josse meant. He tried a different tack.

'He was the one who killed Mr. Abernethy. It wasn't attackers after their money at all. It was Mr. Ogilvie. He lied to us, Josse!'

'Yes, I did say ... well, well. He does not seem to have been a very nice man.'

'Well, no, he wasn't, I don't think. But ... Josse, I think he was frightened, too.'

Josse shrugged.

'Fear makes many men do silly things,' he said. 'Some manage not to, and some are just too frightened. I suppose none of us knows what we would do until it came to the moment.'

'I didn't shoot him because I was afraid,' said Charlie earnestly. 'I shot him because he was going to shoot me, and I tried to get the pistol away from him, and then I knocked the candle over, and he grabbed the pistol back again but it went off and there he was, dead on the floor! And then I really was afraid,' he added, the weight of sorrow pressing on his chest.

'Then you didn't shoot him,' said Josse. 'You didn't kill him. He really killed himself, when it comes down to it. He was holding the gun, and it went off. He would have been more than happy if the shot had hit you. But he shot himself instead. It's not your fault, is it?'

Charlie said nothing. It was a tempting theory, but how could it possibly be right? He thought again of Mr. Ogilvie standing there pointing the gun at him, telling him what had happened to Mr. Abernethy, and about the letter from Tonley. Mr. Ogilvie wouldn't have told him all that and then just said good night to him, would he? He had every intention of shooting Charlie there and then. But did that really make him responsible for his own death?

'What were you doing over at Pijlsteeg anyway?' Josse was asking. 'It's not a place to wander on your own, even when you know where you're going.'

'I was looking for you. The girls were worried ...'

'Were they?' He turned to Anna Katerina and asked something. She shrugged and shook her head.

'Oh. Well, I thought they were, and I thought you must have gone to try to find out more about Mr. Ogilvie and so I followed you, and I found my way to the end of Mr. Ogilvie's alley, and then went about looking for you, and instead he saw me and began to follow me, as it turned out ... But what were you doing there?'

'Ah, well ...' said Josse, with an edge of discomfort and a slight smile. 'I have a friend I sometimes visit, in that direction.' He cleared his throat, tilting his head towards his daughters as they busied themselves about the room. 'I miss their mother, you know.'

'Oh. Of course,' said Charlie, slightly surprised at this turn in the conversation. Then he remembered Josse half-waving a greeting to a woman at a window. Perhaps his friend lived there. In any case, it was none of his business if his friend was courting – except that he wished him very happy.

'So,' said Josse, leaning back, 'you have found Mr. Abernethy, and you have found what happened to him, and you have found the man who killed him, and he is dead. What will you do now? I may say that as far as we are concerned you may stay here as long as you wish.'

'Oh, I can't do that!' cried Charlie. 'I mean, unless you have a job for me. I can't just stay here doing nothing!'

Josse smiled.

'No, I suspect you can't!' He thought for a moment, tapping his large jaw. 'I could find some work for you if you like: it would allow you to save up for your passage home, if that is what you want. Or I could give you, or lend you the money. Or you could take the work here and stay. It is up to you.' He rose to his feet and stretched. 'And now I need a little sleep before I begin the day's work, I think! It has been a long night, though mostly a pleasant one.' He grinned at Charlie and winked. 'Rest for now: your night was more alarming than mine. The girls will fetch anything you need.'

He pushed the door of the box bed a little to, so that Charlie would have a bit more peace and shadow, and disappeared. Charlie sank back on the pillows though he felt not the least bit restful. He had killed a man. But the man had killed Mr. Abernethy, and not even in a fair fight. He tried to put that aside.

What should he do? Should he go back? Stay here? He tried to lay out the arguments on both sides. If he went back he would be going home: that was important. He would see Lang Tam and Phoebe again – he was sure Tam was all right, though he had probably returned to Aberdeen by now - and maybe even Leith Hall. He would have to go to Mayen and tell Mrs. Abernethy all that had happened: he had promised her.

And then there was the matter of Tonley.

Tonley had sent Mr. Abernethy to Amsterdam and to stay with Jeemsie Ogilvie. And he had sent him with a letter telling Mr. Ogilvie to dispose of him, saying that – what was it? He had no further use for him. Charlie's skin crawled again at the thought of the heartless words. But it did make him wonder – what use had Tonley had for Mr. Abernethy in the first place? Could it even be ... could it even be that Tonley had put Mr. Abernethy up to the duel, and to killing John Leith?

Charlie had to stop thinking for a moment and just let that thought lie, until he felt he could face it properly. But then memories filled his head: was that what Lowrie Leith had meant, however drunk he had been, when he talked about hearing someone mention slaughtering Leith Hall? And that look on Mr. Abernethy's face in the inn that morning: reluctant, sober, waiting – and Tonley was sitting opposite him, and it was Tonley who seconded him, and helped him, when he was apparently drunk, to call out John Leith. Was Tonley directing it all, as if Mr. Abernethy was a kitchen boy and Tonley the majordomo? But why? Why might Byres of Tonley want the master dead?

Well, and then the reasons for staying, for not going home: to his surprise he had liked what he had seen so far of Amsterdam, and he thought he might grow used to all that water in time. And he very much liked Josse and his family, and if they gave him money he would want to come and pay them back, anyway. And then it seemed rash, having survived it once, to venture on the sea again.

And he was scared – very scared - of Mr. Byres of Tonley.

He drifted off to sleep, softly on the sweet-scented pillows. In his dream he stayed in Amsterdam – became a rich merchant, married a pretty girl, lived in a house not far from Josse's ... his life was spread out as if he were watching himself in a painting, little figures in fancy clothes. And then there came other little figures, with guns and with knives, and they came into his fine house by force and seized him by the arms, and began to drag him out into the sodden streets.

'You know you murdered Jeemsie Ogilvie,' they said, one after the other. 'You know you murdered Jeemsie Ogilvie. And now you'll pay the penalty – you'll be put to the horn, just as James Abernethy was put to the horn.'

And they dragged him out, leaving his fine coat behind, and pointed to the canal.

'This is the horn,' they said, with the kind of assured nonsense that only comes in dreams. 'Now we'll put you to it.' And with grim efficiency, they ran him forward and flung him into the icy water. He screamed, and woke up panting.

And so, only a few days later when Josse and his daughters finally conceded that he was fit to travel, and Josse had paid for his passage and he had solemnly made out a letter saying that he owed Josse the money, and Josse had found not only a ship for him to sail in but also a kindly, elderly minister off to visit a brother of the church in Stirling to travel with, Charlie ventured on board a ship for the second time in his life, in borrowed linen with his own well-laundered clothing in a bundle under his arm. He had food provided by Josse's daughters and a flask of wine from Josse himself, and the memory of Josse's hug and the girls' smiles telling him to return any time, and soon if he could.

'If nothing else, come and tell us the rest of your story!' Josse cried as the ship set sail, his voice clear even over the sailors' shouts and the creaks of wood and canvas. 'And if you need anything, go to my son in Leith! Remember, Charlie! Good luck go with you! God go with you!'

Charlie, waving, saw Luzie tug her father's sleeve and say something. Josse frowned, and turned to shout again.

'She says she mended your coat ... your letter and the brooch are in your bundle!'

My letter? Charlie wondered, nodding all the same. And what was that about mending his coat? He had hardly worn it for the last week, spending his time in bed or propped by that wonderful black stove.

'Charlie?' An unsteady hand clutched at his arm and he dismissed thoughts of coats and letters, turning to meet loose blue eyes and an anxious expression.

The elderly minister had sailed before, but only once, long ago, and was nervous: Josse had chosen him well, for Charlie's respect and concern for his travelling companion dulled his own anxieties, and doing him small services occupied much of his time during the four days of the voyage. Even when the waves grew greater one night, and the minister prayed with great volume and fervour, Charlie managed to reassure him, thus calming his own fears. The minister was very grateful the next morning when dawn blossomed bright and clear on the eastern side of the ship: he talked with Charlie at some length about his own childhood and the Kennethmont minister, though he did not seem to have any interest in Charlie's more recent existence. Charlie did not wish to speak of anything relating to his master, to Mr. Abernethy or to Tonley to anyone for now. At night, as the minister snored benevolently nearby, Charlie lay awake wondering what to do when he reached Scotland again: he would have to find Lang Tam, certainly, and seek his advice. But what else? He must go to Mayen and tell Mrs. Abernethy all he had discovered. He should tell Andrew Hay of Rannes, too, wherever he might be, for he felt he should account to Rannes for the money he had spent. But then what? Where was he to go?

Each night his mind wrestled with the same problem, and each morning he woke less certain than before. Would he be welcome if he gave his account at Leith Hall? He was far from sure, and in any case he knew well the hatred Mrs. Leith bore for James Abernethy of Mayen. He was not sure he could face it.

Charlie's eyes were damp when he saw the busy port of Leith before him. It was Wednesday morning, just after dawn, a fortnight to the day since he had first arrived in Edinburgh. Ironic, then, that he had spent much more time out of it than in it.

He sorted out the minister's luggage and his own bits and pieces, and went over with the minister his remembered words of Scots before he would meet his colleague, waiting for him there on the quay. And not far from the minister from Stirling, lounging against a barrel, was Lang Tam.

Charlie caught his breath, then began to wave madly. Tam caught sight of him and waved back, grinning and already laughing, and holding up, like a fisherman with a particularly splendid catch, Charlie's pack.

Once the gangplank was secured Charlie helped his elderly minister over to his friend, bade him goodbye, then turned to Tam patiently waiting at his side.

'Tam,' he said in the face of his friend's grin.

'Charlie, lad, I never thought I'd see you on a ship!'

'No, listen, Tam. Mr. Abernethy's dead. He was murdered.'

'What?' Tam looked about, hurriedly, and tugged Charlie away to a quieter place on the quay. 'What do you mean, he was murdered?' He gave Charlie a particularly intense look. 'Did you kill him?'

'Me? No! No, never!' Charlie rubbed his forehead, still not quite able to cope with what he had done. 'But I did kill the man that killed him.'

'Well, good for you, Charlie lad! Who was that, then? A Dutchman?'

'No, a Scot. Jeemsie Ogilvie. I don't think I ever heard where he was from. But listen, Tam, it's more complicated than that, and I'll have to tell Lady Mayen everything. Mr. Abernethy went to Amsterdam with a letter to Mr. Ogilvie, and the letter told Mr. Ogilvie to kill Mr. Abernethy.'

'Oh,' said Tam, 'that's no very polite, is it? Asking a man to deliver his own death warrant?' He thought about it for a minute. 'Who would do a thing like that? Or could I maybe guess?'

'Mr. Byres of Tonley.'

'Aye. Well, it's the like of the man,' said Tam, almost sadly. 'But Charlie, lad, it's grand to see you safely back! And you were away to Amsterdam?'

'Yes – how did you know what ship I'd be on?'

'Well, I didna,' Tam admitted. 'I found out by chance that was where you'd gone, so I thought I'd give you a fortnight and be here for any ship coming back from there. My, there's a gey busy trade betwixt us and them, I'll tell you! I've a lodging just over there, though, so I hadna to walk far. This was to be my last ship, so if you hadna been on this one I'd have been away back up to Aberdeen and told anyone who needed to know that you were away to foreign parts and no coming back.'

Charlie laughed, mostly with relief.

'And would you have taken my pack with you?'

'No, of course not,' said Tam, blandly. 'I'd have sold anything worth selling and drunk a toast to your health with the proceeds. Now, come on and buy me some breakfast, if you've any money left that isna Dutch. And tell me all about Amsterdam!'

They sat on a crate on the quayside to eat, away from interested ears. Charlie marvelled at how he could now look at the ships in Leith harbour with so little concern: he had crossed the sea twice, and his ship had not been smashed to firewood. Not that he was tempted to try his luck again any time soon: he was just very grateful to be alive.

'So you've seen at least a bit of the world, then, Charlie lad,' said Lang Tam comfortably when Charlie had given him quite a short account of his travels. 'Mayen is dead, the man who killed him is dead. Now what will you do?'

'I need to tell Mr. Hay of Rannes, and Lady Mayen, anyway.'

'And then what – find a new place with some gentleman?'

Charlie sighed.

'That depends on what Mr. Hay and Lady Mayen say, I suppose. If they want me to do anything for them to bring Mr. Byres to justice.'

'You!' Tam laughed out loud. 'What use would you be against Tonley?'

It was true, but it stung.

'I'm at their service, whatever task they might give me,' he said, stubbornly.

'Aye, but Charlie lad, he'd eat you for breakfast and then finish a plate of eggs and ham! It'd be his own men Rannes would use. And you can go and hold the widow Abernethy's hand if you like, but she's no money to pay you.'

Charlie opened his mouth, but could not speak. And Tam seemed to realise he had gone a bit too far: he fell silent, too, and kicked his heels against the crate once or twice, looking about him. Then he found his change of subject.

'Man, what happened to your coat?'

He pointed down at the front of Charlie's coat. Charlie blinked down at it, then shifted it to show the waistcoat underneath.

'I think it was when they were chasing me here, that night,' he said, happy, too, to talk of something else. 'I felt something hit me when the man ran past, and Josse reckoned it was a knife, trying to get me in the thigh. But my waistcoat saved me, see?'

'Oh, aye, that's a grand thick winter waistcoat, that one,' agreed Tam, feeling the depth of the padding. 'I doubt that saved your leg, indeed.'

'It was the master's,' said Charlie. 'He left it to me.'

'Did he, indeed? He must have thought well of you.' Tam was struggling, Charlie noticed, to be particularly kind, making up for his last remarks. He would have smiled, but he was still a little hurt. Surely he would be useful for something? And in any case, how could a decent man walk away now, without at least offering his services to Mr. Hay or Lady Mayen?

'Well ...' was all he could manage. 'It's a fine warm waistcoat, anyway.'

'And well mended,' Tam went on. 'Did you find a sweetheart in Amsterdam, then, too?'

Charlie laughed, a little annoyed at the remark but pleased that Lang Tam had reverted to gentle teasing.

'I dinna seek my sweethearts among wee lassies! No, it was one of Josse's daughters mended it for me. They're dab hands at everything, those two,' he added happily, and if Lang Tam noted the reminiscent smile on Charlie's face, he made no comment. Charlie was remembering the way the Gheertzoon family had waved him off at the harbour, little Luzie tugging on Josse's sleeve to say – oh, to say what? About the coat and the waistcoat, yes, and her mending. But that was not it, for he already knew that she had mended them, and had thanked her for it. What had it been?

'What's the matter?' asked Lang Tam, throwing the last of his breakfast to a herring gull. 'Missing them?'

But Charlie had reached for the small bundle he had brought back from Amsterdam with him. In it should be his clean linen, a piece of the Dutch cheese he had taken a fancy to, and a letter to Josse's son in Leith – he would have to deliver that, too. Letters, though ...

He felt the crisp wrapper for Josse's letter under his fingers, and drew it out. It was not sealed: Josse, knowing how Charlie had felt about the letter directing Mr. Abernethy's fate, had left it open, written a note to his son to explain why, and told Charlie he could read the whole thing if he wanted to. But wrapped within it, presumably to protect it, was an older, softer piece of paper, so thin the brown ink showed through. Charlie turned it over.

The address at the top was short, so short that for a moment he had difficulty making it out. York? No: Cork. Hadn't the master been in Cork, on his way back from America? The regimental headquarters was there.

The thoughts ran through his head as he began to read the letter.

'*My dearest Johnnie,*

'*This place is grown mournful indeed since you left, and sometimes I wonder what I shall do on my own and when I might ever see you again. I intend to travel to North Britain soon, but I know it will not be easy for us to meet and I must content myself with news of you via Lady Glastirum.*

'*Yet there is something on which I should very much value your opinion just now. It concerns me deeply, and for that if nothing else I miss you at every moment. A letter has arrived here, pursuing me from America, a letter sent by my dear husband before his death. I should retain it as a memento of him but that it contains information that should somehow I am sure be made known to the proper authorities – but that cannot happen here in Ireland. I shall not send it to you as an enclosure here in case it miscarries: I shall try to find a more secure way for it to come to you.*

'*My dearest, the post is ready and I have only time to address this and assure you that my love for you will not diminish, and I remain,*

'*Your own,*
'*Sarah Dilley.*'

Chapter Twenty-Four

'What's that?' asked Tam, breathless. 'Sarah Dilley? Is that not the Captain Dilley's widow?'

'Um,' said Charlie, 'I suppose so.' There was something else wrapped in the soft paper: his fingers worked at it to free it.

'Ho ho!' said Tam. 'Looks like your master had a warm reception there! I suppose they did sail home together, right enough. Very comfortable!'

'Please, Tam, don't tell anyone of this!'

'Why not? Your master's dead – your mistress canna kill him now!'

'No, but what of the lady?'

'She's – well,' said Tam, reconsidering. 'I suppose. I wonder where she is, anyway? Hey, she says she wants to come back up here to North Britain – what if she's the reason for the duel? How would that fit?'

'Aye, how would it?' asked Charlie. But the idea took hold to an extent. 'I suppose it could have been something to do with her honour, couldn't it?'

'I was thinking more that maybe Mayen or Tonley knew about her, and Leith Hall tried to stop them telling anyone.'

'Hm,' said Charlie, 'but how would Mr. Abernethy challenging my master to a duel, pushed into it by Mr. Byres, fit with that? If Mr. Byres had been, um, connected with Mrs. Dilley, that might do it. But it was the other way round.'

Tam considered.

'Aye, I suppose. Will you tell Hay of Rannes, when you're giving him your report?'

'I dinna ken. I'll have to think about that. What do you think?'

'I dinna think I would, if I were you,' said Tam. 'Rannes is a bit of a strict character, and he was your master's uncle: he might well disapprove, and think that Leith Hall brought the whole business on himself. And then how would he treat Leith Hall's sons and widow?'

'Hm,' said Charlie. He could not see, somehow, Mr. Hay treating Mrs. Leith and the boys badly, even if he thought his nephew had deserved to die. But Tam no doubt knew more of Mr. Hay than he did. He pulled out the round, hard thing he had been fiddling with, and held it to the light, away from Tam. It was a miniature painting, the head and shoulders of a handsome woman with smiling eyes. Was this Mrs. Dilley? But Tam was paying no attention, and Charlie slipped the miniature safely into his pocket.

'I wonder what she was worried about?' Tam went on. 'And did he get the letter?'

'He could have got it years ago,' said Charlie. 'There's no date on this one to tell us.' He read through the letter once more, then folded it into his pocket. He felt he ought to destroy it, but that was a big step to take until he had thought about it more deeply.

'So she could be in Scotland already?'

'I suppose.'

'She could be somewhere waiting for him to come to her!' said Tam, eyes wide. 'She might not even know he's dead?'

'I think half the country knows he's dead now,' said Charlie, unaccustomedly grim. He slid down off the crate and picked up his pack, undoing it just enough to slip his extra bundle into it. 'I'd better deliver this letter to Josse's son, anyway.'

'And then back up north?'

'Aye,' said Charlie, 'That's what's next.'

Josse's son Jakob was a smaller, slightly less bony, version of his father, and gave Charlie and Tam a glass of genever each and then, as they realised they would not be able to take a coach north until the following morning, invited them to stay with him that night. His bunkwife, a Scot, was an excellent cook and for a while Charlie could almost believe he was back in Amsterdam in Josse's hospitable home. But early the next morning they had to make their way back over the hill to the Grassmarket to board the coach again. It felt to Charlie as if he had not seen the place for years, the high lights in the Castle, the buildings plump and straight by comparison with the Amsterdam houses, though they had seemed so tall and thin when he had arrived.

They had the roof of the coach to themselves again, and Charlie banked up the baggage behind him, wriggling into his nest.

'Tam, what do you really think is going on? All this business – the duel, missing letters, Mr. Abernethy being killed, too – what do you think it's all about?'

Tam considered, comfortable in his own perch.

'See, Charlie, it might be near twenty year since Culloden, but there's plenty hard feelings still amongst the Jacobites, and no so far under the skin, ken? I doubt it has something to do with that.'

'That would mean Mr. Byres again, wouldn't it?' Charlie readjusted his muffler, thinking. 'But what was it your master Mr. Dalgarno said? He said he had that old watch with Prince Charles' hair in it, that had saved him in America –'

'Oh, aye, that!' Tam laughed. 'If the house was on fire he'd save that before anything else!'

'But even he didn't seem – well, really fervent, not the way Mr. Byres was.'

'Aye,' said Tam, 'but the chief love of Mr. Byres' life is trouble. That's what keeps him warm at night. We'll have to make do with dreams of willing lassies, Charlie, eh?'

And he couried into his baggage neuk, and fell into a reverie.

The coach drew out of the town and headed north once again, Charlie lost in his thoughts. Tam seemed disinclined to interrupt him, and they travelled pretty much in silence up to the Queensferry, across the Forth – now that Charlie could see it he knew he would have been terrified to cross it on the way down, but it held few fears for him now – through Fife and over the Tay as dusk and snow descended together, the flakes great white spots in the greying air. Charlie's hands were already tucked well under his arms and his pack on his lap protected most of his legs from the snow: at each stop they had to shake white heaps off their shoulders and hats, and took bowls of broth greedily, feeling the steam melt the frost on their faces.

They were stiff again when they reached Aberdeen before dawn, rounding St. Katherine's Hill and drawing into the Castlegate. Charlie looked about him, expecting the place to have changed utterly though it was less than three weeks since he had last seen it. He squinted over at the Leith Hall town house and thought he glimpsed a light between the shutters, but he had no wish to introduce Lowrie Leith to Lang Tam again – that would mean more drinking than he had a head for at this time of the morning. No: no doubt Tam would go home to his masters, and he himself would have to try to track down Mr. Hay of Rannes.

Mr. Hay had told him to write to him at Rannes, which as far as Charlie knew was up in Banffshire, not that far from Leith Hall. Charlie had written once, a few days before he had left Amsterdam, but there was no knowing how quickly that letter might have reached Rannes: he himself might have overtaken it. But if Mr. Hay still happened to be in Aberdeen, it would be daft to take himself up to Banffshire looking for him. Or he could be at Leith Hall. Charlie had pondered on his journey where best to find out Mr. Hay's whereabouts, and had hit on a plan that appealed to him even as it made him nervous: he would go to call on the household of Lady Glastirum, if she was in town, and ask her if she would be kind enough to tell him the whereabouts of her brother. Again, the thought of the lovely, delicate Lady Glastirum being any relation to the enormous, oddly angled Andrew Hay was staggering, but it was apparently a fact and it was no business of his.

'Will you come and tell me what Rannes says, if you find him?' Tam asked. 'I mean, if he asks you to do more, and if you think I could maybe be of any help ...'

'Oh!' said Charlie, amazed at how much effort Tam was going to to show how sorry he was for what he had said. He was touched. 'Of course I'll come and tell you! If I find him. I'll have to go north to Mayen, somehow, but I'll come and see you before then.'

He did want to go and break the bad news to Mrs. Abernethy, but something made him want to find out more, first. It was all very well describing how her husband had met his end, but if only he could find out if Mr. Byres of Tonley had really pushed him into the duel and why, it would be much more satisfactory. As it was it was a half-told affair. He was sure Mr. Hay would feel the same.

His hand trembled a little as he rattled the risp at the door of Lady Glastirum's School Hill house: he was hardly likely to see the lady herself, but the thought of being in the same house as that angel was enough to bring a flush to his face and warm his heart as he stood in the snow. While he waited he noted the clear distance between this building and the flat where he had unsuccessfully tried to prise information from Mr. Gordon of Cobairdy and Mr. Forbes of Brux: he thought of it as a division between Lady Glastirum's true quality and the puffed up Cobairdy. Then he caught himself: it was not up to him to compare different gentlefolk. Well, not unless one of them was Mr. Byres of Tonley.

But to his enormous surprise, he was ushered up to the parlour where the master had spoken with his mother before, and Lady Glastirum, as beautiful as ever even in her mourning weeds, sat on the same chair and greeted him by name. It was all he could do to bow: his throat appeared to have something substantial stuck in it.

'My dear Charlie, what a dreadful thing has happened! I saw you from the window,' she explained, 'and called for you to be sent up. I hope I have not made you feel uncomfortable.'

'Not at all, my lady,' Charlie squeaked. He could barely swallow.

'My brother tells me you have left Leith Hall's service, and why,' she went on. Her voice was like honey on a spring breeze, light and sweet. 'I was very sorry to hear it. I know my daughter in law needs loyal supporters around her at this time.'

'I am sorry, too, to have left the household,' said Charlie, finding his voice again to defend himself. 'But my lady, I could not support Mrs. Leith in pursuing Mr. Abernethy when I thought that he was not guilty.'

Lady Glastirum observed him for a moment, and he dropped his gaze hurriedly. He had been too bold.

'My brother has explained your theory to me,' she said. 'The two shots ... there is something in it, no doubt. And they were always such friends. Poor Mrs. Abernethy: Harriot has no right to pursue her. In law, yes, but in the eyes of the good Lord, not an ounce of a right.'

'Ma'am, I have found out more about the matter and would tell Mr. Hay as soon as I can. He asked me to write to him at Rannes, but I thought if I could find him myself it would be quicker. Do you know – would you be able to tell me where he is?'

'Andrew? Yes, of course: he is staying at Campbell's at present.'

'Thank you, my lady. I'll go and ask if he'll see me.'

'He will, Charlie. I can see you're eager to go and make your report: I should let you go.'

He bowed, but she seemed to hesitate.

'It is a matter of the very deepest regret to me that I did not see him before he died, nor attend him before his burial. My only son ...' Charlie felt tears pricking at his own eyes at the look on her lovely face: at that moment if he could have brought Leith Hall's killer in and thrown him at her feet, he would have done so at once. But she had cleared her throat and straightened her back. 'Tell me, did my son say anything before he died? I have not heard that he said anything that made any sense at all, but if there was anything ...'

'He only said one thing, my lady,' said Charlie, suddenly remembering. 'He said – I think "Dilly, dilly, come and be killed".'

'Did he?' Deep surprise buckled her words, one hand to her lips.

'Do you know, my lady, if this is Mrs. Dilley? For I have never seen her.'

He held out the miniature painting that had been found in his waistcoat – the 'brooch' that Luzie had mentioned to her father.

'Yes,' said Lady Glastirum curiously, 'that is Sarah Dilley.' She looked as if she would have liked to have asked him how he had come by it, but she did not. Charlie drew breath again.

'My lady,' – the words tumbled out before he had even thought of them, 'do you know where Mrs. Dilley is?'

'Mrs. Dilley?' She was pale, he noticed suddenly. 'As far as I can tell, Mrs. Dilley has vanished from this earth.'

Had she really? Charlie wondered, as he tramped through the snow back towards the Castlegate, rather proudly choosing from two different routes rather than just following the only path he knew. But had Mrs. Dilley vanished? Old Margaret thought so, and now Lady Glastirum said the same. When had she written the letter to the master? It was soft and thin and could have been hidden in that waistcoat for years – since the master had returned from America, or nearly. Charlie wondered if that was why he had left that particular waistcoat to Charlie – not to keep him warm, but to keep that letter safe from Mrs. Leith's eyes if anything happened to him. That seemed to imply that there had been no further letters, or the master would have hidden them with the miniature in the same place, wouldn't he?

As he reached the front door of Campbell's inn he could not resist a glance at the wooden lamp post where the second ball was lodged. If he had never heard that story, where would he be now?

In the inn, Andrew Hay of Rannes was just finished seeing to his horse in the stables and returning through the main room when he caught sight of Charlie.

'Good heavens, man, it's good to see you safe and well! I was starting to wonder if I would hear news from you!'

'I wrote you, sir,' said Charlie quickly, 'but I might have overtaken the letter.'

'How was Edinburgh?' Rannes asked, then looked about him. The inn's servants were tidying tables and benches, making ready for the busy dinner time, and one or two men were already propped in corners with bottles of wine. None of them, Charlie noted as an aside, was Lowrie Leith. 'Come upstairs, though, and tell me all about it. I have a room here just now.'

Rannes led the way, making the broad inn staircase look as frail as a ladder. Charlie trotted behind him. Rannes' room was an ordinary size, and Charlie puzzled how he ever fitted on to the bed. But he sat on it now, and gestured Charlie to a stool to perch on.

'Tell me all about Edinburgh,' he said again. 'It's a while since I've been, myself. Did you find anything? Did you find Abernethy?'

'I was barely in Edinburgh, sir,' said Charlie, 'but we did go to the law courts, and we found that there's been no sign of Mr. Abernethy there. But then by chance I did hit on the trail, and – well, sir, I'm afraid I found him.'

'Dead?' asked Rannes after a moment, interpreting Charlie's tone.

'Aye, sir. I'm afraid so. I went to his grave.'

'And where's he buried?'

'At the Oude Kerk, in Amsterdam.'

'Amsterdam?' Mr. Hay's odd black eyebrows danced a jig of incredulity. 'You've been to Amsterdam? But you've only been away – what, a fortnight?'

'Aye, sir ... well, it was all a bit unexpected.' He considered: he had been wondering how much to tell Mr. Hay, but thought in the end it might be best just to lay everything out in the open. After all, Mr. Hay was family. 'Well, first, I found out before I left that the master and Mr. Abernethy, and others, had been attending an Episcopalian service the night of the duel. And that's in secret, sir.'

'Aye, of course it is. You found that out, did you? Well done: you'll not be spreading it further, I daresay.' Obviously this was not news to Rannes, but Charlie was glad that Rannes knew that Charlie knew. Of course he would not tell anyone else, but it made conversations between them much easier.

'Then I went on to Edinburgh,' Charlie went on, and told him in more detail about their visit to the law courts, then Charlie's urge to do a little sight-seeing, which had led to the visit to the luckenbooths and to the High Kirk. Rannes listened patiently, though he seemed unsure as to where the story was going. But when Charlie mentioned first the two thugs, then the encounter with Mr. Byres of Tonley, he sat up a little.

'Is that where Tonley is?' he asked. 'No one has seen him up here for twa-three weeks.'

'Well, sir, there's more on that account,' said Charlie, quite gratified at his attentive audience. 'But first, I'm sure it was the same two fellows that chased Lang Tam and me through Leith. I dropped my pack and lost Tam, and – well, I ended up on a ship to Amsterdam.'

Rannes laughed out loud, a great bellow that made Charlie jump.

'I wish I had been there! I visited that city myself a few years back and liked it very well.'

'My friend Josse says it's not what it used to be,' said Charlie. 'But I liked it myself, sir. Though my stay was not without incident.'

'Go on, then,' said Rannes, waving a huge hand encouragingly. And Charlie went on, telling of their search for Mr. Abernethy, the discovery of Jeemsie Ogilvie, the sorrowful news of Mr. Abernethy's death, and the further disclosure of Mr. Ogilvie's actual involvement in it.

'Ogilvie killed Abernethy, then?' Rannes did not seem entirely surprised, only a little bewildered. 'Why would he do that?'

'He was told to.'

'Told to?'

'By someone who scared him, unless he was a very good liar,' said Charlie. 'And it was Mr. Byres of Tonley.'

'Tonley told this man to kill Abernethy? After he had helped Abernethy escape? Why – why would he do that?'

Charlie swallowed: he was still upset at the words Jeemsie Ogilvie had reported to him.

'He had no further use for him, he said.'

'Aye,' said Rannes after a moment, 'well, that sounds like Tonley, right enough.'

'Sir,' said Charlie, struck by the thought of something he had not told Mr. Hay, 'someone told me they had heard someone tell someone else to arrange for Leith Hall's death in a duel.'

'Someone in Edinburgh? In Amsterdam?'

'No, sir, here. It's – I didn't say anything before, sir, because ... because ...' Why was it again? He was suddenly scared that he had made a mistake.

'Who was it?' Rannes was stern. A man his size had no need to be angry, Charlie thought: a brief grim look was all he had to give to turn anyone's bones to water.

'It was,' he swallowed hard again, 'it was Mr. Leith. Um, Mr. Lawrence Leith.'

'Lowrie Leith?' Rannes' eyebrows rose again. 'At the town house after Johnnie died?'

'At the town house, aye, sir, but not then. Later.'

Rannes frowned this time, and Charlie thought that was even more frightening.

'How did that happen?'

Charlie explained, to the best of his ability: torn between family loyalty, a sense of duty, doubts as to Lowrie's reliability – Rannes nodded – and fear of Mrs. Leith's anger ... all spilled out and Rannes received them thoughtfully.

'Right, I see what happened,' he said, mercifully. 'That makes sense. And as to what Lowrie heard, well, aye, it's anyone's guess whether he was right or havering.'

'So I thought if I told Mrs. Leith ...'

'Aye, aye. I doubt she would have listened to you. But I might have. Right, then,' he said with a sigh, spreading out one great pale hand in front of him. 'I reckon we need to go and see if Lowrie Leith is still in residence across the Castlegate – and if no one has actually come and thrown him out, or made him a better offer, I can't see why he shouldn't still be there.'

Charlie had to leave the room to allow Rannes to rise and pull on his coat and boots – there simply was not room for another person in there when such manoeuvres were going on – but soon Rannes joined him on the landing, hunched below the ceiling, and led the way downstairs and out into the Castlegate. Charlie scuttled beside him over the snowy cobbles, a sudden recollection of running after his father when he was very small. He could barely remember his father's face.

As they approached the town house, Charlie could see that the door was once again ajar.

'Be careful, sir,' he called up to Rannes. 'Once before he just forgot to close it, but another time he was lying in wait inside – ken when I said it looked as if he had been threatened some way?'

Rannes smiled.

'Thank you, Charlie, but he's unlikely to do me much damage.'

'Aye, but sir, with a pistol – I mean, it's no as if your blood is frozen!'

Rannes gave Charlie a puzzled look, and he blushed as Rannes pushed open the door and stood back, in case of attack. But there was no sound inside. A little warily, Rannes folded himself under the doorway and moved inside, surprisingly quietly. Charlie followed, though if anything had happened ahead he would have seen nothing past Rannes' broad back.

The parlour showed some signs of Lowrie-like habitation: an empty wine bottle stood on the little table by the armchair, which was equally empty.

'Go and look in the kitchen and down that way,' said Rannes, 'and I shall see if he is upstairs.'

Charlie went as bidden. In the kitchen a pot of broth had been pulled off the fire and there were signs that the fire had had water poured over it, the quick way of putting it out. He poked his nose into the broth pot, and reeled backwards: it had been there for a few days, anyway. The door to the yard at the back was firmly locked and bolted from the inside, and the windows were latched – not that it had been any different before. Charlie doubted that Lowrie Leith had done much in the kitchen beyond heating broth.

He heard footsteps on the stairs, and hurried back into the hall.

'Not a sign,' said Rannes, 'and I even checked under the beds. But his clothes are still there, and his shaving things – dry as bones, of course, for I don't think he likes to wear them out too quickly.'

'He's put the fire out in the kitchen with water. And the broth that's there is inedible.'

'Let's look at the parlour again,' said Rannes, and thoughtfully ushered Charlie ahead of him so that the lad had a chance of seeing what was there. Almost at once Charlie's foot hit something, and it rolled under the chair. He crouched down to see what it was.

'Another wine bottle, sir. Only this one's near half full.'

He pulled it out and handed it up to Rannes. Rannes looked at it thoughtfully.

'You've met my brother in law a few times, have you not, Charlie?'

'Aye, sir.'

'Then does anything strike you as a bit queer, here?'

Charlie thought. The kitchen fire was odd enough: was Lowrie ever that careful? His gaze wandered to the parlour fireplace.

'Sir, this fire's been put out with water, too!'

Black trails of long-dried runnels lined the hearth. Charlie tried to picture Lowrie here drinking, then rising to put out the fire ...

'And I cannot imagine him stopping when there's wine still in the bottle, sir,' he added, and Rannes nodded at once.

'That's what I was thinking. And when he's in his cups he doesn't tend to think too clearly about fires and safety, that I've ever seen. It looks to me, Charlie, as if our friend here left in a bit of a hurry. Now, why would he do that?

Chapter Twenty-Five

'You said he acted the last time as if he had been threatened? Or attacked?'

'Aye, sir, he had me pinned to the floor before he saw who I was,' said Charlie, touching his bruises. 'And he had a black eye – he said that he had fallen down the stairs. Do you really think he's fled, sir? He wouldn't be – well, would anyone have murdered him?' He would never have suggested such a thing before the last few weeks, he thought.

'It looks to me more likely that he's gone,' said Rannes. 'He's lived an uneasy sort of life: he's very good at disappearing.'

'But why would he do that, sir?'

'Well, it could be half a dozen things, with Lowrie. Debt would be favourite,' said Rannes, staring at the half-empty wine bottle as he held it up to the light. 'But it could be politics, too. Lowrie was a fierce one in the '45, he and his brothers. And if it hadn't been for that, he would have been fierce in something else. He gets bored easily, you see.'

'He thought the master was involved in something secret,' said Charlie, 'and he was dead keen to be in on it, sir. He asked him a couple of times, and he was not best pleased when the master said no.'

Rannes turned his gaze to Charlie.

'Did he?' he asked. 'And do you think, Charlie, that Johnnie was involved in anything secret?'

Charlie's mind sprang off to Mrs. Dilley. That was secret enough. If Mrs. Leith had found out about Mrs. Dilley, it suddenly struck him, would she have arranged a duel to have Mr. Leith killed? But Mrs. Dilley was the one secret he was not going to share even with Mr. Hay: he needed to find the lady, and tell her the bad news

251

of John Leith's death, but he was sure that the master would not have wanted any information about her spread about, for the lady's sake as well as for his own. He was still not entirely convinced that the master had felt about Mrs. Dilley as Mrs. Dilley had evidently felt about him, to judge by her letter.

'Mr. Leith mentioned the Commissioners of Supply,' he said at last, 'but that was no very secret.'

Rannes emitted a burst of laughter.

'No, I don't think so!'

'So apart from the – well, the meeting that night, I canna see what he might have been involved in, sir.'

'No.' Rannes was sombre again. 'No, Johnnie was not cut from the same cloth as his uncle Lowrie, that's true. He liked well enough his home and his family and his estate: he should have made old bones. For him to be the one in the family to die in a duel – and at the hands of a good friend. It just makes no sense, does it? You know that as well as I do.'

Charlie nodded.

'But then if you add in Mr. Byres, sir – that makes a difference, doesn't it?'

'I'd have thought Lowrie would have recognised Tonley's voice, if it were Tonley putting Mayen up to the duel,' said Rannes. 'But I agree it makes the whole thing more suspect than ever. Tonley arranged for Mayen to kill – no, not to kill, as your evidence proves. Tonley put Mayen up to challenging Johnnie, who knows how – money, maybe, and a promise that no harm would come of it.'

'I never saw a man so shocked as Mr. Abernethy was as Mr. Byres took him away that night, sir,' Charlie put in, nodding.

'So Tonley put him up to it, Mayen drew Johnnie outside and fired at him, and missed and hit the lamp post. And Tonley, for whatever reason, shot Johnnie.'

'No, sir, I dinna think he did.'

Rannes, mouth open to continue with his account, shut it. 'Why not?'

'Well, sir, I was there.' Charlie went over it again, stubbornly. 'I saw Mr. Byres fairly clearly for the night – he was wearing a kind of buff coat and breeches, and he stood out. I mean, I could see Mr. Abernethy clearly enough with the lamplight, and he was in a much darker coat.'

'You saw Mayen's shot.'

'I did: I saw the flash from his pistol. But sir, I saw nothing from Mr. Byres, and at that point his hands were in his pockets, and when I got up to them his hands were empty. I mean, he might have dropped it, or slid his pistol into his pocket, but I saw no sign of one.'

Rannes leaned back against the wall, baffled again by this information. Charlie wondered fleetingly if the wall could bear his weight, but beyond a bit of creaking it seemed to be holding.

'Yet we believe that Tonley arranged the duel,' Mr. Hay said slowly, 'and Johnnie is dead. So who killed him?'

'And why would anyone want him dead?' asked Charlie, ignoring the possibility of Mrs. Leith wreaking revenge. Daringly, he added, 'Sir, you would know better than I if he had any enemies.'

'I don't believe he had, Charlie. As I said, he was the last of the Leiths I should ever have expected to die this way. He was generous, amiable, kind – and I am not just listing the words to inscribe on his memorial. It's all true. He was a good man, with many friends, and without a single enemy that I can think of.'

'Yet, sir,' said Charlie, harking back to what Rannes had said, 'he is dead.'

Mr. Hay eased his back, shuffling his massive feet.

'We need to talk to Tonley.'

Charlie turned cold.

'I suppose so, sir.'

Rannes turned and grinned at him.

'Not appealing, is it?' He sighed. 'I don't fancy it much, myself. But someone is going to have to, and we're the ones who know most about it ... I'd bring my brother in, but I want him at Leith Hall to keep an eye on Harriot – Mrs. Leith – for her own safety, and maybe for others, too.' He made a face. 'So it's up to us. But we have to find him, first. Have you any idea where he might be? Do you think he might still be in Edinburgh?'

Charlie might have been flattered at being asked for his advice like that, if he had not been so alarmed at the thought of speaking to Mr. Byres. Surely it was not his place to ask a gentleman questions like that? But Rannes seemed confident he would do as well as Rannes himself. Charlie did not agree.

'I've no idea where he might be, sir,' he admitted. 'I barely stopped in Edinburgh on the way back and I wouldna have expected to see him, anyway. It was pure chance we saw him in the High Kirk.'

'Of course. But it seems to me it would be the sensible place for him to be, and to stay, with all that's going on: he's well to be clear of Aberdeen for now.'

'He might have gone further, sir.'

'Aye, he might ... or he might have doubled back, and headed for Tonley like a rat to his hole. Hm.' He considered for a moment. 'Right, I'll try Edinburgh, and points south. Charlie, are you willing to go to Tonley, maybe, and see if he is at home? You can take a friend with you if you want – that Lang Tam seems handy enough.'

'Aye, sir: well, if Lang Tam can come I'd be happier,' he said truthfully.

'How's your purse? Have you enough to see you through?'

'I have, sir, thank you.'

'Well, then, I suppose we'd better make our preparations. I'll set out now: I can be a fair enough distance on my way, I believe, before dark.'

'Tam's masters might not allow him to go straightaway, sir,' said Charlie, 'not when he's only just back.'

'Well, see if you can get away tomorrow, maybe,' said Rannes. 'Tonley's less than thirty miles away, parish of Tough. Hire a couple of horses, or even a chaise.'

Because of the snow, they decided on horses, and left before dawn.

Charlie had had very little trouble tempting Tam to come with him. Clearly Tam suffered from boredom, too. It was kind of his employers to indulge him, Charlie thought, but Tam was less grateful.

'They're still argifying about what to do when Dalgarno marries Lady Kee-Ho,' he grumbled. 'They're happy enough to get me out of the flat.'

'Is it settled then?' asked Charlie, surprised. 'Is the marriage arranged?'

Lang Tam spat impressively into the snow.

'Aye, in Dalgarno's mind it's all over and done with, and all he has to do is count his money. And father a bairn on her, if he has it in him. Which he swears he does, whatever her other husbands might have managed.' He let his horse put on a little speed, and Charlie had to dig his heels in to catch up. 'Aye, but I dinna ken that his Lordship her brother is as keen on the match. Keracher says he's teetering.'

'What do you think?' Charlie asked.

'Well, she's twice widowed and no bairns – that doesna look good. But she's rich, and that looks awful good. She's pretty enough, too, though she's a bit like his lordship, quiet and solemn-like. But there's those that like a quiet wife. I think she could do a good deal better than Dalgarno, when it comes down to it. But she's taken a fancy to him, it appears, and that counts for a lot with a widow – they ken their own minds.' He whistled briefly. 'Like yon Mrs. Dilley, no doubt.'

'Och, dinna say anything about her, Tam!' Charlie begged. 'Even if there was anything in it I wouldna like word getting back to his family.'

'No to yon Mrs. Leith, any road,' Tam agreed. 'I wonder where Mrs. Dilley is now, though? Does she even know that Leith Hall is dead, or is she biding somewhere, waiting on him coming in to sweep her off her feet?'

'Don't be daft,' said Charlie. 'There was nothing in that letter to say there was anything between them any more.'

Nothing in the letter, perhaps, he thought – though he wished Tam had never seen it: but there was the miniature, and there was the way his master had waited so faithfully outside Mrs. Dilley's rooms in the snow, dressed in his best ... No, Mrs. Leith should never find out about all that. She would be furious.

'So anyway,' said Tam, feeling a change of subject might be necessary, 'what's this we're looking for here?'

'We're looking for Mr. Byres of Tonley,' said Charlie, relieved to be away from Mrs. Dilley but not too happy to think about what might be ahead of them. 'The road to Tough, Mr. Hay said.'

'And what are we to do with him if we find him?' was Tam's very reasonable question. 'Are we going to say here, Mr. Byres, sir, what have you been up to, talking Mr. Abernethy into a duel and then having his throat cut across the seas?'

His tone was a passable imitation of Charlie's most subservient voice, and Charlie gave a quick grin.

'We just ask him if he'll come back to Aberdeen to talk to Mr. Hay, I think,' he said.

'And what if he says no?'

Again, a reasonable question.

'Well, at least we'll know where he is, and I can tell Mr. Hay.'

'Are you going to tell him just to stay where he is until Rannes turns up? For if I thought Rannes was after me, I'd flee. The man's the size of a gentleman's house.'

'Maybe he'll just be curious enough to want to see what it's all about,' said Charlie. This had sounded convincing when he had thought of it late last night, but in the cold light of day it rang a bit less likely.

'Aye, well, right enough,' said Tam. 'I'm sure you're right.'

At the village of Kirkton of Tough, they stopped to find food and ask for directions for the last few miles. Tam would have liked something more than bannocks and ale, but Charlie was content with the quality, and tried to be content with the quantity, too, making himself chew slowly. The woman who had provided the refreshments leaned on her door jamb as they ate, eager for news from somewhere that was not the tiny village of Tough.

'We're looking for Tonley House,' Charlie told her. 'That's not far away from here, is it?'

'Tonley House? Oh, aye – is your master maybe wanting to buy it?'

'To buy it?' asked Tam, as Charlie, more sensitive to the phrase, said 'My master?'

'We've been wondering if it's maybe for sale. There's been nobody in it this long time only when Mr. Byres maybe appears for a day or two on his way somewhere. It's been empty this long time, since Mr. Byres took the family away to Italy at the '45.'

Tam and Charlie looked at each other.

'Are we chasing shadows?' asked Tam.

'We'd better just make sure, though,' said Charlie, not quite allowing himself to feel the relief that threatened to course through him. If Tonley were not here that would be the end of his part in chasing him, wouldn't it?

'Oh, aye, of course,' Tam agreed. 'So which way do we go, then, mistress? Or if you're not too busy maybe you could set us on our way? I'd let you ride my horse,' he added, with an outrageous wink. Charlie thought the woman would slap him, but she giggled.

'I doubt my husband would like that too much!' she said. 'But the way is easy enough,' and she stepped out from her doorway to point them in the right direction.

Dusk had crept over them by the time they reached the house, and Charlie was grateful for Lang Tam's easy company. The place was a great grey block, with the look of an untended grave: no smoke trickled from the chimneys on this cold night, and you could see, even with the snow, where weeds had grown and seeded and died around the great front door. No footprints disturbed them. Lang Tam shrugged.

'There'll be a kitchen door, no doubt. If a'body's here they'll have used that.'

'What do you mean, if a'body's here?' Charlie's heart jumped. 'They said the place was empty!'

'Aye, well,' said Lang Tam, stepping back to give the blank, blind windows a considered survey, 'it looks empty, wouldn't you say?'

The snow around the kitchen door was ambiguous, disturbed by animals, it seemed. Lang Tam tried the handle: it was locked. Charlie, caught between frustration and relief, waited for his friend to say, 'Right, that's it, let's go home.' But Lang Tam showed no sign of admitting defeat. He stepped past the door, and tried a small window. It slid up with a shove, and Tam inserted one long leg, ducked, and drew the other after him. Charlie, after a moment's agitation, followed. After all, if the place was deserted, who would know? And they were not there to steal. He found himself mumbling 'Who would know? Who would know?' to himself until Lang Tam laid a hand on his arm to hush him gently.

The kitchen was bare, and not over-clean: there was mud dried on the stone floor, and traces of oatmeal on the long table. They moved quietly, but still every scrape and tap echoed: Charlie swallowed hard and thought the sound would bring down the ceiling. Lang Tam nodded at a doorway in the far wall, and they headed out into a narrow passage, so dark they had to touch each side to be sure of their way. In a moment they found themselves in the entrance hall of the house, and stopped, even Tam not sure where to go next. The hearth was empty. A clock stood on the mantel above it, hoping to persuade them that it was noon. A couple of paintings, curling out of their gilded frames, had been left to adorn the panelled walls where mould grew in the cracks. The place smelled cold and damp, of old, chilled woodsmoke and wet wool. Charlie took a moment to reassure himself again, silently this time. This was no ancient, haunted castle: it was likely no more than fifty years old, and empty. A poor, abandoned place, with no one looking after it since the family fled after Culloden. No one could be living here: all they had to do was take a look around, see if they could find any trace of Mr. Byres having been here recently – it seemed impossible – and then leave. He was about to say as much to Lang Tam – after all, it had been Charlie's idea to come here, at first, so he could say when they were done – when a sound came from upstairs. A footstep.

'My, yon was a big rat,' murmured Lang Tam after a moment's silence. Charlie stared at him. Lang Tam looked a great deal less confident than he had climbing through the window. 'Or maybe your man is here, after all?'

Charlie frowned.

'I need to find out,' he said. 'I need to find him.'

'Call out, then,' Lang Tam suggested, but Charlie's voice jammed in his throat at the thought.

'No,' he said, when he could speak again, 'no. I'll go up the stairs and see for myself. Only ... will you come with me?'

Lang Tam took a second or too.

'Aye, aye, of course I will.' He made a move towards the staircase, then stopped. 'Have you a knife about you, at all?'

'We're just here to ask him to come to Aberdeen with us. We'll no need a knife, surely?' said Charlie. Drawing a knife seemed likely to bring all kinds of trouble after it.

'And if it's no him?'

If it was not Byres, who could it be, moving so stealthily?

Charlie sighed, and drew his knife. Lang Tam nodded approval, and drew his own. They stepped softly to the staircase.

The first floor: a gallery, overlooking the hall below. Some worn rugs, allowing them to walk quietly. Doors, some closed, some ajar. The nearest room was a study, a solid desk in the middle of it, bare shelves around the walls. They walked right around the desk, but there was nothing of note. Charlie nodded to himself: one room checked.

A parlour, then. Two high-backed chairs, a woman's shawl tossed over one as if forgotten in the haste of departure. A sewing box, furred with dust. The shawl was not dusty, though. Charlie felt his heart skip, and speed up. That could not belong to Mr. Byres. But it was a fine piece - not the garment of a poor wanderer seeking shelter in an abandoned house. Lang Tam fingered an elegant pastille burner on the mantelpiece, carving a line through the dust on it to reveal bright colours below.

'Nothing,' he said. 'Next room?'

A bedroom, the windows shuttered, the air somehow hard to breathe. Lang Tam brought out his flint and after a moment they had light, darting uncertainly into the shadows. The bed had been left made up, the hangings grey and stale. The candle light caught on a mirror, darted back at them, showed them a curtain hanging in the corner of the room.

'That'll be a closet,' Lang Tam said.

'No, the closet's here.' Charlie pointed to the other corner, where a door lay open to a tiny chamber beyond. 'It'll be the servants' stair.' They stood for a moment, eyeing the curtain, neither wanting to say anything. Then at last, Lang Tam said,

'It's a gey strange shape. There's something behind that.'

The curtain bulged at the bottom, its hem wrapped about something hidden. Charlie's hands shook as he reached out to draw the fine, filthy fabric to one side.

If he squealed as the woman's arm flailed out and fell, it was only understandable. Her shoulders and head, too, when the curtain was shifted, landed heavily. For a moment in the flickering light he thought she lived, but even as he wondered, he took in the mottled flesh, the sightless eyes, the black curls escaped from her cap, and he knew. He pressed his nose and mouth hard into his sleeve. They had found Mrs. Dilley, tangled and bloody at the foot of a winding stair, but they were days too late.

Lang Tam must have reached the same conclusion, and then jumped on, for in a shaky voice he said at last,

'That was no her footstep, then, was it?'

'That'll be Mr. Byres. What's he doing in a house with a dead body?'

Chapter Twenty-Six

'There were only two storeys to this house, from the front, weren't there?' said Charlie, looking up apprehensively at what they could see of the top of the stair. 'That must just be servants' rooms, do you think?'

'I think so.' Tam was whispering, which Charlie thought was wise: he wished he had kept his own voice down, but it had made him feel braver to speak up. 'But that'll no be the only stair, will it? Or will it? You ken more about big houses than I do.'

'There could easily be another,' said Charlie, frowning. 'This is nearly at this end of the house. There could be another one at the other end.'

'Good, I suppose,' said Tam, 'for if there's somebody up there – and I'm inclined to hope, just now, that there is somebody up there – then they'd not have got down easily past – past that.' He waved a distressed hand at the broken body on the stairs. It was true, what with skirts and spread-eagled limbs, she would have been hard to pass by, upways or down.

'I think there's only the one person up there,' said Charlie after a moment's thought. 'What do you think?'

'There could be any number, if they're keeping still and quiet,' said Tam ominously, 'but no, I think we've only heard the one moving about.'

'And we both have knives. What is there to be afraid of?'
Charlie could think of a number of things, but it was Tam who
suggested,

'Pistols?'

'Aye, true,' Charlie agreed. 'We should maybe just go now,
quietly.'

'I thought you needed to tell Tonley Rannes wanted to see
him?'

'That was before we knew he was keeping dead women on his
servants' stair, do you no think?' said Charlie. His teeth chattered and
he clamped them shut. 'I mean,' he ventured on, 'that sort of changes
my thoughts on the subject.'

'Then aye,' said Tam, 'let's go.'

'Gentlemen!'

The light in the room had changed. They both spun, knives
in their hands, and Tam's candle went out. Byres of Tonley, never
still, was toying with the dusty hangings of the bed behind them. He
had set his own candlestick down on a low table.

'Mr. Byres!' exclaimed Charlie. He looked quickly up and
down the mobile figure: there was no immediate sign of a pistol.

'You sound surprised. It is my house, though. I think I should
be a little more surprised to see you here, don't you?' He narrowed
his light blue eyes. 'But what is that behind the curtain? You – pull
the curtain back a little, would you?'

Charlie, always obedient, did as he was told.

'Good gracious! A dead woman! I don't suppose either of you
knows anything about this, do you? Have you been making use of my
absence to store corpses about the family home?' The expression on
his face told its own story: he was teasing them, not accusing them.
'And she has been here some time, too: well, that will have to be
removed, or the rats will be straight in. It's a wonder she has not been
nibbled already, but I supposed it has been chilly. Fortunate, that.'

'Do you know why she's here, sir?' Charlie heard himself
asking.

'How on earth should I know?' Byres gave a slight laugh, then
studied Charlie more closely. 'You're Leith Hall's man, are you not?
Or you were, before Mayen took it into his foolish head to play pistols
with him. A sad affair, indeed.'

'Why did you put Mr. Abernethy up to it, sir?' Charlie's

mouth was operating independently, it seemed. Tam gave him a hard nudge to tell him to close it, but Charlie seemed to have no power over it. 'And then you had Mr. Abernethy killed, too. Why was that, sir?'

'I like your manners, little Leith Hall man,' said Byres. 'You accuse me of orchestrating – would that be a good word for it? – two killings, but you still call me sir. A nice sense of your own position. Don't you think so?'

'Mr. Hay of Rannes would like answers to these questions, sir,' Charlie ploughed on, head down. 'He would very much appreciate it if you could meet him in Aberdeen, and discuss the matter.'

'Hay of Rannes? That creature that's built like Gulliver in the land of the Lilliputians. I have never known him to discuss anything, to my recollection. How interesting that he has now developed some kind of reason!'

'Will you come to Aberdeen with us?'

'I don't think so,' said Mr. Byres, quite as if he had considered the possibility. 'I feel the need for a change from busy towns for a while – and besides, it seems there is some tidying up to do here.'

Tidying up – what a way to speak of a dead woman in your house! It was like saying he had no further need for Mr. Abernethy. Charlie felt an unaccustomed anger begin to well in his stomach.

'Your pal Jeemsie Ogilvie ...' he said.

'Ogilvie? Is that the fellow in Amsterdam?'

'You ken rightly that it is. He's dead.'

'Is he?' For a moment Tonley looked – well, surprised.

'I hope he wasna still useful to you,' said Charlie, with emphasis. He felt strange, outside himself, watching as a cold anger, alien and uncomfortable, built up inside him.

'Oh,' said Byres, 'I shouldn't have thought so, no. Anyone can outlive their usefulness, can't they?'

'Aye, now that he's killed Mr. Abernethy on your behalf, I suppose so.'

A smile slithered over Tonley's pale face, as mobile as the rest of him.

'Jeemsie Ogilvie was another one that needed to remember he was there to obey orders. He was not, by any means, the only one.'

Charlie frowned.

'You mean you had orders to obey, too?'

For a moment, Byres seemed to take things more seriously, though his fingers wandered endlessly along the carvings of the bedpost.

'Everyone obeys orders. Until there are no more, and then one is no longer useful. Isn't that right? You've no master now, after all, have you? You must be wondering about your own usefulness.'

'Who gave you the orders?' Charlie asked, listening to himself, to his nerve, in disbelief.

The smile whipped back again, and vanished as quickly.

'Well, you had to ask!' He drew out a battered silver watch on a chain, opened and considered it, then snapped it shut. 'I'm afraid I'm much too busy to talk any further with you, gentlemen. You'd better be off, or you'll never find your way back to Aberdeen in the dark. Tell that great oaf Rannes we'll have a little chat, sometime, no doubt, but I don't think he'll find it of much use, do you?'

He gave a little laugh, and stood back to allow them to make for the door. Charlie and Tam both made sure the table with the candle was between them and Tonley, and hurried back to the stairs, now lit by a few candles in sconces. Halfway down the stairs they saw a figure emerge from the kitchen doorway.

'Hi! You! What are you doing here?' cried the man sharply. He wore, Charlie noted as he froze, a yellowish buff coat.

'No, Paul, let them go this time,' came Byres' light voice from behind them. 'There is plenty still to do!'

The man, cross to be reined in like this, instead stalked to the front door and opened it wide. It was clear as they passed him that he would have liked nothing better than to help them on their way with a foot in the seat of their breeches, but the presence of Tonley on the landing was, for once, their salvation. They stumbled through the dark to where they remembered leaving their horses, and found them unharmed.

'Come on, let's go back to that bonnie wee woman in Tough and see if she can put us up for the night,' said Tam, his jaw sounding tight.

'Tam, did you see his watch?'

'What?'

'Did you see Mr. Byres' watch?'

'No, what about it? Here,' he said, interrupting himself, 'you ken that was Mrs. Dilley?'

'I know,' said Charlie. 'She must have been there almost since she disappeared ...'

'What do you mean? How do you know here? When did you see her?'

'Oh,' said Charlie, taken aback by Tam's sudden questions, still not wanting to tell anyone about the miniature, 'I think someone described her to me. Mr. Holland, I think it was. Mind he was telling me all about what Lord Watt did in America and who was there?'

'Mr. Holland,' said Tam. 'Oh, aye, so he did. We'll have to lead these fellows: it's black as soot out here.'

They as good as felt their way back towards the village: Charlie's head was buzzing with thoughts and memories. Tam's must have been working, too.

'Why would anybody want to kill Mrs. Dilley?' he asked. 'She was a bonnie quine, and kindly with it. We were that sorry when Captain Dilley died.'

'Were you there?'

'When he died? Aye, I was in that action.' There was a pause while they negotiated a spot where a stream had burst its banks and frozen under the snow: the horses were not at all keen on the idea. 'Aye, poor man. And then his Lordship had to write to Mrs. Dilley, for she was already up the line, heading for home.'

'So,' said Charlie, thinking hard, 'when she told the master in that letter that she had had a letter from her husband, he could well have written it and sent it to her but it missed her before she sailed, and followed her on to Cork?'

'Aye, I suppose,' said Tam, 'but did she no say she was going to send Captain Dilley's letter to your master?'

'She did, aye. But if she did, I have no idea where it might be.'

'What was it she said? That it had some odd information in it?'

'I think so. Why do you think she might have sent it to my master? She wasna even sure she would see him again. Why would it have been of interest to him?'

'We canna tell that until we find it, Charlie lad. Was there somewhere at Leith Hall he kept his papers?'

'Of course: the bookroom.'

'Of course, says he!' Tam laughed. 'One of my masters has a

writing slope that even he doesna ken what's in it, and the other has his coat pockets for a desk.'

'Aye, well, the master had his bookroom,' said Charlie, not without some pride. 'But Mrs. Leith's been through it, I think.'

Silence fell again for a little. Ahead, they could see one or two lights that must be the village.

'See, Charlie lad,' said Tam, 'what you have to ask yourself is who wanted Mrs. Dilley killed. Isn't that so?'

'Aye, that's true. But it looked to me as if Mr. Byres killed her. He was barely even trying to pretend he hadn't seen her before on his stairs. Och, Tam, to leave her lying there for days!'

'I ken, I ken,' said Tam. 'Nobody ever said that Tonley was a nice man – I doubt even his mother loved him. But look at what he said – he was doing what he was tellt. And what if there was someone wanted Mrs. Dilley dead and told him to do the deed?'

'And who would that be?'

'Well,' said Tam, 'the obvious person would be your mistress, would it no? Your erstwhile mistress,' he added precisely. 'Mrs. Leith.'

And so it was that after some further debate as to what Mr. Hay of Rannes' views on this might be (Tam felt that since he was likely only just arriving in Edinburgh there was no point in waiting to canvas them), the next morning they bade a fond farewell to the hospitable woman in Tough and her watchful husband, and headed not back east towards Aberdeen, but north towards Kennethmont and Leith Hall.

'Aye, it's not much more than ten miles, though it's a bittie up and down,' said the husband, clearly keen to see them on their way.

Ten miles it might have been, but it was not easy going in the snow. The hospitable woman had given them bread to carry with them but they almost feared to stop in case they and the horses grew too chilled. Though they had left early enough, it was almost dusk again when at last they came to Kennethmont village, and Charlie, breathless with delight, nodded a greeting to every face he saw and every animal and building, too.

'Charlie, lad, it's no so long since you left!' Tam said, laughing.

'It feels like a long time,' said Charlie, and grinned. He had wondered if he would ever see the place again, and here he was, riding through with all his arms and legs in place and money still in his pocket – though he was well aware that it was not his, and would have to be returned or accounted for when his work was done. And then where would he end up?

'We'd best go round the back,' said Tam, and turned his horse on to a shortcut to avoid the long driveway. Charlie was impressed that he knew it – he had not spent that much time around Leith Hall, surely.

'Aye, if I can get in and get out again without Mrs. Leith seeing me at all, that would be best. I wonder who she's put in to my old job?'

'She's maybe not got anyone yet,' said Tam, 'with all the other things on her mind. I thought maybe your wee friend might be happy to help us. To help you, anyway: she never seems that impressed with me, for some reason.'

Well, Phoebe's a wise girl, Charlie thought, but did not say. She would not fall for the charms of a fellow like Tam. The trouble was he was still far from convinced that she would fall for someone like him, either. He was not, he was sure, clever enough to woo Phoebe.

But she had kissed him, and he had treasured that kiss all the way to Amsterdam and back. He shivered at the thought that in a few minutes he might see her again.

At Tam's suggestion, they left the horses tethered at the edge of a field under the trees.

'We can bring them in later for food and shelter,' he said, as Charlie found some scraps of straw to rub them down. 'I'd say you have no wish to draw attention to your arrival, have you?'

'I'm not going to go up to Mrs. Leith and ask if I can look around in the master's papers for a letter from Mrs. Dilley, no,' said Charlie, feeling his nerves growing. When he had dreamed of returning home, it had never been quite like this. Tam was looking up at the house admiringly.

'Mind the last time I was here? Not the funeral: no, that night we all arrived out of the blue, Mayen and my masters and me. I thought then it was a gey fine place Leith Hall had bigged for himself. Better off than any of them, was he no?'

'Saving Lord Watt, yes, maybe,' said Charlie. His mind had wandered back to that evening: Mrs. Leith looking stern, Abernethy apologetic. They had sat up so late after the mistress had retired, talking of marriage, of women, of that mysterious powder horn from America ...

'Oh, my,' said Charlie. 'I think I might just know where the letter is.'

Tam's face split into a grin.

'That'll save us all a lot of time, then! Well done - lead on, Charlie lad!'

The more he thought, as they made their way around the back of the house and into the yard, the more sure he was. For it was after the powder horn arrived that the master had rushed off to Aberdeen on odd excuses, only to spend the best part of a day in that lane off Ship Row in the snow. He had asked his friends, aye, if any of them had had the horn sent, but even Charlie had seen how little interest he had taken in the replies, as if he knew perfectly well who had sent it. The question was, had the master looked inside it? He had shaken it, true, but had said it was empty – a letter, curled into it, would doubtless make no sound. He felt his heart hammer. Where would the horn be now? He had last seen it that evening in the dining room. How would they get there without Mrs. Leith knowing?

He remembered Mr. Keracher and Mr. Abernethy and Mr. Dalgarno handling the horn that evening, and the master's anxious expression. And he remembered, once again, the matter of Dalgarno's watch.

'Tam, did you see that watch that Mr. Byres had yesterday?'

'What watch?' said Tam. They had arrived at a good time of the day: there were few people about even in the yard.

'He looked at his watch before he sent us away. It was a battered, silvery one.'

'Aye?' Tam took a good look about the yard before venturing across to the kitchen door.

'Aye. Tam, it looked awfully like that one your Mr. Dalgarno had. Do you think Mr. Byres could have stolen it?'

'Won it in a bet, more likely,' Tam said casually, and made a mock bow as he ushered Charlie into the house before him.

'Charlie!'

Phoebe sank back against the wall in shock.

'Aye, indeed,' said Tam from behind him. 'The prodigal son is home.'

Charlie would have protested at this ungenerous description, but he was too busy gazing wordlessly at Phoebe. His memory had not exaggerated her prettiness, the glint of her eyes or the shine on her curls, nipped up on the crown of her head with a gleaming dark red ribbon. His heart seemed to be dancing some kind of reel. And she was paying no attention to Tam at all: she was looking – and smiling – right at him.

'Aye, well,' Tam went on, clearing his throat heavily, 'this is all gey bonnie, ken, but some of us would like to be well out of here before we get caught, eh?'

'Oh, aye, sorry, Tam,' said Charlie, breaking away from gazing at Phoebe. Phoebe turned with a sharp sigh to Tam.

'Well, then, what is it you want, Mr. Main?'

'What is it we're looking for, Charlie lad?'

'The powder horn,' said Charlie on a deep breath. He prayed he was right. 'The carved one – it was in the dining room.'

'As far as I know it's still there,' said Phoebe in surprise. 'What do you want with that?'

'If I'm right, you'll see! Is there anybody in the room just now?'

'No, there's no: the mistress is on her own apart from Mr. Alexander Hay, and they just have supper in her parlour, quietlike. Come on, then! I want to see what it is!'

She led the way, as though Charlie might have forgotten, and as they neared the parlour she took his hand, pressing a finger to her lips to hush them. She slid the dining room door open, hurried them inside, and pressed it shut, leaning back on it and allowing herself a light chuckle.

'It's exciting!' she whispered. 'Is this what you do with your life, now, Charlie? Sneaking into people's houses to steal their treasures? That has to be more thrilling than emptying cludgies!'

'We're not stealing it,' said Charlie, cautiously lighting one candle from a taper he had picked up on the way. 'I just think there might be something inside it.'

'Ooh!'

He stepped across to the cold fireplace, and gently lifted the elaborate horn down from the mantelpiece. The candle was on the table and he brought the horn over, already admiring again the clever carving. The place names must all be in America – there was the one the master had mentioned, and the one where Lang Tam had fought, and Captain Dilley had died – and hadn't that been the place where Lord Watt's little son had been killed, too? If Mrs. Dilley had sent this, she must have had someone make it for her in America and sent to Ireland for her to give John Leith. There was his name, squarely carved into the horn. What kind of memories must it have conjured up for her? And then she had decided to use it for this letter from her late husband – hadn't she?

The lid of the horn was silver and as pretty as a lady's button. He tried to twist it, then realised all he had to do was to prise it up. Next to him Tam and Phoebe were hardly breathing.

He set the lid down on the table. Inside the horn, just as he had pictured it, was a double curl of paper.

'Oh!' Tam puffed out a frustrated breath, 'this is too much for me!' He took three steps down the room, drumming on the other end of table. 'If there's aught on it, read it out, Charlie lad, for the love of patience!'

Charlie pulled the two whorled sheets apart.

'It's from that place again, Tam – where Captain Dilley died. Fort Frédéric, isn't that right?'

'Aye, of course it is. What does he say?'

'"*My dear wife,*" he says. Oh ...'

'What? What?'

'"*I'm writing to you because something terrible has occurred,*" he says, "*and I'm half afraid that what I saw will be the death of me. Lord Watt's little lad is dead, and whatever they say it was no accident, nor the action of the enemy, though it may have begun as unlucky chance.*"'

'What?' asked Phoebe. 'Is that Lord Watt that was at the funeral?'

'Aye. Go on, Charlie.' Tam's voice was flat with shock.

'"*Lady Watt is much affected, as you can imagine. The boy ran out apparently to try to fight during an attack made on the headquarters. It was dark, and some of our men thought he was one of the enemy. But they only wounded him. The tragedy came, my dear, when their officer, afraid of Lord Watt finding their mistake, completed the assault and murdered the boy – for murder it undoubtedly was, even in a skirmish.*

"*The trouble is that this officer is well known to me and to*" *you, and I fear that if the enemy returns tonight, as seems likely, the opportunity will be taken to dispose of me, too. I shall try to send word to Lord Watt who has taken his wife and his son's body further towards the coast, but I fear that any letter I am seen to send may miscarry, so I write to you, too, as insurance.*

"My dear, I am more than sorry to burden you with this matter, the more so as I fear you will be a widow by the time you receive this. Be assured that you are in my heart on this, perhaps my final night on this earth, and that I am reconciled with my God. But it is my best hope that we shall meet again in this world, before we might meet in the next."'

There was silence, then Tam said,

'But the name, Charlie? Who was the officer who killed the lad? Does he not say?'

'He has written it very clearly at the foot of the letter,' said Charlie. 'There can be no doubt about.'

'And what is it?'

'It says "Captain Walter Dalgarno". Your master, Tam, and the man who wants to marry Lord Watt's sister. Captain Dalgarno killed Lord Watt's son.'

But Phoebe's attention had been elsewhere. She had turned to face the dining room door, listening hard.

'Someone's coming,' she hissed, and snatching the paper from Charlie's hand she folded it and slipped it into the bodice of her gown, backing over to the wall away from both of them. She looked at Tam.

'Right, then, Charlie lad,' said Tam, 'that's just grand. And to use those words that affected you so much, you're of no further use to me.'

'What?' Charlie gasped. Tam had pulled his knife, and was stepping towards him on those long, ungainly legs that suddenly seemed very useful. 'Phoebe, run away! Go, now!'

Tam paused, and stretched out a hand to Phoebe. She drew the letter out from her bodice, and laid it on his palm. His fingers closed around it, and he drew it to his nose, giving it an appreciative sniff. And Phoebe went to stand behind him.

They had betrayed him.

Chapter Twenty-Seven

The candlelight flickered and settled after Phoebe moved past it. The single candle set on the table reminded Charlie of Jeemsie Ogilvie's house – and look what had happened there. Charlie noted that now she was behind Tam, there was nothing between him and the door – which would be handy, but he would still have to open it and get through.

'Och, Charlie lad, you're always so trusting!' said Tam with a grin. 'You led us straight to this, for which we're mighty grateful.'

'Aye, well,' said Charlie, and shoved his hands into his deep coat pockets, letting his shoulders slump. 'You were always the clever one, Tam.' But you taught me quite well, he thought silently. Tam had been strangely quiet over Dalgarno's watch – and where had he been in Leith when Charlie found himself on the quayside? – but he had really underestimated Charlie when he had bought that dark red ribbon for Phoebe's hair. He must have sent it to her from Edinburgh.

'Will you please give me the letter, Tam? I don't really understand what you're doing.'

Charlie was not sure whether or not to be pleased that Tam was quite prepared to accept his stupidity.

'The letter,' he said, still grinning but adopting a formal stance, his version of a village dominie, 'this letter is what we've been looking for. We knew Captain Dilley had sent it before we – before he was killed in action. I chased it all the way to the coast, but Mrs. Dilley and your master had already sailed. Turns out the letter missed her, too, and followed her, but we only found that out when Mrs. Dilley and your master tried to see each other again. Och, young love!'

'But who's "we"?'

'Mr. Keracher, of course, and Mr. Dalgarno. What they

thought they were doing when they killed that lad ... but he should never have been out wandering around, the fool. Anyway, what was done was done and they thought no one had seen, until they realised Dilley had been around. It can be confusing in a battle, even a small one. Well, obviously if Lord Watt found out what they had done he'd no be too happy with Dalgarno wedding his sister, do you think? So I'm going to burn this now,' he went on, and came round the table to the candle. 'That means Dalgarno can marry the lady, and I'll get my reward – and I'll no have to spend any more time nursemaiding you, Charlie lad, either!'

He was now closer to the door, but intent on the candle. Was that a footstep on the landing outside? Charlie prayed that it was Alexander Hay, Rannes' brother.

Tam allowed the candle flame to slide and run up over the folded paper, smoking black for a second. Charlie winced, not quite watching it, fingers busy in his pocket.

'I wish you hadna done that, Tam,' he said, really quite loudly for a man in a house where he shouldn't be.

'Och, do you?' said Tam. Phoebe gave a little giggle, watching the ashes fall. 'The thing is, lad, that it'll no matter to you much longer. We'll have to decide what to do with you.'

'But I thought you were my friend!' cried Charlie. Whatever he did from now on, he knew that he could never be an actor. But Tam seemed convinced, standing coolly with one hand on the table.

'Aye, well, Charlie lad, you're always the innocent, are you no? Now, come here.'

And at that, the door opened.

Mrs. Leith stood there, solid as a wall press.

'What is going on here?' she demanded.

Then things happened more quickly than Charlie could have hoped. He whipped the knife from his pocket and thudded it into Tam's hand as it lay on the table. He tipped over the candle. He grabbed Mrs. Leith by the shoulders, shoved her out of the room, and followed, pulling the door hard shut behind him.

'Have you the key?' he demanded. Mrs. Leith's face was a picture.

'Where's yours?' she responded.

'I gave mine back! I don't work here any more!'

'Give him the key, Harriot,' came a deep voice. Alexander

274

Hay was mountainous beside them. 'I'll go round and make sure he doesn't get out by the window.'

'The maid is in there, too!' Charlie called after him as Mrs. Leith handed him her keys. 'Phoebe Clark!'

'She is?' said his erstwhile mistress. 'How?'

'She and Tam – that was Lang Tam Main, servant to Mr. Keracher and Mr. Dalgarno – I think they're sweethearts. And ma'am, I know now why the master died.'

For a moment he thought she was about to faint: after all, she was with child. But there was a hard chair by the dining room door, and she sank on to it, taking a moment.

'How do I know you are telling me the truth?' she asked.

'You can ask Mr. Hay of Rannes, ma'am – and I think he might have been communicating with Mr. Alexander Hay, the rate Mr. Alexander went off just now.'

'But what have you been doing? What business is it of yours? You owe me nothing.'

'No, ma'am, but it's hard to shake loyalty, sometimes.'

Alexander Hay reappeared, with a couple of sturdy stable lads.

'You have somewhere we can lock them? Separately,' he added with a frown. Mrs. Leith gave directions, and Hay and the others marched into the dining room. A roll of smoke emerged, then Tam, his hand bleeding, then Phoebe. The stable lads were not reluctant to make sure Phoebe was securely held, it seemed: her face was pink and stony. Tam stopped.

'I dinna ken whether to be proud of you or not, Charlie lad,' he said, 'but you've no evidence, anyway!' He cackled, and allowed them to lead him away.

'Evidence?' Mrs. Leith turned to Charlie. He shook his head, aware that Tam and Phoebe were still within hearing distance. 'Right, come to the parlour. Mr. Hay will join us.'

'I am most annoyed,' she said when they were settled, 'about Phoebe. She was a good little maid.'

'She's the least of it, ma'am,' said Charlie. He was not sure how much he really wanted to defend the girl. She had always been too clever for him.

Mr. Hay came in, helped himself to a glass of wine, and sat on a low seat that brought his head to about the normal height of a man sitting.

'I am glad to see you safe, Charlie: my brother wrote that you were going to Tonley House. He had hoped that would be the safer option for you but on his way to Edinburgh he heard news that Tonley had been heading home. Rannes is back in Aberdeen by now. Did you meet Tonley?'

'Aye, sir, we did.'

'And was that when you realised that that Tam Main fellow was up to no good?'

'No, sir, not entirely. But I saw that Mr. Byres was wearing a watch I believed was Mr. Dalgarno's, and I wondered why he might have it. And Tam was no very keen to discuss the matter, which made me more suspicious.'

'I think,' said Mrs. Leith, 'you had better tell us the whole story.'

Well, he thought as he lay down on his old bed that night, it was nearly the whole story. He had hedged around Mrs. Dilley to the best of his ability, turning her into a sergeant in the regiment. He thought that Tam would have been proud.

The next day he made his way, taking both hired horses, back to Aberdeen. Mr. Hay and Mrs. Leith had thought it best if he went ahead to meet Rannes before the prisoners were taken in, in case they found a way of warning Mr. Keracher and Mr. Dalgarno, but Charlie was less sure that they would bother. After all, with no evidence what had Mr. Dalgarno to fear?

Mr. Hay of Rannes was, as expected, staying at Campbell's, and looked mightily relieved to see Charlie, though when he realised Charlie had brought both horses back he frowned.

'Is your friend Tam all right?' he asked.

'He'll be away a whiley longer,' said Charlie. 'Can I have a word, sir, somewhere private?'

'Of course,' said Rannes. 'There's some light left in the sky – shall we take a walk up St. Katherine's Hill?'

Rannes measured his stride to Charlie's as they climbed the gentle ascent. From the top, they could see the ships in the harbour. Should he go back to Amsterdam?

'So Mr. Dalgarno used his watch like a deposit – that's what Lowrie Leith said - to get Mr Byres to arrange the duel, probably telling Mr. Abernethy he would pay him. And Mr. Dalgarno would pay Mr. Byres when he got his money. Well, anyway, Tam thought that's what happened, but I'm not sure: I mean, I think Tam himself would do a good deal for money –' it pained him, still, to talk of his friend like that, but he knew it was true, 'so he thinks everyone else would, too. And I think Mr. Byres would have played his part for money and for the fun of it. But I think Mr. Byres persuaded Mr. Abernethy that it was some kind of joke, don't you, sir?' Mr. Abernethy would have had no idea that the plan was to kill Mr. Leith. All he had to do was to aim wide. And Mr. Dalgarno got Mr. Byres to abduct Mrs. Dilley.' He scuffed a toe into the snow: he was still not happy mentioning Mrs. Dilley, but he was sure he could trust Rannes.

'And then to kill her,' said Rannes, bleakly.

'Well, again, Tam's trying to say that Mr. Dalgarno never told Mr. Byres to kill the lady. He says that Mr. Byres took her to Tonley, and then, well, he says that he was awful shocked when we found her dead. Mr. Byres could just have kept her there until the wedding was done. But I'm not so sure, sir. If they let her go again, and she found that the master – that Mr. Leith – had been killed, I wonder if she might not have had her suspicions? And anyway, they abducted her. She could have had them arrested just for that.'

'Until the wedding was done?' Rannes wanted clarification.

'The idea was that they knew Captain Dilley had written a letter about the death of Lord Watt's wee lad. I dinna ken whether it would stand up in law or no, but the letter would have been enough to make Lord Watt stop Miss Ciara marrying Mr. Dalgarno.'

'But the letter was burned, anyway.' Rannes sighed, a sound like a juvenile hurricane.

'No, sir.'

'But didn't you say ...'

'There were two sheets, sir, the letter itself and the cover. The cover was all written over with different directions, I suppose because it had followed Mrs. Dilley to the coast and then to Cork and maybe further, I don't know. That's what was burned. But I slipped the letter into my pocket, and I have it now.'

Which was how Charlie, who really felt it was not his place at all, found himself reporting the whole story (edited again to remove Mrs. Dilley) to Lord Watt in person. Rannes stood by him, ready to assure Lord Watt of Charlie's reliability, but oddly it was Mr.

Holland, Lord Watt's man, who stepped in to say he had always felt Charlie was a good and honourable servant. Charlie was strangely touched – perhaps he would find other friends here even without Lang Tam.

Lord Watt was white as fresh snow as Charlie explained what had happened, downing, without seeming to notice, the contents of the glass Mr. Holland brought him. He no longer seemed to see Charlie, or even Rannes: his gaze seemed far away, perhaps overlooking a scene in America, perhaps the faces of those loved and lost. It made Charlie shiver, and want to wrap his Lordship in a warm plaid, but that was Mr. Holland's place, and Charlie knew he would look after his master.

Charlie himself went alone to the little lanie at the foot of Ship Row, though, and broke the news of Mrs. Dilley's death to Margaret, who wept lavishly over his shoulder. And there he acquired another obligation for himself, for Margaret wanted assurance that Mrs. Dilley had at least had a decent Christian burial, and Charlie promised to do his best to find out.

'And what am I to do with her belongings?' she sobbed. 'Och, she's no coming back for them for sure, poor lady!'

Feeling damp and depressed, he emerged from the lanie and walked the short distance to the Green.

It was easy to spot Rannes in the general crowd, and Charlie hurried to join him. There were soldiers about, and other officials whose appearance made Charlie nervous, and to remember again the death of Jeemsie Ogilvie. But it was not Charlie who was about to be arrested for a murder committed far away.

The crowds stopped and watched with interest as Walter Dalgarno and Matthew Keracher were led away: interest, but not much sign of sympathy. Matthew Keracher objected loudly, demanding to know the names of his accusers, to see the evidence, but Walter Dalgarno moved silently before the officer holding him, his face closed. Charlie's fancy conjured up a little boy, eager for battle, running from the safety of his home into the American dusk, but he could not bear to think of what had happened next, at the hands of these two. And all that Lang Tam had covered up, the lies he must have told, the way he had deceived and misled Charlie – not that Charlie had taken much misleading, he admitted to himself. Tam must have been glad to have such innocent, ignorant material to work with.

The Green was busy, so Charlie was not entirely surprised to feel a breath on the back of his neck and smell an unwashed body, but something made him turn around. Lowrie Leith stood behind him, and if anybody in the crowd was watching the arrest with interest, it was he.

'Do you think they'll swing?' he asked, his casual tone belying the intensity of his gaze. Rannes turned in surprise.

'Lowrie! I never thought I'd be so pleased to see you alive and well, man!'

'Ha!' said Lowrie, looking up at him. 'My, how you've grown!'

'Where did you go, sir?' Charlie could not help asking. 'We went looking for you in the town house and you'd left.'

'Aye, looking for excitement! That's what I said I wanted, and that's what I got. Yon fellow wanted me dead,' he explained, nodding at Dalgarno's miserable progress towards Ship Row. 'Because I overheard him getting yon shilpit Tonley to get Johnnie killed in a duel. Me looking for excitement, and instead it's just something I hear in an inn that near has me murdered in my sleep!'

'How did you get away?' asked Charlie, but Lowrie gave a little shrug, a half smile on his lips.

'Never you mind. Let's just say that Lowrie Leith still has friends, when it comes down to it.'

Charlie smiled, then recognised with surprise that for the first time he had ever known, Lowrie was not drunk. But not bored, either, he supposed. For himself, he would not mind a little boredom for a while.

Rannes went with him – or he went as Rannes' manservant – back to Mayen. If Jeemsie Ogilvie had ever sent a letter to his victim's widow, it had miscarried: they had to break the news to Mrs. Abernethy, of her husband's innocence and of his death. They did not stay long: she had family about her, including her cousin the Earl of Fife. She was not without friends, and had found from somewhere a degree of stoicism, as Rannes said to Charlie later. But when she heard the proof of Mayen's innocence, the story of how he had been used, she rose and clutched Charlie's hand, wordless, gazing into his face as if she could read the whole tale there and print it on her own heart.

The ride back to Leith Hall Charlie and Rannes took gently, going over the whole story again between them, the parts they had freely told and the parts they were, generally, keeping to themselves. Charlie mentioned his obligations – more than he had first thought them – to Josse and his family, and his plans to return to Amsterdam to meet them as soon as he could.

'Well, but what will you do now, Charlie?' Rannes asked, 'for if you are seeking a situation, I think I would be happy to have you in my household. It is not large, but I like a sensible man to run it. And I should allow you leave to visit Josse Gheertzoon, of course.'

Charlie was astonished.

'That is very good of you, sir!'

'But?' Rannes smiled, sensing a problem.

'But Mrs. Leith has said – well, much the same thing, sir. She has offered me my old place back.'

'She has forgiven you, then, for your insubordination?'

Charlie laughed.

'My lady was very gracious,' he said. 'And she said how pleased she was that it had all ended – um – in some degree of satisfaction.'

'Even though she'll get no compensation from Mayen?'

'That is far from my business, sir. My work is in the home.'

'And home is important, isn't it, Charlie?'

'Aye, sir, for me it is. Thank you for your offer, and your kind words, sir, but I'll bide at Leith Hall, where I belong.'

Note, historical and otherwise:

I'm very grateful to Eleanor Rowe, from whom I have callously stolen plot ideas before, for graciously handing this one to me on a plate – and lending me the family history (*Trustie to the End*, Henrietta Leith-Hay and Marion Lochhead, Edinburgh 1957) written just before Leith Hall was handed over to the National Trust for Scotland.

John Leith was indeed shot in a duel with Abernethy of Mayen and died on Christmas Day, 1763. Byres of Tonley, who was actually married to Mayen's aunt, was apparently there, as were Gordon of Cobairdy and Forbes of Brux. Dalgarno and Keracher are figments of my imagination and Lord Watt is a version, no more, of Lord Forbes, who having tried to prevent the duel went home early. There were substantial links between the Jacobites and the followers of the Episcopal Church, but there is no evidence that any of these men was in fact Episcopalian – though there is reference to something of the sort in a ballad written after John Leith's death, his adherence to anything but the Kirk was denied by Henrietta Leith-Hay. The territorial designations of Tonley, Brux, Cobairdy, Leith Hall, and Mayen, along with others, are commemorated on the ceiling of St. Andrew's Episcopal Cathedral in Aberdeen, though this is apparently to do with their Jacobite loyalties and not with their churchmanship.

From the family history, it appears that there was always some suspicion that there was more to the duel than meets the eye, though no one argued that Mayen had fired the fatal shot. From the witness statements it is unclear whether there was one shot or two, and what exactly Tonley picked up from beside the dying John Leith. If it had been a pistol, it is likely that Tonley was concealing the fact that Mayen had fired and Leith had not: the witness statements indicate that Leith had no second, and that the duel had not formally begun, when Mayen fired. However, there was a shot hole in a neighbouring lamp post, pointed out to visitors for many years afterwards. Accounts do mention a slight wound in Mayen's thigh, but do not explain it.

The powder horn described in the book is in Leith Hall and is a fine example of the work – though as to whether or not it was a gift from a lady is speculation on my part. It is more likely, from the inscription, to have been presented by his fellow officers.

Harriot Stuart did her very best to wrest compensation from Abernethy's wife, as Mayen himself had fled the country. The wife, Jane or Jean Duff, though, was indeed extremely poor and had by then ten children, and Lord Fife among others did his best to find funds for her and dissuade Harriot from further persecution.

John's Leith uncles were universally unreliable, if one judges by the family history. Lowrie Leith was, however, quite a character around Aberdeen. The Hays were rather more useful. Andrew Hay of Rannes was indeed over seven feet tall, with huge feet – the Jacobites deployed him at the front of their army approaching Derby in the hope that the English would think all Highlanders were that size, and flee!

Less common words in The Slaughter of Leith Hall

Ashet	serving platter (from assiette (Fr.))
Big (verb)	to build
Bunkwife	landlady
Carline	crone
Cassie	cobblestone or squareset
Chap	knock (on a door, for example)
Clout	cloth
Cludgie	chamber pot
Courie	cuddle
Creepie stool	simple stool made from five short planks
Dominie	village schoolmaster
Fank	sheep pen
Gey	very
High heidyins	high-up people, people in charge
Keek	peep
Kist	a chest or box. But for someone to be kisted means that they are being laid into their coffin.
Lepping-on stane	mounting block
Mains farm	the English equivalent would be 'home farm'
Mintie	minute (many words in the North East have '-ie' added as a diminutive)
Neb	nose
News	a news, a gossip (North East)
Pech	pant
Press	cupboard
Quine	woman
Red	to clean or tidy
Shilpit	worthless, shambolic, shabby
Sleekit	smooth, sly, sneaky
Strathbogie	the old name for Huntly
Thole	put up with, endure
Yow	ewe

About the Author

Lexie Conyngham is a historian living in the shadow of the Highlands. Her historical crime novels are born of a life amidst Scotland's old cities, ancient universities and hidden-away aristocratic estates, but she has written since the day she found out that people were allowed to do such a thing. Beyond teaching and research, her days are spent with wool, wild allotments and a wee bit of whisky.

We hope you've enjoyed this instalment. Reviews are important to authors, so it would be lovely if you could post a review where you bought it!

There are several free Murray of Letho short stories, Murray's World Tour of Edinburgh, and the chance to follow Lexie Conyngham's meandering thoughts on writing, gardening and knitting, at www.murrayofletho.blogspot.co.uk. You can also follow Lexie, should such a thing appeal, on Facebook, Pinterest or Instagram.

Finally! If you'd like to be kept up to date with Lexie and her writing, please join our mailing list at: contact@kellascatpress.co.uk. There's a quarterly newsletter, often with a short story attached, and fair warning of any new books coming out.

Murray of Letho

We first meet Charles Murray when he's a student at St. Andrews University in Fife in 1802, resisting his father's attempts to force him home to the family estate to learn how it's run. Pushed into involvement in the investigation of a professor's death, he solves his first murder before taking up a post as tutor to Lord Scoggie. This series takes us around Georgian Scotland as well as India, Italy and Norway (so far!), in the company of Murray, his manservant Robbins, his father's old friend Blair, the enigmatic Mary, and other members of his occasionally shambolic household.

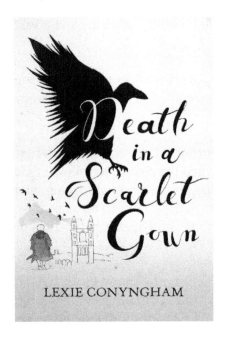

LEXIE CONYNGHAM

Death in a Scarlet Gown

Knowledge of Sins Past

Service of the Heir – an Edinburgh murder

An Abandoned Woman

Fellowship with Demons

The Tender Herb – a Murder in Mughal India

Death of an Officer's Lady

Out of a Dark Reflection

A Dark Night at Midsummer (novella)

Slow Death by Quicksilver

Thicker than Water

A Deficit of Bones

Hippolyta Napier

Hippolyta Napier is only nineteen when she arrives in Ballater, on Deeside, in 1829, the new wife of the local doctor. Blessed with a love of animals, a talent for painting, a helpless instinct for hospitality, and insatiable curiosity, Hippolyta finds her feet in her new home and role in society, making friends and enemies as she goes. Ballater may be small but it attracts great numbers of visitors, so the issues of the time, politics, slavery, medical advances, all affect the locals. Hippolyta, despite her loving husband and their friend Durris, the sheriff's officer, manages to involve herself in all kinds of dangerous adventures in her efforts to solve every mystery that presents itself.

A Knife in Darkness

Death of a False Physician

A Murderous Game

The Thankless Child

A Lochgorm Lament

Orkneyinga Murders

Orkney, c.1050 A.D.: Thorfinn Sigurdarson, Earl of Orkney, rules from the Brough of Birsay on the western edges of these islands. Ketal Gunnarson is his man, representing his interests in any part of his extended realm. When Sigri, a childhood friend of Ketil's, finds a dead man on her land, Ketil, despite his distrust of islands, is commissioned to investigate. Sigrid, though she has quite enough to do, decides he cannot manage on his own, and insists on helping – which Ketil might or might not appreciate.

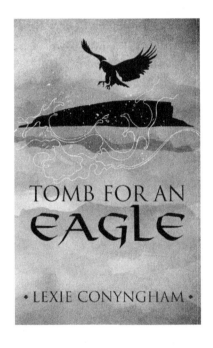

Tomb for an Eagle

A Wolf at the Gate

Other books by Lexie Conyngham:

Windhorse Burning

'I'm not mad, for a start, and I'm about as far from violent as you can get.'
When Toby's mother, Tibet activist Susan Hepplewhite, dies, he is determined to honour her memory. He finds her diaries and decides to have them translated into English. But his mother had a secret, and she was not the only one: Toby's decision will lead to obsession and murder.

The War, The Bones, and Dr. Cowie

Far from the London Blitz, Marian Cowie is reluctantly resting in rural Aberdeenshire when a German 'plane crashes nearby. An airman goes missing, and old bones are revealed. Marian is sure she could solve the mystery if only the villagers would stop telling her useless stories – but then the crisis comes, and Marian finds the stories may have a use after all.

Jail Fever

It's the year 2000, and millennium paranoia is everywhere.
Eliot is a bad-tempered merchant with a shady past, feeling under the weather.
Catriona is an archaeologist at a student dig, when she finds something unexpected.
Tom is a microbiologist, investigating a new and terrible disease with a stigma.
Together, their knowledge could save thousands of lives – but someone does not want them to …

Thrawn Thoughts and Blithe Bits

A collection of short stories, some featuring Scottish Georgian detective Murray of Letho, some not; some seen before, some not; some long, some very short. Find a whole new dimension to car theft, the life history of an unfortunate Victorian rebel, a problem with dragons and a problem with draugens, and what happens when you advertise that you've found somebody's leg.

Printed in Great Britain
by Amazon